I0776930

POSSESS ME!

(I WANT YOU TO)

BOOK TWO
Spooky BOYS

FAE QUIN

Possess Me!

(I WANT YOU TO)

SPOOKY BOYS #2

Cover Art and Interior Artwork by Fae Loves Art

WWW.FAELOVESART.COM

Typography and Interior Formatting by We Got You Covered Book Design

WWW.WEGOTYOUCOVEREDBOOKDESIGN.COM

Editing by Angela O'Connell

INDIE AUTHOR CREATIVE

Dedicated to my husband,
my partner in crime

for all my fellow cereal criers

Author's Note

HELLO EVERYONE! THANK YOU so much for picking up this copy of *Possess Me*! This book was so much fun to write and Prudence and Luca swiftly became my favorite characters I've created thus far. They have their own special brand of weird that, for me, was highly addicting. I hope you enjoy reading it as much as I enjoyed writing it! While this book has a lot of humor throughout, it deals with dark elements. A full content list is up on my website and my instagram for anyone that would like to know what they're diving into before they begin. I can't wait to hear what you all think! As always, feel free to reach out to me while you're reading, and all reviews, comments, and shares are greatly appreciated.

If you'd like to keep in touch with me and receive free content including a free ebook of *There's a Monster in the Woods* and exclusive chapters of my serial *Cloudy with a Chance of Dildos*, you can sign up at faelovesart.com/newsletter. Or join my Facebook group, Fae's Faves! You can also find me on Instagram @fae.loves.art.

I love you all so much, enjoy!

Chapter One

Luca

THE FIRST TIME I got soap in my eyes I was nine years old. I'd been bathing with my two siblings for most of my life and as the oldest, I figured it was finally time to grow up, put my big boy pants on, and shower alone like the independent badass I thought I was.

For months leading up to that moment I'd begged my mom to let me, shooting confidence out my eyeballs like laser beams any time she caught me in the bath. *Look at me, all responsible,* I'd project toward where she sat sentinel on the closed toilet seat, presumably to make sure none of us drowned. I'd squint, my grin positively manic—but all Mom ever did was roll her eyes in response and go back to whatever book she was reading.

At the time, I thought she didn't trust me.

In reality, she was debating whether my independence was worth the addition to our water bill.

When—after a century (a few months) of begging—she finally said yes, I'd been too nervous to ask questions, terrified she'd change her mind and decide if I entered the shower stall with anything but the utmost confidence that meant I wasn't ready. Adam had just turned three and he'd developed an annoying habit of shooting me with his bath toys every time we shared, and I was more than ready to never be squirted in the eyeball by a rubber ducky ever again.

The knob that controlled the water was easy enough to navigate on my own, so maybe I was feeling a bit *too* confident as I piled two handfuls of shampoo in my palms and lathered them up. I figured the hard part was over. Battle won. This was the shower of champions. Then, after checking to make sure the door was shut and I was alone for probably the sixtieth time—a product of having two nosy siblings under the age of six—I ambitiously began the meticulous process of turning myself into Jimmy Neutron.

My emotional high was short-lived when only three minutes into my first independent adventure, I experienced the worst betrayal of my young life. You guessed it. Motherfucking soap in the eyes. Maliciously, the suds dripped from my forehead and seeped into my lashes, eating away at my eyeballs like the soap was made from acid.

It burned *so fucking bad*—and I'd held back my pained cries as I shoved my face blindly into the pelting water, utterly crushed. Like Icarus, I'd flown too close to the sun. My eyes were practically bleeding, the pain was so intense. When drowning my eyeballs in water didn't help quickly enough, I thrust the fat side of my palms into my eye sockets, my nails digging into my now squashed—no longer cartoon-worthy—hair. More pain. Liquid fire. A revolution battling out between the soap and the water attempting to cleanse me of it. Somehow the harder I pushed, the more the soap spilled down into my eyes, almost like my desperation made it multiply.

Though, luckily like all things, even this had to end.

Eons later the soap washed away, and I sat broken, bewildered, and betrayed. I was tear-sticky with my ass plastered to the damp tile, my eyes blurry and swollen, my naked knees wobbling. The warm water had run out ages ago.

As I huddled, shivering and staring up at the shower head, I swore to myself that I'd never, in all my life, feel *worse* than I did in that moment.

I was wrong.

Sitting shakily in my empty car outside the Rain family manor in Elmwood, Maine I felt that same horrid burning at the back of my eyes that I'd felt all those years ago. Only this time it wasn't soap that had killed my dream, but reality, my own stupidity, and one really uptight— horribly dressed—brunette heiress.

My last painting sat strapped into the passenger seat as I rolled down the long gravel driveway toward the unknown, fighting the burning tightness in my chest. If I'd thought the pain I felt sitting on the shower floor at nine was bad, this was lightyears worse.

This meeting had been my last hope.

My last chance to set things right.

I'd been counting on this sale to get me somewhere. At least far enough that I could pretend like I hadn't royally fucked up six months before. But…just like when I was a kid, I'd gone in too confidently. Funny now, how the emotion my painting was supposed to depict was hope. I stifled a bitter laugh as I pulled onto the long winding road that led out of Elmwood.

What a joke.

Hope was a dirty, rotten liar.

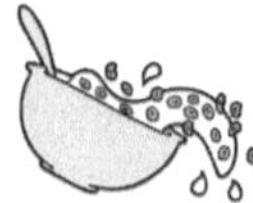

The club in Ridgefield was packed. I don't know what I'd been expecting, all things considered. It was a club, after all. People tended to be squashed like sardines from wall to wall. I knew that, but still, I was somehow surprised and overwhelmed as I clutched my painting to my chest and zeroed in on the bar. Maybe I'd hoped that a club in a tiny town like this would be different. Though Ridgefield was larger than Elmwood, the town I'd just driven an hour north from, it was still minuscule in comparison to the kind of cityscapes I was used to.

Actually, it wasn't the town's fault I was underprepared, I realized belatedly as I bumped into someone's elbow that was somehow both sweaty and glittery. I just wasn't ready for polite company in general, so I would've found any excuse to complain. Anything that would get me out of there faster so I could wallow in salt and calories and drink my sorrows away *alone.* Well, as alone as I could be considering the fact I was sharing a hotel room with my roommate.

It was her fault I'd come to Elmwood to meet Temperance Rain in the first place. Violet had grown up here. And when she'd proudly proclaimed that everyone knew that Temperance was both stupid-*stupid* rich, and a collector of fine art? I'd decided hey—it was worth a shot. Wasn't like I had any other options.

Violet was waiting for me, double-fisting two giant martinis, her back ramrod straight, dark hair perfectly coiffed. She'd texted me as I'd been pulling into the McDonald's parking lot in Ridgefield, determined to eat my feelings in the form of three McFlurries and a large fry.

Come to the club, she'd said.

It'll be fun, she'd said.

It's been six months, Luca. And god knows how much you need to get laid.

As if I wanted to spend my last fucking pennies on cheap alcohol and even cheaper entertainment. To be honest, this pessimistic side of me was unfamiliar. I'd always been a sunshine kinda guy. The kinda guy who looked at a rainy day and talked about how excited I was for the excuse to stay in, prior plans be damned. The kind of guy who sang along to musicals and always had something positive to say. Your grandma died? Well hey, at least your hair looks great. That was me! Sunshine McGee. Smile trooper. Happy-go-lucky extraordinaire.

Until recently.

Sunrise follows even the darkest night.

That had been my motto.

I'd repeated that my entire life. When I'd stolen granola bars from the gas station to feed Adam after school. When my mom's card had bounced when I was tasked to buy Betty a birthday cake. When Mom had told me she'd met Paul and all I could think about was how the fuck any of us were going to survive if he was anything like the last six boyfriends.

Sunrise follows even the darkest night.

I'd sang it to my siblings as we curled up together to conserve heat while Mom worked the night shift to pay to get it switched back on. And even then I'd managed to muster the courage to smile. But now…now the reason I was fucked was entirely my own fault. I'd been too trusting. The fact I'd been a sunshine-kinda-guy had been my downfall.

What's the sun supposed to do when it forgets what it's like to shine?

Stupid shit apparently.

Sunshine McGee was now Sunshine McIdiot.

I rammed into another guy, distracted by my own internal dramatics. He was laughing, his head tossed back, glitter decorating his cheekbones. What was *with* all the glitter? Wasn't tonight supposed to be Swap Night? As in, swap items on a blind date, not swap glitter like craft herpes. Laughing dude had a choker around his neck that spelled "daddy" in silver letters and I stared at it, dumbfounded, watching his throat bob as he stumbled. Belatedly I reached out to steady him, noting the fact the smell of his sweat was tinged with the musky sweet scent of weed.

"Shit, dude." My fingers wrapped around his sweaty wrists as I righted him, my painting squeezed into the dip between my shoulder and elbow so I wouldn't drop it. "I'm so sorry."

"S'all good, man. Don't worry about it." Blond-and-too-pretty-for-his-own-good perked right back up. I could see the bar behind him. Just twenty more steps and I could've avoided this catastrophe and spent the next hour being dramatic with an audience (Violet) and what would be my last bottle of tequila for a while. "*Woah.*"

Woah, what?

"That is a sick painting!" Blondie flashed his pearly whites at me and an uncomfortable flush buzzed across my cheeks as I took a hasty step back. I didn't want to be rude, but despite Violet's urgings I wasn't really ready to get up close and personal with anyone's dicks at the moment. *I didn't think so anyway.* I was in a no-dicking-zone. Even though, admittedly,

I was horny as fuck and blondie looked like the exact kind of guy that wouldn't mind bending me over the back of a couch in a dark room and showing me exactly how much he liked my art.

"Thank you." Normally I'd try to be eloquent, but I still had the remnants of salt on my cheeks from my earlier cry-fest. I wasn't proud of the amount of fries that I had managed to shove into my mouth all at once as I had sobbed myself silly against the steering wheel of Violet's mom's car.

"You here for singles-swap-night?" he asked, and I shook my head.

I'd seen a sign or two on my way to the club but it wasn't like I'd been paying attention. I'd been more focused on my impending doom.

"Oh," Blondie blinked, "I just figured, you know—with the painting and all—that must be why you're here."

"Are *you* here for singles-swap-night?" I asked, not because I was particularly invested in the answer, but because it was the polite thing to do.

"Abso-*fucking*-lutely I am." Blondie flashed his teeth at me and for a moment I reconsidered my no-fucking rule. Maybe what I needed was a distraction? Sex was free. Right?

I turned on the charm, the way I'd learned to when I turned fifteen and figured out exactly what face to make to get the gas station cashier to pay attention to me and not my little brother so he could shove boxes of instant ramen in his backpack.

"You're too pretty to be single," I told him, bringing out my dimples full-force because I knew just how crazy guys got for them. *Hunter* had liked them too. Fuck. *Don't think about Hunter. Don't think about the ring you pawned for last month's rent. Don't.*

"You're cute." Blondie grinned. "But you're right. I'm not."

Ah. *Damn.*

"Though. My boyfriend and I have a lot of fun playing the field, if you know what I mean."

I didn't, so I just smiled.

"He's into…" he leaned in close, the scent of too much cologne filling my nose as he whispered the last word like a secret, "*watching.*"

Oh.

So was sex on or off the table?

"We have a third for tonight but…" Blondie cocked his head, "he can wait for a bit." Something glittered where it sat around his neck, a silver chain catching the neon of the flashing lights. An elbow jostled me and my grip on my painting grew tighter as Blondie wrapped his fingers around the necklace hidden inside his black V-neck and pulled it up over his head. "I like your painting."

So we've established.

"Thank you," I repeated because I wasn't sure what he was expecting from me.

"I got this in the swap—" Blondie held his hand out toward me, palm facing down, the chain inside his fist dangling where it glittered, heavier than it looked. "But I'll swap you for it if you want."

"What is it?" I wasn't sure why I was even considering this. But…I'd spent the past hour choking on salt and sorrow and staring at my last salvation like it had turned into a demon itself. I was pretty okay with the idea of parting with the painting considering the fact it was apparently fucking hideous anyway—or so Temperance Rain had said. Fuck hope. And fuck Temperance. (Not literally, ew.)

"It's a lucky necklace."

"A lucky—"

"Yeah," Blondie's lips curled up and he shook the necklace at me, clearly getting a kick out of the way my eyes chased the movement of the chain. There was a bone-white cross dangling from the end, and it swung back and forth, back and forth like a pendulum as I stared. "*Super* lucky. I mean, I put this thing on and not even five minutes later a girl walked up to me and told me her hot brother was looking for fun."

That didn't necessarily mean it was lucky.

Only that he was hot and in a club full of people ready to fuck.

I stared at him dubiously, and he leaned closer to try to convince me.

"I also found a twenty-dollar bill. Annnnnd…" He waggled the cross at me again. "I found *you*, didn't I? With a painting that has the exact same color palette as my living room." Blondie blinked. "If that's not lucky then I don't know what is."

"And the person you swapped with?" I asked, more than a little intrigued, even though I was kind of embarrassed to admit it. "They don't mind you giving it to me?" Actually no, I didn't really care about that. What I cared more about was— "They think the necklace is lucky too?"

"Oh, fuck yeah. The girl who traded me was the cutest little pastel goth. Told me she's had nothing but good luck since she found it."

"So why give it away then?" This had to be a trick. I narrowed my eyes at him.

"I dunno man." His eyes narrowed right back and his fist shifted away from me a fraction. The necklace swung out of reach. I wasn't stupid. It was obvious he was playing me, pretending to change his mind so I'd jump head first without thinking. Even though I knew that, my heart still began to race and the greedy little monster that rose up inside me screamed that I was about to lose a once in a lifetime opportunity. *What if the necklace really was lucky?* This could be exactly what I needed.

"Maybe you're right…maybe I *should* keep it." Blondie was really laying it on thick. *What a bitch.* He was playing me and I *knew* it, but I fell right into the trap anyway. Hook, line, and sinker.

"No, no." I shook my head, holding my painting toward him in defeat. "You wanted this, right? Matches your interior?" Now it was my turn to lay it on thick. I fluttered my lashes. "It's one of a kind."

His eyes glimmered in the flashing lights as he seemed to debate with himself. I knew he'd already made up his mind, but this was part of the game. It always was. Someone else knocked into my shoulder and I clutched my painting tighter, knuckles white as it wavered in the space between us, terrified a wayward elbow was going to knock the canvas right off the wooden frame.

The yellow, almost petal-like paint strokes mocked me.

"You're right." Blondie grinned, reaching out to snag the painting from me before I could change my mind. For a second I worried he was about to run off with both items, but he didn't. When the painting was secured beneath his arm, he dropped the necklace gingerly into my open palm. It was warm from the heat of his hand, and slightly sweaty too. I clutched it, pulling it close to my chest for fear he'd change his mind.

He didn't.

Now that I'd committed to this, there was no way in hell I was backing out.

That lucky necklace was mine, goddamn it. Blond twunks be damned.

Blondie was gone before I could blink, and for a moment I worried that I'd made a horrible decision. I stared out at the thriving throng of bodies, ignoring their laughter as the white cross in my palm dug into the skin. I could feel eyes prickling on the back of my neck, and when I turned there was no one there.

Just my imagination then.

Probably.

Finally, I made my way to the bar, the niggling feeling that I'd missed something important tickling at the back of my mind. Quickly, before Violet could see what I'd just traded my last salvation for, I plucked the necklace over my head and tucked it under the collar of my t-shirt. It sat hot against my collarbone, a stark reminder of what I'd done as I dodged elbows and surrendered to the call of booze and morning after regrets.

Maybe this had been just another in the long list of my fuck-ups, but I figured it would all work out in the end. I didn't know what the future held.

All I knew was that I could use some luck.

Chapter Two

Prudence

BEING A GHOST made it hard to get laid. There were hoops to jump through, rules to twist, and laws to break. Vanity and Chastity were helpful in acquiring my conquests, but despite the relative frequency of them, there was always something lacking from the encounters. I didn't mind the necessary espionage. I didn't mind the lying. I didn't mind the extra work. What I *minded* was the fact that—just like when I'd been alive—after all was said and done, everyone was still fucking boring.

I'd spent sixteen years attached to a murderous bitch. You'd think I'd be tired of the drama.

But in a fucked up way, I missed it. At least strapped to Lydia, I felt… *something*. It was easier to ignore the way the world and I didn't seem to mesh when all I had to worry about was whose life I'd fuck up next, or what shitty thing I'd have to endure afterward. Being "free" as my sisters called it, only made it obvious there was something very off about me.

I should be happy.

But I was missing the pieces necessary to make that happen.

Even before I'd recognized that I was different, people had told me I was. As if we needed anything extra to alienate us from the rest of the misfits and freaks that inhabited Elmwood.

Helpful assholes.

Our money had always set us apart from the so-called peasants that made up the rest of the population. Our family tree consisted of a long line of too-rich, too-holy assholes with standards so high it was impossible for anyone to meet them.

Gleefully, my mother had driven that wedge between us and the throbbing veins of the community that thrived on the other side of town. For years her holier-than-thou attitude had acted as a tourniquet on our social standing. And that was *before* I'd been framed for murder. Where we'd once been revered, feared, and respected, now we were pariahs, and I had no one to blame but myself.

My regrets, however, had nothing to do with my mother's reputation.

I'd gladly tarnish it to get my dick wet.

I'd gladly tarnish it in general.

Just like I had every Friday night for the past month, I stared out at the blur of bodies in the crowd and wondered why the hell I couldn't have been lucky enough to actually fucking die when I'd been killed. The tedium was worse than my execution.

I was a mannequin in a store window watching the world move on without me while my sisters played dress up with my body. Wearing a people-suit as armor, I died a little more inside with every day that passed.

I spotted a familiar pink head and was spurred into action. The steady throb of the bass pulsed through the room, the scent of sweat and too much body spray in the air as I made my way through the crowd, careful not to touch, for fear of sinking through the bodies. I could feel the pull of my talisman like a siren's call as I hunted the bob of pink through the crowd.

Chastity must've found a new mark.

Her picks were usually prettier than Vanity's, though she tended to choose the utterly vapid. I didn't mind though. Wasn't like I wanted to discuss the meaning of life when I had my cock buried inside a tight ass. Everyone was equally annoying the second my dick was no longer inside them.

Pretty was good.

Boring.

But predictable.

Easy to manipulate.

For those brief few seconds as I pressed inside someone else's heat their heartbeat became my own, the throb of their pulse almost as heady as the warmth sucking at my cock. Sometimes it almost felt like being alive again.

Almost.

Found her.

I dipped between a couple whose tongues and hips were welded together, pushing past a throng of giggling bimbos until a break in the crowd revealed the pink head I'd been following. Annoyingly, I'd made a mistake—which was unlike me—because now that I could see more clearly I realized the pink haired figure wasn't my sister at all. It was someone else entirely.

Whoever he was, stood chatting with another man, his gray eyes lit up like fireworks in the flickering of the club lights. His face twisted as he deliberated, scrunching up expressively before he handed a canvas over to the stranger.

Pinkie was interesting looking. Like an old painting, or a Fae creature.

Unlike the man he was talking to, he wasn't what most would consider conventionally attractive. His upper lip was too thin, his eyes too round, his ears too large, his cheekbones too sharp. *Pretty*—like the kind of thing that would've stopped Van Gogh or Monet in their tracks. There was sadness etched in the creases of his expression, though his face remained charismatically friendly. The beacon of his pink hair had caught my attention, but the depth in his stormy eyes was what trapped me.

Drawn to him, like a shark to blood. *Mona Lisa*. Something you could stare at for hours unable to figure out why you couldn't look away. Secrets hidden in the corners of that smile.

My fists clenched.

The talisman pulled at me like it always did when I got too far away from it, so I took another step closer, blinking away the disconnection that followed the necklace being passed to someone new. My equilibrium was shot as I stared at the glimmer of silver that now hung from Pinkie's fingers, the off-white of the cross taunting me.

Apparently the blond had been Chastity's target. Not unsurprising. He was exactly the kind of idiot she usually picked. I couldn't help but be glad, however, that I wouldn't be going home with him tonight, a new plan falling into place as I watched the pink-haired man slip my necklace over his neck and tuck it beneath his t-shirt. Safely hidden.

His long legs ate up the space between him and the bar, and I couldn't help the way I grinned after him.

He didn't know it yet, but he had just become my golden ticket.

This wasn't going according to my sisters' plans. The chaos that would ensue would be memorable to say the least. If I was a better man, I'd feel bad about what I was about to do. But I wasn't. Death had taken the last of my empathy and I had my own agenda to attend to.

Pinkie sat at the bar for over two hours with what I could only assume was his friend. Despite her dark hair, general air of judgmental punk-ish-ness, and the fact her wardrobe was better than his was, she wasn't as interesting as him. She was too loud, too quiet, too…*something*. Something I couldn't name, but seemed to be a personality trait for every person ever.

I didn't understand the easy way she bunched her fingers in the back of his hair and pulled him close. They shared a single glass of tequila, abandoned martini glasses scattered beside them. Despite the fact I'd been staring, neither had noticed me. Too caught up in their conversation as I leaned against a pillar at the end of the bar, my arms crossed. I could hear their voices over the noise, echoing through the ever-present fog in my mind.

Freedom was like that sometimes.

Foggy. Directionless.

With Lydia I'd always had a purpose. A mission. No matter how fucked up it was. And on the rare occasion she didn't have a task for me, I'd been commanded away. The Nothing sucked me back in, the void slipping its icy fingers around my disjointed existence.

This was what they'd meant when they dubbed the term the "living dead."

This was why what had been done to me was considered a curse.

"*Luca.*" The dark-haired woman shoved at Pinkie's shoulder, her pale eyes wide and ringed with smudged eyeliner. "You *didn't.*" The entire time they sat they'd been discussing what seemed to be a popular TV show. After a few minutes, I'd tuned them out. Finally. Something interesting was happening.

Luca.

Derived from the Latin name Lucas.

Meaning: Bringer of Light.

An interesting name for a man that had doom and gloom written all over his sunny face.

"It doesn't matter now, anyway." Luca shrugged then downed the rest of their shared glass. The woman smacked his arm in retaliation, and I cocked my head, interested to see what he'd do next. Against my better judgment I was curious. He was my golden ticket after all. Manipulating him would be easier if I could find out what made him tick.

What had he done that caused her to act so aghast?

Did it have something to do with the painting he'd swapped for my talisman?

He'd probably stolen it. That level of skill was hard to come by.

Maybe the painting had been hers.

Curiosity tingled at my fingertips and I clenched my hands into fists to abate it. If I listened long enough, maybe I could use this to get what I wanted from him.

"It's done. It's gone. Done-zo. *Gone-zo.* Whatever way you want to put it." Luca signaled the bartender for another drink, glaring at his friend till she rolled her eyes and slid another bill across the counter to pay for his drink. Was he poor then? "Besides, apparently it was 'hideous' and 'looked like it had been created by a kindergartner with finger paints.'"

So he'd been trying to sell the painting. Didn't mean it hadn't been stolen, but it was becoming more likely he'd created it himself. He was even more interesting than I'd first thought. This conversation was enlightening to say the least. Bargaining chips were swiftly falling into place. If he was struggling financially then I had my in.

Money was always an excellent motivator.

"It *wasn't* hideous. Fuck that bitch." The woman smacked him again, and I watched Luca throw his hands up to block her anger. With a swiftness that was entirely unexpected, and clearly practiced, he reached over and viciously pinched the skin above her elbow in retaliation. The familiarity of the interaction made me wonder for a moment. Siblings maybe?

No.

I hoped not anyway. That would complicate things.

Besides, they looked too different to be blood related.

Luca was all willowy muscle. Gangly and fairly tall—though not ridiculously so. He had long fingers, long legs, a long throat that bobbed as he swallowed. Sweat glistened in the hollow at the base of his neck and my teeth began to ache with the need to bite the vulnerable sliver of skin. I wanted to sink myself inside him, make him wear my marks like a necklace. A paper trail of brutality, bruises strung like pearls.

Yes.

Yes, he'd do.

Tonight wasn't so boring after all.

Chapter Three

Luca

MAYBE THE DINGY hotel bathroom wasn't the best place to jerk off, but I was horny, distressed, and more than a little tipsy, so I figured it worked just fine. It had been nearly two weeks since I'd had a moment alone like this, and the turmoil brewing inside me only amped up my need for release. My fingers blurred along my body, scratching along sensitive skin, pinching my nipples till I gasped.

I hoped if I was rough enough I could convince my body that someone else was touching me.

I was certainly drunk enough to believe the lie. To believe that I wasn't alone. That I wasn't lonely or sad. To believe that self-loathing wasn't festering like disease under the surface of my skin.

The fog of my breath concealed my blurry reflection in the mirror as

I braced my body against the counter. Cheek to the glass, the difference in temperature made my overheated skin burn. The unpleasant sensation was a welcome diversion—I'd accept anything that would help me forget what I'd done, and who it would hurt.

As I touched myself I missed the happy person I used to be. I missed the way I turned my petals toward the sun and opened myself up to rays of possibility. Now I was withered, and even in the privacy of my own mind, I knew I wasn't worth the sunshine.

"C'mon Luca—" I groaned, frustrated when I couldn't stop the poisonous thoughts that welled up inside me. Pinching my nipples harder didn't distract my mind. It only hurt, and not in the way I craved. *This wasn't working.* Even the promise of an orgasm wasn't enough. I softened my touch, my thumb tickling across the puffy, pink abused flesh of my nipple in apology. My skin was hot to the touch, oversensitized. Somehow the gentle pressure only made me feel worse.

Disappointment tasted like battery acid on my tongue as I glared blearily at my reflection, a vicious hate bubbling up inside my chest.

Why couldn't I stop thinking? Why couldn't I— "Just—"

Just what?

Fuck.

Just *shut up.*

Shut your goddamn brain up for two fucking seconds you worthless piece of—

Touch yourself.

A voice echoed in the back of my head and I responded without thinking, desperate for anything other than the desolation of my own thoughts. This was pitiful and I was running out of time. Violet could come back any minute, and I wouldn't be alone again till I got home to

California without her. Annoyed, I abandoned the abuse of my chest, and instead let my palm rest warm and sweaty against my racing heart. There. *Fuck.* Yes. Finally something that didn't make me want to peel off my own skin.

Stroke, the voice whispered, commanding, dominating, detached.

Figuring my nipples deserved a do-over, I followed the command, whimpering quietly as I thumbed hard over the already abused flesh and winced.

Softer.

Softer?

Softer.

Softer was good. Amazing actually. My cock twitched to life as I rubbed a soothing circular motion over my nipple. It pebbled beneath my touch, a jolt of pleasure causing a quiet exhale to burst from my lips.

More.

Feeling emboldened, my fingers slipped gently along my breastbone moving upward, thumb dipping into the hollow at the base of my throat. I wasn't the most sensitive there but my nerve endings were alight with pent up energy and I was sure just a few strokes of my cock would have me spilling against the cheap laminate counter.

Maybe for once it wouldn't be hard to get off.

I just needed to distract myself long enough to do it.

Fuck, and now I was in my own head again.

Harder.

Right. Yes. Touching.

Focus on the touching.

I could do that. I could definitely do that. Touch. *Yes.* Touching. Keep touching—

Harder, Luca.

Harder. Okay. Yep. Solid plan. My thumb dug into the hollow at the base of my throat. My nail briefly caught, and the sensation of it scratching sent all prior thoughts skittering away. I gasped and shifted my weight, spreading my palm wide and stroking upward till my thumb slipped into squishy flesh beneath my jaw, and my hand burned hot against my windpipe. A trail of gooseflesh tingled in its wake. This was good. Nice. But it wasn't enough—

Choke yourself.

I immediately tightened the grip I had on my neck and gave it a gentle, experimental squeeze. Even pressure this light caused panic and pleasure to tingle like electricity through my body as my windpipe compressed delicately beneath my fluttering fingers.

Why did this feel so good?

I'd never been choked before.

Shouldn't it hurt?

Maybe it should, but it didn't.

I released a broken breath, my leaking cock pressed insistently against the lip of the counter as I gave an aborted, desperate little thrust. My dick was so hard it hurt. Zero to one hundred in less than ten minutes. When I arched my hips back a fraction I could see the slick red tip of my dick, pointing eagerly up at me through the slit in my UFO themed boxers.

The reminder of how bad I needed this only made me spread my legs wider so I could properly watch in fascination as precum slipped down the crown of my cock. I'd seen this before hundreds of times, but I'd never felt like this. My whole body quivered as I licked my lips, mesmerized by the way my cock jerked in response every time I tightened the grip on my throat. Hunger, unfamiliar—dark, and delicious curled in the back of my mind, waiting.

Tighter, tighter, *tighter.*

Till my vision blurred, spots swimming in front of trembling lashes.

That's it.

Take it.

Fuck.

Wow.

You *like* the pain.

Fuck.

You're a slut for it, aren't you?

"God yes—" I whimpered, lips rubbing against the icy glass mirror. Finally out of my head, I was able to appreciate how good this felt. My Adam's apple clicked when I swallowed, my vocal cords vibrating against my palm every time I made a noise. I'd never paid such close attention to my body before, and the feeling was addictive. Overwhelming. Intense. Fucking earth-shattering.

I needed more.

The lack of oxygen was making me lightheaded.

I couldn't breathe. I couldn't—

I couldn't believe how close I was to coming from this alone.

My dick jerked eagerly, spurring me into action as I used my free hand to fumble with the hem of my boxers, tucking them beneath my swollen balls. I needed release, but I needed to tease more. Giving in momentarily, I curled my fist around my length, marveling at the velvety texture of the skin. Hot to the touch. Sticky pleasure smearing along my palm as I spread my fingers wide and the dark blond curls at my pelvis tickled their pads. Sliding lower, I dug my nails *hard* into the fragile skin a few inches to the left of my dick.

It hurt so good I could hardly believe it.

The grip I had on my neck loosened as I explored myself for what felt like the first time, only for the exploration to be cut short as that same unfamiliar voice that had made its home inside me echoed in reprimand.

Pathetic.

Harder.

Harder…yeah. I could do harder. Harder was good—

God. It hurt. My nails dug deep enough into my thigh to leave crescents behind before impatience got the better of me. *No more teasing.* Spots swarmed across my vision. I squeezed my eyes tight and finally, *blissfully,* wrapped my fingers around my aching dick. Pleasure burst bright red behind my eyelids, and I slumped forward in relief, my lips dragging against the mirror. Hopefully I wouldn't leave marks all over the glass— buuut, honestly? It felt too good for me to really care.

That's what Windex was for, right?

Hold on to that feeling.

It felt so good to be touched, felt so good to be present in the moment, my body thrumming like an instrument beneath my hand. Pleasure was a foreign but distantly familiar sensation.

Squeeze yourself.

I squeezed.

I'd always been messy. Most of the time I barely needed lube to get myself off, my own precum more than enough to slick the way. Now was no different, my cock dripping eagerly while I played with it, thumb digging into the leaking slit till a broken whine escaped my throat. The sound vibrated against where my palm held my neck—loosely now—and I trembled, weak-kneed.

I needed more.

No.

Not there.

Not…what?

I said *squeeze* yourself.

Squeeze? I *was* squeezing. And my dick was enthusiastically thanking me with the way it jerked in response. God. *Yes.* I fucked into my fist, the pleasure making me sex-stupid for a few blinding seconds before I finally realized what the voice in my head had meant.

Right.

My neck.

Squeeze my neck.

I didn't need to be reminded twice. I followed the command with enthusiasm. My nails bit into the sides of my throat while I swallowed back a groan and shoved my palm hard enough against my windpipe I saw stars. I knew I was doing this wrong. The choking bit. There were articles about it on the internet—oxygen wasn't supposed to be inhibited, just the blood, but God…even though I was doing it wrong it still felt so *right*. I couldn't stop, even if I wanted to.

Everything was spinning, spinning, *spinning*.

My lips were chapped, my tongue needy, mouth too empty as the chill from the glass pressed against them. I'd never been this kinky before. Never touched myself so roughly—never been so demanding.

This was new and terrifying.

And I liked it, probably too much.

Too soon, my orgasm rushed toward me. My hips were helplessly pumping into my fist, upper body wedged sweaty and slick with my own desire against the counter as my pace quickened and the slick sounds of sex made my mind buzz with a primal sort of want. I wanted to fuck. To slide somewhere tight and hot, and release all over my fingers. My grip tightened and I swore, pelvis snapping forward at the thought.

Look at yourself.

My eyelids didn't want to open, but I forced them to anyway. The voice hadn't led me astray yet, after all.

Look at what a whore you are. So desperate you'd fuck anything, wouldn't you?

God…

Fuck your fist, that's it.

You're such a needy little bitch.

Desperate for a good dicking, aren't you Pinkie?

The derogatory words only spurred me closer and closer to orgasm. I'd never known I would be into this—but fuck. Here I was, totally into it.

Look at yourself, slut.

Open your eyes.

Unable to be anything but obedient, I opened them. My broken cry weaved through the slick sounds of my fist around my dick as pleasure burst like fireworks inside me, and cum leaked eager and hot between my fingers. Staring at my reflection, I really *did* look like a whore, all half-lidded pleasure, my cock wet and slutty where the angry red crown popped through the loop of my fingers. Fuck. Fuck-fuck-*fuck*.

God, I looked good.

I hissed through my teeth, fumbling away from my throat to scrape my fingers past the sensitive skin of my balls, lower, lower. I pressed hard against the sweat sticky skin behind them as pleasure trembled through my body and my eyes rolled back as I jerked into my fist. *Fuuuuck.* Coming felt like a religious experience, my lashes fluttering as my tongue lolled, and my toes curled against the cold bathroom tile. Somehow my cum slick fingers ended up in my mouth and I sucked on them gratefully, shoving them far enough back I choked a little, salt on my tongue.

Why did this feel so…so fucking amazing?

Why hadn't I ever been able to do this before?

Good boy.

Pleasure tasted salty-sweet on my tongue as I trembled, knees weak, head full of bees.

My entire body had been rebooted.

Unable to let go too soon, I basked in the overstimulation, gasping as my slick fingers twisted around the sensitive tip of my cock and the deep scratch of the voice in my mind commanded me to keep going—to keep playing till it hurt, till I couldn't take it anymore. Till I was a sobbing mess and my dick was raw.

Only when I was too exhausted to move, did I open my eyes again. Half flopped over the counter, my body trembling, my cock twitching feebly, I had never looked more satisfied. When the fog of my breath on the mirror cleared however, I was greeted with a sight that chilled me to the bone. At first glance nothing was wrong. Same familiar cheekbones. Same freckle-smattered nose. That cut in my lip from the time I'd ran into an open kitchen cupboard.

Something was wrong though.

Different.

It took me a moment too long to realize what had changed. My face stared back at me, sure, but—it was wrong—all wrong. Set beneath dark brows should've been gray eyes, cloudy as a rainy day. But instead, what stared back at me was a mismatched pair. One was still gray, but the other…no. The other wasn't mine. How could it be?

The foreign eye flickered icy, glacial blue. Nearly fluorescent in color, the iris glowing softly. There was something about it that was demanding, despite the fact it was foreign. Like it wasn't going anywhere. Defiant. Like it owned me. Like it had any right to be there at all.

Chapter Four

Luca

I PROBABLY SHOULD'VE realized I was being haunted sooner. I didn't though. Sunshine McIdiot, remember? Honestly, at first I really thought I was lucky—just like the blond man at the club back in Maine had made me think I would be. Apparently my optimism wasn't all the way dead.

This was karma or some shit.

Yeah.

Freaking.

Right.

It started with little things.

I'd forgotten sweetener for my coffee at the airport, and only realized after I'd already made myself at home waiting for my plane to arrive. After muttering about it, I rose to my feet, slung my duffle bag over my shoulder, and began the arduous trek through the terminal back to the cafe.

Except, when I finally arrived at the tiny little corner shop, the line had been incredibly long.

Too long.

Dejectedly, I turned right back around. I'd rather gag my way through the bitter bean juice than wait behind fourteen people just so I could be wired up for the plane ride home.

My abandoned seat was still empty so I plopped into it for the second time that day. Some guy two rows over snored peacefully with his headphones on. Squeezing my cup tight in one hand I did what I always did when out in public, looping my backpack straps through my legs so no one could steal it.

A flash of color caught my eye as I fidgeted, and I paused, jaw slack when I realized what it was. On top of the cheap navy pleather of the seat next to mine was a handful of sweetener packets and a few cups of hazelnut creamer.

Huh.

Lucky me.

I squinted down at it suspiciously then casually peeked around the gate looking for my unlikely savior. Someone had obviously left these behind. Or…maybe they'd overheard my complaining and took mercy on me in my painfully un-caffeinated state. Kinda stalker-y? But hey, at least I had drinkable coffee.

Ultimately I didn't give a fuck how the sweetener had come to be in my possession. Only that it was, and I was going to enjoy the hell out of it. Because *coffee.* Duh. I dumped everything in, startled when a new guy sat down a few chairs over while I swirled my cup to mix it. Aha! Mystery solved. I raised my cup toward him in thanks, figuring he must've been my good Samaritan. His brow furrowed and his eyes narrowed in annoyance before he rose from his seat, and headed to another row, far, far away from me.

Okay.

Maybe he wasn't coffee Jesus.

Shrugging the awkwardness off even though my eyes were stinging, I finished my coffee in peace. Lately it seemed a stiff breeze was all it took to make me cry, but I refused to ugly sob surrounded by jet-lagged civilians. No. I'd save that for home.

Because there was nothing better to do I checked my bank account while I waited, fiddling nervously with the strings on my hoodie as I absorbed the too-cold air conditioning and tried not to think about how utterly fucked I was. For a guy that had been sitting pretty with nearly a million cash just a year ago I was feeling pretty abysmal.

Three thousand dollars.

That was it.

All that was left.

Aaaaand like an idiot I'd just traded my last painting to a random dude at a club because I'd been feeling sad. So, yeah. Go me. Yay. Excellent decision making skills. Ten out of ten.

Realistically I *could* paint something new but…ever since I'd realized the extent of Hunter's betrayal I'd been unable to muster up the will to create anything. My creative river had run dry. Not to mention the fact that lately it seemed no one was interested in buying abstract art. I'd been a trend, only I hadn't known it till everyone else had decided I was no longer relevant.

With clammy hands I shoved my phone into my pocket. The empty airport somehow managed to feel oppressive. I was suddenly glad I'd decided to go home ahead of Violet. The idea of staying here a few more weeks was far too overwhelming for my fragile mind to comprehend. I wasn't used to being so brittle. Like anything—no matter how small— was enough to cause me to shatter.

I missed home.

I'd gotten used to San Diego and its crowds. Elmwood reminded me too much of the tiny town I'd grown up in Oregon and thinking about *that* only made me sick to my stomach.

Speaking of things that made me want to throw up—I needed to call my mom back. She'd been leaving me messages all week about something her and Paul didn't want to text me about. But fuck—As much as I loved her I didn't have the spoons for that conversation, not when I knew the second I spoke to her I was bound to break the fuck down and confess everything.

I was letting them down. *All* of them.

Mom, Paul, Betty, Adam.

Especially Adam.

Tall, gangly, grouchy as hell—and young. So fucking young. Too young to stop looking at his big brother with stars in his eyes. Too young to realize I wasn't who he thought I was, and the confidence I'd always projected was a fat fucking lie.

I couldn't…admit what I'd done.

What I'd let *him* do.

Maybe part of me was still in denial, or maybe I was still trying not to cry in the middle of the airport.

Trust no one. That's what Violet had told me after I'd explained what happened. A little too late though, all things considered. Since then, I had taken that advice to heart. Aside from Violet of course. She was the exception, as always. Though even where she was concerned there were some things I was still skeptical about.

It wasn't often I spent the weekend with witches after all.

That's what she claimed they were, anyway.

After the painful ride home with my phone sitting like a lead weight in my pocket, the plane finally descended into sunny San Diego. Inhaling the scent of salt and sunscreen wafting through the air, the flip in my belly finally settled. Home at last.

Chewing my lip raw, I waited for my Uber to arrive. It'd be sixty bucks to ride to our dinky little apartment, which was a shit ton, but…I didn't really have a choice at this point. My piece of shit car was still sitting abandoned on the street outside my apartment downtown.

Hitting the confirm to pay button killed a part of my soul.

I pulled down the brim of my baseball cap, wishing for a moment I could disappear inside its shadows, just as coppery blood burst on my tongue and I released my abused lip with a wince.

"Shit, ow." Nowadays, unconsciously—and consciously—I was always punishing myself. In a weird way the pain made me feel better. It distracted me. A finger tapped at my shoulder and I jolted to attention, turning around swiftly, ready for attack. *Fuck. Can't believe I let my guard down! I knew better than that.* If there was one thing living in the city had taught me it was to never turn my back on the crowds. Especially when I was alone.

I had no reason to fear though, apparently. The man was smiling at me, his brown eyes flashing, shaved head glistening as the sunrise caught on his dark skin in a way that made my insides flip. Cute-cute-cute.

He's not hitting on you.

Stop it.

Well, maybe…

"You dropped this," the man hummed, holding out his hand. And I—unthinkingly—grabbed what he was giving me without even looking, too mesmerized by the flash of his white teeth and the way he cocked his eyebrow at me.

"Thank you." My jaw was on the floor somewhere. Damn, he was cute.

After I stared my fill, curiosity got the better of me and I glanced down to see what he'd placed gingerly inside my grip. *Shit.* A crisp twenty-dollar bill winked up at me. This would've been fucking awesome except for the fact I knew I hadn't been carrying cash so… I glanced up to tell him the money wasn't mine only to discover that he was long gone. I was alone again.

Weird.

My Uber arrived before I could do anything about it, so I pocketed the cash and shrugged my way into the back seat after checking that the license plate matched the app. Red roofed buildings blurred on either side of the vehicle as I pressed my cheek to the cool glass and watched the world spin by. Twice in one day something out of the ordinary had occurred.

Once was a coincidence. *Twice though?*

Maybe the necklace was lucky after all.

The next morning I picked my way through Violet's last box of granola as I stared blankly at the street outside the lonely kitchen window. We lived in the busy part of downtown. Far enough away from the ocean that it took me a good fifteen minutes to jog there. I spent most of my mornings pounding across the sand and inhaling ocean-scented freedom as my bare feet tingled from the force of my steps, and the thrumming of the blood in my veins made my head blissfully blank.

Running as much as I did had the added benefit of keeping me lean and muscular. It was convenient that at least one of my forms of therapy wasn't going to give me clogged arteries.

McDonald's though…

Today I wasn't at the beach. Obviously. Instead, I sat in a puddle of sunshine in our apartment as a dark oppressive cloud hung over me.

It was eleven a.m. Which was way later than I usually got up. My skin felt too tight and I could still smell the airport clinging to my body. I should be at the beach by now—self-medicating with sunshine—but I was too depressed to do anything other than shovel dry granola into my mouth and mope wearing a stolen pair of Violet's lilac-colored silk pajamas.

When the box was nearly empty I tipped it upside down and inhaled the crumbs, choking a little when a wayward almond got caught in my throat. The next five minutes were spent regurgitating like a baby bird until my throat was clear and my eyes burned. Which was, of course, when my mother decided to call.

Again.

Shower.

I needed to shower.

Then I'd call her back.

I wasn't procrastinating. Totally not.

The water pressure was abysmal and I tried to muster up the energy to jerk off again, hoping for a repeat of my drunken night in the hotel. To be honest, my thoughts that night had almost felt like they'd come from another person. I wasn't normally that assertive.

Not that I was necessarily *passive* in bed, but I did have a preference. I liked receiving. In every definition of the word. Affection? *Yes.* Blowjobs? Double *yes.* Dirty talk? Oh, hell yeah. Dicks? Give them all to me. Seriously. The sky was the limit.

What I *didn't* like was being the one in charge of what was going on. For me there was nothing less sexy than being asked what I wanted in bed. Which was why *that night* had been so wildly out of character for me.

My dick didn't want to rise to the occasion, which was fair.

It probably wanted a vacation from me as much as I did. I was tired of moping too, but I had yet to discover a solution to my growing list of problems. I figured the death of my career and life savings deserved at least a few days of grieving. Not that I hadn't already been doing that for months.

So, instead of jerking off—which is what I *really* wanted to do—I slapped more pink in my hair with the tinted conditioner that Violet had crafted for me. She was nice like that. She claimed pink was my color and told me having bright hair canceled out the fact I dressed like a dude-bro. I liked the pink. I also liked looking less—in her words, not mine—"straight."

Out of habit, I spritzed some cologne, a new baseball cap, and my favorite pair of joggers before I forced myself out of the apartment and out to the sidewalk. There. Running would give me endorphins, right? I'd feel better. *Hopefully.* Better late than never.

You didn't call Mom back.

Later.

Okay, so maybe the run was less for endorphins, and more so I could continue to procrastinate.

The sun beat on my shoulders and I welcomed its warmth. Still moist from my shower, the afternoon heat made me feel like a damp t-shirt tossed around a drier. Despite this, for the first time in days things were finally looking up. Almost cheerful, I soaked up sunshine and headed toward the beach.

There was a crosswalk up ahead and I calculated whether or not I'd benefit from crossing now or later.

My phone buzzed.

"Goddamn it."

I answered it, already knowing who it was going to be.

"Hi, baby." My mom's sweet crooning echoed on the other end of the line and I sighed, relaxing a little as the familiar scratch made my heart throb. Even though I was avoiding her I missed her. Hearing her voice only highlighted the fact I'd barely called her since shit hit the fan. "We've been playing phone tag."

I didn't correct her. We both knew for a proper game of phone tag I would've had to have called her back at least once. Which I hadn't done. In…six weeks? Yeah.

I was a shitty son.

"Hi, Mom." I forced a smile into my voice, staring down at my beat-up sneakers with a frown. I'd meant to buy new ones but that—like everything else on my financial agenda—had flown out the window the second I realized my savings were gone. All my extra cash had been spent running around trying to sell the rest of my backstock and well…look how well that had gone.

"Ah, there's my chipper-skipper."

God, I hated that nickname.

"Why are you calling, Mom?" I asked, going for polite, though I couldn't hide the tension in my own voice. *Don't fucking cry, man.* It was like she had this magic-mom-voodoo. All I had to do was listen to her voice long enough and the secrets and tears would flow out.

"It's been so long since we've talked."

Ah, and there the guilt-tripping came in. She had this way of delivering her blows—all soft and sweet, *kind*, the way she was. Mom didn't have a single bad or manipulative bone in her body. It's why for most of my life it had been my job to protect her from the men that wanted to take advantage of that. Thank God, she'd met Paul.

I loved her for her naivety, but I hated her for it too.

It was because of that innocence that I'd been forced to grow up lying. It was because of her forever bleeding heart that I'd ended up sixteen, stranded at a gas station in the middle of the woods, with two hungry younger siblings as night fell, and her latest boyfriend drove off without us. Worst of all, it was because I was just like her that Hunter had been able to fool me in the first place.

Still, though.

I loved her more than I loved air.

"I've been really busy. I meant to call." I explained, trying to soften the blow. We both knew I was lying but, since she was the best, she didn't push.

"Adam's only got a week left of school." She said instead of bothering me and that horrible gnawing guilt latched on to me once again. *Nibble, nibble, nibble. Fuck you, Luca you sad-faced bitch.*

"It's his last year, right?"

"Yes sir! He's valedictorian. We just found out."

"Good for him."

"Paul says he takes after you."

"I wasn't valedictorian."

"You were—are—a good boy though. Adam wants to be like you," she laughed. "Thank the lord Paul finds it cute. He's always fucking askin' if Adam wants to be adopted and move to California with you."

My heartbeat stuttered.

"Does he?" I asked, honestly terrified of the answer. I could barely take care of myself. Violet's stolen granola sat like a rock in my belly. I didn't want anyone in my family to see the reality of my situation. Not when they were so proud. Not when they still believed the lie I'd been breaking my back to keep up.

"He's still set on Harvard." She clucked her tongue with a laugh, though the silence grew oppressing as her words sunk talons into my already wounded heart. I don't know what I'd been expecting. Maybe I'd hoped he'd changed his mind—maybe-maybe-*maybe.*

But no.

Sunrise follows even the darkest night.

What a fat fucking lie.

There was no sunrise for me, not now.

The stop light turned red, and I stepped out onto the street, blinking through the blurriness of my tears. I swallowed bile, trying to figure out what to say. Blank. I had no words that could explain how monumentally

I'd fucked up.

I had to say something.

"Mom—" I opened my mouth, hopelessness crushing my heart as my feet hit the asphalt and my head began to spin.

I didn't see the car speeding toward me until it was too late.

Chapter Five

Luca

I FROZE.

My phone fell to the ground with a clatter, the screen no doubt cracking as I stared in horror at the vehicle careening toward me. It was clear whoever was driving was about to blast through the red light. There was nothing I could do—no amount of heart-attack-inducing terror that could get my feet to move.

I was a block of ice, stationary and static as my pulse thundered and my life flashed before my eyes. I was gonna die, and there was nothing I could do about it. I was gonna die with nothing to my name and no chance to explain how I'd lost everything in the first place. A giant disappointment. The big brother who promised too much. A failure.

Liar, liar, liar.

Tires screeched.

Something hard and cold wrapped around my wrist. Distantly, I recognized the sensation as fingers, but I was too far gone to understand what was happening as the breath jerked from my lungs and I was thrown halfway across the street. Hot asphalt scraped my knees, my baseball cap flapping to the ground, as the side of my face slammed hard enough stars burst behind my eyelids.

The car drove past with a loud honk.

Silence.

I lay motionless, numb. The pain hadn't caught up to me yet as I blinked till the empty street came into focus. My wrist burned where the phantom fingers had jerked it, but when I turned to look for the person that had pulled me out of the way, I was shocked to find the street completely empty. I closed my eyes again, pressing my head to the hot ground as a broken gasp escaped my throat.

What. The. *Fuck?*

By the time I'd scraped myself off the pavement and gathered my shattered phone I was too shaky to do anything but head home. I walked back in a daze, my face numb, pain prickling like ants beneath my skin as I clambered up the front steps to our building. My hands burned as I pushed through the door to our apartment and collapsed with a groan onto the lumpy sofa.

I stared at my broken phone screen for far longer than was probably healthy.

It had been the first and only thing Hunter had ever bought me.

I'd only kept it because I hadn't had the money to replace it six months ago when shit went down, even though looking at it at first had made me want to hurl. *Maybe it would still work?* I tried to turn it on but the shitty screen stayed black.

Yay.

"Fuck!" I threw my phone at the wall, pulling my hair till pain zinged from my scalp, only to realize belatedly—that my hat was missing—and in my rush to get home I'd left it behind. Great. Another thing I couldn't afford to replace. "Being poor is so fucking expensive."

Ice.

Ice?

Put ice on your face. It's swollen as hell.

I gently prodded my cheek. *Ow.* Shit. The shock was wearing off, and with every passing second the pain would only get worse. Ice. Huh. That wasn't such a bad idea. Maybe if I caught it soon enough I could stop my face from feeling like I'd spent half the day making out with a meat grinder.

We didn't have ice packs, because of course we didn't. So I grabbed a bag of freezer-burned peas and pressed it to my cheek. It smelled funny. Chemically. The moment the cold plastic met my feverish flesh I winced but didn't let go, tapping my fingers on the counter as I slumped in relief. The pain melted away, as a cool numbness settled over the area. Better. This was better. I was a genius apparently.

Painkillers.

Right. Painkillers. That wasn't a bad idea either. I fumbled my way into our medicine cupboard and popped a bottle of ibuprofen open. It was tricky working the childproof lid one handed, but I managed.

Maybe I should take extra?

Yeah. Extra was a good idea. The back of the bottle was really only a suggestion, right?

No.

Okay, fine. One it was.

After popping the pill, I sprawled across the couch with the peas pressed to my face. I did feel better. My phone lay accusatorially on the floor where I'd thrown it. Fuck. Maybe I shouldn't have done that? But it wasn't like I could shatter it *more*. The thing was already broken.

"You got any advice?" I asked no one in particular, staring up at the ceiling, wondering how the hell I'd even survived in the first place. At the time I'd been so sure someone had grabbed me—but…there'd been no one there.

I'd been lucky.

Again.

And suddenly…*it* occurred to me.

The necklace.

What if it had fallen?

I scrambled my free hand up to grab it, surprised to find it still around my neck. Sure, I'd been the one to put it there—but I'd forgotten as I'd wallowed around like a lumpy sad-sack. The white cross was warm from where it had been pressing against my skin and I clutched at it, shocked and more than a little excited.

Isn't that what the guy had said?

That it was lucky?

I thought about the coffee, the twenty-dollar bill, the car—and wow.

Wow.

Wow-wow-wow.

Holy cannoli.

Hope burst through me and a startled laugh bubbled out. Maybe my luck *was* turning around. Maybe there was a sunrise after all.

Chapter Six

Prudence

LUCA HAD THE weirdest habit of walking into rooms, staring blankly at the wall, and spontaneously bursting into tears. It didn't matter what time of day it was, what room it was, or what he'd been doing previously. His tears, apparently, didn't have the decency to conform to a nine to five schedule.

Though every room in the house had been christened by sobbing, Luca's favorite spot to cry was huddled over a bowl of cereal, while he sat at the wobbly kitchen table. The wood was covered in hand-painted astrology symbols. It looked like it had spent the last hundred years collecting dust in the back of a thrift shop before it had been resurrected from furniture Hell and adopted into Luca and Violet's horror show of an apartment.

I'd learned Violet's name that first night I'd inhabited his body, watching impassively as Luca had flopped next to her on the hotel's horribly flat mattress. She'd talked his ear off about hot blonde women and the dangers for youth today, caused by consuming hormone-altering chemicals in common everyday food.

Both of them were annoying.

Dramatic.

I thought the waterworks would finally be over when Luca ran out of cereal to cry into. I'd been wrong. Undeterred, he gathered the crumbs from the hollow skeletons of the mostly empty boxes he found scrounging through the dark recesses of his pantry. When *that* was gone, he went to the store and bought more.

With my talisman swinging from his neck—his gray eyes lost, muscular arms flexing—he ate his way through three different boxes before I decided enough was enough and began hiding them away when he was asleep.

It did no good.

Any time he was hungry, he found them.

He was like a starving raccoon, muttering away, his pink curls tucked inside a baseball cap that had the logo of a sports team I didn't care to recognize on it. After he choked his way through a few more bowls, instead of being happy he had located the missing cereal, fifteen minutes later he would be settled on his bed covered in crumbs, crying.

Again.

He wandered around the apartment like a fluffy pink zombie-snail oozing emotion behind him. *Sad, sad, sad,* he leaked as he stared morosely at the walls and popped painkillers like candy every time I commanded him to. The swelling in his face was going away. Maybe it was the salt from his tears. Keeping track of days was difficult for me. Keeping track of people's moods was even harder.

I hadn't been the most emotionally in-tune person even when I was alive.

In fact, I actively avoided emotion.

It was oftentimes confusing. People's faces said one thing, but their words said another. Traps. Everywhere. It was easier to understand expressions when I'd known someone for a long time, but I hadn't had that luxury since before my death. That was why, at first, Luca's tears made me uneasy. I tried to ignore them, but that soon became impossible. Especially on days he'd freeze, stare out the window, and cease to function for what felt like hours at a time. (Not that I'd call his normal moping and crying "functioning.")

Even I was becoming concerned.

I didn't *care* about him. At least that's what I said to make myself feel better. I was paying attention because the more I observed—the more I learned about what made him tick—the easier it would be to take advantage of his weakness.

I'd already learned he was susceptible to basic superstition.

Lucky. That's what I wanted him to think the necklace was. If it was lucky he wouldn't throw it away. He'd covet it. Cherish it. Keep it safe. I'd laid the bread crumbs for him to follow, in the hopes that when I finally revealed myself he would be less frightened and more…complacent.

If he thought I was a lucky ghost there would be less fighting over what I planned to do. Positive manipulation at its finest. I could convince him, control him, lie—whatever I needed to get what I desired without handing him my secret. He'd believe me if it meant more twenty-dollar bills were slipped into the pockets of his horrible baggy jeans.

People were greedy.

That I could count on.

Maybe it would benefit me to figure out why he was so emotional?

But no.

I didn't care enough for that.

It would still work.

It had to.

I just wished he'd stop crying long enough to notice the money I'd hidden in his sock drawer. If he was smart, he'd use it to replace his broken phone. I didn't want to hold my breath for that though. Clearly, he wasn't the sharpest tool in the shed. It had been days and he still hadn't realized that I'd taken his body for a spin. Though, in his defense, robbing an ATM downtown had only taken an hour max.

One week in and I already knew that Luca was…*useless*. A dumb blond in a pink disguise, with a massive collection of painting supplies he never fucking used.

Perfect.

I wouldn't feel bad about killing him.

"Look, I swear to god." Luca's voice echoed in the back of my mind as I slowly became conscious. Sometimes it was like that. Sucked into the darkness, my existence flickering like a candle in the wind until I'd gathered enough energy to appear. There was another way to bring me to the surface, but I refused to sink that low ever again. Even if it meant remaining inside the brutal grip of limbo.

It was cold there, in the Nothing.

Icy.

Uncomfortable.

When I was corporeal I hardly felt the temperature. Trapped in the Nothing, that changed. My senses were heightened, magnified by an emptiness so vast I lost all perception of myself. Immobile, I had no choice but to become one with the frost and bitter things, my essence fracturing like scattered glass while I waited for time to move again, and my pieces to gather. The cold was wicked but it wasn't the worst part. The loss of time was. The disorientation. Weeks could pass, months, years and I'd never know it.

Once, in a fit of rage, Lydia had banished me to the Nothing for an entire year. When I'd finally been released, it had taken a full week of her gloating to realize just how much time had been stolen from me.

Not that time should even matter to me anymore.

I was dead after all.

Who cared if I disappeared?

That was what I wanted anyway, so why did it matter *how* it happened?

Except, even *I* knew that without an anchor, eventually being stuck in the Nothing was sure to drive me insane. My sense of self was all I had left, and with each trip into the darkness I lost a little more of it. Technically, becoming permanently corporeal was a fairly simple fix. The fact I existed at all meant I still had an anchor to cling to. The twist? The bearer of my talisman had to actively wish me beside them—which meant they had to be *aware* of the power they held over me.

I wasn't willing to give that away again.

I could deal with the Nothing when I knew firsthand that being held by a knowing host held dangers far worse than the darkness.

Lydia had proven that.

I could still remember the eyes of the little boy I'd been forced to help Lydia torment. The way he'd stared unseeingly at me, trembling, tear stains streaking his pale cheeks, as I'd held him immobile. I'd known him. Before the mess. Before I'd died. Amanda's son.

Which was why it gave the murderous bitch great joy to watch how hurting him affected me. Angry, bitter, then numb as I accepted that I had no choice but to do as she said. The kid had been the spitting image of the person who had taught me what kindness was. To crush him felt like defiling her memory.

Lydia had tortured us both simultaneously. She was efficient like that.

Why do one thing when you can do two?

I chose not to think of the boy's name. I didn't like being reminded of that time in my un-life. It didn't help. Nothing would. It was a thing that had happened that I couldn't change.

"I'm being haunted—" Luca's voice was getting louder, and I chased after it, wandering through the empty inky-black. I sifted through the strands of reality. Every word he spoke was a sunbeam breaking through the clouds of my captivity.

When I finally burst free the scents and smells of the real-world rushed forward. Bright. Loud. Colorful. Blurs of shapes that shifted and evolved until the first thing I recognized was the scent of—

Cereal.

We were eating cereal again.

Why was I surprised?

Like always, Luca was talking to Violet. His phone had been fixed—or replaced, it was hard to tell. Though I figured all I would have to do to find out was check whether or not he still had the *I'm a lucky little ducky* sticker stuck to the back of his phone.

"Yes, I'm sure." Luca continued, poking at a stray piece of marshmallow from his current bowl of Lucky Charms. "No, I don't know how it happened, or who is haunting me."

Huh.

He wasn't as stupid as I'd thought.

"Kinda hard not to notice when money is appearing all over the fucking place—and you catch a photo of yourself on the *Five O'clock News* that— *miraculously*—explains exactly where it all came from." Luca blinked, then shuddered as I exited his body and floated to the kitchen sink. Right now I was too weak to be tangible, so I simply observed, curious to see the effects of my handiwork.

Luca didn't seem relieved.

You'd think, considering the amount of zeros that populated his bank statements, he would be glad to receive money unsolicited. There was no reason to be upset. I'd worn a disguise. *How had he recognized himself in the first place?*

Besides, it wasn't like I'd had a choice.

Before—when my only goal had been getting my cock wet, those few hours of physicality had been a walk in the park. My targets always wanted me to touch them after all, even going as far as to command me to do so, unaware that with every uttered plea they made me more tangible.

This—what I was doing with Luca—was new territory.

I'd never had an unaware host before.

Which was fine by me. I could still get what I wanted. Even if I was, admittedly, the weakest I'd ever been. I could still make this work. *I could.* Though…apparently my assumption that he was easily tricked might have been premature.

Luca was smarter than I'd given him credit for.

The fact he'd noticed my presence was a testament to that.

"No, the ghost isn't hurting me. No, it doesn't appear to be malicious. No flickering lights. Yes, I'm sure. But also—how the hell do I exorcise it?" Luca continued speaking, his hands gesticulating wildly, long legs sprawled, his broad shoulders encased in a silken violet robe with a fluffy fur collar. It was clearly not his, judging by how ill-fitting it was.

He wanted to exorcise me?

No. That wouldn't do. To emphasize my point, I reached for the light switch, summoning every ounce of strength I had to give it a few rapid, angry little flicks with my finger.

No exorcising.

"Motherfucker." The white of Luca's eyes flashed as he whipped around to glare suspiciously behind him, before blurting a quick, "I gotta go, Violet. Text me."

He hung up, placing his phone flat on the table. The ducky sticker was missing. *Interesting.* So he had a problem with me stealing, but didn't have one with spending the money? I liked that. A little too much.

"Hello?" Luca spun the other way, still searching. He wouldn't find me, no matter how many times he dramatically twisted. His naivety was… amusing, which wasn't an emotion I felt often.

I didn't answer him.

Why would I?

Clearly my silence wasn't enough of a deterrent.

"Are you…gonna murder me?" Luca asked, gray eyes wide. He bunched the stolen silk robe he wore like a cloak around himself. His long legs poked out the bottom, dark blond hair flickering along his exposed shins, feet bare—vulnerable. "Because like—I've seen *The Exorcist*," Luca continued to ramble, "and *Supernatural*. Also, my roommate is a witch."

So he was *threatening* me now.

"So, yeah. You really don't want to hurt me. I know shit. And my roommate? Yeah—she'll…totally…um." Luca blinked, scrubbing his hands nervously on his thighs. "She'll totally get you."

As far as threats went this one was pretty tame.

I'm very frightened, I deadpanned.

"*Aha!*" Luca leapt from his seat, pointing accusingly at the fridge to my left like he expected me to be there. "I knew it! I *knew* you were talking to me! It took me a second but—"

You're pointing at the wrong place.

I'm over here.

"Over where?" Paranoid, he spun around to check over his shoulder. I could practically taste the fear buzzing beneath his skin. Even separated, his emotions simmered within me, our connection undeniable in light of his strong emotions. An itch in the back of my mind that I couldn't scratch.

I don't know why I told the truth, but I did.

The light switch.

Luca whipped to face me, his pink hair bouncing, robe flickering as he glared right where my cock would be if he could see me. It was…again. *Amusing.*

His cereal was getting soggy.

Up.

Luca dragged his gaze higher, his eyes meeting mine—not that *he* knew that. My mouth suddenly grew dry as I looked my fill. There were freckles across the bridge of his nose. Like a paint splatter. His chapped pink lips trembled. A bead of sweat trickled down the side of his temple and into the groove beneath his jawline. Bravery bolstered by fear. I could taste it as clearly as I could see it flickering under the surface of his stormy silver gaze. Brown lashes, thick and straight. Doe-ish. Like prey. A sheep parading as a wolf.

"Who are you?" Luca repeated his earlier question, but again I didn't answer. My strength was slipping already and I sighed, disappearing toward the call of his body, resigned to be pulled into the Nothing once again.

I hadn't realized how much it would affect me to be with a host that was unaware of my presence.

I would have to get used to it.

The curse was unforgiving.

Unforgiving as the dark.

I was spread thin once more, my molecules separating and scattering as my thoughts fell away, my essence devoured, and I became nothing once again.

Chapter Seven

Prudence

THE NEXT TIME I came to the surface I was stronger. Which…was interesting considering the fact that Luca was actively trying to get rid of me. Floating at the edge of the room, I had a front row seat as he burned sage in a circle, chanting a spell I could clearly see glowing from a Google page open on his laptop screen.

He looked determined.

Frazzled.

Fluffy.

Hilariously earnest as he waved his hands in the air, robe swaying, long muscular legs encased in a new pair of pajama pants, that had the fortune of riding up his supple calves. The fuzzy purple bear slippers really gave the whole ensemble a frightening kick.

For the first time in eons, my heart burst to life as I abandoned my post and wandered the apartment to inspect all the traps he'd laid out for me while I'd been lost.

Salt.

There was salt *everywhere*.

A grocery bag full of generic bottles of salt sat abandoned on the counter, clearly ready to embark on another salt spreading adventure. The trash bin beside it was already full of what I could only assume were the containers he'd emptied.

Damn.

It looked like it had taken hours.

That was some dedication.

"*Begone!*" Luca yelled as he finished his Google spell. Immediately, banging sounded beneath his feet and Luca jumped in surprise, then swore as the neighbor in the apartment beneath his admonished him by whacking their shared floor/ceiling with what sounded like a broom. "Ghosty?" He called much quieter this time. He waited, but I didn't respond.

The tantalizing aroma of Luca's sweat wafted through the air, making my cock twitch and my hands clench into fists. Something primal inside me purred as I tipped my head toward the scent, soaking up the mix of coconut, pineapple, sunscreen, and musk with curiosity.

I finished examining the apartment and stopped in front of him, cocking my head. His shoulders sagged with relief now that he believed the spell had gotten rid of me. Ha. As if something so simple could banish me. As long as Luca still wore my necklace, dangling sweet as sin against his breastbone, he was mine. *Why* he wanted to get rid of me so badly, I had no idea.

All I'd done was give him money and force him to take care of himself.

Not that I particularly excelled at the *whole caring for another human* kind of thing.

I was shit at it, actually. Even *I* knew that.

Sighing dramatically, Luca wandered into the kitchen and flopped into his favorite rickety wooden chair. It teetered, and he placed a hand on the pitiful little dining table to his left to steady himself. As he wiped the sweat from his forehead, I admired the way his tank top dipped low enough I could sneak a glance at his hard pink nipples.

I wanted to bite them till he cried.

"Are you gone?" Luca asked the air—me—his body slipping lower in the seat till his legs were spread and his puffy slippers skidded on the stained linoleum.

I don't think you want me to leave, I replied.

He flinched, glancing around again before he reached up and plunged his fingers into his already frazzled hair in alarm.

"Are you in my head?"

What do you think?

"Oh my fucking God." Luca pulled at his hair, shaking his head in disbelief. "*Why is this happening to me?*" he muttered, clearly distressed. "I pay my taxes on time. I haven't stolen in ages—karma should be on my side, shouldn't it?" He pulled tighter on his hair, quaking in a way that made me want to force his hands away, so I could see the look of pain more clearly. "I fucking *hate* ghosts," he added under his breath.

Why are you so sure I'm a ghost?

"Well, aren't you?"

I suppose he had me there.

"You know. It would really help me out if you would stop fucking ignoring every question I ask. I have no idea if you're like—malicious or whatever. Of malicious intent, I mean. Yes." He snapped his fingers. "That's it! The internet said some of you are here for that—to be *malicious*. So are you?" He could've won an award for most uses of the word malicious in a single sentence.

Do you think I am?

"Oh my god. Stop answering my questions with questions, you dick."

I don't plan on hurting you any time soon.

"But you might hurt me later?" Luca squawked. "Not exactly reassuring, dude."

That isn't what I said.

He wasn't entirely wrong, but I wasn't going to tell him that. For my plan to work it was important he trusted me enough to take his body for a spin. I kept losing time, and it was getting more and more annoying. If I could possess his body for long enough, maybe I could accomplish what I needed to do and then fuck off to whatever hole in Hell would have me.

I already knew I wasn't strong enough for that though.

At least not yet.

"Why can't I see you?" Luca asked, shaking his head as he squinted around the room suspiciously like he thought by squinting he'd be able to break through the fog between our dimensions. He released his poor abused hair, and I relaxed a fraction when none pulled out.

Why would you want to?

"I'd like to put a face to the voice I've been hearing in my head for two weeks," Luca pointed out. "I mean—" A burst of splotchy red blossomed outward from his tanned cheeks, caressing his ears, his neck, till it disappeared beneath his collar. "We had…sex, didn't we? It seems only polite."

Ah. So he'd caught that too.

No. You're too emotional right now. Later.

"Too emo—" Luca spluttered in offense, flapping his hands around like a sexy pink Big Bird. "I'm not emotional! I am a perfectly functional member of society." He blinked, eyes narrowing. "Wait, have you been watching me?"

Obviously.

"Oh. *Fuck*. I can't believe I'm stuck to a nosy ghost," Luca lamented, dragging his hands over his face in frustration.

It's not my fault you excrete emotion like a sweaty man in a sauna.

"First of all, gross. Second, fuck you." Luca huffed, crossing his arms over his chest, his cheeks puffing up as he blew his floppy bangs out of his face. "I resent that. I'm just…going through a rough patch."

Why?

"Why—" Luca blinked, clearly confused. "Why am I having a hard time?"

Yes.

"Um—I'm *literally* being haunted," Luca pointed out. "Do you need another reason?" He was hiding the truth, but I figured I'd find out soon enough so I didn't push. Instead, I just observed him. After a moment his eyes lit up, and he popped out of his seat and began strutting around the kitchen, peeking in the cupboards.

What are you doing?

"Looking for speakers. Or like…a phone? Just because I hear you doesn't mean you're not just a prank."

You were so sure earlier that I was a ghost.

"Well, yeah. But I mean. I'm open to other possibilities. Maybe someone is fucking with me." Luca's eyes narrowed. "But…No." He wilted, shutting the cupboard he was inspecting. "No, I don't think you're pranking me. I'm pretty sure you really are a ghost."

Why do you say that?

He was honestly fascinating. I couldn't help but poke, curious to see if I could get him to react. Unpredictable. Even more unpredictable than *I* was.

"A gut feeling I guess? I don't know." Luca shuddered. "I just…" His cheeks grew pink again and he began to shuffle in this awkward little dance that made me bite my tongue. "I just *know*, okay? Maybe that's dumb of me but…"

Following your instincts isn't dumb.

"Thank you! That's the first nice thing you've said to me." Luca's grin wilted as quickly as it had come. With a sigh he slunk his way to the cluttered yellow counter, unknowingly walking right toward me. He leaned his back against it, with all of his considerable, long-legged weight, his head dropping in defeat. Up close like this I could count the freckles on his nose.

He was taller than me, by a fair margin. I cocked my head as a wayward pink curl that snuggled around the shell of his ear broke free. He exhaled raggedly. He had no idea how close our bodies were, and I wasn't sure I *wanted* him to.

If he knew, he'd move.

The single window cast beams of sunlight, painting Luca's sun kissed skin gold as the potted plants that sat in a string atop the run down cabinetry drooped their leaves toward him. The long slope of his nose scrunched up in disgust as his lashes practically glowed.

He was a walking contradiction. As pretty as he was masculine. Probably unaware of how obscene his muscular ass looked in his clearly borrowed pajama pants. Blind to the fact that the way his broad shoulders pulled his violet robe taut was even more provocative than if he'd been wearing nothing but his freckles.

Everything about him screamed *fuck me.*

"It's just my luck that I've had a fucking audience during the worst two weeks of my life."

An unfamiliar feeling bubbled up inside me.

Guilt?

Guilt.

I'd never felt that before.

It sucked.

That sucks.

"Nah." Luca shrugged, tipping his head back, the long line of his throat exposed in the light. I wanted to lick the sweat glistening on his skin as his Adam's apple bobbed. Desire for him made me both dazed and ravenous. "I guess it's not that bad. I mean, now that you've seen me at my lowest, at least I don't have to lie to you, right?"

Do you lie often?

"Often enough." Luca grimaced, then back-pedaled. "Not about anything important, though. Just normal stuff. People are like, 'Are you okay?' and I'm like, 'Oh, I'm fucking fantastic! Thanks!' Even though on the inside I actually want to die."

Wow.

The more Luca spoke, the more animated he became. His sadness seeped away. It was like watching the sun peep through clouds on a stormy day.

"Actually the more I think about it, having you around might be kinda nice. Cuz even though it's gross you've seen me snotty and emotional, at least with you I don't have to pretend like I'm happy, you know?"

Oh.

"So yeah. Um, hi. Please don't murder me in my sleep. My name's Luca—in case you didn't already know that—and I'm a twenty-four-year-old hot mess with trust issues."

I didn't ask.

"Dick." Luca laughed, more genuinely this time. His eyes flickered with emotion and he blew his bangs out of his face with a sigh. "Please, for the love of all things unholy, at least give me your name?"

Maybe it was the fact he'd said please.

Maybe it was because when he moved like that all I could think about was how stunning he'd looked with his fingers shoved down his throat and his cock tucked hot-wet and pleasure-sweet between his long, capable fingers.

Prudence.

"Prudence?" He blinked, brow furrowing, "That's a weird name."

Tell that to my mother.

"Sure," Luca grinned bright enough he chased away his own shadows. "I'll tell her the next time I see her. You know, after sex." He blinked, frowned, then frowned even more. The lines multiplied. "In case you couldn't tell, that was supposed to be a 'your mom' joke."

I could tell.

"It wasn't very good, was it?"

No.

Luca laughed again, the sound loud and uninhibited as he shook his head. "Well, okay then. Fuck you too, Prudence." He tipped his head to the side, his pink curls spilling, lips twisted into a naughty little smile that made me want to fuck him till his eyes crossed.

My cheeks hurt and when I reached up to investigate why, I was shocked and a little disgusted to discover that I was smiling right back.

Chapter Eight

Luca

IN MY DEFENSE, jerking off wasn't the first thing I did after I found out I was being haunted. I ate dinner first. *Then* I jerked off. I mean… who could blame me? That night in the hotel had lived rent free in my head for two weeks now and I'd been unable to get myself off since. *Now* I knew why. Injustice, thy name is: Toppy Ghosts.

Prudence wouldn't mind.

Probably.

Maybe…if I was reaaaally good he'd lend a helping hand?

Maybe…I could entice him to show his face with the magic of my dick? Man, *that* was optimistic even for me. It was probably weird that I wanted him the fuck out of my life, my head, my apartment—and yet simultaneously wanted him the fuck inside of me. Priorities.

So, yeah.

Confusing.

Wait.

Could he hear my thoughts?

Scratch that—more importantly—was he even human? Was I seriously about to get off thinking about a dude that I didn't even know the species of? Or how old he was? *Oh, god.* What if Prudence was like…a super creepy old man with droopy jowls and ear hair and—fuck. Now my boner was definitely gone. I pulled my hand out of my boxers with an annoyed huff.

Think happy thoughts.

Sexy thoughts.

"What do you look like?" I asked the air, only to be greeted by silence. Since the last time we'd spoken he'd barely been around, so it was no surprise to me now that Prudence was missing again. It was almost like sometimes he got zapped away. Poof, like he'd never been there to begin with. The first time he'd disappeared he'd been gone for long enough I'd contemplated calling up a priest and asking them to cleanse the entire apartment. But I decided against it when his absence started to convince me that I'd imagined the whole thing. I was self-aware enough to understand the unholy crying I'd been experiencing may not have been the only symptom of my current mental breakdown.

If I was a sane person, I would've been relieved he wasn't always present. It was one step closer to not having him around at all. Buuuut honestly, I wasn't sure I *wanted* to get rid of him. As much as I hated ghosts—which I did—thank you, *Supernatural.* I didn't think Prudence was *actually* bad. I still had bruises around my wrist to prove that fact. Not that I was one hundred percent certain he'd been the one to save me from the murder-car—because I wasn't—but, at this point, it was the likeliest possibility.

So far he'd basically been a shit-head but…good things had been happening often since I'd left Elmwood, and I could only assume that they had something to do with our attachment. So…maybe I figured he deserved the benefit of the doubt.

Plus the orgasm he'd given me had made me see Jesus.

Hard to hate a dude that made you cum out your eyeballs.

A lucky ghost indeed.

Violet was not impressed with my ghostly angst. I'd texted her about him about sixty times now and it was clear that she didn't believe I was telling the truth. Kinda like how I didn't believe her when she told me that her family was full of witches. Hypocritical, I know.

Except—this was a bit more serious, wasn't it?

That was why her easy dismissals really made my blood boil.

The longer she patronized me, the more annoying it became. *Actually*! Now that I thought about it, this wasn't the first time she'd done this. Ever since Hunter had left me, she'd started to act like she thought I couldn't be trusted to make my own decisions.

Which *pissed* me off.

I loved her but, God—

Nothing made me more upset than being treated like I was incapable. I'd been chopping my way through the jungles of life since I was a wee embryo, for God's sake. In fact, not only had I been responsible for myself, but also for the livelihood of Betty and Adam too. *Damn*. The more I thought about it the more angry I became. I shook off the frustrating thoughts, glaring down at my limp dick with disgust.

Boner-ville was now a ghost town. And I blamed Prudence, since thinking of him was what had reminded me of Violet in the first place.

"This is your fault, you know." I accused the empty room, receiving the answer I expected, which was once again…nothing.

Fuck.

There would be no ghost-sex for me, apparently. It was funny how so recently I'd declared myself in a no-dicking-zone and yet here I was… mourning the lack of paranormal penis in my life.

I rolled onto my belly, burying my face in the pile of pillows on my bed with a frustrated groan. The sheets were worn and soft and still smelled like laundry detergent from the last time I'd washed them. *Why was it so hard to do such simple shit sometimes?* God knows I could use the dopamine high a good orgasm would give me. I was pretty sure my overused tear ducts were about ready to evict me from my own body. Form a union. Start a revolution.

I just needed to feel good for *one fucking second.*

Like always when things didn't work out the way I wanted them to, I resorted to violence. Hopefully the bite of pain would shock my dick into waking up. Tentatively, I slipped my hand inside my boxers again, scratching a trail over the top of my thigh till gooseflesh formed in its wake. The familiar prickle of the hair on my legs against the pads of my fingers lulled me into a state of calm. Just me and my dick. We could do this. *Totally.*

I'd always liked how it felt when I pulled on the hair, as weird as that sounded. I was sensitive all over down there. Every twinge of pain sent a direct signal to my cock. Maybe if I teased my body enough I could get little Luca on board again?

Several frustrating, tantalizing minutes passed as I toyed with myself to no avail. When scratching didn't work, I gave up on that and began to stroke my dick. Despite my enthusiasm, it remained stubbornly limp in my grip. I loosened my hold on it, when it became obvious my evil plan wasn't working.

"Fuuuck," I whined pitifully into the mattress. No matter what I did, I still couldn't get hard. *Damn it.* Too bad I couldn't just…tap into my inner Prudence and fuck myself dumb like he had the other night. How the hell had he made me feel so…present? In the moment. Without being distracted by my own mind?

Before our first time together, I honestly hadn't known that I was so *into* the whole *be mean to me in bed* thing. Toxic was apparently the hottest thing ever. And now that I did, I should be grateful, right? That he'd shown me the light.

It was wild how much I craved being called a slut again while he choked me silly. Maybe it made me fucked in the head to crave that buuuut just thinking about a repeat *really* got me off. I could try to do it myself—yes! That was a good plan. Go, me!

"Jerk yourself off, you stupid slut," I attempted, the words unnatural and stilted on their way out. *Nope. Nope. Nooope. Absolutely not.* I cringed. Definitely couldn't pull off a Prudence.

Well, it was worth a shot.

That desperate, are you? Little ducky's trying to howl.

"*Oh, thank fuck.*" I perked up, and my dick did too—to my relief. It twitched inside my loose hold as I exhaled the tension away, Prudence's now familiar scratchy drawl filling my ear.

What do you want?

"*Ugh*. Don't make me ask."

Prudence was silent. *Was I supposed to beg?* I waited for all of fifteen seconds before my will to get off became stronger than my pride. "Please, Prudence," I implored. "I just want…*fuck*." Words. Why were words so hard? I swallowed. "*I wanna feel good.*"

Are you prepared for it to hurt?

"Oh God, yes." The words escaped before I was able to filter them, my own enthusiasm surprising me as my hips flexed and precum made the inside of my boxers slick where my cock head pressed against the cotton fabric. *When had I gotten hard?* I'd been so distracted I hadn't noticed. My dick throbbed in my grip and I gave it a soothing squeeze right at the base, suddenly breathless.

Man. Apparently begging really did it for me too. I was learning all sorts of new things about myself lately.

Hard limits?

"Um…none?" I squeaked, squirming a little, my balls beginning to ache as I slipped my fingers down to toy with the sensitive skin pulled taught overtop them. *Jesus.* Why did the act of simply talking to Prudence get me so fucking hard? There was something naughty about it. Taboo. I shouldn't be doing this. My cock jerked and I whimpered, lips rubbing against the bedsheets. Was he watching me? Was he inside me? Could he feel how good it felt when he talked to me like that?

Safeword.

"Uhhhhh." I chewed on my lip. I'd never had to use a safeword before. I knew *what* they were, obviously. Porn could be very informative that way. Not that I'd ever thought I'd do anything like the stuff I saw online. Those videos had always felt like a fantasy far removed from the world I lived in. How naive I'd been. For once, I was glad things weren't going to plan.

I was starting to think maybe Prudence knew what I needed better than I did.

"Fruit Loops?" I offered tentatively.

Typical.

"What is *that* supposed to mean?"

Nothing. Get on your knees.

I got on my knees.

Following Prudence's demands was the easiest thing I'd ever done. Sure, he was dead. Sure, I was like *fundamentally* freaked-the-fuck-out—but hell! I was horny too. And who would say no to sex with a bossy ghost? Not me, apparently. Possible jowls be damned.

"What now?"

Don't move.

I swallowed, holding myself perfectly still as I lay on my belly, weirdly desperate to please him. Maybe in the future I'd push back—just to see what he'd do—but for now I was too eager to feel the rumble of his words inside my head to be anything but compliant.

I wished he could touch me for real.

The longer I held still, the longer I began to overthink. *Had the sheets always felt this scratchy? Were these the boxers with the hole in the crotch? I couldn't remember. Damn I should've showered.*

I squirmed.

Should I arch my back more? Shake my ass a little? Was he looking?

Oh god. Was he even gay?

"Um…this might be a weird question. But—do you like…*like* me?" I asked, my bare back trembling as I kept my face pinned to the mattress.

My cheeks were hot. I was uncomfortable, and not in a fun way—though my dick *because it was a dick*—remained stubbornly hard inside my grip. "Because, if this is a pity thing, I'll still take it. I just…would rather *know* that before we start."

Needy much?

"I'd like you more if you shut up." A dark rumbling voice echoed from behind me and I jolted, my whole body tensing as something cool brushed against my back. A hand, maybe? I released my cock to push onto my hands, startled, as my pulse beat an angry staccato against my ribs. "*Don't look,*" Prudence commanded. I recognized his voice. I'd heard that same smooth drawl spout vitriol sporadically in the back of my mind for the last few weeks.

Holy shit.

Prudence was behind me.

"Wait— But—" I shook my head in confusion. "*Are you…?*"

"Solid. Here. *Annoyed.*" Prudence's hand—because that was what it was, wasn't it?—pressed hard against my back, pushing between my shoulder blades until I got the point and sunk down onto my elbows again. He removed his hand. I felt the bed shift. My breath expelled in a panicked-excited puff.

What was he doing back there?

Did this mean he was a poltergeist? Poltergeists were the ones that could touch things, right?

Oh-my-god. What if he was looking at my ass? *He was probably looking at my ass. There was a ghost looking at my ass!*

"Are you looking at my ass?" I asked, sounding properly scandalized, even though literally *all* I wanted from this goddamn life was for Prudence to ogle me. Insecure? Yeah, right. Not about this. I knew I had a fantastic ass. All the hills and miles I hiked meant I'd built my glutes to beyond perky levels. It was one of the things I was actually confident about. That and my superior lying skills. Not that I had used them in a long-ass time.

That was beside the point though. Because Prudence. And asses. My ass, in particular. I was dying to hear his answer. And I had no idea how he would reply, but I was shaking in my hypothetical boots as I waited to find out.

"Do I need to gag you?" Prudence deadpanned, clearly amused though his voice remained unimpressed. Or maybe I just hoped he was amused?

I swallowed. *I swallowed again.* My cheeks grew even hotter, and a little whimper left my lips without permission. "I wouldn't complain." Outside the single bedroom window starlight crept between the clouds, painting the bedsheets silver as I trembled.

This was all so new, so surprising.

I hadn't known Prudence could become…whatever it was he'd become. Solid, like he'd said? With a body? Wait, shit. Now that he was behind me my earlier paranoia came back full force. Oh god, what if he really *was* an old man? He was refusing to let me look at him after all. Maybe there was something he didn't want me to see.

"Are you like…super terrifying? Grotesque? Is that why you won't let me look?" I fretted, wiggling uncomfortably, my nipples hard where they rubbed against the cool sheets.

Prudence huffed, an irritated, put-upon sound. He was a man of few words, which made our dynamic chaotic—since I spewed nonsense like a dictionary holding a megaphone.

"I won't repeat myself again, Luca."

"Okay." My pulse fluttered. My name on his lips sounded like sin and smoke, and I was weak, desperate to hear what he had to say next.

"*Be quiet.*"

Quiet. I could be quiet. I could totally do that.

"I'll answer your questions when, and *if,* I feel like it. *You* are not in charge here. Nod if you understand." I nodded, my dick sloppy wet and hard enough to pound nails where it pushed against the slit in my boxers. The elastic hem clung to my wrist as I tried not to pant, hips primally circling, aching for something hot to fuck into.

"I'm going to touch you now." There was no inflection in Prudence's voice to warn me of what was coming. Because I still had some sense of self-preservation, I didn't point out the fact that he already did.

The cool slide of a calloused palm scratched its way up my spine, dominating, possessive, like it had the right to do whatever it desired and I had no choice but to take what I was given. With his thick fingers spread wide, Prudence's hand climbed inch by inch, till his fingers closed around the back of my neck and he squeezed tight. "Take your hand off your cock."

I pulled my hand out of my boxers, even though that simple action made me want to sob.

I wasn't sure why, but that one almost innocent touch forced my worrisome thoughts to take flight and all the tension bled from my body. Prudence was surprisingly gentle—though firm—as he tangled his fingers in the back of my hair, closed his fist, and pulled tight from the root till sparks of pleasure shot down my spine and my toes curled.

"Shit," I hiccuped.

The pain shot directly to my dick as a rumbling, almost mean chuckle echoed behind me.

"You like it hard, don't you?" Prudence murmured, lips teasing against the shell of my ear. He crowded in close behind me, every brush of his body against mine, tingly more than anything. Like parts of him weren't truly solid yet—at least not right now. "*Don't you,* Luca?" Prudence's voice was a threat I gladly succumbed to as he pulled harder and I gasped.

"*Yes.*" The word escaped my lips breathlessly and Prudence hummed his approval.

"You're greedy," he decided. I couldn't deny it. Because he was right. I *was* greedy. Now that he was touching me I craved more, more, *more.* It wasn't enough. Sure, I hadn't even known I could have this until thirty seconds ago, but I needed it just as much as I needed my next breath. Little shock waves of pleasure shot through my body as I arched my back and shoved my ass toward the empty space behind me that Prudence's body would've taken up if he'd been fully corporeal.

I never should've taken my hand off my dick.

My quads were beginning to strain and shake as I squirmed for him. The ache in my balls had become nearly painful, they were pulled so tight. Slick fabric teased the crown of my cock and I humped forward desperately, scratching at the cool sheets till my fingers felt raw to the touch. The scent of sex and sweat danced through the air, making me nearly drunk with lust.

I wanted to jerk my cock again. No—I wanted *Prudence* to jerk it. *Yes.* That.

"Please touch my dick," I gasped, surprised by how easily I gave in. I wasn't normally like this in bed. It was a game of masks until I inevitably released physically. I hadn't ever been able to let go like this, to be uninhibited. Authentic. One hundred percent myself.

But I could now.

Prudence had *chosen* me.

Not the other way around.

Besides, even if this went south, he could leave and no one would know just how much I'd begged for it. Begged for the pain, the tears—the pleasure. I could be his slut and the world would stay ignorant to the fact.

"Stay present," Prudence admonished, his growl emphasized by the sting of teeth as they sunk icy-cold into the soft flesh just below my ear.

"Oh, fuck." I twisted my head to the side to give him room to work, but there was no need. His teeth were gone as quickly as they'd come, his hand still pulling my hair taut.

A fresh drop of precum leaked down my shaft as my hips flexed, once again searching for friction. Every touch was electrifying. I could feel the imprint of his teeth like the spot he'd bitten was hardwired directly to my cock. *God, I needed to be touched.* "My dick, Prudence—Please—" I groaned low, only for his teeth to sink in a second time a few inches below the first bite.

It hurt so good my eyes rolled back.

"*Quiet,*" Prudence murmured, sweet as smoke. "I'll touch your cock when you've earned it."

"Oh god," I whispered, a prayer.

"I like the way you beg," Prudence's hand slid up till he could fist the longer strands at the top of my head. This time, when he pulled my head back—hard—his teeth pressed threateningly against my jugular. I wasn't sure if he was going to fuck me or eat me. Was it bad I didn't care which one he picked?

"I like the way you make me," I admitted.

"Tell me what you desire," Prudence commanded. My dick twitched and a fresh drop of precum tickled down my shaft as I waited. I could practically feel how much I was dripping, how badly I desired him.

"What I desire?" I desired him to touch my dick.

"Your darkest fantasy. Something you've never told anyone." Prudence's breath tickled my skin and I shuddered, distracted as his words hit me. Immediately I knew what he was after. To humiliate me. To drive me higher than anyone ever had before. My skin was hot and tight, my chest constricting as I imagined how powerful he would feel the second I gave him what he wanted.

How did he know I liked this?

The squirming. The shame.

It made my dick so fucking hard.

"I don't have any," I lied, just to see what he'd do.

"Liar," he whispered, a threat trembling beneath the simple word. My cock jumped and my fists clenched. Shit. I needed him so fucking bad. *Why was I resisting, again?*

Right.

I liked the chase.

I thought so, anyway. This was all so new.

"I swear, man. There's nothing. I'm normal. Totally. No secrets. Nada. Zip."

Prudence didn't dignify my words with a response. He just held still, all touch ceasing as he waited, and waited, and waited—and fuck. I really was a greedy bitch. The longer I had to wait, the more I squirmed, the harder my cock got and fuck-fuck-fuck. I just wanted—

"Okay. Fine. *Fine*, fuck. Will you touch my dick if I tell you?" I hardly recognized my own voice. I could practically hear him rolling his eyes at me. "You have to swear not to judge me."

Even though this was a game, very real humiliation simmered under the surface of my skin. What if he thought…shit. What if he didn't like what I had to say? I'd never admitted it. Not even to myself. I swallowed the lump in my throat, a drop of sweat trickling down the side of my neck as I bit my lip hard and waited.

The moon had fully risen now, its light filling the room with an almost ethereal glow. It lit up the posters on the wall, the silhouette of my baseball cap tower stacked on the bed posts. My hands were nearly white where they bunched inside the sheets.

"Fine." Prudence's voice was a relief, even though realistically I knew if he was going to judge me, a stupid promise wasn't going to stop him.

"Okay…" Was I really doing this? I sucked in a deep fortifying breath. I could lie. I could definitely lie. I could say what I thought he wanted me to say. Buuuut I wasn't going to. I'd rather be humiliated and honest with him, than manipulate the fragile bond between us. I was tired of lying to people. And besides…he'd already seen me at my worst. Which was weirdly freeing. "I…uh." Shit, even though I'd decided to tell the truth, that didn't make this any easier.

My cheeks were so hot they could scramble eggs. Probably, anyway.

"I've never told anyone this." I squirmed.

"Stop stalling," Prudence growled, and I shuddered, my cock jerking at the threat in his words. I bit my lip again and forced myself to breathe.

Just do it.

Like ripping off a Band-Aid.

"I want…" I swallowed. "I want to do nothing."

Silence.

More squirming.

"Explain."

Oh good. If there was anything I was excellent at, it was rambling. "I know that sounds bad—who wants to do nothing, right? But I can't help it. I want to lie back. I want to take it. I want to be worshiped, just because someone likes me that much. I want teeth, and tongue. I want to be licked, and sucked, choked—fucked. I want to be edged over, and over, and over again. And after I've come so many times I'm sex-stupid, I want to be cleaned up, tucked in, and worshiped again."

The itching under my skin for once settled. My secret out in the open. I felt raw, nervous, relieved.

Prudence was silent for a few long seconds before he made a hungry, *dangerous* noise that had my eyes rolling back and gooseflesh shivering up my skin. He was a predator, and I had just walked into his trap.

"Princess," he said, in that same scratchy drawl I was quickly becoming used to. The nickname didn't sound like an insult. Just an observation. One I couldn't even be mad about.

"Fuck, it sounds bad, right?" I licked my lips, my mouth suddenly dry. *What if it wasn't enough?* Even though I'd given him all I had. My cheeks burned. "It's not that I don't like reciprocating. Not at all. I love that. I really do—I just…sometimes, wish to be…"

"Owned."

"I was gonna say wanted? But I guess 'owned' works too." God, every word out of his mouth was pure sin. My hips fucked forward of their own accord, seeking friction, and the last dregs of my patience slipped through my fingers. "Now will you please, for the love of all things unholy, please-please-*please*—with a cherry on top touch my—*ohhhh fuuuuck.*"

When his hand wrapped around my dick it was bliss. Tight. Cold. Sadistic bliss. All it took was a single brush of his finger over my hole to have me seeing stars. And when I lay spent, Prudence's presence gone once again, I couldn't help but hide my laughter against the scratchy cotton sheets.

The truth was, I *needed* him.

And I knew this wouldn't end well—it couldn't. I *knew* it couldn't. It would crash and burn—but hell—it would be one wild, delicious ride.

Chapter Nine

Luca

"DID YOU 'EXORCISE your ghost' yet?" I had my phone propped against a box of cereal on the table, and it buzzed against the cardboard as Violet's tinny voice echoed on speakerphone. I debated how to answer as I shoveled Lucky Charms into my mouth, stomach growling impatiently. For me, sex was a one-way ticket to hunger town. And I was *starving*.

Speaking of sex…

Prudence was…*holy cannoli.*

He was mean, demanding, detached, hot-as-all-hell and without a doubt the *best thing* to ever happen to me.

"Yeah…so—*about* that," I hummed, crunching through my spoonful before I poked it—now empty—at my phone with vehemence. I knew Violet couldn't see me but that didn't stop my gesticulating. "I've decided to keep him."

"Okay, Luca." I could practically hear her eyes roll. *Okay.* So we were *still* doing the whole *Luca is mentally unstable* thing. Cool. Cool-cool-cool-cool.

Actually, no. *Not cool.*

I needed to take a stand, and now was as good a time as any.

"Look—I love you—But if you don't stop being a dick about this then I'm not going to tell you all the juicy bits." My voice was probably a little harsh, all things considered. *Crap.* Instant regret. And *this* was exactly why I never stood up for myself.

"Shit—" *Ah, fuck. I'd hurt her feelings.* "I'm sorry if I've been…'dick-ish' I just…know more about this stuff than you. The likelihood of you actually being haunted by a ghost is literally so low it's just hard for me to believe."

"And who made *you* the expert on paranormal activity?" My cheeks flushed and I shoved my spoon in my bowl, pushing it away, no longer hungry. Colorful little cereal blob shapes slopped back and forth as the milk settled into place. "We literally binged *Supernatural* together. I know the same shit you do. And besides—you don't have the same hyper-fixation I have with Dean's ass, so I bet I was paying closer attention."

"Dean's ass is not the plot, Luca. That's besides the point, though. I'm a witch. *Remember?*"

"Okay I get that. But like—"

"*Do* you get it?" Violet sighed, muttering something over her shoulder before her end of the line got quieter and her voice grew clearer. I hadn't realized she'd been in public until suddenly she wasn't. Living in the city had taught me to automatically tune out background noise.

"I *know* you're a witch."

"I don't think you do," Violet's voice was threaded with impatience, and I quieted as I waited for her to continue. "You say that, but you don't get what it *actually* means."

The hypocrisy of this argument was hilarious. Here I was—not believing her—when I was currently pissed at her for not believing me. Man. A pit sat heavy in my stomach as I chewed on my lip, trying to decide how to navigate the rest of the conversation.

She was kinda right.

I didn't get what she meant when she said she was a witch. To be fair, she'd never really explained what she meant. I'd just accepted it like I'd accepted her horrible country music—or the fact that she was obsessed with the worst flavor of ice cream ever. Pistachio. Ew.

Buuuut…clearly ghosts were real.

And if ghosts were real then maybe witches were too?

Shit.

I was a dick.

"Yeah…" I agreed, chewing on my lip as I kicked a leg up and wedged my foot under the back of my knee, wiggling to get comfortable. My chest hurt. My hands were all sweaty. "You're right. I'm sorry."

Remorse tasted like ash on my tongue.

Even though I knew Violet was kinda being a jerk about the whole ghost thing she was still my best friend. I missed her. I hated when she left home to spend the summers in Maine with her family. Even halfway across the country, Violet was dependable as hell. Unlike me. I couldn't even pay my own portion of rent without scraping my bank account clean with a toothbrush.

Maybe I should start an *Only Fans* like she had? Except who would pay to see my socially awkward ass?

Prudence, maybe.

Huh.

Except I still didn't know if he liked me because he hadn't fucking answered me earlier. And also—he was dead. So how the hell could he pay me anyway? Ghosts didn't have money. *Man.* Did his family even know he was still here?

If he stopped being a stoic asshole I could ask him.

But…that might kill the mood.

And I kinda hoped if Prudence were to show up again, we wouldn't waste time talking. Sure, maybe wanting him for his dick was shitty of me. But at least I was being shitty *and* sexually-satisfied at the same time. Like a cat who caught the canary, or however that saying went.

Sunrise follows even the darkest night.

Hell yeah, it does.

And my sunrise sounded like sex, smelled like leather, and knew exactly how to torture me into getting off. My neck tingled just thinking about the bruises he'd left behind as he'd choked me to completion. Yeaahhh… It was probably good Violet couldn't see me right now. I was grinning way too hard, and looked like I'd been mauled.

"*Hellooo?*" Violet's voice filtered through my thoughts. Shit. I hadn't meant to ignore her.

"Sorry! I was thinking about ghost sex," I blurted, unthinkingly.

There was an awkward pause that seemed to go on for ages. I squirmed, tapping my fingers nervously against the lip of the table. I hadn't meant to say that. Fuck. If she didn't believe me before, she definitely wouldn't now that I'd brought Prudence's dick into the equation. It was one thing to be haunted, and something entirely else to be haunted by a ghost that wanted to rail you.

"Wait—" Violet's voice grew hard, the amusement bleeding away as she spoke. "*Ghost sex?* You didn't tell me about ghost sex."

"I told you I hadn't gotten to the juicy bits yet!"

"You're not fucking around with Patrick Swayze, Luca. If you're having sex with a ghost I should definitely be the first person to know."

"Um, pardon me, Miss-Condescending-Mc-Witchy-Pants. You have made it incredibly uncomfortable to talk to you about the whole thing because you've made it obvious you're just humoring me." Obviously, she hadn't realized I'd caught on to what she was doing. Her silence was flabbergasted.

It hadn't hit me how hurt I was until that moment. The words were already out. That was the shitty thing about words. Once you said them they couldn't be unsaid.

Violet was a bitch sometimes but she always meant well. She'd been the person to stop me from shaving my head during a bad emotional spiral. She'd been the person who had slathered bleach on my hair, then gently rinsed it away while I stuck my head under the tub faucet. She was the person that watched reruns with me just because she liked to sit beside me. She was the person that had held my hand as I sobbed over bank statements—and the person that had curled up on my bed with me for weeks while I cried my way into sobriety, cursing the very ground Hunter walked on.

So, yeah.

This was out of character for her.

"I'm sorry I made you feel that way," Violet said softly, remorse coloring her tone indigo. The drive to paint the emotion tingled at my fingertips, and I fiddled with my—her—robe absent-mindedly, aware that the desire to paint would flee the second I left the phone call.

Nothing had been clicking for me lately.

It was a tease, a glimpse at what I had been able to easily reach before, but could no longer touch.

I missed the release that came from painting the emotions that scattered like confetti inside my head. My thoughts were piles of yarn, jumbled together in a mishmash of color that only ever detangled when I was in the middle of a project.

"Look. I get it. You think I'm emotional—" I sighed. Apparently everyone thought I was emotional lately.

"To be fair, baby, you're a *little* emotional."

"Well *yes*," I agreed, "But I'm working on it. Working through my emotions is healthy, right?"

"Of course."

"So yeah. *This*—the ghost thing? It's real. And it has absolutely nothing to do with *that*—or Hunter. Hunter can go suck a dick covered in warts for all I care."

"Ew."

"I'm emotional, not delusional, Violet. When I told you I was being fucking haunted I meant it."

"I believe you."

"Yeah, but only after I told you about the sex. Which—what's up with that?" I blinked, "Ghost sex, I mean. I didn't even know that was possible. Is this like a common thing? Do ghosts just walk around and decide to fuck people all the time?"

"It's not unheard of." She was quiet for a few seconds that felt like lifetimes before she exhaled raggedly, concern leaking into her tone. "I don't think it's a good idea for you to interact with your ghost, Luca. Something about this is just…not right."

Ah. So *now* she believed me.

Weird.

Maybe the ghost-fucking was more common than I'd thought?

"Sure, yeah. You're right. I probably shouldn't have sex with something I don't understand, right?" *Lies.* Yeah, right. As if I was going to suddenly not crave Prudence's touch just because she told me it was dangerous. You know what was also dangerous? Even more dangerous than ghosts? A serious lack of orgasms. I was *suffering.* I had tons of pleasure I needed to catch up on.

"I'm serious. If I need to come home I'll—" *Cockblock me? No, thank you.*

"Thanks, but I've got this. No more ghost-dicking for me."

"You swear?"

"Abso-posu-tutely." *Lies, more lies. Oh my god.* I wasn't normally this shady, but fuck. I would give Prudence up over my dead body, literally.

"Chances are if he's there he wants something from you—" Orgasms. "And it's better if you limit your interactions as much as possible while I figure out how to get rid of him—"

"Woah." I blinked, alarm making my chest tight, and my hands clammy as I sat up straight in my chair, soggy cereal still sitting abandoned. "Wait, *what?* Get rid of him?"

"Of course. That's what you wanted—" She plowed forward and a sick feeling of loss filled me at the thought of Prudence disappearing. She was right though. As far as she knew that was what I wanted. For nearly two weeks that's all I'd talked about. But now…things were different.

I had bruises to prove it.

"That's really not necessary. He's not bothering me." Maybe I sounded too frantic, but I couldn't help myself.

"Luca." Violet's voice darkened, a thread of fear and trepidation sneaking in. "You need to let him go."

"It's only been two weeks, it's not like I'm attached. Who cares if he sticks around a little longer?" Lies, lies, *lies*.

"If I need to fly home early I will. We'll take care of this together. You're…well. Never mind. I just mean—after everything you've gone through this year—this isn't a healthy place for you to be in. With a normal dude? Sure. With a ghost? Absolutely not. They aren't what you think they are."

They're better?

Sexier?

Meaner?

Sign me the fuck up.

"He can't be *that* dangerous."

"You don't know that," Violet raised her voice over mine. "I'm only telling you this because I love you, Luca. Seriously. Ghosts *are* dangerous. Getting rid of them isn't simple. It's not like it is on TV. Freeing him from the spell he is under is a complicated, maybe even impossible process. Which you can't do because you don't even know how to do it. He could hurt you. In fact, he could kill you, depending on what it is he wants." Her breath stuttered. "*Promise me* you'll tell him to go away."

Prudence's earlier words echoed in my mind, and I shuddered.

Are you prepared for it to hurt?

Somehow I didn't think *that* was the kind of hurt that Violet was talking about.

I'd always been the responsible one, the one in charge of everyone's happiness at the detriment of my own. Even now, every day was filled with the guilt of letting my family down and for once in my fucking life I was ready to take what I wanted. What I *deserved*.

So, I lied right to her figurative fucking face.

"You're right. I'll be careful," I promised, discarding the honesty I'd worn like a mask for years, as I embraced the part of me that had long been buried. The part born from hunger and necessity. The manipulative part. The one that knew how to lie and get exactly what he wanted.

"Okay," Violet sighed, relaxing, and I unconsciously mirrored her, even though my heart was racing and my lips were dry. I hadn't realized how tensed up I'd become. "You'll call me if something happens?"

"Of course."

"I promise I'll believe you this time. I really am sorry about before. It wasn't cool."

"I forgive you." My heart thumped and I squirmed, the wooden chair I was sitting on suddenly completely uncomfortable as the weight of my dishonesty settled over me. "I'm sorry too."

As my now mushy cereal sat in the bowl beside me, only steadily getting softer, I could only think one thing.

Liar, liar, liar.

There was an awkward pause that went on for long enough I thought Violet had hung up the phone. But when I checked, she was still there. Quiet. I couldn't bring myself to end the call, even though I had the feeling that staying on the line meant I was about to hear something I didn't want to hear.

When she spoke, I wasn't wrong. "I trust you, but…before I go, I need to tell you what the real risks are."

Chapter Ten

Luca

I WAS STILL reeling from what Violet had told me, but—in typical me fashion—I'd decided the hot ghost was worth the risk. It had taken an embarrassingly short amount of time to come to that conclusion. Sure the risks were…honestly pretty fucking high, but… Ghost booty? *Boo*-ty? Yeah. Hashtag, worth it.

Unfortunately, after I'd decided to fuck everything else (and Prudence) and take what I wanted, things didn't work out that way. Prudence didn't come back. For days I waited, ready to drop my pants at any moment like a horny pink porn star.

Without his penis to distract me I was forced to confront the fact that I only had a hundred bucks left from the money Prudence made me steal—stolen for me? I wasn't sure what the ghostly logistics were. Either way, cash was dwindling—along with my cereal stash. Maybe it made me a bad person, but I was seriously contemplating selling the watch Paul had given me for Christmas to cover next month's expenses.

Not that I didn't *love* the watch. It was great. Totally a Paul gift. And I meant that in the nicest way possible. As great as it was though, rent and food—*those* were my priorities, and I was quickly running out of a way to pay for both.

I mean—fuck. Since I'd been home I'd already plowed through my snack stash, my emergency snack stash, and my extra-emergency snack stash. Ramen was pretty much the only option I had going forward if I didn't want to starve. And it was *that* scary thought that finally made me realize something needed to give. I couldn't keep wallowing like this.

The time for sadness was over.

Instead, I had to move forward.

But how?

Blinking blankly at the canvas laying on the ground in front of me, palette full of paint, brushes lined up in a pretty little row, I waited for inspiration to strike. I stared, and stared, and *stared*—but nothing happened. With my creative juices clogged, I was about as useful as a dried up lakebed in the desert.

So, I contemplated my options.

I could get a job. In fact, I'd have to.

But before that I'd give painting this one last, final try. If I couldn't do it, I'd move on. *Simple.*

As I sat pretzel-legged on the scratchy carpet in my bedroom, my fingers itched to tell the world how I was feeling. I wanted to paint the turmoil, to splatter and slash the paper in a red so bright people would be forced to look at it—to understand how it felt to hit rock bottom. To discover the loneliness that accompanied personal failure.

My fingers twitched. My eyes burned. My chest was tight.

I wanted this so bad—

But I couldn't do it.

Reaching for the paintbrush just felt wrong.

After spending half the afternoon wasting time, I had no choice but to give up. So I abandoned my paints in favor of applying for jobs online. Flopped over on my mattress, art supplies kicked unceremoniously under the bed, I submitted application, after application. Enough time passed that my stomach began to growl, and a tension headache throbbed at the base of my skull. The sun crept high in the sky, the sunny summer heat creeping through the cracks in the window.

Submitting resumes was a familiar process. Before I'd made it big in the art world, I'd done this at least a dozen times. I tried not to think about how sad it was that I was back where I started again, repeating a process I hadn't done since I'd turned twenty.

Realistically, even if I started working immediately, whatever money I made wouldn't be enough to pay my portion of rent—there just wasn't enough time. But at least it would be something, right?

I might have to give in to Violet's offer just this once, even though I'd rather take a fist to the face than accept help. I'd just have to pay her back.

Violet was making a good chunk of money on *Only Fans*. Her following was loyal and wildly enthusiastic, and she'd been offering for months to cover my portion of rent with the extra cash she earned. I'd always refused. Even though refusing had meant selling my last few paintings for far less than they were worth, in my desperation not to lean on someone else. I was running out of options though, and we'd lose the apartment if I stalled any longer. I wasn't sure why the thought of relying on someone else made me want to gouge out my own eyeballs but hey—knowing I was fucked up mentally?

Yeah, *that* wasn't really a surprise.

I'd never really outgrown who I'd been. A scared little boy, robbing gas stations, his palms sweaty, as he fought tooth and nail for every good thing he'd ever had in life. All I had now was my pride, and even *that* wasn't worth much anymore.

What had happened to me?

What had happened to the prodigy? The artist? The son that my mother bragged about all over town. The man that had paid for not only college for his little sister but his mother's minivan too. The man that everyone was in awe of—virile and colorful—full of life and a vision for the future.

My future now was scarily blank.

I saw no way out of the pit I'd fallen inside.

There was no ladder.

No rope.

No handholds.

Only the teasing flicker of a future overhead that wasn't mine anymore.

I shut my laptop with an aggrieved huff and laid it gently on the floor beside the bed before I flopped down again with a sigh. Violet's robe caught around my shoulders and I wiggled some more to un bunch the fabric. Rolling around on my belly atop the covers and whining didn't fix my problems, but it did make me feel just a little better. At least until the chill of another presence filled the room, and I stopped my depressed-worm wiggling, my head popping up, cheeks pink with embarrassment.

He was back.

"Dramatic." Prudence's voice electrified me into action and I jumped about a foot in the air. My heart was racing, and I slapped a hand over it as if that would stop it from leaping out of my chest. I struggled to my knees.

"Holy shit," I gasped, the pounding against my ribs vibrating my palm.

"Don't turn around." Prudence was behind me, just as he had been that night that felt like eons ago. It didn't escape my notice that I had been in this exact same position the last time he'd appeared. On my knees for him. Quivering in anticipation. His voice rumbled through the air, musky, dark, and impossibly sexy. He was a rainstorm. He was the fathomless depths of the ocean. Deep, deep blue. Like turbulent waters.

The pile of baseball caps stacked on top of my bedposts were not nearly as interesting as the man—ghost?—behind me, but I somehow managed to stay obediently still while I faced them. I'd had days to wonder about my ghostly companion. Days to come up with questions.

So I blurted out the first thing that came to mind.

"Why do you care if I see you?" I asked, unable to help myself. The curiosity had been killing me. I was an artist. Visuals had always been important to me.

"I don't."

"Then why—"

I felt the brush of lips against the shell of my ear and I shuddered, holding carefully still for fear of scaring Prudence away again. He was a cool presence behind me. Solid, yet still icy-cold. Prudence's voice blanketed my body, familiar as an old friend, tickling my senses, exploding heat through my veins till my cock was hard and my toes curled.

"I like the way your heart races when you're scared," he murmured, toying with me, like always. A cat playing with a mouse.

"I'm not scared of you." *That was ridiculous.*

"You're trembling. Your breathing is erratic. What else could it be?" His voice was almost playful. As playful as he got anyway. I was coming to learn that Prudence had about two emotions. Blank and horny.

"Excitement." I swallowed, my throat bobbing as I felt the tickle of his hair brush my cheek. So close and yet so far. The baseball caps blurred. "You make me *so* fucking excited."

"*Fuck*," Prudence hissed, low and throaty. A hand closed around my neck, fingers digging into my windpipe. He squeezed in a soft pulse that had me breathless for a few agonizingly glorious seconds before he slackened the grip enough I could breathe again. "You know just how to push my buttons, don't you, Pinkie?"

"I'm not trying to."

"*Liar*," Prudence tsked almost fondly, pressing his teeth threateningly against the sensitive hollow beneath my ear for the second time since I'd met him. *Liar* was quickly becoming my favorite insult. I melted, tipping my head invitingly to the side as much as I could with him holding my neck in place. Slutty. Overeager. All the things I'd been too self-conscious to be with anyone else.

I'd worn the bruises he'd left behind with pride, though they had sadly already started to heal splotchy yellow. Soon enough they'd be gone altogether. Maybe, I'd be lucky he'd leave more.

There were no masks between us. All his sharp edges fit against mine. It wasn't fair that I'd met my perfect match and he was already dead.

And yet...I couldn't stop myself from craving him.

"Are you ashamed?" Prudence hummed, his teeth digging into my jugular hard enough I was sure their impression would be left behind, his voice turned to rubble. The promise of pain was all I needed to let go. Like a string had been cut, I sagged into the possessive, familiar grip he had on my throat, my lashes fluttering. "Are you ashamed that you let me touch you like this? That you let me talk to you like this? That you like it?"

"What do you want from me?" I asked, my voice barely a whisper, croaky and weak as I felt his teeth slowly release the grip they had on the tendon in my neck. A shudder ran up my spine and I couldn't suppress the breathless whimper that left me. He was a predator, it didn't take a genius to figure out that one. I was willing prey.

Tingles. Tingly. Tingly-tingly-tingles all over.

My belly flipped, my cock weeping—like just feeling the cool grip of his fingers, the bite of his teeth, the whisper of his breath, was enough to make me sex-stupid.

"I want you to take your cock out." Prudence almost sounded bored. The possessive grip he had on my neck betrayed him.

"No—" I whimpered, because what the fuck? But also—why was I saying no? "No, sorry. I don't—I don't mean, *no*. I just mean…that's not what I was asking." *What had I even asked?*

Right. I'd asked what he wanted from me.

Prudence was silent and I squirmed. He made no move to continue without my permission though, and a giant green flag flared as I trembled. Shit. *Why was I saying no again?*

Clearly, I was stupid.

Or Violet's words were getting to me.

I swallowed, too aware of the way my Adam's apple pressed against the scratch of his cold palm. "I want to know more about you than what it feels like to be bossed around."

"'Bossed around?'" I could practically feel his amusement making the air between us flicker with static before he gave my neck a playful squeeze and spoke again. "You would rather *chat* than let me touch your cock?" *Oh. Oh. Fuck. Was he offering?* God, what was I doing, passing up an opportunity like this?

"How about chatting and then cock touching?" I offered hopefully.

"Pick one." Prudence cut off my air supply, and my whole body lit up like a firework. *Sex, sex, sex,* it chanted. But my stupid-whore mouth betrayed me again.

"I want you to answer my questions," I managed.

Idiot.

God, I was an idiot.

Prudence sighed, his grip slackening as he pulled back, fingers still teasingly brushing the sensitive goose pebbled flesh. A rush of air filled my lungs and I gasped. Prudence stroked appraisingly over the bob of my Adam's apple and I immediately missed the restriction of his tight grip. *How fucked up was that?*

I could feel his saliva drying on my neck, the chill made me shiver all over.

How was that even possible? How could he have saliva at all? How… how…how…?

"You get three questions."

There was no way in hell that was enough.

"Five."

"Three," he growled, releasing my neck completely. Despite the lack of contact, I could tell he was still behind me by the chill in the air. It made my hair stand on end. There was a predator at my back and the danger was more than thrilling.

"Four?" I asked, hopefully.

Prudence made an annoyed little sound.

Then…nothing.

Nothing.

I waited, and he remained quiet. It was a battle of wills. Which I lost. Embarrassingly quickly. I *hated* silence. "Okay, three," I gave in with a huff.

"Choose wisely."

"Okay. Fuck. No pressure or anything." I rolled my eyes sarcastically, squirming because I was way too aware that all I had to do was turn around and I'd finally get to see him. He was *right there.* Solid and real, hovering behind me like he was alive after all. I swallowed the lump in my throat, bunching my hands tight into fists to keep myself still, before I wriggled to get comfy. Sitting on my knees I stared at the UFO posters tacked to the wall right above my bed.

Patience.

I could do patience.

I could totally do patience.

"I'm waiting," Prudence taunted me.

Shit. I was supposed to be coming up with questions, not thinking about sneaking a peek at him. "Give me a sec!" I waved him away, well aware I looked absolutely fucking ridiculous in my purple silk robe, and pink *Looney Tunes* boxers, gesticulating at the wall while I had a conversation with someone I wasn't sure was even real. I squirmed. "I *have* questions. Lots of them. I just…need a second to think of them."

"Why did you ask for answers if you didn't have questions?"

"Like I said, I have some. Just—" I shook my head. "*Shush*, for a second?"

"You're *shushing* me?" His tone was colored in disbelief and the desire to paint it made my skin itch.

"Shush!"

Prudence snorted. It was a parody of a laugh, and I startled, honestly surprised he was even capable of that much emotion. Wow. It made me wonder what his real laugh would sound like. But then I realized I was stalling again and time was ticking—

What should I ask?

Hmmm.

We sat in silence for a solid five minutes before I came up with my first question.

"Why are you haunting me?" I blurted without preamble.

There, that was a good, solid question right?

Prudence was quiet for long enough I worried he'd disappeared again. But he hadn't. His fingers brushed against my nape and I jumped as I felt him twist the curl of hair at the back of my neck. Gooseflesh tickled up my arms and I shuddered, right before he pulled hard enough my head tipped back and a soft pained noise escaped my lips. My cock was still definitely ready to go and I ached to reach down and give it a squeeze.

Why didn't I want sex again?

Right.

Because questions.

Answers.

All that horrible but important shit.

"Ugh you're taking forever," I complained after a few more centuries of painful waiting. Prudence's fingers playing with my hair were incredibly distracting, and also super fucking rude. Because wow, it was like every time it hurt even just a *little* my cock jerked.

"Shush." He was mocking me and I didn't even fucking care.

More silence. More waiting.

He trailed his nails behind my ear and I twitched, shivering, as the hair on my arms stood on end and I tried not to stare at the wet spot where the tip of my cock pressed against my boxers. God, it hurt so good to be teased like this. Prudence knew exactly what he was doing to me and he clearly got off on the torture as much as I did.

God, I liked him so much.

I wanted him to bully me more.

Eventually I stopped anticipating his answer. Instead, I let my lashes flutter shut and tipped toward his questing fingers, hyper-aware of his every move. It felt so good to be touched like this, explored. Like he was mapping out my freckles as he toyed with my heart.

An eon passed and then finally, *finally* Prudence spoke. When he did, his words were smoke and rainfall, trickling over me, as he played me like a fiddle till my head drooped and I sunk into a foggy state of lust-addled curiosity.

"You looked stupid enough to want to help me."

Okay, *rude.*

I couldn't muster up enough fight to do much more than tremble.

"Asshole." I gasped, but Prudence ignored me, his fingers slipping around the front of my neck again till they dipped into the hollow at the base of my throat. *God, why was that so hot?* When he grew bored with my collarbone they teased at the neckline of my robe, slipping beneath the fabric to toy at my sparse chest hair.

"You're not special," Prudence added, as if he didn't care how the words would affect me. Jokes on him though, because his condescension only made my dick harder.

"What do you need help with?" I asked, curiosity buzzing beneath my skin, at war with the desire to be touched, and touch in return. I wanted to reach up and snag his fingers, suck them into my mouth, choke on them to show him how good I'd make him feel if he let me warm his cock inside my throat.

"Is that your second question?"

"Yes." I desperately needed to know why he was here, Violet's cautious words lingering in the back of my head. Even though, admittedly, I was distracted, still thinking about his fingers. I could feel them teasing, teasing, teasing as he slid further and further under my robe. Inch by inch. Till finally they brushed up against one of my nipples and I grit my teeth to keep from groaning.

So he wanted to play it this way, huh?

Shithead.

Man, I was pretty sure I was in love with him already.

"I want to die," Prudence murmured, his words tickling across my skin.

Oh. Wow. Boner killer. I jolted from him in surprise and Prudence made an angry, low noise that had me immediately cowering back into place. *Okay, so, no moving. Got it.*

"You want to...die?" I blinked. "But aren't you already dead?"

"I am." Aggressively he shoved against my back, both threatening and tantalizing. The full length of his body crowded against mine, solid, strong, and entirely too delicious for me to resist. I rubbed back, unable to help myself. Full pecs rubbed against my shoulder blades. My nipples hardened, tingling as I bit my lip till it burned.

Apparently, fucking and chatting were things that could totally happen at the same time. Thick, callused fingers pinched my nipples hard enough to sting, torturing them till my eyes rolled back, and my cock jerked. I couldn't help the way I shoved my chest up, chasing his touch like the slut he accused me of being.

No one had ever touched me like this before.

Like I was their sole focus.

"And yet…I'm still here." He breathed, his tongue wet and cold as it snuck along the shell of my ear. I couldn't help but whimper, my body twitching as I tried to simultaneously shove into the fingers plucking my nipples and back against his mouth. "I don't want to be."

Simmering beneath my skin was a flicker of shame. Prudence had been right about that. But there was something else there too. Something new. Just like I'd never done any of this before, I'd never been *this way* with anyone else.

Uninhibited.

Unhinged.

Absolutely fucking ready to submit.

"Why do you think I can help with that?"

"Third question?"

Prudence's free hand slid around my body to my hip, squeezing me tightly enough I swore it would bruise. God, I *wanted* that. The bruises. I wanted to wear them around like a badge of honor. Something to remind me of him the next time he disappeared.

"Wait, no." I shook my head. Distracted as I decided to bend the rules…

just a little. I couldn't look at him—buuuut…he hadn't said anything about touching so I tipped my head to the side far enough that I was able to brush my lips against Prudence's cheek. Desperate to touch him, but not desperate enough to become completely disobedient.

Just a taste—a tease.

It would be so easy to peek—but I didn't. Somehow I managed to keep my eyes firmly shut. Obedient. I didn't want to know what Prudence would do to me if I directly disobeyed him. Part of me knew he wouldn't go easy on me either way. Even though this was just a game. *I hadn't looked, had I?* Despite the undercurrent of anticipation, I could not deny the fact that my actions made it clear that I *wanted* to be punished.

Pushing Prudence's buttons was my new favorite hobby.

I kissed his cheek.

"Naughty," Prudence murmured, the apple of his cheek jumping against my lips as he spoke. The skin was petal soft, just as chilly as his hands, and…weirdly human. The scratch of barely there stubble tickled against my lips. Deliciously prickly, as I laced another eager kiss against the scratch of his cheek, yearning for more of him. Already, this wasn't enough.

Prudence's nails bit into my hip punishingly. I gasped as he gave my nipple a vicious rub, soothing the touch with the pad of his thumb before he moved on to the other side, evening out the pleasure as he flicked my already aching nubs till I was a gasping, shuddery mess. I liked it rough. *Apparently.* The more my chest hurt the more my dick leaked.

So fucking much.

"Third question, Luca." Oh god, my name on his lips was sin itself. If he said it enough, maybe I could forget what it meant to be anything other than Prudence's Luca. I wouldn't be a failure anymore, a fuck-up. Washed up, watered down, dried up.

I wanted to ask him where he went when he disappeared.

But I figured that sort of question wouldn't get me anything more than empty words as an answer. I needed *action*, that was what today had taught me. Thirty job applications later and I knew what I needed more than anything was a path to follow.

"What can I do to make it so you don't leave again?" I asked softly, surprised by how sweetly the words left my lips. I hadn't realized I could sound like that. Docile. It was…*strange*.

Prudence must have been surprised too, because he stilled, his pleasure-filled torture ending for a moment as his fingers ceased their rubbing, and I felt his breath ruffle my hair. I wanted to peek at him. The desire to see his face was so bad it made my teeth ache and my body itch.

Somehow I knew if I did, he'd leave me.

So I stayed still.

"Tell me to stay," Prudence finally murmured, his nose brushing along the shell of my ear, then my cheek, until he was able to nip sharply at the corner of my jaw. "Say it."

"I want you to stay," I told him softly, lashes fluttering. He was right there. *Right there*—all I had to do was open my eyes—

Don't look, don't look, don't look.

"Stay with me, Prudence."

Let me look at you. Please.

"Fine."

Apparently chatting time was over because thirty seconds later I was on my knees and elbows again, and I had Prudence's hand down my pants. His grip was slick and cold as he played with my quads, scratching along the sensitive skin, gripping at the squishy parts on the inside of my thighs in the way he'd already deduced I liked.

I was louder than I meant to be, sobbing into the comforter as I shoved my hips back against him, desperate for anything—

He was a *tease*.

A complete fucking tease.

The torture of my sensitive thighs was worse than the nipples. Sometimes his forearm would brush up against the sticky crown of my cock and my hips would jerk forward searching for friction, only for him to pull back again. I swear he was doing it on purpose to fuck with me. "Prudence—" What was supposed to be a threat came out as a plea. *Why wasn't he annoyed?* I felt like all I ever did was whine and beg. *Maybe he…maybe he liked that?*

"Quiet," Prudence commanded, his voice scratchy and low. "Hold still or I'll stop."

I swallowed, nodding my head before he even began to move. Anything. I'd do anything to get him to touch me for real. My balls were drawn up tight, my hole clenching as more precum dribbled down the throbbing shaft. I didn't dare look, because he'd told me not to, even though my curiosity was slowly killing me.

What would his hand look like?

Ohh fuck. Fuuuck.

Prudence's finger dipped into the tip of my dick, and I laser-focused on the sensation as he rubbed at the sticky slick at my slit till my hips were jumping on their own to chase him, and my toes curled.

Don't come, don't come, don't come.

It was easier to ignore the need to see him now that I had a face full of bedsheet and I could feel his thighs up against mine. I needed to know if he was as into this as I was. So I pushed back experimentally, and my ass brushed against a bulge in his jeans. His cock was hard, thick, and felt eager enough my confidence boosted. Ah. *So he wasn't as unaffected as he sounded.*

"You're hard—" I blurted, stupidly.

"You're squirming."

Prudence pinched the loose skin at the top of my cock and electricity shot through my body. I didn't even recognize the choked sound I made as he released me, fanning his fingers along my length like he was measuring it.

Fuck.

He felt so good.

Firm. Dominating.

My cheeks were uncomfortably hot as I drooled onto the mattress. Shame crept up on me as I realized just how much I was grinding my ass against him. I hadn't noticed till he pointed it out. As embarrassed as I was, I couldn't bring myself to stop. A greedy slut, indeed.

"Do you like your hole played with, Luca? You don't look like the type," Prudence asked, his voice a quiet, curious scratch.

I nodded, surprised by my own enthusiasm.

It wasn't that I was surprised I liked it—what surprised me was that for some indiscernible reason, honesty came so easily when I was talking to him. I loved being fucked actually—but I'd only played with my ass a handful of times, and all of them had been with Hunter.

It was something I'd never been comfortable doing with a stranger. When Prudence had brushed my hole the last time we'd been together it had felt almost forbidden.

It felt intimate.

Too intimate.

"Are you going to touch me there?" I asked, swallowing around the sudden dryness in my throat. Even *I* could tell how hopeful I sounded. Prudence huffed in what I guessed to be amusement, a soft little noise that made my dick weep. He rubbed his finger through the fresh drop of precum at the tip of my cock, a contemplative sound rumbling in his chest as he gathered the sticky liquid thoughtfully before smearing it down the shaft.

Fuck yeah.

My abs tightened and I hissed.

I bucked desperately into the touch, my mouth hanging open as I drooled against the bedsheets. Instead of teasing, like I expected, he just tightened his grip, forming a circle around the root of my cock. I humped again, just to feel the way he squeezed all the way up. Tight. Cold. Just the right amount of scratch.

"Nnnng," I groaned.

My eyes rolled back, voice deepening an octave as I humped forward, caught between shoving back against Prudence's dick—the only indicator of his desire—or forward into his vise-like grip.

God, he was going to be the death of me.

Chapter Eleven

Prudence

LUCA WAS DELICIOUS when he was horny. All long-limbed debauchery, his pink hair flopping forward, his elegant neck glistening with sweat. Dappled sunlight slipped from the window, decorating his broad, freckled shoulders as they tensed with each panted breath. The muscles in his back rippled, and I had to bite back my groan at the sight. I hadn't been lying when I said he didn't look like the kind of man who liked getting fucked. Not that stereotypes were ever based on fact, even I knew that.

It was the way he held himself.

Everything about Luca screamed "normal, straight, vanilla" aside from his pastel pink hair. Passing him by on the street you'd never know the way he quivered at the promise of his hole being played with. The way his hips rolled forward like a dog in heat at the slightest touch. The way he begged for pain with the lost look in his pale gray eyes. Everything about him came to life under my attention.

It was addicting.

The noises Luca made when I squeezed the crown of his cock were especially lovely.

I wasn't normally the kind of person that called *anything* lovely.

It was a word I hadn't even realized I knew how to use.

But there was no other word that accurately described the way he opened up for me, vulnerable and uninhibited.

How had I been lucky enough that this gangly artist had stumbled into my web?

Horny as fuck, and ready to hump his way into oblivion, Luca was the loveliest thing I'd ever seen. I loved the way his ass flexed, the way his muscles tensed, the way his robe slipped off his shoulder far enough that I could sink my teeth into the freckled skin at his nape.

The handjob was on the wrong side of too dry, but Luca didn't seem to mind. In fact, I suspected he liked it. He craved pain mixed in with his pleasure—and that made me…*well.*

That made me want to fucking hurt him till he came.

"You don't know what to think, do you?" I purred, unfairly turned on by the sight of him losing himself beneath my touch. *That's it, puppy. Fuck my fist. Arch that sexy little ass back.* "You can't even admit you like it—and yet here you are—presenting yourself like a bitch." I used my free hand to grip one of his cheeks, squeezing hard enough I could feel the muscle give as he hiccuped his pleasure into the ridiculous pink sheets on his bed. His boxers had slipped down his thighs the more he wriggled, and the rounded curves of each sweet ass cheek were fully on display.

My cock ached to bury between them. To sink into all that pink, sticky heat and give him something real to cry about. Distantly, I recognized that Luca had fresh tears on his cheeks. My dick throbbed, testing the seam of my jeans as I watched those sweet cheeks spread to accommodate the swell of it. Shit. Fuck. That was nice. He had a nice round ass, a long thick dick. I gave his balls a little tug and the sound of his sobs were enough to make my cock weep.

If he cried long enough I was sure one glance at his tear-streaked, pink-cheeked face would have me coming untouched.

He made me feral.

My teeth ached to bite, my hands to maim, my hips to fuck.

The baser instincts were as frightening as they were liberating. No one had ever made me feel this much before. No one had ever made me feel this possessive urge to dominate.

How was it possible that I had finally found someone that suited my more depraved tastes? We were two puzzle pieces, shaped to fit, a perfect match.

It made no sense.

He made no sense.

But here he was anyway.

Confusing.

Annoying.

Absolutely fucking pretty when he cried.

"Prudence—" My name on Luca's lips sounded like a prayer, and I couldn't help the way I gripped his cock tighter, movements growing rougher in response, as I jerked him from root to tip with an enthusiasm

I'd never felt for a prior partner. Slick noises filled the air along with his whimpers. I'd slept with as many people as I could since I'd been freed from Lydia's hold but…

No one—before or after death—could compare to Luca.

I wanted to *own* him.

If I had my way he'd never sit again without feeling the sting of where I'd touched his body.

When Luca finally came it was with a desperate cry so heart-wrenching even my icy heart stuttered. He was a mess, his cum slick as I rubbed it around the base of his dick, toying with his balls, slipping down beneath them to the darker sensitive skin of his taint. He jumped away, and his ass clenched, but he didn't tell me no, as I played with him there. I grew bolder, my fingers slipping back further till I reached what I wanted.

His hole was soft beneath my touch. It fluttered, clenched, kissing at the pads of my fingers as I contemplated what to do with him.

He was sweaty and shaking, and the way he continued to hump forward, shoulders drawn tight despite his softening cock, made me figure he'd had enough for today.

Fine.

I released his hole and moved my attention to his neck.

When I was finished, he had bite marks all over his pretty tanned shoulders. They stood out stark, red-angry, and more than likely painful on his tan, freckle-coated skin. I grinned, a vicious smile, as I admired my work.

"I'm good," Luca blurted, his voice fucked-out and breathless, muffled against the bed. "In case you're worried."

"I'm not." Maybe I was lying, but I didn't overthink my response as I gave his neck one last lingering perusal before I sat back on my heels. My cock was still hard, jutting toward his ass like an arrow. The desire to sink inside him remained strong, but I resisted. His command to stay with him simmered under my skin, the ache of the Nothing no longer pulling my leash quite so tight.

My thighs trembled, and I almost wanted to laugh. It was weird. All of this was. Sometimes seeing my own body gave me emotional whiplash. I stared at my thighs, shaking my head to clear away the fog of disassociation before I focused my attention on my pretty pink toy, his muscular back quivering.

He stayed face down, obediently. Stupid pink colored boxers tucked beneath the globes of his ass, a drop of cum connecting his cock to the now wet bedsheets.

"Are you…?" Luca shoved his hips back inquisitively, surprising me when his ass met the swell of my throbbing dick and he gave an experimental little grind. My lashes fluttered and I indulged him for half a second before the practiced way he arched his back began to piss me off.

Who else had he done this for?

How many men had seen him like this?

He was *mine*. A masterpiece that belonged in a private gallery. The idea of sharing him with anyone else made me want to kill something.

"I'm good." I pushed Luca unceremoniously off, watching him flounder then fall forward into the puddle of his own cum with a surprised little gasp. What I *really* wanted was to rub my cock against all that naked skin, but I didn't.

It wasn't time.

There was so much emotion inside me it was making me feel antsy and overwhelmed and I resented the feeling.

He'd only want more if I touched him the way I craved to and all of this was…surprisingly raw for me. Jealousy was a new emotion. I didn't think I'd ever felt it before. I needed to process. The Nothing was still my cage, but at least it was a familiar one. I needed some time to come to terms with the new life he'd breathed into me.

My chest felt tight. My tongue was too big for my mouth.

"Stubborn dick," Luca muttered under his breath, still sounding just as fucked-out, still looking just as delicious with his robe shoved up beneath his pits. His half-bare back flexing.

I didn't want him to see me like this.

Unsure.

As much as my dick wanted to fuck him I realized that I wasn't ready to sink inside his heat yet. To become one with something living for only a moment. Chasing heartbeats, like he was just another body. As much as I'd sought that back home, this felt…different. I didn't want to analyze why that was.

Maybe it was Luca.

There was something wrong with him.

There had to be.

"Can I look at you now?" Luca practically begged, still obediently lying in his own mess.

"No." I wasn't sure why it mattered so much to me. My chest was still tight. Sweat beaded at my temple and the falsity of it pissed me off. It wasn't like I was alive. I didn't need to sweat. The intricacies of the spell woven around me just made me feel worse. A parody of the living. A production.

Despite this, I wasn't insecure.

I knew what I looked like. Being handsome was just another asset like any other. My good looks had always made it easy to get what I wanted. Men were eager to trust when they thought you were pretty enough to fuck. Somehow…I didn't want Luca to think of me like that though. As a petty fuck.

He was my golden ticket, even if he didn't know it. Annoying as he was.

"*When* can I look?" Luca whined, petulant as always.

Jesus. "Stop asking."

"No."

I slapped his ass in retaliation. It jiggled, and forced him deeper into the puddle of his cum. He muttered more complaints, and I grinned. *Maybe he'd shut up now?* I thought, meanly.

I should've known a little slap wouldn't deter him.

Instead of backing off, Luca just shoved his hips back for more, his round ass flexing in a way that made it incredibly difficult to resist grinding against it. How was it possible that I was still hard? *Fuck.*

"But what if I *really* want to know what you look like?" Luca complained. W*hiney-whiney-whiney.*

I wanted to shut him up with my dick, stick it down his throat deep enough he couldn't ask me any more questions.

Brat.

I slapped his ass again, harder, even though it hadn't worked last time. A pink hand print slowly began to settle on his skin and my grin turned wolfish. He was trembling. The prospect of a new way to mark him made my blood sing.

"What can I do to get you to show me?" He was bargaining now, sugary sweet, and a weird fluttery feeling was flickering in my chest in response.

"I'll show you when I show you. Stop. *Asking.*"

"Ugh." I could practically hear his pout. Somehow this time, just hearing it wasn't enough. I wanted to see it. See his pale eyes grow dark and annoyed. See the jut of his lower lip, powdery sweet. Desperation bubbled inside me at the thought. Staring down at Luca's broad shoulders and trim waist was…admittedly incredibly gratifying. But…

I liked his pouty lips more. *Especially* when he was being bratty.

Annoying, annoying, annoying.

Overwhelming emotion threatened to make me run again, but Luca had mercy.

"I'm hungry."

Finally. Something I could work with. "No more cereal."

"God, what are you, the cereal police?"

"I would rather you not die of diabetes before you fulfill my purpose for you."

"Look—I'm doing my best here, dude. Normally my coping mechanism of choice is going for a run, but now I'm like…fundamentally terrified of it because I almost got hit by a fucking car."

"Your face healed." I pointed out. I didn't see his point.

"Yeah but my ego hasn't."

The more Luca argued, the harder my dick got, and the more tempting his freckled ass became. I could slip inside him. He'd like that. Maybe he'd squeal a bit, but ultimately I already knew he was willing.

"So, just watch for cars." It wasn't that hard.

"Yeah okay, easy enough for you to say. You don't know what it felt like seeing my life flash before my eyes."

"Death isn't the worst thing in the world."

"Yeah, and how would you know? You're not actually dead."

Wow.

He must've realized he crossed a line because he stopped trying to sneakily wiggle on my dick and settled down, even the set of shoulders apologetic. "Shit, sorry," Luca murmured, contrite. "That was rude of me. I don't…actually know what it's like for you. Or what you've been through. Sometimes I just get caught up in the fight, and words come out I don't really mean."

No one had ever apologized to me so sincerely before over something so stupid.

I was silent.

Silent for long enough I expected him to get impatient and begin annoying me again. He didn't though. He waited for me. To forgive him. Fucking idiot.

My chest didn't feel so tight anymore.

"What happened to the money I got you?" I asked, changing the subject. I wasn't ready to dive into that part of my un-life. I probably never would be, and certainly not with him. His apology wrapped like a warm blanket around my heart, despite how hard I tried to shove it off.

"I spent it."

"If you say you spent it on cereal—"

"It wasn't on cereal. Well—" Luca wiggled uncomfortably again, and for some reason that only made my dick harder. I liked him squirming. It was my comfort zone. "I bought a few boxes. But most of it I used to replace my phone."

"Good." I'd already known that, but this was proving to be a perfect distraction from our previous conversation.

"Actually!" Luca wriggled, then stilled, stopping himself from sitting up. I was prepared to shove him back down if needed, but clearly he knew how to be obedient. "Speaking of the whole body-snatch-a-palooza you hosted, we need to have an important conversation about boundaries."

My stomach flipped.

"You didn't like the se—"

"No, no. Don't get me wrong. The sex is perfect. Be as bossy and mean as you'd like. I know my safeword—" Luca was quick to interrupt. "I mean…if we're going to be sharing my body sometimes, I would really like to set some rules."

"Fine."

"Really?" He perked up, the tension in his shoulders melting away. "Damn, I really thought this would be harder."

"It's your body."

"Okay." Luca wiggled again, thoughtfully. It was clear to me the longer I got to know him that he had no problem demanding things before his brain caught up. "So." He was quiet again for a solid minute before he spoke, "Obviously, number one. No stealing things."

"You had no problem using the money—"

"Um, yeah. Before I knew it was stolen." I didn't need to see his face to hear the sass in his tone. I smacked his ass and he yelped.

"You need money. I got you money." I didn't see the problem.

"Okay. But there's like—a line, Prudence. I'd rather not end up in prison, thank you." Luca growled into the comforter and I was…weirdly charmed by how firm he was being about the whole thing. Also the fact he was more concerned about being caught and going to prison than he was about the morality of stealing from an ATM.

Huh.

"Fine. No stealing money with your body."

It was interesting that he'd decided we have this discussion at all. None of his words felt like commands. I knew if needed, I could break them. And that fact was what truly clued me into the fact that I still had a choice in all of this. He hadn't stolen my agency yet. That didn't mean it wouldn't change if he became aware of the power he held over me but…

"Thank you." Luca shifted awkwardly for a moment, "Also… Um—with the whole…body stealing thing? Can you let me decide when you do that?"

He was asking for a lot, and it was clear he knew that.

He thought I'd say no.

"Fine."

"Oh-my-god, really?" Luca perked up, then mumbled to himself, "I didn't think you'd say yes to that one."

"Like I already said, it's your body."

"Fine! Okay." He squirmed. "Last rule for now." *Jesus Christ. There was more?* "When I ask you ghost questions, I need answers."

That was where I drew the line.

There were things I didn't want him to know.

He wouldn't help me if he did.

"No."

"Yes! I need to know stuff, Prudence. If you're going to be a permanent roommate in my body I deserve to know what I'm getting into."

I'd already told him this was temporary.

What part of the fact I wanted to die, did he not get?

Though…the idea of being permanently attached to the pink-haired weirdo wasn't entirely unappealing.

"What if I want you to do something for me in exchange? It seems to me you're asking for an awful lot when you have little to offer."

"Um, excuse you. I'm offering you an apartment in my head? I think that's enough, don't you?"

I guess he had a point.

"Fine."

"Awesome-sauce!" Luca wiggled happily, still smashed in his own mess like the world's sluttiest worm. I couldn't help but stare. It was like he didn't even remember that his ass was on display anymore. Or maybe he did. Maybe he *liked* the fact that I was looking.

Shameless.

Why did I like that?

This was not "awesome-sauce" at all.

Chapter Twelve

Luca

EVEN THOUGH I'D asked him to stay, Prudence wasn't physically present like I'd hoped he would be. Clearly, despite what Violet had told me, I knew shit about ghosts. It could've been a placebo effect but I swore I could feel the tickle of his presence in the back of my mind, watching my every move.

After we'd had sex he'd disappeared—again—go figure. I'd wasted time on my computer for a while, but ultimately given up stalking my little brother's Facebook in favor of getting ready for bed. I probably should've texted Adam back—since I'd left him on read. But every time I thought about talking to anyone in my family my stomach twisted in knots.

I still hadn't called Mom back since my accident the other day.

And, because I was the worst son in the history of the world, I'd been "forgetting" to charge my phone so I wouldn't have to deal with her phone calls.

The moon rose above the city skyline, and the scent of salt water crept through the cracked bathroom window as I brushed my teeth, just waiting for the other shoe to drop.

This afternoon had been too good to be true. It really had. Distantly, I wondered if I'd look happier now that I'd gotten laid. Violet had been pushing me to get out of my funk and meet someone for months—and now that I had…well…maybe I wouldn't look so tragic. Glancing up at the mirror, I was startled to catch the flicker of an electric blue eye staring back from my reflection. The first time I'd seen this back in Elmwood it had made me feel vaguely terrified. Now though? I only felt excited, because I knew what I was looking at.

Prudence's eye.

I wasn't *stupid*.

Some things were obvious, even to me. This whole thing was weird as hell, and should not have been physically possible. Someone else's eyeball was literally glowing at me from my face. It should've freaked me out, but mostly I was just…curious.

Questions itched beneath the surface of my skin. Belatedly, I recognized that I should've bargained for more answers from Prudence. Not that he'd probably give me any, let's be real, I'd had to fight tooth and nail for the first three. The dude was as tight lipped as a sexually promiscuous nun.

Too many questions. Not enough time.

Was Prudence like those little people in *Inside Out*? With his own teensy-tiny desk in the back of my head, watching out my eyeballs like a bossy-as-fuck lil creep?

I snorted, then sighed. I couldn't really picture him. Even tiny. It still bugged me that I didn't know what he looked like, or even what his age was. His eye was the only part of him I'd seen thus far—and oh. Oh. *That* sudden realization made an excited quiver tremble through my body. Shit. This was *his* eye. I was literally looking at it—through it? Whatever. Didn't matter.

Ha!

Maybe I couldn't see all of him, but I sure as shit could stare his eyeball down. (Yes, I was self-aware enough to know I was acting a bit…insane. But that wasn't enough to stop me from doing it.)

I cocked my head, bit down on my toothbrush to hold it in place, and squinted at myself thoughtfully. Despite the color change, both eyes seemed to work the same. I closed one at a time, testing them out individually, before I ultimately decided that they were functioning just fine.

Icy teal-ish blue. Almost like a glowy popsicle. It was hard to imagine a face that could pull off a color so…striking.

"Is that you?" I asked around the barrel of my toothbrush…except it sounded more like *ish-thab-yew?*

Hopefully Prudence spoke toothbrush.

No.

Oh good. Still a dick.

A little thrill flipped in my belly as I nodded, then decided it wasn't realistic to expect a full conversation when I had mint-flavored foam coating my lips and plastic between my teeth. When I'd spit and rinsed I turned back to the mirror again, unsurprised that my eyes were still abnormal. They weren't the only thing that caught my attention this time, though. At least now that I knew Prudence could see me.

Fuck. My hair was a hot mess. Bubblegum pink, and sticking up like I'd been electrocuted—or—spent a good hour getting it pulled on by a ghost.

"Do you see what I see when you're inside me like that?" I asked, a little horrified.

Yes.

Even though I'd literally told him he needed to answer ghost-related questions, it still surprised me that he did. Prudence respected my wishes better than half the boyfriends—let's be real, all of them—that I'd ever had. It made me feel powerful. Like a ghost whisperer. Or an asshole whisperer. *Shit, that was disgusting.* I cringed.

"Why aren't you out?" I blurted a second later. He didn't answer that question, so I tried again. "I thought you said if I asked you to stay, you would stick around?"

I am around.

"Yeah, okay, sass-man. But you're not…*here*-here, you know? You're *there*-here." I pointed accusingly at my reflection in the mirror, only for the ridiculousness of the moment to catch up to me the second I realized what I was doing. Man. I looked out of my mind right now. Scolding my own reflection—

A laugh bubbled up my throat and I snorted, hiding inside my elbow as that one little noise evolved into a full on snicker, that I had no choice but to surrender to.

By the time I finished laughing, my cheeks were flushed, and my heart was fluttering. I couldn't remember the last time I laughed that hard.

I turned back to the mirror to talk to Prudence again buuuut looking at myself just made me laugh again. *This was so wild. Abso-posu-tutely wild.*

What's so funny?

"You? Me? *Us?*" I gestured between my body and its reflection—and then laughed again as my wet toothbrush dripped on the counter from where it remained firmly gripped inside my other hand. "The fact that I'm like—literally talking to myself right now."

No you aren't.

"I kinda am though? I mean, I know you're there but like…c'mon, dude. Don't you think this is just a *little bit* funny?"

Silence.

And then…to my surprise Prudence huffed. It was the closest thing to a laugh I thought he was probably capable of. This beat out the half snort he'd given me before by miles.

"See?"

It is a bit weird.

"Yeah, understatement of the century." I was quiet for a few more minutes as I tried to get my own amusement under control. When I'd finally stopped laughing I rose from where I'd collapsed to my elbows on the wet counter, toothbrush abandoned.

"I want to look at you. Please?"

I hadn't expected him to respond so immediately.

But he did.

Because the second my eyes flickered to the mirror again, I saw a man staring back at me in place of my reflection.

My heart stuttered to life as a gasp left my lips. *Thump, thump, thump.* Distantly, I recognized that I was gaping at him, and a startled, amazed squawk escaped my lips. This was some real Belle-in-the-Beast's-castle-discovering-the-portrait-on-the-wall shit.

Prudence was…*fuck.*

He was beautiful.

Beautiful in the way a snowstorm was. A shark. A wolf closing in on its newest kill. Vicious, deadly, gorgeous.

His eyes were the same electric blue that I'd seen reflected in my own. Striking. Brutal. Glacial as an iceberg. His thin dark brows were lowered in what I assumed to be a permanent scowl, his lips pulled thin with tension. The tip of his button nose could've been called cute if it had belonged on someone else's face. On him however, it somehow perfectly complemented the sharp angles of his jaw, his cheekbones, and the slope of his nose.

He looked young. About my age. Pale too. So pale he was nearly blue. Tattoos covered almost every inch of his body, spaced apart like his skin was just a frame for the art that was so meticulously painted upon him. Symbols of the grim reaper, ravens, and scythes decorated his arms and neck in a traditional tattoo style I'd always found effortlessly sexy. A moth fluttered along the base of his throat, black spiderwebs covering his neck everywhere the moth couldn't reach.

I stared.

I stared, and stared, and stared.

Happy? His voice was angry, detached. I watched the way his lips moved with fascination but instead of hearing his voice with my ears the words echoed inside me. Was this…an illusion then? Why was he showing this to me? He clearly didn't want to.

Just because I'd asked?

That was weirdly polite of him.

"You're way younger than I thought you'd be—" I blurted, more than a little surprised as I realized that I was looking down at him. "Shorter too." I blinked. He was shorter than me—by a good seven or so inches. Prudence glared up at me, and a jolt of want so visceral it made my knees weak, bolted through my body. "Tater top," I muttered under my breath in dazed appreciation.

Then it hit me. The fact he was so young meant that Prudence couldn't have been more than twenty when he died. Wow. That was…so fucking sad.

Disappointed?

"Um. No." I shook my head to clear the emotional whiplash, dragging my gaze over the swell of his pecs where they tested the fabric of his pulled-tight white t-shirt. "I am very-very-very much not disappointed." I blinked. His throat bobbed when he swallowed, and my eyes nearly rolled back at the sight of the moth fluttering in response. "Holy shit. I wanna *taste* your tattoos—with my tongue."

Prudence cocked his head at me, nostrils flaring. He looked mad. *Mad-mad.* Oh god. I wanted him to beat me up—with his dick. His eyebrow twitched. Silver glinted.

"Sweet baby Jesus, you have an eyebrow piercing." I blurted out, clearly having lost my mind.

And?

"And—" My gaze dragged over his stocky figure and I felt my cock twitch and my toes curl against the cold tile floor as I tried to anchor myself. If I'd thought I was obsessed with Prudence before this—wow. *Wow.* There was no fucking way I was getting rid of him now, risks be damned. "Finger tattoos," I gasped in reverence. "I *love* finger tattoos." I wanted to paint him—my hands twitched helplessly till I was distracted as another realization struck me like a blow to the face.

Those fingers had totally touched my ass earlier.

Oh god.

Oh-god-oh-god-oh-god.

Prudence's nostrils flared again and he leaned closer to his side of the mirror, clearly trying to intimidate me. Posturing, like a peacock. I knew there was glass between us, that he wasn't real. But fuck. He was intense. I should've been scared, but I wasn't. His plan to frighten me into submission didn't work because instead of falling back in fear, I just honest-to-god *whimpered.*

"Oh my Lord," I groaned softly, soaking him up like he was water and I was a sponge on a diet.

What now?

"You're like—the prettiest thing I've ever seen in my entire life, and I am pretty damn sure you can't be real."

Idiot.

"Prudence!" I stabbed my finger at him. "You didn't tell me you were hot! I am having a full-blown crisis right now." My cheeks were hot as I flapped around like an angry bird. "I wouldn't have asked to see you if I knew you were this sexy! *Jesus.* I needed to mentally prepare for this. *Why didn't I mentally prepare?"*

What did you think I'd look like?

His blank expression shifted till it was almost curious. Looking at his face was making me want to implode.

"*I don't know.* An old man? I thought you might be wrinkly—or gray— or like…weirdly sexy in a terrifying creature type of way." I blinked. "I guess the last bit is kinda true. Because *wow.* It shouldn't be possible for you to be this sexy and this good in bed. What the hell. The probability is just crazy."

Are you done?

"Um, no? I will never be done. I feel blindsided. Like—holy shit." I shook my head, scrubbing hands up over my eyes, my cheeks bright red. "Okay. I changed my mind. I don't want to see you anymore, goodbye," I declared dramatically as I squeezed my eyes shut tight to fortify myself against his gloriousness. When I dropped my hands and opened my eyes my face was staring back at me again.

Okaaaay.

"I didn't mean literally," I blinked. "Come baaaack."

He came back.

"Wait—Okay." I pressed my hand to the mirror, stupidly shocked when cool glass touched my palm. I should've been touching his pec, the solid swell of the muscle tucked beneath my hand. He looked so real. If I moved my hand to the right I could brush his nipple. He's just…just a reflection though, I reminded myself as Prudence glared up at me, his chest flexing in fury beneath my palm. I felt cheated that I wasn't actually touching him. "I…" I blinked, shaking my head again to clear it. "You look like you could bench press five of me."

Prudence didn't dignify this with a response.

"Sorry, sorry. I'll stop freaking out—just give me a second."

He nodded.

And then I noticed the fact his ears were pierced—multiple times— *multiple times!* And I had another mini panic attack.

Eventually, I calmed down, though my heart remained stubbornly fluttery. I swallowed around the dryness in my throat as it finally hit me that Prudence had been watching the whole fucking time I freaked out. How embarrassing. My cheeks burned as I released the mirror and took a shaky step back. I let him soak up my humiliation greedily. It was only fair since he'd let me ogle him. His unnaturally pale gaze was hungry but detached as he inspected me through the glass like I was a slab of meat on a butcher table.

Why was that so hot?

"So—it is really really *really* important to me right now that you answer my earlier question. The one you totally ignored."

Which one?

"Whether or not you like me."

Prudence's eyes narrowed into slits. Now that I saw him actually pissed off it made me aware that apparently the murder stare he'd been giving me before was probably just his face. A permanent *I will kill you* kinda vibe. Effortlessly gorgeous and deadly at the same time.

My heart thundered in my chest as I waited with baited breath for his response.

Please, please say yes.

I want to fuck you.

"Oh, thank god." That was good enough for me. I slumped in relief. Hearing those words cut through the tension that had crept into my body the moment I'd realized he was way out of my league. "Are you sure?"

God, I was annoying. I winced at myself.

He devoured my shame with his eyes.

If I didn't want to fuck you I wouldn't have chosen you.

For some reason…that made me feel incredibly good. I flushed a little and nodded, squirming as I glanced down at my silky stolen pajama pants self-consciously. *Fuck.* He'd seen me in the robe—he'd seen me cry—*oh no.*

How could he be attracted to me if he knew what I looked like snot-covered and tear-streaked?

Maybe I should stop stealing Violet's stuff. Maybe I should make an effort to be sexier? To try and fix the damage I'd already done to my image.

I wasn't normally like this.

I usually dressed in athleisure and was covered in paint. Though, now I wasn't even sure that could be considered my "normal" since I'd been existing as a sad lump of stolen silk for nearly six months. I had nice clothes. Sure, they were sitting in a dirty pile under my bed next to my abandoned art supplies—but I *could* resurrect them.

"I should probably put more effort into my appearance," I muttered softly to myself. "Gotta change so I—" Prudence's voice immediately cut through my morose thoughts like a blade, all vicious, sure, and effortlessly commanding.

No.

Don't you dare.

Wow.

Wow.

My heart quivered like crazy as I looked up at his reflection and saw the quiet fury on his face. So he…he liked me like this then? I swallowed the lump in my throat at the thought that anyone could find me attractive when I was at an all-time low. Clearly, Prudence did though. And I could definitely see myself getting way too attached to him already. Maybe Violet had been right? This *was* dangerous.

But not in the way she'd warned.

Chapter Thirteen

Luca

MIRACULOUSLY, I DISCOVERED twenty dollars hidden under a couch pillow the next day. I'd scanned the room for signs of ghost-thievery—found none—then proceeded to drive my shitty car all the way to the nearest McDonalds to buy two large fries. Back home, I munched away, typing one-handed as I sat pretzel-style at my dining table, and whipped through another fifteen job applications.

So far I hadn't heard anything back, but I was still holding out hope I'd start getting calls today. It was just a numbers game, wasn't it? All I had to do was submit enough applications and eventually someone would offer me a position.

I'd lied my way through my resume but as far as *they* knew I was overqualified.

Most people didn't have a background as colorful as mine. Rich at eighteen. Viral artist—turned has-been.

I didn't include that on the applications.

I had a mouthful of fries when Prudence appeared again. One second I was alone and the next there he was, standing across the table from me, framed by aged cream wallpaper.

Prudence stared at my fries.

I stared at him.

The red fry carton sat to the left of my hand, still full, and I shook off the salt on my fingers before I grabbed it and offered it to him. His eyes narrowed at me and I tried not to be too overwhelmed by the fact that he was *right there*. All five foot three of his gorgeously muscled frame.

Real. Solid. Tangible.

All I had to do to touch him was reach across the tabletop. I didn't. But I *could.*

Why he'd decided to pop out of my head for the time being, I had no idea. I liked that he was able to be around more. Even though there was no rhyme or reason to his visits.

"Do ghosts eat?" I asked curiously, wagging the box toward him till it made a little *shh, shh, shh* noise.

"We can."

Okay. Unhelpful, much?

"Do *you* like to eat?"

Prudence's lips thinned and he glanced away, the tense muscle at the corner of his jaw tick, tick, ticking as he seemed to process the question. Finally—after a million years—he responded in a low, scratchy drawl. His words were stilted and forced, like they'd been literally dragged out of him.

"I don't know."

Oh.

"You don't…know?" I blinked, then set the fries down because my arm was getting tired. "How do you not know? Wait. Scratch that. Dumb question. Exactly how long have you been a ghost?"

Fuck, had he recently died? Is that why he hadn't tried it yet? Shit, that was sad.

"No one has ever offered me food before." *Shit that was even more sad.* Prudence's words once again sounded like they were being tortured out of him. Despite how clearly he hated the small talk, he was still answering, so I figured he should get points for that.

In fact, now that I thought about it, he hadn't taken over my body again either.

He was following all my rules to a T and it was…weirdly nice? It made me *want* to trust him.

"So…how does this work? The whole possessing people thing." I blinked. "Do you have to always be attached to someone? And if you aren't…is there limbo?"

Prudence glared at me, his dark brow flickering. Light played off of his piercings and I licked my lips in fascination. The grim reaper tattooed on his arm flexed where it was half covered by the hem of his sleeve as he stared me down, Adam's apple bobbing. Yum.

"I have to be attached to someone," he repeated, holding perfectly still, though it didn't take a genius to see that he wanted to run from the conversation. I wasn't sure why this was so hard for him. But then again, I'd never been a ghost before, so what did I know about how hard it was?

"Eat a fry, Prudence." I picked up the fries again, waving them at him with an eyebrow wiggle that made him roll his eyes. He did as I said, his fingers immediately reaching for the box. The way he moved was…almost shy. I stared at the designs he had tattooed around his thick knuckles as he squeezed a fry between his pointer and thumb and brought it apprehensively up to soft-looking lips. L-I-A-R. Liar spelled across his knuckles, a letter on each finger. Huh. I wondered why he'd had that tattooed? It gave more meaning to the fact he'd called me a liar at least twice since we'd met.

Maybe for him, it was less an insult, and more a warning.

My lungs froze as Prudence's nostrils flared. He brought the fry to his lips and chomped the golden-potatoey-straw-of-goodness with a flash of white teeth.

He chewed.

My lungs expanded again.

I had no idea something as simple as chewing could be so captivating. But I figured…for Prudence—if this was truly his first time eating after death—maybe this moment was more important than it seemed. Monumental even.

He finished the fry in silence.

When he was done Prudence crossed his arms, pale eyes all murder-y, dark crush of bangs falling across his brow. His hair was long enough on top that it flopped spikily forward. The shaved sides gave it an effortless punk feel that had me foaming at the mouth.

Hello emo phase I thought I'd outgrown.

The more I stared at him the more I realized that he was actually kinda cute in an…angry way. Terrifying too. Like one of those bulldogs that look sweet until they try to bite you through a fence.

I offered the full container to him again, but he didn't take any more. He did, however, turn his attention to it, instead of me. I wasn't sure if I missed the weight of his gaze or if I was relieved to get a break from it.

Prudence made me *feel* things.

All sorts of things.

I didn't care what Violet had told me. This, right here. This was worth it.

"You want more?" I asked, *shh, shh, shh-ing* the box at him as he glared way too seriously at the fries, his lip curling in what looked like disgust. "You can have some—" I singsonged as I *shh, shh, shh-ed* the salt again. Quicker than I could blink, he struck forward, fingers wrapping around my wrist. His skin was icy to the touch but surprisingly supple as he squeezed hard enough that I nearly dropped the box entirely.

"*Luca.*" My name was a warning on his lips.

I'd always been good at ignoring those.

"Prudence." I wiggled my eyebrows at him again, though I did follow his unspoken command to stop waving the fry box around. "Eat the fries, Prudence." I blinked. "If you want to." I tacked on, suddenly worried I was reading him wrong.

But…I wasn't.

My people skills, once again, did not fail me.

Because the second he was given permission, he snatched the box out of my hand and retreated to stand on his side of the table again. I felt the distance between us keenly. I never thought I'd get so attached to his presence but hey—here we were. Only a few weeks and some change in and *BAM*. I was attached as fuck.

Prudence glared at the fry box like it was about to grow arms and pop him one right in the face.

Betrayed by potato.

A true tragedy.

And then…he brought the box to his mouth, tipped it back, and put away the entire remainder of its contents like a pint-sized garbage disposal. I watched in fascination, then surreptitiously peeked at the floor to see if maybe it had passed right through him and left a pile of fries on the ground—but nope.

Nothin'.

When he finished he set the carton back down on the table and glared at me for the zillionth time that day, challenging me to speak. If I was a smarter man I probably would've gone back to working on my job applications and let him process his McDonald's in peace. But I wasn't that smart. And besides…I was curious.

"Where do the fries go?" I asked. "When you eat them."

Prudence's nostrils flared and his lip curled again. Oh god. Why was pissing him off quickly becoming my favorite pastime? *Man.* I wished I could be hired as his personal gnat. Just *buzz, buzz, buzzing* away around his shoulders so I could watch the way his face shifted into an expression that said *I'm going to tear you apart.*

Delicious.

"That's between the fries and God," Prudence deadpanned.

It took me a solid minute to realize he was joking. And then I laughed, a horrible, disgusting snort choking its way up my throat as I wagged my head in disbelief. I hadn't laughed this much in ages.

"You know jokes?!" I slapped a hand against my chest in mock-surprise. "I didn't know you knew jokes."

"There's a lot you don't know about me."

"Yeah, yeah." I grinned and then dug around inside the empty McDonald's bag for the fry stragglers. I offered them to him, weirdly excited his fingers might brush mine. The man had quite literally explored almost every part of me and yet the idea of touching his hand like middle-schoolers on a first date, made me weak in the knees. Once again, Prudence didn't respond.

I blinked expectantly, cocking my head in confusion.

Was he being shy again?

Could Prudence even *be* shy?

"C'mon, you know you want them." I waggled my fistful enticingly at him one last time, gasping in surprise when Prudence lunged forward and snatched them away immediately, chowing down like a starving man.

Wow.

I never knew it could be sexy to watch someone scarf down potato-shaped-heart-attacks but, man. Prudence could make anything look like a prelude to a porn scene. Even snorting fries.

My laptop screen blinked off. Just another reminder that I was allowing myself to be distracted from my true goals. I jiggled the mouse with a sigh till the screensaver came back on.

"Okay, so—" I blinked. "This was fun—and also weirdly informational. But I really need to finish these applications or you—and I—are no longer going to have somewhere to live."

I moved to wipe my hands off on my jeans (real pants today) but Prudence's fingers wrapped around my wrist to stop me. He squeezed, and my heart rate kicked up a notch. It rabbited around my chest as Prudence shuffled close, his hungry eyes dark with intent, the light playing games with the shadows beneath his cheekbones as he brought my fingers to his lips.

What was he—

Oh.

His tongue flickered out, wet and shockingly frigid as he dragged it up the length of my middle finger. He was tentative at first. Then he grew bolder, tracing the slippery appendage along the sensitive skin between my fingers as he chased the leftover salt.

By the time he was finished, I was flushed and breathing a little too hard.

I offered him my other hand eagerly and he arched an eyebrow before he pushed my hand away in denial and retreated. He stood next to the table again, awkwardly statuesque and I picked my jaw up off the ground, shocked and more than a little turned on from his little display. I wiped my hand off on my pants.

Did I have a finger fetish?

No.

Maybe?

Probably, if my dick was any indicator.

Prudence continued to stand sentinel, and I shook my head to clear it, flushed all over and semi-hard. Job applications. C'mon. Job. Jobs. Jobbity-jobs. I glared down at my dick. Then at Prudence, because he was still hovering.

"Sit, Casper the-not-so-friendly ghost. Just watching you stand is making me tired." I'd always been a bit bossy. It came with being the oldest, and the person that did most of the caregiving. Mom had done her best, but that also meant most of the time she was working to make ends meet. And when she wasn't working she was catching up on much needed sleep.

She'd been present as much as she could.

But...I'd picked up the slack for most of our lives. Especially when Mom went on another bender with some random boyfriend she was "so sure would make a great father for us." Spoiler alert: they never had. At least until Paul came along when I was in high school.

Paul was…kind of a miracle, for all of us.

He was gentle, kind, and just as hopelessly in love with my mom as she was with him. He adopted us all, didn't even bat an eye, and worked his ass off to get the promotion needed for my mom to finally quit her many—life-sucking—jobs.

They weren't rich by any means, but he made enough every year to give each of us something nice for Christmas.

Paul was a sweetheart.

Then, as per usual, thinking of my family was quickly followed with gut-clenching guilt. I wilted, my smile falling away like it had never been there at all.

"What's your problem?" Prudence's voice interrupted my wallowing. I hadn't even noticed he'd sat down across from me like I'd commanded, but he had. His thick thighs were splayed wide, one of his booted feet propped up on the rung of my chair, his head tipped back as he stared through his lashes at me. Effortlessly pretty. Effortlessly cunning. Effortlessly sexy.

The bastard.

"My problem?" I played dumb as my shoulders rose up to my ears and tension bled through my body.

"You look like you're sucking on a lemon."

I smoothed out my features, embarrassed to realize he was right. I'd been squeezing myself tight all over. Wrinkles-galore.

"It's just…" I shook my head, my heart giving a sick little lurch in my chest. "I was thinking about my family."

"Are they dead?"

"What? No!" I glared at him, and then sighed, because I knew it wasn't his fault he didn't know.

"Then why are you sad?"

Why am I sad? What a good question.

Maybe because I was a liar.

Maybe because I was a failure.

Maybe because even though all my life I'd strived to be different, at the end of the day I was just as naive, just as trusting, just as stupid as my mom was.

"I fucked up."

Prudence cocked his head and I stared at the little black cross tattooed underneath his left eye, too raw to look him in the eyes. He was waiting, but I didn't know what to say so I remained silent.

"If they're not dead," Prudence said, stilted, and clearly struggling to soothe me. My sweet sadistic little robot. "It seems to me that whatever you've done…isn't irreparable."

I guess he was right.

At least they weren't dead.

Weirdly enough, despite how bluntly he delivered the words, I felt better. Shifting in my seat, I bit my lip as I glanced at his mouth, oddly charmed by the way one side pulled up farther than the other when he talked.

"What did you do?" Prudence asked, surprising me once again by inquiring further. I squirmed in my seat as I debated whether or not I should reply.

I hadn't told anyone other than Violet what had happened.

Because…

Because saying it out loud would make it more real.

Then again…Prudence was my lucky ghost. If anyone could make me feel better it was probably him.

"I'm going to let them down. They don't know it yet. But they're never going to want to talk to me again. And I deserve it." Nope. I was right. It didn't make me feel any better to say the words out loud. I wilted, slumping forward till my head thunked against the keyboard of my hand-me-down laptop. I'd sold my other one to make rent a few months ago, and Violet had given me her old one in the interim.

Prudence was quiet.

I didn't want to see the look on his face.

I didn't want to see the judgment I was sure would be there.

"What happened?" he finally asked. It was clear he was trying to be sympathetic, but the man had no idea how to properly infuse emotion into his tone. He always sounded equally blank, equally growly—aside from when he was turned on. Then he got really-really growly.

It seemed *I want to fuck you* was the only emotion he was well-versed in expressing.

"I trusted the wrong person." I shook my head, sick all over. "I don't…I really don't want to talk about this."

I thought he'd push.

I thought he'd say something—anything that would make me feel worse.

But he didn't.

Instead, he just…stayed mercifully quiet.

And when I glanced at him he was watching me with that same dark, assessing gaze I was coming to crave. Like a panther waiting to pounce.

"Okay," he grunted.

And that was it.

Nothing else.

My laptop screen blinked to life as I jiggled the mouse, some of the weight that had settled on my shoulders lifting as I began to type again. Every few minutes I'd glance over at Prudence only to find him still watching me. His gaze was just as heavy, just as predatory as it always was, despite what I'd admitted. He didn't interrupt me.

I was grateful.

Honestly, I was grateful to him for more than just *this*.

I hadn't cried in three days now, and I knew a lot of that had to do with the fact that he'd shown up in my life. Sure, he'd been here before but… talking to him? Being with him? Was the most normal I'd felt in months. I didn't have to hide. I didn't have to lie. Not like when I talked to my mom—not like when I talked to Violet.

Prudence accepted me.

He told me not to change.

He was mean, and dominant, and more than a little sadistic—and he was kinda fucking sweet, actually.

Chapter Fourteen

Prudence

THE NEXT WEEK felt like stepping into a sitcom. The German philosopher Friedrich Nietzsche once said, "The future influences the present just as much as the past." That quote hung around my neck like a noose as I calculated every decision I made, trying to find the opportunity to spring my plan on my unsuspecting pink-haired companion. I was playing the long game. Unfortunately, I knew time was not on my side. Soon enough my sisters would discover where I was. I needed to be long gone before then.

At least one thing seemed to be improving, despite my anticipation for the future. The Nothing buzzed at the back of my mind, dark inky fingers reaching to claim me once again, but the longer I stayed away, the weaker its grip became.

This feeling of…peace was unfamiliar.

Luca didn't seem to understand the power he held over me.

Every command he uttered was to improve my existence, not take from it.

Eat whatever you want, Prudence.

What's mine is yours.

Touch whatever you want.

Sit on the couch, for god's sake. Didn't I tell you what's mine is yours?

You don't need to ask to change the channel, dude. Just do it.

You want another Oreo? Sure! Eat as many as you want.

Luca was a giver. Which was why it was hard for me to believe he'd fucked up so horribly with his family. Curiosity was foreign to me. As foreign as the slick oil of guilt that sat heavy in my belly every time he smiled at me like I deserved it. He didn't like seeing me uncomfortable. Even though he was fully aware that I was dead, and therefore incapable of feeling discomfort the same way he did.

He did what he could to make me feel at home. Each command was carefully cultivated to build me from the ground up. To give me back the freedom that death had taken. It was exactly what the original creators of my spell had intended. Only…he did it unaware. Confusing. He was confusing.

What was his angle?

Soon enough, through the web of his demands, I was beginning to grow solid—able to interact not just with him, but with the world around me.

It was the closest to living I'd felt in a very long time.

Sometimes when he was sleeping I would stare at him and try to figure out whether or not he was incredibly stupid, or just…kind. Tonight was no different. He lay slumbering beside me, snuffling into his pillow, his long limbs akimbo. The numbers on the clock glared red as I found myself lost in thought once again.

Stupid or kind.

Luca began to snore, and I rubbed at the unfamiliar ache in my chest with a frown.

Maybe both.

He kept bending over backward for me but never extended himself the same courtesy. Sometimes his kindness was honestly ridiculous. Exhibit A: He'd blown up a fucking air mattress for me, ignoring the fact I'd literally told him I didn't need it. He'd glared till I'd given in and let him arrange the spare blankets and pillows on top of the rubber monstrosity. The sheets he'd painstakingly tucked overtop it were covered in little rocket ships full of various dog breeds wearing astronaut suits. It was very Luca. *Was it too late to tell him I was allergic to color?*

He clearly had a hard-on for alien-core.

"Are you judging my sheets?" He'd said, all incredulously, like judging the fact he decorated like a toddler was the rudest thing I'd ever done to him. I'd just arched my brow, and let him grumble his disgust. Despite his bluster, I caught the lost look in his eyes as he'd fingered the corner of the sheets, like my disapproval hurt him more than he'd said. Like the person who was really judging him was himself.

I'd kicked him to get him to stop, and he'd squawked at me indignantly. But the light flooded back into his eyes, and the self-hatred that had flickered inside his gaze fled. He could be so kind to others, but to himself? There were demons hiding beneath the surface. I didn't have to care to notice that.

The double standard pissed me off. Contradictory. Sometimes it was almost like he purposefully chased the things that made him hurt.

Phone calls upset him, and yet he never stopped taking them. His hands would shake in agitation. His lips bitten red and raw. It made me regret giving him money for a phone in the first place. Only because his turmoil complicated things, of course. Not because seeing him upset bothered me.

That would be as stupid as his stupid pink hair.

He'd opened up to me a lot during this past week but there was still so much he was hiding. Secrets on secrets on secrets. Every time Violet called he would shoo me away, a constipated look on his face that meant she was about to question him about me again.

The second Luca had mentioned that she was born and raised in Elmwood, I knew she was a threat. As a sanctuary, even the humans who occupied the tiny shit-hole were aware of the secret.

What *exactly* she knew was yet to be discovered.

He was being incredibly cagey about the whole thing.

Which…made it difficult to know whether or not she was telling him the risks of helping me. Or worse, about the spell itself. Not that information regarding ghosts was widely spread. There were few left who even knew the mechanics, and even fewer who knew how to create one. She may be a witch, but that didn't necessarily mean that she was an educated one.

Besides, the spell had been banned years ago, for good reason.

I only hoped that the fact I answered all Luca's questions now meant he would bring any inquiries my way, rather than hers. Now, more than ever, it was important I curate every answer to suit my purposes.

There was a flaw in my plan.

Which only became more apparent the longer I spent with the pink-haired twunk. The more I got to know him the worse I felt about using him. Once again, guilt climbed my insides like rot. Made my skin tight, and my stomach flip.

Feeling bad…was foreign.

I wasn't used to feeling much of anything at all.

Luca was sleeping when I heard the noise.

It echoed through the house, quiet and unassuming, but I knew exactly what it was. The front door. It had made that same *screech-thud* sound every time Luca had gone in and out the month I'd spent with him.

Oblivious to danger, Luca remained unbothered, drooling on his pillow, his fluffy hair a mess around his face. There were six baseball caps stacked together laying by his lax hand. He'd fallen asleep nearly an hour ago while organizing them. He had too many. Apparently he had a system. Which was hard to believe just looking at where they lay stacked haphazardly on top of his bed posts. He'd explained, but I'd tuned him out.

Something about baseball teams.

Color.

Region.

Blah, blah, blah.

Luca snuffled, wriggling to get comfortable, his supple muscular legs sprawled wide in a way that made me want to crowd up between them and bite his ass cheeks. He reminded me of the effortlessly athletic kids in high school, destined for full-ride scholarships and a white picket fence as soon as graduation was over. Exactly the kind of guy I'd wanted to fuck from the moment I figured out how my dick worked. I didn't bite, even though I wanted to. Instead I turned toward the threat, rising from my spot on the useless air mattress.

The clock read one a.m.

Too late for guests.

Something more nefarious was at work. I slipped through the wall, slinking along the hallway, quiet—the way I'd learned how to be out of necessity.

The light in the kitchen was on and I knew for a fact Luca had turned it off.

He'd flipped the switch, sweat gathered at his temples, his eyes bright after he'd literally wrestled me on the ground for the last Oreo in the packet he'd found in the back of the cupboard. I'd won. He'd pouted. I refused to sympathize. It was his own damn fault for telling me I could eat anything in the house. He'd brought this upon himself.

A cupboard thudded open in the kitchen. *Thud, thump.* Then shut. Someone was definitely here. If it was a thief I wasn't sure what they'd be stealing. Chipped bowls? Mismatched mugs? Luca's piece of shit laptop?

It didn't matter.

He was mine to protect until I had what I wanted. By extension, that meant guarding his things as well as his body. I couldn't harm someone without his go-ahead. Not with my hands, anyway. But there were a lot of other ways I could incapacitate our visitor. Which made an interesting thought arise. *Huh. Would Luca help me hide a body?*

Yes.

Despite his general…everything-ness, the kid had backbone. I could see strength flickering inside his eyes, especially when he'd been at his lowest. Behind the tears something else lurked. A curious sort of thing.

How I instinctively knew that, I couldn't explain.

But my cheeks were hurting from smiling again and it was pissing me off.

The wood supports and plaster inside the wall almost tickled as I phased enough of my body through it that I could see inside the kitchen to the threat that awaited.

"I know you're there, Prudence," a voice echoed.

A female voice.

Familiar.

I recognized it from Luca's many phone calls even before I saw the woman who spoke. Violet.

She was back. Two weeks early.

Shit.

This meant I was officially out of time.

Why the hell had I waited so long? Why had I been lured into a false sense of security? Why had I entertained Oreo wrestling, rom-coms, and hours of babbled nonsense? All this time, fucking wasted if I couldn't get Luca out of here before Violet ruined everything.

The fact she wasn't a burglar made me relax, despite the even more real threat to my plan. My thoughts whirred. I'd have to amp things up. The stakes were higher than ever now. *How could I get Luca to take me where I needed to go?* Oregon wasn't just hours away, it was an entirely fucking different state.

Guard dog duties no longer necessary for now, I ignored Violet, confident she wouldn't be a problem tonight at least, before I moved back toward Luca's room.

This was a problem for tomorrow.

I'd have to convince him that getting rid of me was a bad idea. Convince him to take me where I needed to go. To do what I needed him to do. And I'd need to do all of that before Violet informed him of the risks.

I'd heard Luca rant enough about Violet's witch-i-ness to know he wasn't talking about being a bitch. I'd never met a witch before. There were a few that lived in Elmwood, but I'd had no reason to interact with them when I was alive—and after death there was nothing anyone could do to break my spell, aside from Lydia, so there had been no point.

That didn't mean they couldn't take me from Luca though.

I refused to let that happen.

I was so close.

So fucking close.

Maybe I could solve his problems and my own at the same time. I knew he needed money, and that was one thing I had in abundance. I still wasn't sure why he needed it, but with how big his mouth was—*fuuuck don't think about his mouth*—I figured he'd blab at some point. Sure he might die, but at the end of the day, based on the clear devastation he'd been fighting for weeks, I didn't think he'd hesitate to make the choice. I'd just thought I had more time to…

To what?

To get him to like me?

I traveled through the apartment in a daze, blinking when I realized I was back safely in the bedroom, and Luca lay prone on the bed exactly where I'd left him just a few minutes earlier. His body was relaxed as he nuzzled into his pillow, his t-shirt riding up his back high enough that I could admire the dimples at the top of his ass. It was a nice fucking ass. Round. Bouncy. Firm. Encased in a teeny-tiny pair of outer space print boxer-briefs that were clearly way too fucking little for those supple thighs.

The crease between his cheeks and his hamstrings flickered as he shifted, briefs stretching to accommodate his thick ass. Luca's sleepy scent tickled my nose—sweat, saltwater, and coconut. I inhaled greedily, my breath escaping in an overwhelmed puff as I fought back the urge to bury my face between his cheeks to inhale the clean musk directly from his shorts. If his briefs were any more see-through, and if he spread his legs just a liiittle more I was sure I'd catch a glimpse of the shy little hole hidden away beneath them. *Had he put these on knowing I'd look?*

I wouldn't be surprised.

As guarded as Luca was, he was shameless too.

My cock perked up and I shoved the heel of my palm against it to soothe the ache.

I hadn't expected Luca to be so…

So, *him*.

But he was.

The list of his transgressions was longer than the Bible. He sang all the fucking time—horribly off-key with an obscene amount of jazz hands. He wore his emotions practically tattooed across his face. His eating habits were abysmal. And the man spent way too long reapplying pink dye to his hair every time he showered. Unfortunately, all these objectively negative things didn't stop him from growing on me like a fungus.

He didn't wake up.

671. That was how many breaths he took before Violet retreated to her room, the door across the hall shutting with a quiet *snick*.

I'd snooped around inside her room before while Luca slept, so I felt no need to do so again. It wasn't unheard of for witches or hunters to carry artifacts meant for ghost collection. And I was certain she didn't have anything of importance. At least nothing that could trap me.

Besides, my talisman still hung safely around Luca's neck. Coveted like he truly thought it was lucky, just as I'd planned.

1,921 breaths later, Luca stirred. Except this time the movement was followed by a desperate little sob. It had been so long since I'd last heard him cry that the sound startled me. I hadn't realized how long I'd been standing, staring at him till that moment. Within seconds I knelt beside his head, knee to the mattress—unsure what I was doing—only that I wanted to help.

That sick feeling was back again, and I was at a loss for what to do.

The only real experience I had with crying had been when I'd babysat the kids in my social circle when I'd been alive. But I'd never felt affected by their emotions. It was a nuisance. A problem to be solved, at most. Easily forgotten.

Tears glistened as they dripped down angular cheekbones. Soft pink bangs stuck to Luca's sweaty forehead, his chapped lips parted like he'd been biting them in his sleep. There were freckles everywhere. It would take hours to count them. They splattered his lips like paint spots. He didn't make another sound. Completely silent as tears continued to fall and my pulse fluttered in fascination as his face twisted up all over again. Normally his crying elicited a much different response from my body.

This time my cock didn't react.

Which…*surprised* me.

Until now Luca's crying face alone was enough to get me off.

But *this* was different. It was intimate. Private. It wasn't something he meant to show me—but he had gifted it to me anyway, unaware.

I swallowed, unsure.

More tears fell.

His pillow was growing damp.

I'd never…comforted someone before. Especially not while they were unconscious. I'd never wanted to. Truthfully, I didn't know how. Maybe my past was to blame. My mother and her icy personality. The parade of nannies I'd gone through so quickly I'd never learned their names. The too-large age gap between my sisters and me. The standard I'd always had to uphold as the oldest Rain sibling, till the day I'd decided enough was enough and burned it to the ground.

If not that, then maybe it was the years I'd been kept prisoner by a madwoman. All the twisted things I'd done to please her. All the tears I'd caused. The cruelty I'd given birth to. In the end it didn't matter why I was the way I was. My weaknesses were my own. And for the first time in my life I felt the need to do something about someone else's pain.

I wasn't sure if it was empathy, or possession. Anger that something else could elicit such a strong reaction from him.

Luca's hair was downy soft as I carded my fingers through it, startled— like always—by how very warm he was. Even his sweat was fascinating as I detangled his bangs, gently swiping away his tears with my thumbs till they stopped flowing and his lips ceased wobbling.

I didn't know why he was crying.

I wished I did.

Maybe then I could stop it.

It was annoying. It was all annoying. I hated it. That's why my chest was so tight. And that's why my hands didn't feel like my own. Not because I hated when he was upset. He was just annoying. Yes. That was it.

His wet lashes clumped together like spiderwebs.

At some point Luca woke up. His breathing pattern changed. Long fingers twitched as consciousness flickered behind his bruised eyelids. The damage from his kiss with the asphalt was gone, all that remained was a faint scar along the swell of his cheek.

Luca's furrowed brow was still present and even though I knew he was conscious now and everything inside me screamed to move back, I couldn't help myself. I pressed my thumb against the tensed muscle and gently rubbed it away, my heart stuttering, desire trickling through my veins. My heartbeat was just an illusion. A trick of the mind. A mechanism of the spell meant to keep the dead alive but… It felt real. Sickeningly so.

Luca didn't speak.

He didn't have to.

Without opening his eyes he leaned into my hand, and fanned a gentle kiss against the fragile skin on the inside of my wrist in thanks. Irritated, I slipped my hand in a line down his chest, and under the hem of his tiny underwear till my fingers settled on his cock, and the turned-on little whimper that left his lips rocketed us officially back into familiar territory.

Tears glistened on his cheeks as his face scrunched up, and he spread those long legs wide in invitation. The second his eyes fluttered open and his gaze met mine it finally hit me that there was no way in hell I was letting him go.

Chapter Fifteen

Luca

IT WASN'T FAIR that the morning after Prudence had comforted me for the first time, I was accosted with Violet's ire before I'd even had breakfast. Being awoken by a Prudence-patented hand job the previous night had gone a long way in fixing my dark mood, buuuut orgasms did not Hunter-flavored nightmares fix. Sadly. I'd gone back to bed hopeful, only to be disappointed by fate.

"What are you doing?" Violet's voice was way too loud and I grimaced, covering my ears in a way that was probably childish, but fuck—*did she have to yell?*

"It's like nine a.m., Violet. My ears are not awake yet." I complained, though—that was about how long it took me to realize that she was standing right in front of me, very real, and very exhausted. "Woah!"

I removed my hands, stared down at her pixie-esque face as a grin split my cheeks hard enough they burned, and I wrapped her up in my arms. "You're here! Early! When did you get back?"

I gave her body a happy shake, more than pleased by the indignant little noise she released. I swore I could hear her piercings rattle. Despite her annoyance, Violet hugged me back. Her blood-orange perfume was just as delicious as I remembered and I huffed it up like a greedy pig snuffling the forest floor for snacks.

"Oh my god I missed you!" I gave her another shake and Violet laughed, clearly forgetting she was supposed to be irritated by the hug because she squeezed me back just as tight. She was smaller than me, though not by much height-wise. The real difference came in the size of our frames. I was long and gangly with muscle built from years enjoying the great outdoors, and a few sweaty, baseball-filled summers in high school. Violet was all sharp elbows, and paper-thin bone. My shoulders were nearly twice as broad as hers, and yes, we'd measured. "How the fuck are you, dude? How was your flight? Did you Uber here?"

Violet had a natural layer of softness that made her more than appealing to hug.

Even though it was early, she'd already donned her goth armor. Black fishnets over a black tube top, paired with a pleated purple skirt. Her chunky platforms easily gave her an extra six inches in height. I rarely saw her without them. Apparently, the fact it was nine a.m. and she more than likely had jet-lag wasn't a strong enough deterrent to go without. I was honestly glad to see she'd dressed up. It meant she wasn't too tired—or too angry. *Good.* Things between us had been a bit awkward since she'd taken up a vendetta against my ghost-man-friend. With a snort, Violet eyed the robe I'd stolen from her, shaking her head, her eyes alight.

"I don't know how you haven't torn the seams on that thing, getting your big ass shoulders inside."

I'd torn a stitch.

Or two.

Not that I'd tell her that.

Shoving aside how irked I'd been with her for all the lecturing I'd received over the past few weeks, I shook my head and laughed. She may be overprotective and a little on the judgmental side, but…she was *still* my best friend. And I knew she was just looking out for me. Even though I was a grown-ass man and didn't need her to.

"I got in late last night. Didn't want to wake you," Violet finally answered when I set her down. "I'm fine, aside from nursing the regrets of a hookup from Elmwood I shouldn't have enjoyed as much as I did. And also what feels like an entire bottle of tequila that I don't remember drinking when I got back home. The flight was boring, but good. And yes, I got an *Uber*. Also, what the fuck happened to all my granola?"

"Violet!" I grinned, evading her last question like a pro as I slapped her cheerfully on the back. She stumbled a little then glared, though her prickly expression quickly became a smile, the piercings in her cheeks pulling up before she whacked me right back, way harder than I'd hit her.

"Luca!" We grinned at each other for a solid minute before I watched the smile on her face slowly die as she got a good look at me. Shit. I wasn't sure what she'd see on my face but…it couldn't be good. My belly flipped nervously, guilt digging its nails in as I pushed past her quickly, not capable of dealing with whatever was making her angry. At least not yet. My stomach was growling and I was still buzzing from my most recent ghost-orgasm. Prudence was waiting in my room, which probably meant he'd known Violet was here and didn't warn me.

Dick move.

But okay. I wasn't surprised, that was right on-brand for him.

Food. All of this would be easier to handle if my stomach wasn't trying to eat me.

Except…Violet gasped, a wretched little sound that had me whipping around with alarm. Her eyes were wide, lips parted. I glanced behind myself to see what was freaking her out. Please, God. Don't let Prudence be naked behind me or something. Not that I'd even been blessed enough to see him that way—but still. This would be the worst possible time ever for that.

But nope. Nothing was behind me.

Huh.

"*Luca*," Violet repeated, horrified.

"What?" I turned my attention back to her as soon as I was sure no ghost peen was in sight. Her eyes were on my neck. It only took a second for the realization of why she'd freaked out to hit me like a sledgehammer.

Mother-*fucker*.

The hickeys.

The goddamn hickeys Prudence had been sucking into a necklace around the back of my neck. He was a bitey-little-biter. I'd gotten so used to his chompy-ness I'd honestly forgotten the marks were there. It wasn't my fault that for weeks there had been no one to hide from—nothing to lie about. We'd been alone together, and I'd very much enjoyed—and encouraged— the fact he'd been turning me into his own personal chew toy.

I felt regret keenly now.

"Violet—it's not what it—" I flushed, an angry upset feeling bubbling up. I wasn't hungry anymore. *Okay, that was a lie.* "Fuck. Okay, it's exactly what it looks like." There was no lying. I couldn't. Not anymore. She wasn't stupid. I was stuck. Besides…if there was one person I didn't want to lie to it was her. "I told you I wanted to keep him." My voice didn't even sound like my own. It was soft, hoarse. Resigned.

"You promised!"

"I know, I'm sorry. I feel like total shit about lying but you gotta know that I—"

"I *told* you how dangerous he is." Violet pushed against me, the whites of her eyes flashing. Realistically I knew she was only acting this way because she was scared for me. But my hackles raised anyway. The wild look in her eyes felt like a threat. "All he has to do is get you to release him and the likelihood of you dying is—"

"Look." I held on to her shoulders, giving them a squeeze to silence her. We'd been close so long that the simple touch alone was enough to get her to stop. "I *know*."

"You don't."

"I do," I shook my head. "I *know*, Violet. Believe me, I listened to everything you said about him. I couldn't forget even if I tried. Every known Prudence fact is voluntarily tattooed inside my brain. I just… God, I don't know how to say this without sounding like a complete idiot. But I genuinely don't care about the risks. He's worth it."

"You can't mean that. You don't want to die."

"I mean, yeah. Dying would suck. But Prudence isn't going to kill me. Even if he was? Honestly? This time with him has made me the happiest I've ever been. I won't give him up. I *can't.*"

"Luca…" Her voice trembled and her eyes were wet. She wouldn't look at me. But I forced her to anyway. Her skin was sweaty. Her cheeks squished beneath my palm. "Is this because of Hunter? I know that you've been through a lot this year but you can't give up because of it."

"Vi, seriously. I appreciate your concern but 'this' and 'that' are totally different issues. I'm not giving up. I'm fine." I smiled, even though anxiety was bubbling up inside me. I felt like we'd had this same argument a thousand times and I was getting tired of it. "I'm just—really well-fucked." I dropped her face, my hands clenching into fists as I waited for her response with baited breath.

"I…" Violet clammed up, her whole expression shuddering before turning to cement. Still. Determined. Stubborn. Fucking hell. "I…can't let you keep him."

"And I'm not going to let you take him away." We were at an impasse. But I knew I'd win. She loved me too much to hurt me like that. I kissed her cheek and pulled away, heading toward the kitchen, my skin crawling. Pretending like everything was normal took every ounce of my control, but I managed.

I rummaged through the cupboards. My hands shook as I tossed two plastic bowls onto the dining table we'd painted together two years ago while drunk. *Thunk, thunk.* I stared at the lopsided yellow squiggles Violet had scribbled, willing them to teach me how to act normal, when my thoughts were spinning like a tornado. The squiggles were supposed to be stars, but she'd gotten frustrated and given up halfway through painting. It was funny, how she'd always struggled following through, and yet here she was—ready to drive my ghost away from me, no matter what it took.

"Come eat breakfast," I called, unable to look at her as I gathered the cereal boxes and poured the last of the Fruit Loops into our bowls. I needed to focus. I needed to fix this. I needed to stop thinking about Prudence. Except, I couldn't help it, because looking at the Fruit Loops only made me want to laugh—for obvious reasons—and like my eyes were magnetized to him my attention was pulled back toward my bedroom.

Prudence was in there.

Snooping through my painting supplies like he didn't know I knew.

I could feel his curiosity, bright silver in the air.

Violet sat in her chair across from me, ankles tucked together as she shoveled cereal into her mouth and smiled. It was a bit stiff, but hey. She was trying. To her credit she didn't bring Prudence up again for the entirety of the meal. I asked about her family, her brother, Avery—the wooded recluse who recently decided to open an occult spell shop—and her mother's herbal tea business she ran on the side.

Violet chatted away, her raven-colored bob tucked behind her ears as she explained what exactly "intention" tea was. Then spent five minutes complaining about Avery's bleeding heart and his colorful menagerie of random ass pets. By the time she'd finished her rant, I'd almost forgotten why we'd been fighting in the first place.

Unfortunately, I was reminded again when her dark gaze dragged over my collarbone and she stared a little too long at the hickeys that were purpling along my throat. I swallowed, suddenly a little sick to my stomach all over again.

My phone buzzed, saving me from whatever awkward conversation we would've been forced to have if I stayed. Excellent timing, telemarketer my friend. Cheerily, I leapt to my feet, interrupting what I was sure was about to be another fight as I cocked my head toward the back of the apartment with a put upon grimace.

"Sorry! Gotta take this." Distracted, I didn't actually check the caller ID as I fled down the hallway toward my bedroom for privacy to answer. *Buzz, buzz.* I stumbled to a halt right outside the door with a grimace. Prudence. Right. He was still inside—and I wasn't really in the mood to be spied on right then—so I popped into the shared bathroom instead, shut the door, and answered.

"Hello!" I chirped, extra loud, in case Violet thought I was lying about the call. I cocked my head, listening for her response. But nothing came.

To my horror, Mom's voice filled my ear and immediately the sickness festering beneath my skin multiplied. The tiny bathroom grew even smaller, as the walls closed in. My breath stuttered out, and I gripped the counter tight with my free hand, reflection staring back at me, horror-stricken.

How long had it been since the last time I'd talked to her?

Right.

I'd been ignoring her calls since the car accident and…well.

Clearly, she could tell.

"Have I done something wrong?" Her voice wobbled. No "hello." No "hi, baby." Not for me. Not this time. I swallowed bile, dropped my head, and leaned my body heavily against the cool counter. My arm shook from the weight of holding myself up. I'd never felt so heavy.

"Hi, Mom."

"Luca."

"No. You haven't done anything wrong." Jesus-god. Luca-this, Luca-that. That was all I was hearing today. Did *everyone* think I was a basket case? My skin itched, ants biting their way through my carefully collected control. There were lies on lies on lies, fogged like glass, between me and the rest of the people in my life.

I couldn't breathe—

I couldn't—

I—

"Then why have you been ignoring my calls?"

Jesus. Fuck. Fucking. Fucking. Fuckfuckfuckfuck.

"I've been busy." More lies, more lies, lies, lies, lies, *lies*. Trailed like corpses behind me.

"I know you're busy, baby. But I'm your mom. I want to know what's going on with you. You don't call, you don't text. Adam says you left him 'on read' or something last week. I don't know what that means, but it can't be good." She inhaled, and more words poured out. "We're *all* concerned. You didn't even reply when Paul texted you the stats for the Bears game! You love talking baseball with him—I just…don't understand what's been going on with you lately. This isn't like you." Her voice was wobbling again and I felt my heart begin to shred itself into a million tiny pieces. "I get that something must be happening, that you're busy—like you said—" We both knew that was an excuse. "We used to talk all the time…I miss that. I don't need anything else. I don't know what I've done to cut myself out of your life but, Luca, please. Please give me a chance to fix it."

Mom.

Mom and her bleeding heart.

Acid burned its way up my throat and I made a hurt little noise. "I'm sorry, Mom." God. I was so fucking sorry. She had no idea how sorry I was. "I'm sorry. I didn't mean to—I just…"

"You've always been my most sensitive baby. I know breaking up with

Hunter was hard for you. But I hope you know my negative reaction to him had nothing to do with you and everything to do with me. I felt… something was off. I've wondered…"

No.

No, no, no, no.

"I've wondered if maybe because I said something…" Mom's voice only got wetter, shakier. "I pushed you away?"

This. *This* was the exact phone call I'd been avoiding. And the fact it was happening at all was my fault. I could see that now. If I'd answered her calls—If I'd pretended harder, then maybe…maybe she wouldn't sound so hurt right now.

One thing was for certain.

No matter how big my problems were I couldn't let her think the rift between us was her fault. Not for even a second longer. "No. That isn't it." I shook my head hard enough my vision swam, breaths shallow, too fast. Fast enough I had to force myself to count to regulate them. One, two, three—*fuckfuckfuck. Act normal. Act normal! Breathe, Luca. Breathe!*

She couldn't know how this was affecting me.

I was supposed to be strong.

Reliable.

Solid.

The one she could count on.

Her golden boy.

Her sunshine.

Sunrise follows even the darkest night.

Sunrise follows even the darkest night.

Sunrise follows even the darkest ni—

"I swear." I somehow managed to keep my voice steady when I spoke. "Leaving Hunter totally messed me up, but our breakup had nothing to do with you. I love you. I don't blame you at all. You were right, he was a bad egg. I'm glad you said something."

"Are you?" I could practically smell her tears. "Because I worried maybe you thought I didn't approve of the two of you together. But you know that's not it, right? You've always been my baby. Sexuality has never mattered to me like some of those moms you see on TV. Bitches. All of them. That ain't no way to mother your baby. *You're mine.* I could never stop loving you. So if that's why you haven't been talking to me, please know I'm so, so sorry I made you feel that way and I—"

"No." God. What a hot fucking mess.

I couldn't breathe—I couldn't—I—

Each breath choked on its way out. The counter bit into my palm so hard it might as well be cutting it. Chilly fingers bunched around my wrist. Strong. Reliable. Solid. There was only one person I knew that felt like ice and comfort all at once. Prudence squeezed me tight, one hand tangling in the back of my hair, grounding me as I trembled over the empty sink, the blurry drain swimming as dark spots danced in front of my eyes. His touch mended my scattered pieces together. Blearily I lifted my head. Pru's dark figure stood behind me, blocked by my bulk and out of focus through my tears.

My phone trembled in my sweaty grip but I held tight.

He caught my weight easily as I sagged against him, my mother's voice still echoing from the tinny speaker as Prudence held me together. The fact that he could easily hold me up wasn't lost on me. But instead of basking in the feeling as I normally would, I wilted. He pulled my hair tight till I turned all the way around. Then, using the possessive hold he had on me, he forced my face into the hollow at the base of his throat. His skin was cold, but very real. I had to crouch a bit to reach, but I didn't mind.

I knew with us standing this close, Prudence would be able to hear what my mom said. But it didn't matter.

None of it did.

Only him.

His strength, steady as a river.

Prudence's hand in my hair loosened a fraction. I pulled the back of his shirt tight in protest, the inside of my wrist brushing against the chilly strip of skin above the waistline of his jeans. With an annoyed huff he tightened his hold again and I relaxed as my scalp began to tingle.

With him beside me, words were suddenly possible again.

"Mom, listen to me for a second." The walls stopped closing in on me as I inhaled the scent of smoke and leather from Prudence's throat. My lips bumped against the moth tattoo on the center of his neck that I'd admired at least a million times since I'd seen him the first time. "Everything is fine. I'm fine. Everything is going really well, actually. Hunter leaving was great! It really was. I'm happier than ever." Lies, lies, lies.

She quieted.

Could she tell?

My breath stuttered, my pulse beginning to dance again. Prudence's fingers pulled taut, pain zinging up my back. I sagged again, letting him force me into submission. The touch meant *calm down*. I hadn't realized I'd tensed up but *he* had. The steady *thump, thump* of his heart trembled against my cheek, and I nuzzled into it, unable to help myself.

How did he have a heartbeat?

Maybe it was part of the spell he was under.

"I've been really busy because of work," I said softly. "But I'll do better. I'll call more."

"I want to see you." Mom's voice was stubborn, it left no room for argument.

Fuck. No. *No*— "What—?" My shock must've been obvious.

"Luca. If you're telling the truth and nothing is wrong, then you won't have a problem coming home to visit. It's not like we live on Mars. Besides, your birthday is coming up. I've been trying to plan something for you like we always do—which you would know if you had been answering your phone." My breath hitched. "We haven't seen you since Christmas. Betty's even bringing her boyfriend over to meet you, and Adam's out of school for the summer. It's time to come home."

I couldn't *afford* to go home.

But I couldn't admit that without coming clean about all my lies.

She was right. If nothing was wrong, I should've had plenty of money to visit them. It wasn't like I had a job that had me on a strict schedule—not yet, anyway.

Prudence's nose was cold where it pushed against my temple. The touch was weirdly soothing. He probably didn't think I'd notice the way he was sniffing at the sweat there. But I did. It hadn't taken long for me to realize he liked anything that reminded him I was human. He seemed particularly attracted to my scent.

"Okay."

"Good," Mom's voice flooded with relief. "Twenty-five is a big number. We'll make it extra special! Betty's baking!" I was so fucking screwed it wasn't funny. "I'll see you soon, baby. Five days."

"Five days." I echoed obediently. "Love you, Mom," I croaked.

"Love you too, sweetheart."

The second I hung up, Prudence took my phone away. He set it on the counter, then he dragged me out of the crook of his neck, his hands bracketing my cheeks, squeezing till I was forced to look him in the eyes.

I expected judgment.

But he…he just looked at me like he always did.

Sure. Confident. Detached. *Hungry.*

"I can solve your problem."

"What?" My heart wobbled, and my eyes were more than a little wet. I was shaking all over but Prudence didn't seem to mind. He squeezed me tighter, tight enough a trickle of pain tingled beneath my skin. Just enough I could separate away the tangles of anxiety and fear that were still threatening to choke me from the inside out.

"Money. That's what you need, isn't it?" Prudence's voice filtered through the fog in my head. *How had he known?* "If you help me I'll make sure your family is taken care of."

"How?" I had no idea what he was talking about. He was *dead.* Dead men didn't have bank accounts.

"My family—" Prudence grimaced, "and I…have more than enough means to fix the mess you're in, whatever it is."

"You're…"

"Rich, yes."

"And you would…*do* that?" I shook my head dubiously. My lips were dry and my tongue flickered out to wet them. "You would help me?" For a second I almost asked him why he'd robbed a fucking ATM if he was as rich as he claimed he was—but I held myself back.

"Yes."

"I need a *lot* of money."

"Name your price."

My price? Shit…I didn't even know. I did some quick mental math, only possible because I'd gone through the calculations at least fifteen times since I'd lost all my money, trying to figure out a way to make this work.

"Three hundred thousand dollars."

Prudence didn't even blink. "Four hundred thousand."

"Did you just barter higher?" I stared at him, not sure I was hearing right.

"Three hundred thousand for whatever it is you're upset about. One hundred thousand for potential damages."

Potential…damages? Ah. Like Violet had warned me about. I shuddered, but…I wasn't surprised. At least he was honorable enough to compensate me.

How was this real? How was this possible?

"But…" I trailed off, my lashes wet with unshed tears, the tired hollows beneath my eyes felt nearly bruised from the stress. At my temples a tension headache was coming on and crying was only bound to make that worse—but there was nothing I could do to stop myself once I started.

"You have to do something for me in return."

Right. That was only fair.

I already knew what he wanted.

Didn't take a genius to figure that out.

"You…" I swallowed, trying not to be too shaken by the predatory glimmer in his eyes. This was exactly what Violet had been talking about.

The trap. The bargaining. He wanted death and well…I wanted…to fix the mess I'd made, no matter the price. "You want to die, right? Like… *actually* die. Pass on. Be done-zo. Gone-zo."

If Prudence was surprised I remembered his earlier statement he didn't show it. Instead, he nodded. His eyes flickered to my mouth and I could tell he wanted to kiss me. He'd never done it before. But it wouldn't surprise me if the first time he did was when I was in the middle of a full-blown panic attack.

"How can *I* help with that?" I knew what he wanted, but as Violet hadn't known all the details herself, only the risks, I was still a little lost. I couldn't imagine hurting him. The idea made me sick. Murdering someone in cold blood? Yeah, no. I didn't think I could do that. Tiny Betty and Adam popped into my mind, the way they'd clutched at me when I was barely old enough to hold their weight. The way they still looked at me that way, like I could fix everything. Like I was worth relying on. I amended my statement. Well, *maybe*…if I absolutely had to, murder was an option. But not Prudence. I could never kill Prudence.

"I need the key." Oh, thank God.

"The…key?"

"It's a word that was used to trap me. A password," Prudence explained, his voice blank as always. "There's only one person who knows it and she's in prison."

"Prison?" I blinked in confusion. "Why is she in prison?"

Things were starting to fall into place like a fucked up game of Jenga and I didn't know what to do with how tangled my thoughts had become. My turmoil was black, black, black.

"She killed two people," Prudence said.

"Wow. A murderer. Okay. Cool. Cool-cool-cool-cool." I shook my head—or tried to. There wasn't much I could do with the way Prudence was holding me captive. Still though, his possessive grasp was welcome. His icy grip on my face grounded me in the present. "Why does a murderer know your key?"

"She's the one that made me."

"Made you?" My head spun. "Like…in an easy bake oven?" I half joked.

Prudence snorted. "Cursed me. Created me. Trapped me here. Then held me prisoner."

Oh.

Fuck.

"That's…" I swallowed, "super fucked up. Like—super, super, *super* fucked up." His eyes were fathomless. The muscle in his jaw jumped. "And she's the only one that can…free you?" I clarified.

"Yes."

What the fuck.

"Okay, I'm going to need more information about the whole prisoner thing later. But for now…You…" I searched his gaze, chasing the flutter of his lashes, and the stubborn set to his jaw with my eyes. "All you need is the magic password?" The morning sunlight filtered through the foggy glass of the bathroom window as I waited.

"Yes."

"That should be easy enough." I had always been good with people. Maybe not murderous, imprisoning, spell-casting people? But still. How different could she really be? If I flirted hard enough I could get pretty much anyone to give me anything.

Prudence frowned, and I watched the satisfied glint in his steely eyes, more than a little mesmerized. He was so close to getting what he wanted. Loss tickled keenly at the back of my mind as I realized what that would mean for us. No more Prudence. No more sex. No more food fights— He'd be…He'd be *gone*.

Forever.

But…

I couldn't keep him here. Not if he didn't want to stay.

Dead or not, he deserved a choice.

So I did the only thing I could and gave in. "Deal."

Prudence's pale eyes widened in surprise before his lips twitched and a grin stretched wicked as sin across his handsome face. He looked feral and gorgeous and *God…* I needed to know what his smile tasted like.

"Kiss on it?" I asked, probably a little too desperately.

I thought he'd say no.

But he didn't.

Instead, he just…kissed me.

His lips tasted like I'd thought they would. Like fresh spring water, smoke, and something deep and musky that had me chasing him for more. He sucked my tongue into his mouth, squeezing my cheeks hard enough all I could do was whimper, surrendering as he completely devoured me.

By the time he was finished, I had forgotten all about my lies, my promises, and our fate.

All I could think about was him, him, him.

I chased his lips again, and succumbed to his cruelty willingly.

Chapter Sixteen

Luca

"SO BASICALLY." I forced Prudence into my bedroom, shutting the door behind us. I made sure it was locked for good measure before I turned back to him with a thoughtful frown. "We have five days to get up to Oregon for my birthday." I blinked, then narrowed my eyes. "Where is…the prison thingy?"

"Oregon."

"Oh! Awesome!" I perked up. "That's weirdly convenient." Huh. I clapped my hands together, then tapped my lip thoughtfully as I debated our next course of action. "We need a plan."

"We need money."

"Can't you call up your rich family?" I bit my lip, "You know—um. Say you need money or something?"

Wait.

Fuck.

He was dead.

"Scratch that! Dumb question." I was full of those today. "Does your family know…" I waved a hand at him, encompassing all of his very real, muscled-tattooed ghostly glory.

"They know I'm here, yes."

"Oh." Weird. "So are they…"

"Looking for me?"

"Yes?"

"Yes."

"Oh." More blinking. Man. Talking to this guy was like pulling teeth sometimes. "So *can* we call them?"

"No." His lips thinned, and I watched him in fascination as my thoughts whirred. None of this made any sense to me. If his family knew he was here, if they knew he needed help, if they were already looking for him, couldn't we just ask? As much as I hated the idea of relying on anyone I also had no idea how we would accomplish this without some sort of outside influence.

I had hardly any money.

There was no time to earn more—and besides. I hadn't painted anything new in months. My last painting now sat useless but pretty in the living room of that blond twink from the club.

"Why not?" I asked, because clearly Prudence wasn't going to elaborate without a lot of poking from my end.

"Because they'll stop me. I want to die and they're desperately clinging to the fact that I'm here."

Wow. It sounded so dark when he said it like that. But I figured there wasn't a better way to describe it. I just…wow.

Macabre much?

"So that's kaput." My brow furrowed as something struck me, my eyes narrowed suspiciously. "Wait. How are you going to fulfill your end of the deal if you won't talk to them?"

"After we've retrieved the password there will be no need to hide from them anymore. I'll take you to the bank myself, and transfer the money. They'll be too far away to stop me from doing what I need to do."

That made sense. But also—

"If you can just walk into a bank and get money, why don't we do that now?"

"I'm not going to risk it when it's possible they could get my location from the transfer."

"Oh." So *that* was why he'd robbed the ATM all those weeks ago. Damn. Apparently even someone as put together as Prudence had things he was afraid of.

Also…I figured it was fair. Otherwise how would we ensure he got his end of the deal? The thought of Prudence dying still made me feel sick but I wasn't about to tell *him* that. He deserved to make that choice. Even though honestly I wished he'd decide to stay so we could be whatever we were for longer, I understood that I had no idea what it was like to exist for him.

How long had he been dead?

What was that like? To exist without existing. Could he still feel things the way he had when he was alive? Had this cool-detached man always been like this? Or was his personality a side effect of dying?

In fact, how *had* he even died?

Why was he here?

I couldn't shake the thought that what kept Prudence here wasn't a blessing but a curse. He certainly didn't seem happy about it. Not that he ever seemed particularly chipper. If I was being honest, the happiest I ever saw him get was when he was being mean to me (which I liked) or when he was popping rolls of Oreos like a shark on crack.

"They're probably close to finding me," Prudence added, crossing the room before he sat down on the bed. He was all effortless confidence, his legs sprawling wide to take up as much space as possible, his thick thighs filling out his jeans in a way that would make any man cry. Effortlessly commanding. Watching him relax atop my colorful comforter made my belly squirm happily.

I liked the fact he was becoming more comfortable around me. Even if being comfortable also went hand in hand with being a nosy shithead. I could clearly see where he'd been peeping through my paint supplies while I'd been out of the room. He hadn't even bothered to shove the bin back under the bed, it just lay at his feet, torn open and rifled through. The empty canvases mocked me. My dirty laundry lay spread on the floor in accusation.

Prudence was totally unrepentant as I crossed my arms, and debated joining him on the bed.

"So we really are on a time crunch," I tapped my lip in thought, mulling over our options.

"Do you have a car?" Prudence asked.

"Yes." It was a clunker. The thing broke down more often than not, but despite the fact it spewed smoke and blasted music at random times loud enough to burst your eardrums—it was *still* a car. "It's more of a death trap than a vehicle?"

I'd had the thing since I was sixteen. I didn't drive frequently enough that I'd ever felt the need to replace it, even when I'd been doing well financially. Besides, Mom had been the one to get it for me, and I'd always been sentimental.

"Problem solved," Prudence deadpanned, clearly unfazed. I laughed at the joke, only to realize belatedly that he had been totally serious. "We'll take your 'death trap' for a spin."

I could sense Violet somewhere down the hallway, the idea of her overhearing our plan making my skin prickle. She'd stop us, I knew she would. Now that I understood that witches and ghosts were actually a thing, it wouldn't surprise me if she had the magic to do it. Somehow…?

"No!" I yelled, waving my hands around in my panic to shush him as I glanced over my shoulder with a wince. The door was locked, but fuck— the walls here were ridiculously thin. "*Lower your voice.*"

"*You're* the one yelling," Prudence snarked back and my jaw clicked shut in response. Shit. He was right. A soft laugh burst from my lips and I deflated, crossing the distance between us before I flopped onto the mattress beside him. As it dipped beneath my weight, our bodies were forced together. My heart beat stuttered. It was wild that Prudence was here at all. Especially now that he was solid more often than not. Sometimes I wondered if he was just a figment of my lonely imagination, something I'd made up to heal the bits of me that had been torn loose with Hunter's betrayal. But…no. Peeking through my lashes at Prudence's stoic expression, my lip caught between my teeth, I knew for a fact I wasn't imagining him. As artistic as I'd always been, even *I* wasn't creative enough to have conjured up someone this perfect.

I shrugged helplessly, embarrassed by my own antics. Prudence's skin was cold where it brushed tantalizingly against mine. The veins in his forearms rippled as he crossed his arms, biceps bulging.

His expression did not invite argument.

I argued anyway.

"It's going to break down on us and we'll end up stranded. Besides, gas prices are literally atrocious," I added. We both knew this was true (or at least I assumed he did) but Prudence rolled his eyes at me in response.

"Do you have a better idea?"

I blinked. I grimaced. Maybe he was right…I mean, it hadn't broken yet, right? It could probably handle a quick little road trip north to Oregon. It wasn't like it was across the whole country. I'd made the trip before. It was honestly our only option.

My eyes narrowed as I pursed my lips in thought. "I guess not. What if it *does* break though—?"

"Then we'll figure something out." Prudence stared up at me, his dark crush of hair falling across his brow as he leaned closer to meet my gaze. His broad shoulders pulled his t-shirt taut, glorious pecs swelling with each carefully calculated breath. Everything about him was gorgeous. He shouldn't have fit in here, with my space themed posters, and my pastel pink bed set, but he did.

He and I were complementary colors.

His dark lashes fluttered, thick enough he could've been wearing eyeliner. The contrast in color only highlighted how striking his irises were—so pale they might as well have been colorless. Despite how striking his gaze was I couldn't help but turn my attention to his lips, my own tingling in response. I knew what it felt like to kiss him now—and wow. Ten out of ten would recommend. I wanted to do it again, so badly I knew the desire probably wasn't healthy.

Needy.

Maybe toxic?

But fuck. He was mine now, at least until he got what he wanted, right?

This might be my last shot at something like this.

It was okay to want him.

Things never work out well for you when you want them to, a bitter voice reminded me and my mind flashed back to Hunter. My stomach flipped and I bit my lip hard enough the pain distracted me from my thoughts.

I knew I shouldn't trust Prudence.

I'd been burned before.

He was just like Violet had said—he had his own agenda. And based on what she'd rattled away about during her fits of hysteria over the whole thing, at the end of the road his death might end with mine as well. Making that sacrifice though? Didn't feel as hard as it should've. I hadn't lied when I'd told her this was the happiest I'd felt in years. He made me feel…He just—

Yeah.

He made me *feel.*

"Okay." I exhaled raggedly, then flashed him an eager grin. "Road trip? Road trip. No espionage. Just…good ole birthday shenanigans."

"Exactly."

"It'll be great. Totally, completely great. Things will not go to shit. Nope."

Maybe this would work? Maybe it wouldn't. But Prudence was right. It was worth a shot.

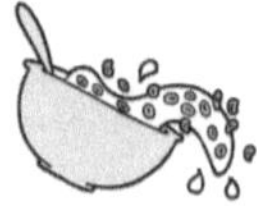

Fifteen minutes later things took a turn for the worse.

I could hear Violet in the kitchen rattling around. Damn. *Had she even left since breakfast?* My stomach was growling again. And after how long my talk with Prudence had taken, I was more than ready to toss a bag of ramen in the microwave, and try my luck.

I paused, halfway down the hallway.

Violet's voice echoed through the air, hushed, like she was speaking quietly on purpose. Because—as much as I made fun of Prudence for being nosy—I was actually pretty nosy myself, I stayed silent. I tip-toed down the hallway till I was close enough to hear clearly without giving myself away.

When I was fifteen I had a similar experience. Hidden in the darkened hallway of our trailer, listening to Mom's hushed whispers as she told Paul, in no uncertain terms, that she wouldn't marry him unless he was willing to love all of us the way we were meant to be loved. I'd never known my dad. Never known any of our dads. That alone had made me wary of Paul from the start. He'd had to woo all three of us kids just as hard as he'd wooed Mom. Except, when she got flowers and nights out on the town, we got a dad that showed up for every spelling bee, baseball game, and art contest we'd ever participated in. Paul had never let me down. Not once.

Hearing her words back then, I'd felt peace.

This situation though—was different.

Instead of feeling excited as I eavesdropped, I was…apprehensive.

So much was going on it felt like there were marbles rattling around inside my head. I shook it to clear it, and held my breath so I could catch the words Violet spoke next.

"He's still here," she hummed.

Who is still here? Me? Or Prudence? This already didn't sound good.

No bueno, no siree.

Scraaape, thud. The familiar sound of Violet pulling out our cutting board, and setting it on the counter filled the air. Ah. Against my better judgment, a smile crept across my lips. No doubt, Violet was probably about to prepare one of her fucking amazing Italian recipes. They were her go-to form of apology after we'd been fighting. A manipulation I welcomed with open arms, and an open mouth. There was nothing a nice, thick lasagna couldn't fix. Not for us. Maybe she was about to ruin that though, because something about her words seemed…off.

I exhaled quietly, then held my breath again.

Anxiety tingled at my fingertips.

"Yes. He's still wearing the necklace," Violet answered whoever she was talking to on the other line. The rattling of cupboards in the kitchen paused as she listened to their response. Icy fingers clenched around my heart as I protectively clutched the cross hanging from my neck. The ivory bit into my palm as I squeezed tight to soothe myself.

Standing in shocked silence, fear buzzed at the edge of my senses, insistent, and all-encompassing. I'd loved and lived with Violet for long enough to understand that if she was conspiring against me, it was only for my own good. She was just that kinda person. Bossy as hell, but good-hearted.

This time though…I couldn't shake the feeling that she was about to betray me. I tried to rationalize her words but…the longer I listened, the clearer it became that Violet was plotting against me.

"If I take it off of him, what happens? Will *he*…you know…disappear?" She was quiet for a moment, oblivious to the fact that my skin was crawling and bile made my mouth taste like battery acid. "Okay, so if *that* won't work, then when can you come get your brother? Tomorrow? The longer they're together, the closer they get, and Luca is… He's too *soft* for this. He'd attach himself to a phone pole if he thought it looked at him twice." I knew she didn't mean to be cruel. I knew she couldn't know I was here, listening like a sneaky little creep—but…*fuck*. Did she really think I was that stupid? Before that moment, I hadn't known a person could be eviscerated with words alone.

My eyes burned.

There was more silence as she listened, and then, "I'll try to distract him until then."

Who was she talking to?

Was this Prudence's family?

I realized now why he'd been so careful to hide his location from them. Clearly, like he'd suspected, they'd figured out where he was through Violet. Maybe they'd overheard one of our many conversations about him? Elmwood was a small town after all. And if that was the case, it meant they'd been hunting for him from the second he'd disappeared. There was no other explanation. Fuck, I was across the entire country, how the hell had they known where he was?

How did Violet know them?

What was going on?

Maybe Prudence wasn't as paranoid as I'd thought he was.

And then…her words finally clicked into place. The necklace. *Duh.*

The necklace belonged to Prudence. He'd appeared in my life the second I'd put it on. I could still remember the way he'd talked me through orgasm, his voice dark as sin in the back of my mind. But *that* had been in Elmwood which…meant it wasn't that weird that Violet might know Prudence's family after all.

Maybe the whole town was in on the supernatural conspiracy.

If witches and ghosts were real, what else was out there?

Dean Winchester's ass had not prepared me for this.

Even though I'd brushed off her warnings of doom and gloom. I'd clung to the facts regardless. Violet had explained that ghosts were cursed beings. Closer to weapons than the specters we'd seen in horror movies, trapped in the living world because of unfinished business or emotional attachment. No. Creating a ghost was difficult. Nearly impossible, especially now that the practice had been banned for hundreds of years. So how…and why had the murderous bitch who made Prudence done it?

If it was so difficult that even Violet, a witch, didn't understand the specifics, how the hell had this woman known how to create him?

And also…

Why the fuck had Prudence been at the club that night I found him, in the first place?

Rare cursed ghosts probably didn't frequent most clubs.

This was all so fucking confusing. My breath came out in stuttered little puffs and I covered my mouth to stifle the noise. *What was going on?* I understood why Violet was hell-bent on getting him away from me, but…didn't she understand that I liked him? Sure, my attachment probably wasn't the healthiest but, fuck… Couldn't she see how badly I wanted him? That he was *helping* me?

She'd told me not to trust anyone.

Apparently she'd been right.

I just hadn't realized she was the one I shouldn't trust.

The sound of the kitchen knife meeting the cutting board made me flinch. A plume of onions and garlic aroma filled the air at the same time I came to the horrible conclusion that we were out of time.

We had no choice but to move forward with our plan.

Some part of me had hoped I'd have more time to at least think it through. But with Violet actively plotting against me, it was clear my time was up.

He'd attach himself to a phone pole if he thought it looked at him twice.

Tomorrow someone was going to arrive to take Prudence away from me. My heartbeat thudded so loudly I could barely think. Violet had decided to steal my agency from me just like Prudence's family was planning on doing to him. Very real sympathy made my breath catch. Or maybe that was the horror I felt as I realized that Violet wasn't cooking apology lasagna after all.

It was…*betrayal* lasagna.

She planned to woo me into a false state of security with cheesy carbs. *It hurt.* So fucking much. I never thought she'd do this to me.

Why couldn't she just…trust me?

Was it because of Hunter?

Was it because of how much I'd cried—because I'd been struggling? When had my turmoil convinced her that I couldn't take care of myself? When was the turning point? When had we stopped being equals? What did this mean for our friendship?

Maybe she was scared of losing me, but that didn't justify this.

Fuck.

One thing was certain—I had to get away—I had to warn Prudence. We had to leave. There wasn't time for more planning, not if Violet was actively plotting against us. His family could arrive at any time, and we'd be completely fucked. He could kiss his freedom goodbye, and I…well, I couldn't handle what that would mean for my future.

There was no time to waffle about anymore. We'd use my savings. We'd have to. Even if we spent every last fucking dime, the pot of gold at the end of our adventure would more than make up for it. So I pushed aside my apprehension. Giving up those last few dollars felt like hacking off a vital part of me. I'd already lost so much. This was all I had left.

It wasn't the money.

No.

It was what it represented.

My shrinking bank account was all that remained of the legacy I'd built, thinking it would last forever. I hadn't known it was Rome until it'd fallen.

Violet couldn't know what we were plotting. Which meant I had to sneak away without her noticing I'd been there at all. If she knew I'd overheard her conversation there was no telling what would happen next. I still didn't understand the rules of the supernatural, or even what being a witch entailed. I didn't want to find out the hard way.

I had to get away.

Quietly.

I turned around, as slowly as possible—terrified she'd hear me. *Don't creak, don't creak, don't creak.* The aged wood of our old-ass apartment was bound to turn against me, and I had no way to stop it. This was some James-Bond-level shit, and I was not mentally prepared to become a master spy today, but here we were.

The first step toward my room went smoothly.

The second step went just as well as the first.

Great.

Now just twenty more.

I could do this.

Violet had started talking again but I blocked her out. There was nothing she could say at this point that would dissuade me. She didn't understand that I was willing to take the risks. All of them. I wasn't going into this blind. I knew what was at stake.

In fact, even Prudence had no idea that I knew what this might mean for me. He was hiding that information. For whatever reason. Maybe he thought I wouldn't help him if I knew. Maybe because the curse was so old, and so obscure, he genuinely didn't understand the risks himself.

Somehow I doubted it was the latter.

I wasn't afraid, not if helping Prudence meant avoiding the misery I was about to inflict on my family. If all went well, they'd never even know what had happened. Water under the bridge. If I didn't do this, my future was a bleak one. I couldn't live with the guilt I was currently feeling. Every day I woke up sicker than the last. It colored everything I did black, black, black till I fell into a void made of pain I had yet to inflict.

Caught in my own web.

I'd do anything if it meant I got to be sunshine Luca again. The big brother. The son. The man my family could rely on, rain or shine. Besides, there was no guarantee I'd die anyway. Violet herself had said that. It was all maybes and mights, what ifs and could bes.

I was willing to take that chance.

I managed to get back to my room in one piece and the moment I stepped across the threshold, Prudence paused, hands caught rifling through my underwear drawer. I blinked, unsure what the fuck to do with what I was witnessing. My morose thoughts were momentarily derailed, as I cocked my head, and he continued to flip through my most private shit, uncaring of his audience.

The door shut with a click behind me.

"What?" Prudence's scratchy voice made my insides do the salsa. Fingering a pair of neon green briefs, his hooded eyes dared me to say something, eyebrow arching in challenge. I had…so much to unpack in that moment. So many questions. Like, why are you going through my underwear drawer? What do you think you're going to find? And also: Did you find my old jock straps? Because I haven't seen them in months. And most importantly: Don't you fucking dare judge me for all the patterns. I like what I like, douchebag.

Maybe, he thought there was more money. After he'd robbed the ATM he'd left a whole pile of it in there, after all. Or…maybe he was simply being a nosy fucker. *Again.*

Was accosting my paint supplies not enough for him?

He just had to know every single little detail of my life.

Ugh, why did that make me want to laugh? It should be creepy. Probably. Not endearing. Nosy ghost.

Reaching down, I grabbed a wayward rolled up sock-ball from the floor by my feet, and chucked it at him in retaliation. It went right through his head, and he growled at me. Actually, fucking growled.

"Why are you—" I shook my head. "You know what? I don't want to know."

Prudence continued to stare at me, though his lips did a downward twist thing I didn't know how to describe. It didn't escape my notice that he hadn't left the room now that Violet was back. Was he worried Violet would hurt him? No. That seemed unlikely. I doubted Prudence was scared of anything.

Or maybe…maybe he wasn't as comfortable around other people as he was with me.

A little smile flickered across my lips and I shook my head.

Then…everything came back to me in a rush and I locked the door behind me with a quiet *snick* before I crossed the room toward him and leaned close enough there was no chance Violet could overhear me.

There were scant inches between us.

I could feel the buzz of energy from Prudence's body as he shifted almost imperceptibly toward me, his eyebrow quirking, his hands stilling their snooping. "*What?*" He asked again, this time softer.

"Violet called your family. I don't know how she knows them, but they know where you are now. I'm sorry."

To his credit he didn't freak out. Instead, I watched his lips thin and his eyes grow icy, *mean*. I hadn't realized how soft he was toward me until that moment. There was something dangerous about the way he grew blank and murderous, fire dancing behind his glacial gaze.

"We have to leave right now or she's going to give you back," I said softly.

"When are they coming?"

"Tomorrow."

There was no time to plan ahead. No time to do anything but run.

"Pru, we have to go—" The nickname slipped from my lips and I was as surprised by it as he was. I jerked my head toward the door, ready to bolt the second he joined me. Instead he surprised me, his fingers latching around my wrist in a possessive, dominant grip that had my head spinning. His pale eyes were blazing and I was mesmerized as my bones creaked within his grasp.

"*No.*" Prudence shook his head, dark hair falling across his brow as his lip curled up in disgust. A shiver ran up my spine. He glanced toward the closed door, his eyes murderous. If I didn't know better, I wouldn't have been surprised if he'd started growling at it. "She'll anticipate that."

"What…"

"Stay for dinner."

"Stay for—"

"I'll pack you a bag. Stay for dinner. Act normal. When she goes to bed we'll sneak out."

"I don't think the car is safe for long distances—" I tried again.

"What would you have us do? Walk?" Prudence arched an eyebrow, his nostrils flaring and I…wilted. He was right. Fuck.

"Fine. But I'm driving." The dude was a ghost after all. "You probably don't even have a valid driver's license."

"Whether or not I'm licensed is the least of our worries right now."

"You'd only say that if you weren't licensed."

"*Luca.*" His voice said, *shut up.* But his eyes were dancing.

He was right. Again. I just liked to argue. My breath hitched, as I realized how close our bodies were. For a single perfect moment, all the fear fled and I was struck with a dazed sort of longing. Prudence was so close. *Right there.* Muscled, glorious. The scent of his smoky musk tickled my nose. His fingers wrapped around my wrist like shackles.

I wanted him.

If we left tonight, did that mean… No.

Did that mean that last night was our last time together?

No more sex?

"Does this mean no more sex?" I parroted my thoughts, sounding more devastated than I'd meant to. Prudence's attention snapped to my lips as my tongue flickered out to wet them. His mouth twisted down. It took me a solid five seconds to realize he was smiling. *Smiling!* Except it wasn't a mean smile like the one he'd worn earlier this one…was soft. Downturned. Sweet. I'd never seen a downturned smile in real life. It charmed me.

Hilarious how in all the time I'd dated him, Hunter had never made me feel as wrong-footed as I did in that moment, enchanted by an unusual smile as I interrupted a ghost going through my underwear drawer.

I'd always had this image in my head of what a heart stopping grin should look like. This didn't look anything like I'd anticipated. Which made it fitting, and even more precious in its own way.

"Where's the fun in that?" Prudence said, and his words were a promise as much as they were a challenge.

"On the run?" I clarified.

"Sure." He reached for the back of my neck with his free hand and yanked me down to his level. When he kissed me it was all teeth and tongue. It stung, sinful, delicious, confusing. Prudence kissed like he did everything else. He was demanding, direct, and most importantly, dominating. Like he thought by fucking me with his tongue he could claim every inch of me. Every brush of his lips had a purpose, and that purpose was to tear me apart, kiss by kiss, till he could make space for himself inside me, whether I wanted him to or not.

Something cool and metallic rubbed against my palette but I ignored the sensation, too enthralled with the way he tongue-fucked me into submission to pay it much attention. By the time he pulled back, I was breathless with desire, I could feel the splotchy heat of a blush all over my cheeks and throat. My lips tingled. My head was spinning. Prudence moved his hand to my chin, gripping it tight. It was the same way he'd held me earlier that day when we'd made our deal. But this was different. This time his eyes were hungry and dark. This time he played with my bottom lip, tugging it down with his thumb, a spark in his eyes that meant sex, sex, *sex*.

"I'm going to fuck you as many times as I can before I die."

"Okay," I croaked. Because what the fuck else was I supposed to say? "Do you mean like—*fuck-me*, fuck-me? Or?"

"Wouldn't you like to know?" His smile turned mean again, the sweet downturned grin gone as he released my lip, with a quiet *thwap*, and rose up on his toes to claim my mouth in another bruising kiss.

He hadn't actually answered the question but…I found it didn't matter. Later, I caught him slipping my still full bottle of lube into the front pocket of the backpack he was packing. I didn't know how I felt about the way he arched his brow at me in challenge for the second time that day, his eyes fiery, his movements purposeful and powerful.

All I knew was that I would take whatever scraps of attention he gave me.

Maybe he was taking advantage of me.

If that was the case, was it really such a bad thing?

Chapter Seventeen

Prudence

TO HIS CREDIT Luca was surprisingly good at lying. Slipping back inside his body for the first time in days felt like melting into a vat of butter. I didn't mind it—not in the way I did with my sisters—or Lydia. Weirdly enough, despite being made of cotton candy and sadness, Luca was the least annoying person I'd been attached to.

I didn't dislike him.

Which was…hard for me to admit.

Not because I wasn't at peace with my bitterness—*I was.* but because it had been so long since I'd met a person that valued kindness above everything else. Amanda had been like that, and look where it had gotten her. Six feet under, without even a tombstone to remember her by. His fate would hopefully be less disastrous.

The juxtaposition between Luca's kindness and his desperation for money was interesting.

Why did he *need* it so badly?

Usually greed and selfless-ness didn't go hand in hand.

There was something he wasn't telling me. A family problem. Maybe something to do with the ex everyone kept bringing up. The money had to be connected. There was a reason behind his tears. A reason he'd walked straight into traffic that day all those weeks ago—so blinded by emotion he hadn't noticed the oncoming vehicle. He'd been lucky I'd been there. He'd been even luckier that I had the strength to separate from him long enough to pull him out of harm's way.

Did he know that I saved him?

Even if he did, it didn't really matter.

At the time I hadn't been doing it for him.

I just…hadn't wanted to find a new host. That was all. Obviously.

Throughout dinner with Violet, Luca had played it cool. He revealed nothing. He laughed at all the right jokes. His compliments to the chef were free flowing. Every gesture, every smile manipulated his roommate into believing all was forgiven.

I couldn't help but begrudgingly respect that about him.

How had he gotten so good at lying?

Why?

For a man that was so overwhelmingly positive, it was kind of sexy to see him fall whole-heartedly into his role as a doting roommate when in reality he was seething on the inside.

I couldn't always feel his emotions when I was occupying his body. It took focused effort for us to communicate. Tonight though, his anger was so loud I almost had to cover my ears.

Fury, betrayal, distrust.

Pain.

Heartbreak.

He passed a bottle of parmesan. Long fingers trailed over the edge of the table. His laughter spilled like summer through the room as the sun grew heavy outside the single window above the sink. All the while, he smiled, chatting away like he wasn't boiling from the inside out.

We snuck out after midnight. Apparently, Luca's roommate usually went to bed early, and after the painless dinner, her guard had been down. It was strange how much they trusted each other. I wondered if Luca would feel just as guilty about lying to her as he did about whatever it was that had driven him to help me in the first place.

His backpack was a steady weight against his back as he tiptoed down the front steps quietly, his breath leaving him in anxious little puffs.

"This feels so wrong," he muttered to himself. The cement was cold enough it bled through his beat-up tennis shoes. "I've never lied to her like this before."

We don't have a choice.

"I know, I know." He paused, glancing longingly back at the apartment building one last time. "I just…I know she's not trying to be a dick, you know?"

Do you always believe the best in everyone?

"Maybe not everyone." Luca laughed, but the sound was short and bitter. He shook his head and I watched the world blur wetly through his eyes as he blinked away tears, before he climbed into the driver's side of the beat-up Honda parked on the street. I'd noticed it a few times. Always just figured the piece of shit had been abandoned. Every single door was a different color, like it had been Frankenstein-ed together, and the interior looked no better. The seats were covered in fast food wrappers and makeup products, and I made a mental note to clear them off when Luca went to sleep.

We'd drive until we ran out of gas. That was the plan. When Luca got too tired, I'd take over. His earlier bluster had been just that. Bluster. No substance. I knew him well enough now not to believe half the argumentative shit that came out of his mouth. Tonight was step one in the plan we'd concocted while waiting anxiously for Violet to finish her goddamn pasta.

Out on the open road the world felt like a much larger place. I hadn't had much time in cars recently—aside from my weekly trips to Ridgefield for clubbing with my sisters. It was…novel. Until I'd hitched a ride inside Luca, my world had been a tiny place. Sure, I'd traveled to Elmwood with Lydia to kill her nephew, but she'd stuck me in the goddamn Nothing the whole time.

I'd never done anything willingly when I'd been with Lydia.

Once again, the memory of green eyes flooded with fear and revulsion, came to my mind. Amanda's son. My greatest regret. No. That wasn't true. My greatest regret was interacting with Amanda at all. She'd been the mother I'd never had, but because of me… No. *No.* I wouldn't think about it. I refused.

No matter what Lydia wanted me to believe, the fate of the Evans family had not been my fault.

"What's up with you?" Luca asked quietly, his gaze still trained on the road in front of him. It was the middle of summer now and during the day the asphalt was hot enough to see the heat waves rolling off it. Even now the warmth in the air tasted like salt and promise as we whipped down narrow streets toward the freeway.

Nothing is "up with me."

"Yeah, okay. Keep your secrets, Mr. Mysterious," Luca scoffed. "It's not like you're in my head, or anything." Honestly, until that moment, I hadn't realized he could feel my emotions the same way I could feel his.

Do you really want to know?

"Duh? I wouldn't have asked if I didn't."

God, I wanted to slap his naughty little ass. Mouthing off like he had any right to do so. He wasn't the one in charge here—even if he was.

"Prudeeeeence." Luca was whining again, and to my annoyance, the sound made my cock twitch. Why was it that even at his most obnoxious, I couldn't help but react this way? I should hate this on principle.

I mulled over whether or not to respond.

Luca clearly had a vendetta against silence, because he broke the quiet once again. "Look. The whole point of all of this is to end your…afterlife right? So does it really hurt to open up a bit? It's not like I'm going to tell anyone. Scout's honor."

If I answer your questions are you going to answer mine?

That seemed to stall him for a moment as he figured out how to reply. Underneath his skin I felt the flicker of unease.

"I guess that's only fair." Luca sighed, then stayed silent for probably the first time in his entire life. There was no sound inside the vehicle—aside from the whisper of the wind trickling in through the windows as Luca rolled them down and tipped his face toward the breeze. It said a lot about him that he could enjoy something as simple as that—even when he was in the middle of running away. Even when his life had turned upside down, and his eyes still shined with unshed tears.

I was thinking about before, I finally answered him when I was ready.

Half an hour had gone by. He hadn't spoken the entire time. He'd just pulled onto the freeway and sped off north like a fire was lit under his ass. Streetlights blurred beside us, streaks of lights like shooting stars in the dark. They painted his high cheekbones with slashes of brilliance.

Now it was my turn to wait for his reply.

It was surprisingly busy on the road considering what time it was. But then again, I'd grown up in Elmwood, so it shouldn't have come as a surprise to me that San Diego was different. Elmwood had a population of three thousand people. No movie theater. No malls. Not even their own Walmart. It was a useless sort of place, and even though I'd lived there for all of my actual life, it had never felt like home.

It was a prison built with trees and smiles. Smiles that were never genuine when they were aimed at me—at least—until I'd met *her*. Amanda.

Funny how now that I was dead, Elmwood was one of the only places I knew of that was safe for someone like me.

"Before…?" Luca trailed off, patiently waiting, the sassy twist to his words from earlier completely absent. The man I was talking to now almost seemed like an entirely different person.

I liked him just as much, which…surprised me. Considering how much I enjoyed it when he was bratty and loud.

Before you.

I was conserving energy for the drive ahead, so I didn't exit his body, despite the fact this conversation felt entirely too intimate.

Guilt, fear, sadness.

Emotions I hadn't even known I *could* feel.

Emotions I'd kept buried as long as I could.

It was funny how death had taught me more about living than being alive had.

"Where were you?" Luca asked quietly, patiently. "You said you were with a…lady?" He didn't want to say *murderer* and I wasn't sure why I thought that was incredibly fucking cute. Like it was a dirty word, and he didn't want to soil our conversation.

A murderer, yes.

"Ah." Luca nodded. "Um." He slowed the car down a little, changed lanes, and then sped up again, his fingers twitching where they squeezed the steering wheel. *Squeeze, squeeze, squeeze.* It was an anxious tick I probably wouldn't have noticed on anyone else. He had a hard time talking to me, I knew it was because I wasn't the most forthcoming with information.

Luca was a ball of restless energy and I…well, I was the absence of it. A void that sucked in the life around it and turned it into something darker than space and heavier than death itself.

A black hole.

"So why did she…you know…create you?" His hands were *squeezing, squeezing, squeezing* again. I wanted to smooth my fingers over his knuckles, to soothe them where they turned white with tension.

What a weird feeling.

I didn't like it.

She wanted a servant.

"A servant? For…" Luca's fingers began to tap nervously, and I stared out at the open road in front of us, curious if by looking through his eyes I'd see the beauty in it. I didn't.

To help with murder, yes. Among other things.

"So you've killed people, then?" Luca said those words in an oddly blasé way, like it didn't matter to him whether or not I'd done it. Like… he'd accept me either way. My throat felt dry and I shrunk in on myself, confused and a little afraid of the fact I was beginning to tingle all over. My heart hurt. *Why did it hurt?*

I've never killed someone outright. Only almost.

"But she made you do other things?"

Worse things.

For the second time that night I thought of green eyes. I thought of sobbing. A tiny boy who resembled the person I cared most about in the entire world, held down by my hand and beaten in front of me. I shuddered.

"What's worse than murder?" Luca asked softly, gently.

Making someone wish they were dead.

"Oh." He blinked and was silent for a while as he processed this. "You didn't want to do that though, right? You wouldn't hurt someone on your own."

I would.

"You would, what? Hurt someone?"

Yes.

If they were a threat.

If they got in my way.

If they hurt what was mine.

"Oh, well." Luca perked up again. "Is it weird that that only makes me like you more? Like, earlier I was thinking about you. And I realized you kinda remind me of a rabid bulldog."

What?

Well that was…random.

"Yes! Because they're all cute until you get up close to the fence and then—if they're a good guard dog—they bite you! But anyway. Sorry. That's beside the point. What I meant was that you're loyal, like dogs are. You decide who your pack is, and you stick to it."

I don't have a pack.

"*I'm* your pack." He said this with such surety it made my heart stutter and that same tingling feeling begin to buzz all over me again. I worried he could feel it too.

You are *not* my pack.

"Yes I am! Look at us—espionage-ing together. Braving life-threatening vehicles. Making secret plans. You *like* me." Man, he sounded so sure about that. "You totally like me, and we're friends now—we shared fries, Prudence. And orgasms—so…yeah. We're a pack!"

We're not wolves, Luca.

"I mean, *yeah*. But that's not the point! The point is, you'd fight for me. I'd fight for you. We're in this together and that makes us…you know… something pretty special."

We're something, alright. He ignored my sarcasm.

"See?! Here I am, putting up with your asshole-ry. Not caring that you'd hurt things, or even kill them, should the situation arise. Because *solidarity*, Prudence. And also because I know you won't hurt me. So *there*.

Tell me I'm wrong. I dare you."

Because I know you won't hurt me.

Guilt gnawed away at my insides. It was syrupy, thick and heavy as it weighed me down, and I struggled to find the words to speak. I wanted to reject him. I wanted to deny what he was saying. The part of me that had always fought, wanted to hurt him just to prove a point.

What he was saying couldn't be true, could it?

I hadn't even felt this loyal to my sisters, and they were…well…*family.*

"It's your turn now, you know." Luca broke the silence, the tension in his shoulders gone, his knuckles no longer pulled tight and white where they gripped the steering wheel. Apparently my lack of response was answer enough. He looked practically chipper. "I asked you a question so it's only fair."

Right.

Momentarily derailed, I decided what I wanted to ask. Something had been bothering me but I hadn't addressed it yet. I'd gone through his bedroom multiple times and found bin after bin of art supplies and yet… no art? It made no sense. I knew he was an artist. The first time I'd seen him he'd been trading his work for my talisman after all.

What happened to all your artwork?

"Oh. Shit. That's a long story. If you really wanna know, I gotta explain a bit." Luca tensed up all over again. I watched in fascination as he glanced in the side mirror to check his blind spot and I got a glimpse of the haggard twist to his lips. They were bitten raw and red and I wanted to soothe the torn skin with my tongue. If I bit him I was sure he'd bleed. My cock twitched.

Later, I reminded myself.

"So, I'm an artist," Luca started, clearly unsure how to begin.

Yeah, I gathered that.

He continued, ignoring me, "It's my career of choice. I've always loved it. And honestly? It was going really well for a while. I was making money, like *looots* of money. People loved my shit. You couldn't catch me without a paintbrush in my hand." He laughed self-deprecatingly. "But when shit hit the fan suddenly I just…couldn't do it anymore. Painting has always been stress relief for me, a way to get my feelings out. I'm lost without it. I've tried. Believe me. I have. But even just *looking* at my art now makes me want to cry. So I sold it all. Which was great. I made up for some of my losses, and I didn't have to see the paintings anymore. I always just figured the money I made would tide me over till inspiration struck again…only it hasn't. And I'm starting to think it won't. So yeah. Artwork, poof. Gone-zo. I may never paint again."

He said the words carelessly but I could feel the way his heart was breaking at the thought.

Amanda had always said you couldn't force inspiration. That it came to you when you least expected it. Maybe if Luca survived this, he'd find our adventure could chase away the last of his demons. For now though, I was still curious.

What did you paint before the art block? I couldn't believe how interested I actually was in his answer. When I'd been alive, there had only been three things that I genuinely cared about. Art. My motorcycle. And food.

"All sorts of stuff," Luca shrugged. "My favorite thing though was…" He fidgeted. "Ugh. You'll probably think it's cheesy."

I won't.

Weirdly enough, I wasn't lying.

I was, for the first time, truly invested.

"I paint emotions?" Luca cringed at himself. "I know, *I know*. That's like—cliche—and very *Pinterest* of me but…still. They always just…hit me—you know? The feeling of them. The colors—the vibrancy—the way they can pause time or speed it up, depending on how you're feeling. The way people experience them so differently. They're never the same. It's all so…"

Fascinating, I finished for him.

"Yes! I always thought so."

Do you paint your own emotions or other people's?

"Both? Either? I like experiencing things through every perspective." The more he talked the more animated Luca became, and I was enraptured as he took one hand off the wheel and began unconsciously tracing shapes against the top of his thigh like he was painting from memory. "The first piece I made that really felt *real* to me I painted for my mom's wedding when I was seventeen."

I wanted him to continue.

What did you paint?

"It was a wedding present for her and Paul—that's her new husband, he's actually super cool. Anyway, it was like…this abstract splash of color. Pinks—yellows—champagne! Twisting, writhing, tangling together. A combination of all of us. Paul, Mom, me, Betty, Adam! Our colors blending like we were about to. Inside every paint stroke I hid my hope for our future, Betty's distrust, Adam's eagerness. All you had to do was look at it, and you'd feel it all. But above that—above the layers and layers of conflicting emotion, there was just…love. The love I saw between them, as cheesy as that sounds. It was bubbly, and bright. Young, in a way I never got to see my mom be before." He took a breath, flashing me a shaky, nervous smile. "Sorry, I'm talking too much, aren't I?"

No.

I couldn't remember ever being this fascinated by someone before.

I don't understand.

"What do you mean?" Luca paused, clearly flummoxed.

How could you recognize love enough to paint it? I clarified. It seemed a ridiculous notion, that he could see love. That he could replicate it.

"Oh." Luca blinked. "I don't know how to explain that. I just… Sometimes when I look at someone I can—*see it?* What they're feeling. Why they're feeling that way. What color it is—what shape—I don't know if it's normal to be like this or maybe I'm just delusional but…putting form to feelings has always come second nature to me." He blinked again. "It's the strong emotions that really get me going, you know?"

You've been sad. Haven't you wanted to paint that emotion?

I wanted to see what his sadness looked like to him.

"Um, yeah." Luca laughed and the noise was sharp and brittle. "I don't know if 'sad' is the word I'd use."

You've been crying.

I wasn't stupid.

Tears equal sad..

"Yeah, but like…" He shook his head, a nervous quirk he did often. It was almost like he thought his brain was an Etch-A-Sketch and shaking himself enough would erase his thoughts. "I haven't been sad. I've been…" he trailed off.

What?

"Desolate maybe? Desperate? Despairing. Lost. Confused. Angry. And worst of all…numb. Lately, I've been feeling like I'm worse than nothing. Like if I hadn't come along, then maybe the people I love wouldn't be hurting."

Worse than nothing? What was that supposed to mean? How could one person feel so many emotions at once?

"Sadness is the addition of melancholy, you know? Blue. Silver. Gray. Heavy as syrup. Gentle as the evening tide. Sadness fades. It has a beginning, and an end. Sometimes it loops, but there's always causation. Not to be confused with depression, because that's a whole different demon."

Okay.

"What I've been feeling isn't sadness. There's no end to it. It's a black hole. Sucking, sucking, sucking at me. Eating away till there's nothing left. It's black, black, black. The absence of light. The absence of feelings in general. Nothingness, in the truest sense of the word." He swallowed. "Even *I* can't paint nothing."

Funny how I'd so recently referred to myself as a black hole.

Was that how he felt too?

Why?

I was getting tired of not knowing what had caused him to feel this way.

"Because—" Luca cut himself off, his fingers twisting nervously around the wheel as his free hand traced frantic patterns on his pant leg. *Swirl, swirl, swirl, jab, jab, swirl.* I couldn't tell what shapes he was forming, but it didn't matter. I could see the emotion clear as day. Turmoil. Like a hurricane. "Because, I lost the part of me that felt like sun? That gave light to everything inside me."

I don't understand.

Fuck. I…wished I did though. I wished I could…what? *Help*? God, what a stupid notion. I couldn't help him. I didn't even understand half the emotions he was talking about.

"Before…" He began to explain, patient as ever. "I was Luca. Sunshine, Luca. I shined everywhere, you know? Lit up emotions, made people laugh, helped my family. Dependable as the sunrise every morning." He glanced in the rearview mirror and visibly startled when he caught his own reflection. One of my eyes glowed back at him—us— and Luca stared at himself for a beat too long before turning back to the road.

"Growing up we didn't have much. Mom did her best, and I did too." He shrugged. "She depended on me to always keep the sun shining. I was *supposed* to be the golden child."

How could you lose such an integral part of who you are?

I needed to know.

Tell me.

"I didn't." Luca's voice grew cold and a feeling of shock twitched through my body at the sound. I'd never heard him so…angry before. "It was *stolen* from me."

Stolen from you?

"Yes." Luca squeezed the wheel tight, his free hand shifting from his thigh back to the wheel as he glared at the dark road in front of him. "I don't want to talk about this anymore."

Okay.

I wasn't sure what I'd said to upset him. Maybe the whole conversation had been too raw. One thing was for certain though. He *would* tell me what had happened. I would force him if I had to. And I would rain hell on whoever it was that had hurt him. For the first time in my life I was grateful for the crash-course in murder Lydia had given me when she'd held my talisman.

Luca didn't speak again for a long time. Not until the radio came to life and Evanescence began blasting loud enough for Hell to hear. Luca jumped nearly a foot in the air and then laughed, a loud barking sort of sound, as he slammed the volume button repeatedly till the damn thing turned off.

His smile was back as he glanced in the rearview mirror again, making eye contact with me.

"Be prepared for that to happen at least a hundred more times on this trip. Fuckin' death trap."

He was grinning, and I couldn't help but think despite what he'd said earlier, he still looked like sunshine.

Chapter Eighteen

Luca

WE ONLY HAD a quarter tank of gas left when Prudence took pity on me and my loudly growling stomach. We'd swapped places driving when my eyes had started to droop, and seeing him again—solid—after the conversation we'd just had was surprisingly scary.

It made it real.

I'd already shared more with him than I'd shared with anyone else, even Violet. Prudence knew me, and hell. I didn't even know his last name.

Without prompting, Prudence took the next exit into a big city, chasing the signs that led to an old school diner right off the freeway. Huddled shadowy figures wandered along the dark sidewalks, chain link fences towering high as we peeled into the parking lot, and Prudence put the car in park. I couldn't help but stare at the tattoos that swept across his thick fingers as he squeezed the steering wheel. My stomach growled again.

On our way through the door, I misjudged the distance between my body and another patron as he was exiting, and we collided with an *oomph*. "Sorry!" I called after him as he flashed me a smile, and headed into the parking lot.

Shit.

I was more tired than I thought.

The inside of the establishment was surprisingly cheerful. A direct contrast to the atmosphere of the street it took residence on. The walls were a jaunty yellow, faded with age. Red vinyl squeaked as I slid into a booth at the back with Prudence across from me. From our seat we could see into the kitchen, and the signs that pointed toward a locked bathroom on the other side of the room.

I stared at his shoulder, tracing over the contour of it with my eyes as I bit my lip and fiddled with the worn edge of the table top. When the waiter came over and handed us the worn laminated menus it only took me five seconds to decide what I wanted. A burger and fries. My stomach growled and my mouth watered just thinking about it.

"Pru," I nudged him with my foot, and he glared at me. It was the first time I'd met his gaze since I'd admitted all that shit in the car. My skin felt a size too small. "Order something."

"I don't need to—"

"C'mon. My treat." Sure, I was poor as hell. But I couldn't deprive him of one of the only pleasures I knew he still had. He didn't fight me, to my surprise. He just ordered the same thing I did, then leaned back, his biceps bulging as he crossed his arms and stared me down.

I squirmed under his gaze, chewing on my lip and chasing headlights through the window rather than look at him.

"What's wrong with you?" Prudence's voice was quiet, deliberately brash.

"Wrong with me?" I played dumb, hoping he'd drop the subject.

"You won't look at me," he accused, and I grimaced. Shit. He'd noticed. I guess it was hard to miss, considering how much I usually drooled over him. My cheeks got hot as I fidgeted uncomfortably beneath his attention.

The waiter offered us a wane smile as he placed a twin set of water dappled glasses in front of us. He looked high. Tired too. And his uniform smelled as much like weed as it did like fries. I smiled back, ignoring the hole Pru was glaring into the side of my head. The waiter disappeared, then returned, setting our plates onto the table with a quiet *thud-thud*. The sweet aroma of grease and salt wafted up from them making my tastebuds tingle.

Pru—the fucker—could wait, goddammit. Hopefully the interruption would distract him.

But, nope. No such luck.

Yay.

Prudence kept staring at me. I could feel the weight of his gaze like a brand on my skin. It made a shiver tremble its way up my limbs as I folded my arms over my chest and mirrored his guarded posture. Without preamble, he reached across the table and stole my motherfucking plate like a thieving little thief.

Fine.

So he wanted to play dirty, huh?

"I talked a lot in the car. You sure you want to hear more?" *Please say no, please say no.* I was too emotionally raw for this right now.

"Yes." Prudence sounded confused for possibly the first time since I'd met him. "What does that have to do with anything?"

I huffed, digging my nails into my biceps hard enough pain zinged from my fingertips. "I just…" Fuck. What the hell did he want from me? *The truth.* He wanted the truth. Fine. If he wanted it so bad, he could have it. "I've never told anyone any of the shit I told you. It's embarrassing."

"Why would that be embarrassing?" Prudence stole one of my fries from the pilfered plate he held hostage. He shoved it into his mouth, his tongue flickering out to swipe the salt from his petal-pink lower lip. Shit. His tongue was pierced. *How the fuck had I never noticed his tongue was pierced?*

"Aren't you annoyed by me?" He was confusing. I squinted at him distrustfully, looking for signs of deceit. But…I saw none. Prudence was an asshole, but he was honest. His pale eyes narrowed right back at me, dark lashes smudging across his cheeks as he blinked. He practically looked like he was wearing eyeliner—and shit. If I kept thinking about Prudence in eyeliner I was going to get a boner regardless of how awkward I felt right now.

"Why? Because you answered the questions I asked you?" he clarified.

"When you put it like that it seems stupid."

"Because it is."

"Okay, rude."

"Maybe, it's stupid to worry so much about what anyone else thinks of you, me included. I'd be an asshole if I was annoyed you answered the questions I fucking asked."

"I think this is the most I've ever heard you talk. Also, for the record? You *are* an asshole. You're literally calling me stupid right now." For some reason the churning in my gut was going away. Damn. Why were his insults comforting? Maybe I was even more fucked up than I thought I was.

"I'm just pointing out your inconsistency."

"Okay…?" What the fuck was that supposed to mean?

"Are *you* annoyed that I answered *your* questions?"

"Well, no." Duh. Obviously.

"Then, why would *I* be?" He stole another fry. Thief! Potato thief! If I didn't get my plate back soon I was sure he'd eat them all.

"You didn't get…ugh!" Words did not want to word. I slapped my hand on the table angrily, more frustrated with myself, than I was with him. "You didn't get all vulnerable, like I did. You told me shit, sure. But like… *Pru.*" Again the nickname escaped unbidden. Without my permission, my lip began to quiver. "You gotta realize you're not like other people. For some reason you're weirdly…into my brand of odd."

Maybe he genuinely didn't understand.

It wasn't actually dickish of him to ask why I was acting off. Normally I was all over him like a sloth with my tongue out. Maybe…in his own Prudence-y way, my silence made him feel insecure. Damn, what a thought.

"Whatever you say." Of course, he wouldn't fess up. He was Prudence. He'd probably rather lose a hand than admit I made him feel something. That didn't really bother me though. I could see it on his face. He thought he had a poker face, but…if you knew where to look. His eyebrows held all his secrets. They twitched a little, signifying his unease. "Stop punishing me for whatever shit is going on in your head." He punctuated his point by jabbing a finger at his own temple, his nostrils flaring. His painted nails were chipped and weirdly charming. The aroma wafting from the two plates Prudence had in front of him should have distracted me, but it didn't.

He probably didn't realize he'd just admitted that me not talking to him was punishment.

Fuck.

That was cute.

"I'm still getting used to your particular brand of honesty," I admitted, charmed.

Prudence clearly sensed the affection because his eyes narrowed and his nostrils flared angrily. Then he growled at me. Actually, fucking growled. I couldn't stamp down my smile quick enough. He did give me back my plate of food though, so I supposed my comment hadn't been negatively received.

Suddenly, I was hungry again.

I shoved a fry into my mouth, groaning as the salty, crispy flavor burst on my tongue. Hell yes. My lashes fluttered as I sighed happily. I hadn't eaten out anywhere but McDonald's in for-freaking-ever. This shit was good.

When I stopped food-gasming I tossed Prudence a smile. He'd already dug into his own plate, munching away like a starved thing. Ten fries in his mouth at once. Amazing. His lashes fluttered as he paused, then picked his burger up, swiping his mouth with the back of his hand.

"It really didn't bother you?" I questioned, just to be sure. He growled again and I couldn't help the giddy feeling that buzzed inside me. "Okay, *okay*." My happiness bubbled over, and the smile I'd been swallowing returned full force. He blinked. Probably blinded by my dimples. They were my other nice feature, aside from my ass. "I get it."

I dug into my food again, my stomach growling its appreciation. It was odd how stubbornly he was trying to cheer me up. It just reminded me of all I'd admitted in the car…and all I hadn't. I really hadn't been this vulnerable with someone else before. I was the kind of person who gave my surface to everyone because I knew it was palatable.

Anything deeper than that? And yeah. You got insecure Luca. Terrified, he'd said too much, too soon. Terrified he was too much in general. The shitty part? No one had ever actually said shit to me about anything like that. No one had bullied me. No one had called me a dork, or made fun of how obsessed I was with art.

The mean person?

The bully?

It was me.

I swallowed the lump in my throat, startled when Prudence's boot hit my shin and I jumped about a foot high. It stung. But the pain rocketed me out of my head. I blinked blearily, realizing that I had been staring down at my plate blank-faced. Half my fries were gone. My head whipped up, and I was met with Prudence's proudest, meanest grin.

His entire plate was fucking empty.

And apparently he'd been sneaking fries from under my nose.

"What the fuck, dude?" I said, belatedly. Prudence regarded me for what felt like an eternity, his eyes dark as he cocked his head to the side, lips thinning. His attention made me squirm.

"Tell me what to do."

"What?" My cheeks grew hot. Naughty ideas flickered through my mind, but I forced them—and my dick—down.

"Tell me what I need to do to get you to act normal again." His gaze was challenging. "I hate when you're quiet."

Shit.

My eyes grew hot and wet, as I realized however bluntly delivered, that was probably the nicest thing anyone had ever said to me. I hadn't known how much I wanted to hear those words. But here I was. Floored. I swallowed the lump in my throat, then offered him a wobbly smile.

"You can't. I just need time to process, okay? I don't get vulnerable with other people often." More like, never. Exhibit A: The fact I'd rather risk my life helping a ghost than admit to my family I lost my fortune and couldn't pay for Adam's college courses anymore.

"What if I tell you something?" Prudence bartered, like this was a problem that was easily fixed. I almost wanted to laugh, but he was trying, so I didn't. It meant something to me that in his own, awkward way he wanted to make me feel better.

Most people would go for a hug.

Not Prudence.

I don't know what I'd do if Prudence tried to hug me. Probably explode into a million tiny pieces.

"You already answered my questions in the car," I stalled. Not sure what he wanted from me. I couldn't just turn off whatever I was feeling, no matter how badly I wanted to.

Or just one?

"Not good enough. You accused me of not being vulnerable enough. So let's even the playing field."

Shit. I had done that, hadn't I? I opened my mouth to apologize, picking through my remaining ten fucking fries. When he reached for my burger, I slid my plate close to my chest, guarding it with both hands and a quiet huff.

The corner of his lip twitched up.

"I don't want you to do something you don't want to do." There. *Words.* Words were good. Just because I felt weird and uncomfortable, didn't mean it was his fault. And it also didn't mean I wanted him to give me something he wasn't ready to give.

I probably shouldn't have worried because I'd barely finished talking when he spoke.

"I hate my mother."

Wow, okay. So he was going to do this no matter what I said. I waved a fry at him to continue, blinking owlishly as I shoved it into my mouth, and waited.

"She's a self-righteous prick. Always has been, always will be." Despite how strong his words were, I couldn't detect actual heat in his voice. His tone was as bland as if he'd been talking about the weather. Not that Prudence would ever be caught dead talking about the weather. Ha! Get it? Caught dead. I hid my smile against my shoulder so he wouldn't see. He must've taken that as a sign that he hadn't given me enough information, and before I could stop him, he started talking again.

"We were raised in a very strict household. My two sisters. Me. I was the oldest, and there were certain standards I was expected to adhere to." He folded his arms again, and his chest tested the fabric of his white t-shirt in a way that had me practically drooling. His tattoos flexed with his muscle. Lord have mercy.

"I'm guessing you didn't like that," I deadpanned. Understatement of the century. Prudence following rules? Yeah, right. I cocked my head toward the tattoos I had just been admiring and my breath stuttered when Prudence's lips pulled into a wide, wolfish grin.

"I fought back at every turn." His grin turned meaner. "Every opportunity I had to undermine her rules, I took." See? *That* was the Prudence I was starting to know. I nodded, taking a big bite of my burger with a happy sigh. Now that he was talking, it felt less awkward. My skin no longer felt quite so tight.

"There was a woman," Prudence continued. I choked on my burger.

"*Not* like that." Prudence kicked me again, and I blinked away the wetness in my eyes as I tried to get my esophagus working again. *Jee*-sus.

"Prudence—" I moved to apologize. He just glared at me, and my jaw clicked shut as I nodded, gesturing for him to continue.

"She taught me about art." Oh. *Oh.* My eyes widened, and I set my burger down and held my breath as I waited for him to continue.

"I didn't know you were an artist," my stupid mouth blurted out before I could stop it. So much was making sense. "So that's why you were nosing through all my art shit," I muttered under my breath. Also why he'd been so damn curious in the car.

He ignored me. "She was too soft. Too kind. Annoying. Like you."

What a ringing endorsement. I rolled my eyes.

"I still think about her."

Oh. Well, that was sweet.

I'd learned not to open my big mouth, so this time I wisely took another bite of burger and waited in silence. It took him a while to get up the nerve to speak again. I watched his face change. The blasé attitude he'd had before morphing, the glint in his eyes dying a slow painful death till no spark remained. He looked gaunt. Older than I'd ever seen him before as he glared out the window and I watched his shoulders tense. When he spoke, the words were quiet, hushed. "She died."

She died.

Those words hit me like a train wreck and I was momentarily stricken as I stared at him. Those two words alone made it clear how much this woman had meant to him. When she died, something must've died within him too.

"It was my fault," Prudence continued, the muscle in his jaw jumping. "I didn't tell her what I'd seen. I didn't warn her."

"Pru…" I reached across the table, commandeering one of his hands and giving it a squeeze. His palm was much broader than mine, but my fingers were longer. We looked like a matching set. Yin and yang. His palm scraped against my skin as I gave it another gentle squeeze. I already knew whatever it was—whatever had happened—it wasn't his fault.

Unless he had outright murdered her, death was one of the only things that was blameless.

I didn't say that though. I could see it wouldn't help. He was closed off to me, his body tense, his hand stiff within my own. Cold. Like always. But in a new way too. My thumb swept over the top of his knuckles, the unfamiliar texture of his skin making my nerves dance. "Do you want to talk about it?" I barely recognized my voice, it was so…gentle. Low. Sweet.

Prudence shook his head.

I thought he would be done now, surely this was enough. Once again, I moved to stop him, but he kept speaking anyway. Maybe he needed to say this, more than I needed to hear it.

My burger was getting cold, and I'd probably gotten ketchup on my shirt leaning over it, but I didn't care. Not when he was looking at me like that. Not when I could see the loneliness trembling inside the icy cavern of his gaze. Prudence grit his teeth, jaw muscle jumping again. I could literally see the moment it hit him that this being vulnerable thing? Yeah.

It sucked.

But also…it was liberating too.

I hadn't felt this light in fucking years.

Like by telling him the things I'd kept close to my chest, I'd let him take some of the weight from my shoulders. I could only hope he felt the same.

When Prudence spoke again, I was surprised by his words. "I hurt her son."

There was very real pain behind that statement, and my grip on his hand grew tighter as I waited to hear what he had to say next. When he didn't continue, I nodded. It was clear he needed the encouragement, because he released a stressed puff of breath, and a little furrow appeared between his dark brows.

The overhead light glinted off of his piercings as Prudence flicked his tongue stud against his teeth with a quiet click. "That wasn't my fault. Not like Amanda's death was." I nodded again, scared of spooking him. Keeping the name Amanda close to my chest so I wouldn't forget. "But I'll never forget the way he cried." I was squeezing his hand so hard at this point I worried it might be hurting him. But he didn't seem to care. "Was that enough?" He asked, voice raw as gravel, almost hopeful. I blinked in confusion, my hand trembling with the tension of squeezing his so hard. "Now, will you talk to me like normal?"

Shit.

My heartbeat rabbited around inside my chest, my eyes burning a little as I nodded. "Sure, Pru." I nodded again, and again. "For sure." I reached for my burger with my free hand, took a bite, and made a happy groaning noise just to prove my point. "Mmmm burger-y." When I stopped fluttering my lashes at him in mock pleasure, Prudence had relaxed somewhat. Which meant this was probably my only opportunity to say this—so. "You can talk to me, you know," I said gently, his hand still gripped tight in mine as burger juice slipped onto my plate. "I'm good at talking. But I'm a passable listener too."

"No." Prudence's response was expected. To my surprise? It didn't sting. Not one single bit.

I grinned at him, unable to help myself. A lock of dark hair fell across his brow, and rather than blow it out of the way, he just let it be. My spooky, emo Clark Kent. "I have a feeling we're going to be getting to know each other reaaaaal well by the time our adventure is over."

He kicked me again. And I laughed.

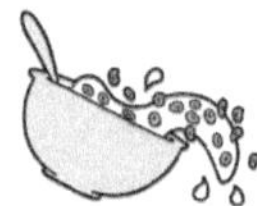

Of course, because I had shit luck, nothing could stay good for long. With my burger finished, and our waiter still serving a massive party of drunk men getting their late night drunchies on, I patted my pockets looking for my wallet, only to discover it was not fucking there. I dropped Prudence's hand.

I slapped my front pockets. Nothing.

Slapped my back pockets a second time. Nothing.

Scrounged around inside my hoodie, just to be sure.

But nope.

"What?" Pru's voice was a quiet hiss. Curious. Concerned.

"My wallet…" I panicked some more as the realization of what had happened hit me square in the face. Here we were, three hours from home—and I'd been… "Shit." The dude. The fucking dude! When we'd come in he'd slammed into me and I'd—oh god. I'd apologized like an idiot to the guy who had fucking robbed me.

"What?" Prudence repeated.

"Shit, shit, shit, shit, shit." I lamented my life. "I got pick-pocketed." I shook my head in despair. "He hit me with the oldest trick in the book, and like a fucking sucker, I fell for it." My scalp tingled as I pulled my hair taut. I was usually better at this. "I am such an idiot."

My legacy gone, quicker than I could blink.

But I had bigger problems brewing.

Prudence growled at me again. This time it didn't comfort me, I was too far gone. "No, you aren't." He was on high-alert already, tension buzzing beneath the swell of his broad shoulders as he glared out the window at the street, like the streetlights had been the ones to fucking rob me. "Tell me to go look for it."

"Um, no?" I sighed, because as much as I appreciated the fact my pint-sized ghost companion wanted to go rough some dude up, there was no point. "No. He's long gone. I appreciate the thought, but the guy peeled out of here the second he got off scot-free." Chasing him would be a waste of time. Prudence huffed but didn't argue, thank god. I didn't think I had the capacity to banter with him right now.

I had to think of a plan.

"We're gonna have to dine and dash," I decided. His eyes widened. It was the first time I'd seen him truly surprised, and a startled laugh threatened to escape my lips. "I'll need a distraction…" I waited for him to get the idea, and when he did, his smile grew wicked. He popped his knuckles, then stretched his neck from side to side, waiting for instruction.

Five minutes, three exploded toilets, and one small kitchen fire later, and I was out the door and back in my piece of shit car.

"Please start, please start, please start," I pleaded with the car gods as I flipped the ignition and the engine roared to life. Behind the glass windows the patrons of the diner were scrambling about, all involved in the distraction of the century, as Prudence climbed into the passenger seat, half phasing through the door, like he'd forgotten people could see him.

Not a hair on his head was out of place despite the chaos he'd just created.

He grinned at me, and I grinned back as we pulled onto the dark street and headed toward the freeway.

"So, what now?" Prudence inquired, surprising me when he asked rather than told me what we were going to do.

While he'd been clogging plumbing and pouring oil on shit, I'd had enough time to come up with a plan. Sure, I hadn't done this in a while. A good long while. But some things were like riding a bike.

We had to save the battery juice on my phone, since I didn't know when the next time I'd get to charge it would be, but this was necessary.

"Pull up to the nearest club." I dug around my hoodie pocket for my phone and tossed it toward Prudence. He caught it effortlessly, typing in my password, despite the fact I'd never fucking told him it. Nosy fucker.

"Why?" He asked, though he did as he was commanded. The fluorescent blue of the screen lit up his face as streetlights flickered through his body. Maybe setting fires tired him out, because he seemed slightly less solid than before. I could almost see the seat through his body. It should've weirded me out, but it didn't.

"We don't have any money. We have hardly any gas." I pointed out our major problems, tapping my fingers on the steering wheel as I explained.

"And that guy who stole my shit?" I flashed him my dimples as I rolled down the window and the cool night breeze whipped through the car. Sure, this was a shitty plan, but it was the only one we had. My belly was full—and Prudence was here. So really, tonight wasn't so bad. Maybe it could even be fun. "Yeah. He gave me an idea."

Chapter Nineteen

Prudence

LUCA WAS RUNNING on fumes by the time we got to the club. There was a slap-happy jerk to his motions, and his eyes were just on the wrong side of wild. According to Google, the whole place would be shutting down in just over two hours, so we didn't have much time. I was still begrudgingly impressed that he'd been the one to come up with this idea.

He was full of surprises today.

It was becoming clear to me, the longer I spent with him, that Luca was not who I'd thought he was. Behind his sunshine and smiles, he was an enigma. Every new discovery I made about him was a gift tangled in ribbons, just ready to be unwrapped.

There were deep bruises beneath his eyes, the kind that only came from true exhaustion, as we pulled into the parking lot and he turned to me, determined. His jaw flickered with tension, his broad shoulders pulled back as he stared me down. Despite the look on his face, when he spoke his words were gentle.

"You gonna be able to stay solid if we go in there?" he asked.

I blinked.

"Because if you can't I—" When I glanced at myself I realized his concern was not unfounded. Unconsciously, I'd relaxed around him, my body morphing into the half-solid state it only became when my guard was down. Immediately, I focused all my energy on my appearance—a skill I'd had to hone while with Lydia—until I was no longer see-through. "Shit. Never mind."

"I was just conserving energy," I arched an eyebrow and Luca smiled.

"Oh. Well, good then." He blinked at me, eyes searching mine for just a moment before the steel in his gaze came back full force. "You know the plan?"

I rolled my eyes. "Yes."

"Awesome. Go rob some dudes, ghosty Mc-Hottie-Pants." He held up his hand for a high-five, which I refused to return. My hands stayed firmly on my thighs as I glared. It would be a cold day in hell before I—

He grabbed my hand.

His skin was hot, almost soft. Long fingers gave my palm a gentle squeeze. It reminded me of the diner. The way his grip had been tight enough to chase away my demons.

"You're such a grouch. Ha. Prudence the Grouch." Luca snorted. I couldn't stop staring at our hands. *Why the hell did I like this? What was happening to me?* I hated physical contact outside of sex. "I'll go in first.

You follow after me. We need to make sure it doesn't look like we came in together."

I rolled my eyes again. He'd already explained the plan five different times. I knew it by heart. I wasn't stupid.

I could hear Luca's grin before I saw it. "Whoever boosts more wallets wins."

"You're such a child."

Luca huffed indignantly, but there was mirth twinkling in his eyes, not annoyance. And then the motherfucker fuckin' tricked me. He pulled my hand into the air, and I blinked at it in confusion, muscle-memory forcing me to hold it in place as he removed his hand from mine and then—slapped my palm. *Hard.*

"Go team!"

An hour passed.

Considering the club was nearing closing time, it remained surprisingly packed. Which was fine, because the crowd suited our purposes perfectly. Bodies pressed together, the scent of sweat in the air, as the neon lights above flickered rapidly enough to need a flash warning.

Two wallets. That was all I'd managed in the hour we'd been separated.

Knowing Luca, he'd probably only grabbed one. Or none. So I wasn't that concerned about losing our bet. The twink I was currently manhandling around the dance floor grinned at me, his eyes alight. Objectively speaking, he was attractive. Well…he *should've* been. He was exactly the kind of guy I would've taken into a back room at the club in Ridgefield.

As it stood though, I only had eyes for one man.

I'd taken to dancing around the room, boosting wallets from the people I wasn't dancing with while I used my twink of choice for cover.

For a while I'd lost sight of Luca. Which I hated.

I'd hunted the crowd for the tall bob of his fluffy pink head, distracted in a way that was entirely unlike me. And when I located him…well. My focus had stuttered, then stopped. A full-on collision between my purpose here, and the man that I found…tolerable.

Luca was dancing.

His long legs were spread, head tipped back, hips doing this circular swivel shake that had me hypnotized. My grip on the guy I held captive tightened and he gasped, but I ignored the sound as I traced the contours of Luca's gorgeous full pecs, and down the rolling twist of his sexy abs with my eyes.

My mouth was dry.

The man behind him had his hands on Luca's hips, maneuvering him, though it was obvious he didn't need the help. They made their way toward us, casual enough that random-dude wouldn't notice. Luca's scent filled my nose again, his body only a few feet away.

Sweat, sex, fruity liquor.

He caught my eye and grinned.

Something secret inside me settled now that I knew he was safe.

The guy groaned as Luca twisted them around, flipping their bodies. The eyeful I got of the broad back of the man he was dancing with blocked my view of Luca. I wanted to yank them apart. Shove a ruler between them. Shove my tongue down Luca's throat—and claim him in front of all of these people.

I'd never wanted to own someone else before.

Funny how I'd possessed, but never felt possessive.

Luca's hands wrapped around his partner's back, fingers tracing down the dude's spine. I was close enough I caught the groan the touch elicited as the asshole tucked his face against Luca's neck.

"You got a boyfriend?" he asked. The pounding bass wasn't loud enough to drown out the words.

My grip grew even tighter. Tight enough I was sure it would leave bruises. I should've cared, but I didn't. Brian? Brett? Budweiser? Whatever the fuck his name was, whined in my ear, and I cringed in response, too hyper-focused on Luca's hands as they slipped slow and sure down the man's back, inch by inch.

"Nah," Luca laughed softly. My teeth clenched.

"Hmm." I watched as the guy fingered the back of Luca's neck, tracing over the bruises I'd left along his throat. "Interesting."

When Luca's hands reached the stout man's waistband I was ready to rip them apart.

But then…his fingers snuck casually into the guy's back pocket. And he slipped his wallet out, quick and easy.

With his hands on the guy's ass I watched in fascination as Luca smoothly flipped around again, tucking the stolen wallet into his waistband under his hoodie in a movement so fluid I never would've caught it if I hadn't known what he was doing. He ground his ass against asshole's hips, turned his head to the side far enough the light hit his cheekbone, and I caught the corner of his smile.

And then he winked at me.

"Ow!" The guy I was holding hissed, shifting uncomfortably. I'd stopped dancing. Which was stupid. I couldn't get us caught. Funny how I'd thought Luca would be the one to fuck us over, but here I was…so enthralled by him I was about to blow our cover.

I could feel his pale gray eyes on me as I turned back to my dance partner with a grimace. I didn't apologize on principle. Just arched my brow and watched the kid simper. Ugh. Apparently he liked the negative attention, because it took me a second too long to respond as his hand slipped up my thigh and he laid his palm flat against my crotch. My dick did not respond.

"You like to be rough, huh?" he asked, his voice grating on my nerves.

I was done with this game.

Three wallets was enough.

Ready to throw the guy off of me, I paused when I glanced up and caught the heated, possessive fire burning bright in Luca's eyes. We were ridiculous. A slow smile crept across my face as his cheeks flushed and he twisted those massive shoulders to face me. He eyed the hand on my crotch pointedly, his nostrils flaring, the muscle in his jaw jumping.

God, he was gorgeous when he was pissed.

I got the feeling he didn't get angry often.

There was a light dusting of gold stubble growing on his jaw and I was suddenly desperate to feel the sandpapery texture against my tongue. Something about him was so effortlessly masculine despite his pink hair, and ridiculously thick brown eyelashes.

Because I was an asshole, I didn't remove Bret-sky's hands. I even let my lashes flutter, to prove a point. If he was going to go around groping people in the search of money, I could too.

Luca's eyes darkened, and he jerked inside the other man's grasp.

"Hey?" Twink guy said, confused when I ignored him.

"Yeah, I like it," I said the words loud enough for Luca to catch them, making sure there was enough growl left in my tone of voice to really get the point across. "What about you?"

"Fuck yeah. You got a boyfriend?"

Luca's eyes burned into mine, my pulse thundered, as something wicked itched beneath my skin. My smile only grew wider. I maintained eye contact as I pointedly provoked the only man I wanted on my cock. "Nah."

Maybe it was petty, to quote him like that.

But the way Luca stormed off made it worth it.

His long legs ate up the dance floor, his date abandoned as he practically stomped his way toward the coatroom at the back of the club. Those broad shoulders flexed, his ass bobbing as I cocked my head to watch. There was a glittery handprint on one ass cheek, and irrational jealousy made my skin itch.

Unceremoniously, I shoved the twink off of me and followed.

Luca should know better than to run from me.

I'd have to teach him.

When I finally caught up to him Luca was standing in the dark, rifling through the pockets of someone's coat. He glanced up at me, a pissed off jut to his clenched jaw that had me panting after him like a dog. God he was gorgeous, his big chest heaving, eyes molten lava. Before I could blink, my back hit the wall. It took conscious effort not to phase right through it.

"What the fuck?" I asked at the same time Luca's voice erupted between us.

"Why'd you let him touch you?"

I felt nearly giddy as Luca's eyes flooded with heat and frustration. His grip on my shirt grew tighter as he crowded up against me, lip curling. Angry Luca was really doing something for me. Unlike when the twink had been touching me earlier, my cock rose to the occasion without so much as a single touch.

Luca licked his lips, and I stared at his bright pink tongue with fascination. My cock twitched as I imagined pushing inside that angry little mouth, hot-slick as he slurped around me. As quickly as it had appeared, his bluster wavered. The softness in his eyes returned. His lip wobbled. *Shit.* He was upset.

"You told me to get wallets," I pointed out.

"I didn't tell you to get felt up."

"Says the guy with a handprint on his ass." Yeah, I'd noticed. And I was petty enough to point it out. Luca's wobbling lip flattened and he glared at me with an angry huff. Yeah, didn't like that, did he? Sexy little hypocrite.

"It isn't fair." Luca clenched his teeth and glared at me.

"What?"

"This was supposed to be fun." Honestly, I was surprised he thought robbing people was fun. I added this to the list of things about him that were fascinating. Who the hell was this man? And what had happened to the cereal crier? "It was supposed to be a game. But instead, all I can think about is the fact that guys are touching you, and I—"

Jealous. He was *jealous.*

"You, what?" I asked, enjoying the way his grip on my shirt flexed as a hot puff of breath met my cheekbone.

"*I* haven't even gotten to do that yet."

His raw words hit me.

He was jealous that someone else had touched me before he had. *Fuuuuck.* My cock jerked and I glared up at his fuck me eyes, using every ounce of concentration I had to hide how absolutely gone for him I was in that moment. He wanted to touch me? Fuck yes. I wasn't sure what had changed—but I was suddenly ready.

Unfortunately for both of us, he'd been too much of a brat to get a reward.

He'd have to earn it first.

"How many wallets did you steal, Luca?" I asked, my voice deliberately low. I clucked my tongue disapprovingly when he released a ragged little whine. There was a thrill to this. The fact that anyone could walk in here. There wasn't even a door, just a lone archway crowded with abandoned jackets. It was dark inside the space, dark enough I could barely make out the shape of the coat rack behind Luca's wide shoulders.

Luca licked his lips, and I fought back a groan.

They looked so soft.

So kissable.

I wanted to bite them.

He dropped his hold on my shirt, reaching for the hem of his hoodie, his big hands shaking as he wrapped his fingers around it and slowly lifted up. One, two, three, four, five. Five wallets sat tucked tight against his flat little belly. His stomach stuttered as he sucked in a breath, and I reached out to trail a solitary finger along the edges of skin bordering the stolen items.

"Tsk," I clucked my tongue at him disparagingly. "Five?" I shook my head. "I thought you could do better." Honestly, I was amazed. But he didn't need the ego boost. My gaze snapped to his face again as I waited for his response. He licked his lips a second time, still holding his shirt up, despite the fact that anyone could walk in.

His eyes were dancing, sweat glistening across his temple, glitter smudged over his lovely cheekbones. Had whoever put the glitter there been the one to touch his ass? I nearly growled at the thought.

"You're not pleased with me?" Luca's words hit me like a sledgehammer to the knees. I glared up at him, my lower abs growing tight as desire shivered deep inside me. It was unlike anything I'd ever felt before, even for him. Ravenous. I was ravenous. He dropped the hem of his hoodie and I mourned the sight of his abs immediately. Staring at me with dark eyes, and parted lips—he was tantalizing. Apparently everything about him provoked me. Clothed or not.

He liked this game just as much as I did.

His eyes said, *fuck me.*

They said, *take from me.*

They said, *remind me who I belong to.*

They said, *you're mine.*

This was supposed to be fun. That's what he had said.

So let's make it fun, then.

I hadn't felt this alive before. Not even when I'd had a real heartbeat, real blood in my veins, a real future. And I knew the immensely satisfying feeling had nothing to do with the stolen wallets, or even the possibility of discovery. The person responsible was the man towering above me, his long throat bobbing as he swallowed, waiting.

You're not pleased with me?

"No." I played his game. There was no choice, really. Not when he was looking at me like that. "I am not."

Luca bit his lip and my hands twitched at my sides. He bent down. Warm lips brushed against my cheekbone, dragging softly as his breath puffed along my skin. "Then…" Luca trailed off, a question in his words. Slowly those sinful lips traveled to the shell of my ear till his breath tickled, and my toes curled inside my boots. "Will you let me please you?"

I didn't respond, even though it took every ounce of my strength not to. My hands itched to form fists, my cock about ready to punch a hole through my jeans. His scent filled my nose. Sweat. Fruity drinks. Sin. I inhaled greedily, nostrils flaring.

"I'll do anything," Luca promised.

He was so warm.

So. Fucking. *Warm.*

A snake in the garden of Eden.

"Get on your knees." My grin was meaner than I'd intended, but I couldn't help it. He wanted mean as much as I wanted to give it to him.

Luca dropped to his knees.

He blinked up at me, his eyes flooded black with desire. Those big shoulders relaxed a fraction now that he was in his rightful place, his hands twitching where they rested atop his lean, muscular thighs. He was panting. *God, he was stunning.* His nostrils flared. His chest heaved with each labored breath as he peered through his lashes at me, the freckles splattering his cheeks catching the echo of the club lights as they bounced through the doorway.

The power Luca surrendered to me in that moment went to both my heads. My cock jerked, as I took the time to truly appreciate the sight of him on his knees. I had never met another man so willing to give himself to me. Especially someone like Luca. A jock. An artist. An enigma. All boyish charm, golden muscles, and pretty lies.

My cheeks hurt I was smiling so hard.

These smiles were the ones I'd always had to swallow back when I was alive. They made people uncomfortable. Not Luca, though. No. At the sight of my grin he grew hotter, needier. He spread his thighs wide in invitation and I couldn't help the way my gaze caught on the obscene way his cock tented his pants, trapped by fabric, long and thick.

"You want to please me?" I'd never been happier than I was in that moment.

"Fuck, yes." He sounded freshly fucked, his voice was so harsh and low.

"Then lick my boots."

Chapter Twenty

Luca

"WHAT?" THE WORD left my lips before I could catch it.

Then lick my boots.

That simple phrase made my head spin as I stared up at Prudence, slack-jawed. "You want me to…?" Surely, I'd heard him wrong. There was no way he actually wanted me to—

"Lick. My. Boots." Prudence's hands clenched into fists. I only noticed because they were right by my face, and I grimaced, squirming on my knees as I debated what to do. My first instinct was to tell him to fuck off. But then again…this was what I'd wanted, wasn't it? I'd promised him I'd do anything.

The question was, was I enough of a whore to get down on the ground and…*ew.*

Ew, *ew*. I couldn't imagine what kind of dirt and grime occupied the floor in a place with this much foot traffic.

"No." I was startled by how weak my protest sounded. Shouldn't I be more offended? Disgusted? I'd wanted to touch his cock, not…this. Whatever this was. We'd played with humiliation a bit, but never like this.

"No?" Prudence arched a brow, and immediately I began to cave.

Besides, I knew my safeword. If I wanted to stop, I could always just say it.

"No?" I laughed nervously, unable to help myself.

"Deny me again and see what happens." Shit. The threat in his voice was really doing it for me. I bit my lip. I could do this. *Hell, who was I kidding?* I already knew I was going to. I'd do anything to touch him, even apparently…this. My nose scrunched unhappily at the thought, buuuut my dick was most definitely on board. It twitched and flexed, and my balls drew up tight as I bit my lip hard enough it stung.

I could've fucked a brick wall, I was that turned on.

First fingers.

Now licking boots.

Who knew?

"You wanted to touch me. I'm giving you what you want," Prudence continued, pretending he couldn't see the war waging on my face. His smile was wicked, like he greatly enjoyed watching me squirm. Clearly, this was doing something for him too, because when I glanced between his legs at my prize longingly, I could see the thick swell of his cock trapped against the side of his leg. He was hard too. So fucking hard. And I wanted to see him—so, so bad. To taste him. To suck the salt from his skin, and choke on his fat length till he came down my throat.

For such a little dude he was most definitely packing heat.

Jeeee-sus.

It wasn't fair.

I wanted my mouth on that thing—like—yesterday.

I was so turned on at the thought of touching him, in whatever capacity, I could barely think. Besides. He was right. I'd asked for this. Repeatedly. It wasn't like he was asking for my kidney.

I also, kinda *did* deserve some punishment. I'd thrown him against the wall, after all. And we both needed him to reset the balance between us. He wanted me underfoot, in my rightful place. (Literally, in this case.) And I was absolutely not going to argue with that. Not when I liked it there. Not when folding to him was my favorite activity.

But.

That didn't mean I wasn't going to take as many liberties as I could getting there.

"Okay," I breathed in defeat, immediately rewarded when Prudence's nostrils flared and his dick twitched. My balls drew up tight in sympathy. My cock head was rubbing, rubbing, rubbing against the already slick fabric of my boxers as my lashes fluttered.

There was something about giving in to our shared depravity that made me lightheaded. There was no confusing what I was about to do. If someone saw me here—shit. *What would they think?* Humiliation made my face heat as I took a fortifying breath before I committed to what I was about to do. *I didn't care.* Let them watch.

Without speaking, I leaned forward, pressing a kiss to his knee, glancing up at him through my lashes as denim scraped against my lips. It was crazy to me how real he felt. Flesh and blood. Just looking at him, I never would've known the bastard was dead.

"Good boy." Prudence's praise went straight to my needy cock, and I hiccuped a whine against his knee, rubbing my cheeks against the fabric just to feel the scratch. Kiss after kiss, I traveled down his leg. Inch by inch. I sucked at the fabric, scraped my teeth against it, took every liberty I could as I made my way down his shin, then ankle, to the edge of his boot.

Dazed with desire, and panting hard, I peered up at him through my lashes.

He was a black and white blur above me, his hands clenched into fists, tattoos rippling as his big chest heaved. I swear I could see a wet spot forming above the head of his cock where it lay trapped against his jeans, and the thought sent a little thrill through my body.

"Tongue out," Prudence urged, his voice trembling, low and rough. His eyes were on me, dark, predatory.

I stuck my tongue out, inches away from the toe of his boot, my eyes crossing as I tried to look up at his reaction.

I'd never seen him like this before.

Every time we'd had sex it had been in the dark, with him behind me, or occupying my body—and it had always centered around my pleasure. Never had I seen the way his lashes fluttered when he was turned on. Seen the way his lip curled, almost in disgust, his brow knit. His nipples were hard where they pushed against the fabric of his tight white t-shirt and I held back a groan. I wanted to suck on them. Lave the fabric with my spit till the pale pink-ish blue color of them bled through.

My tongue trembled as I closed the distance between my mouth and his boot. Four inches, three inches, two inches, one—wait. I blinked, forcing my gaze from his face down to his shoe, only to realize I had licked right through it. Nothing but cool air. But…why—

Oh.

Oh.

It wasn't about actually licking them.

No.

"Nnng." My dick jumped and I whined, unable to help the broken noise that left my lips unbidden. No. It wasn't licking the boots. It was the fact I was *willing* to do it. Something so filthy, so depraved. Submissive. Ridiculous. Completely at his mercy.

Fingers tangled in my hair, and I nearly sobbed with relief as Prudence yanked my head back so I was staring at him again. His boot met my cock with a gentle press of rubber that had my eyes rolling and my tongue hanging out as I panted.

I rutted against the unforgiving leather, fucking his foot with short bursts of my hips as my scalp tingled and that foggy place in the back of my head welcomed me deeper inside its embrace. I probably looked ridiculous, panting hard, my hips jerking. That thought only made my balls ache, as I pumped faster.

"Good boy," Prudence's voice was impossibly low. Rougher than before. I couldn't believe I'd earned his praise twice that night. I'd definitely made the right choice today. I humped his boot, ignoring the way it hurt almost as much as it felt good. Shame made my skin hot. This was wrong. So fucking wrong.

I loved it.

"There's a good, puppy. You need this don't you, you dirty little slut. Show me those fuck me eyes. Slower, Pinkie. That's it. Swivel those pretty goddamn hips. Show me how bad you want this." Prudence's praise went right to my head.

The pressure and praise made me melt, my balls drawing up tight as I whimpered, rutting against him with a desperation I probably should've been self-conscious about. My nipples tingled, hard and sensitive. Too sensitive. My hoodie was too hot, the sticky-sweaty slide of the stolen leather wallets clinging to my abs as my hips jerked.

"You can touch me," Prudence said, and I released a noise I wasn't entirely sure was human. My own pleasure forgotten, I lunged toward the zipper of his pants. Eagerly, I shoved my nose against the swell of his balls, then sucked an eager stripe down the thick shape of his cock where it lay trapped against his thigh. "Tongue only."

I whimpered.

But obeyed.

Two seconds later he freed his cock, his big fingers gripping the base as he slipped his fist up, then twisted around the crown. The head of his dick was flushed red, slick with his own precum, uncut—and genuinely gorgeous. There was a delicious vein that traveled up his length, and I watched the way it pulsed with rapt fascination. I could practically taste him already. His scent was strongest here. My head spun. I'd drooled all over his jeans but he didn't seem to mind as the tattooed flash of his knuckles jerked his cock right in front of me.

There was a line of black piercings down the length of Prudence's cock and just looking at them made my dick jerk. I wanted to touch them. To explore their shape and texture. To suck on each one, just to see what he'd do.

I shouldn't have been surprised he was pierced here too.

"Nothing else," he threatened. "Tongue only." I nodded immediately. I would've promised him anything at that point if it meant getting to taste him. "Do you understand?"

I was too far gone to argue.

"Tongue out," he commanded for the second time that night. I held my tongue out obediently. It trembled from the strain as I waited, eyes crossing as I tried to get a better look at his cock. He stroked it a few more times to take the edge off, then drew it to the left, only to let it swing against the side of my face with a wet slap.

Precum smeared against my glitter-streaked cheekbone and my eyes rolled back as I waited, tongue twitching, his boot still pressing hard against my cock. It was dehumanizing. All of it was. And I had never felt more right in all my fucking life.

I'd tried to be good.

I'd tried to be responsible.

I'd tried to be everything everyone wanted me to be.

This? With Prudence. It didn't feel like any of that. I didn't have to try. It was effortless. It was just him. Just me. No expectations. Nothing but the true essence of us. The parts we'd been too scared to show the world—or in his case, more than likely been punished for.

His cock slapped my cheek a second time, leaving a hot stripe in its wake, before he finally, blissfully pressed the crown onto my tongue. Oh sweet lord. Have mercy. Studs tickled along my tastebuds as I sucked, drooling eagerly around him as he fed inch after inch of his fat dick into my mouth. Salty, sweet. Colder than your average male, but twice as delicious. The velvety skin rubbed against the back of my throat.

It'd been a long time since I'd done this. So I couldn't help the way I choked when he pushed just slightly too far, too fast. Instead of pulling off, he watched me struggle through it with hungry eyes. I'd never been happier than I was then, gagging on his cock, the cold piercings rubbing against the sensitive nerve-endings on my tongue. Eventually I stopped spluttering, settling down as I stared up at him through tear soaked lashes.

A groan filled the air, and it took me a second too long to realize it wasn't mine.

Prudence swore softly under his breath, rucking his shirt up under his chin, his abs sucking in as his hips pressed forward, and his cock sunk deeper, deeper still. With my nose in the dark curls at the base of his pelvis I couldn't help the way the bliss caught up to me once again.

His hips pulled back, and I struggled to breathe through my nose, overwhelmed by sensation. When he pushed back in again, this time I was ready. I relaxed my throat, concentrating on his face as he sunk so deep inside me I wasn't sure where he started, and I ended.

Musky.

Big.

Delicious.

Prudence huffed an annoyed little sound as he tightened the grip he had on my hair, and shoved my head down a few inches. "Too fucking tall," he hissed through his teeth. I slumped lower, realizing belatedly he'd been on his tippy toes till that moment. His legs relaxed a fraction, though his thighs were still tense as he stroked a hand over my cheek, thumbing my spread lips with something akin to wonder flickering in his fiery blue gaze.

I sucked harder, just to watch the way his pecs pulled tight as his ragged breath stuttered. His hard nipples looked particularly bitable, and I had to hold back my desire to tease them, the way he'd teased me just a few days before. Maybe he liked it like I did. Hard. Mean. "That's it," Prudence crooned, sounding equal parts condescending and approving. "Get it nice and wet."

I choked on him a little, drool slipping down my chin as my eyes strained in an effort to keep meeting his gaze. His lip curled again in response, his head thunking back against the wall as his chest shuddered with a ragged exhale. There was something intoxicating about seeing Prudence lose some of his carefully cultivated control. God he smelled good. Carnal. Delicious. The scent of sex fogged my mind as I tasted the sweat on skin. Every time the piercings that acted as a ladder down his cock scraped against my tongue, my dick leaked in sympathy. It felt so fucking good to be owned like this. So. Fucking. Good.

Bliss.

Prudence's hands climbed into my hair again. Both of them this time. He held me tight, forcing me to stay still as his hips began to stutter. In and out, we moved in perfect synchronization. A rhythm that was predictable enough I lost myself in it. Hypnotized by ghost cock, *who knew?*

Distantly, I recognized that tears were slipping down my cheeks. That my nose was running. That I'd leaked cum all over the inside of my pants, and that the crowd outside the coatroom was getting quieter and quieter as people exited the club. Maybe no one was coming in here, because they could hear me choking on Prudence's cock?

Whatever.

I didn't care.

When Prudence came there was no indication he was about to do it. One second he was pounding my face, sloppy and brutal, my scalp tingling as he pulled my hair taut. The ragged hiss of his breath, the slurp of his thick cock squishing inside my throat filling the air. The next, salt erupted on my tongue, slipping down my throat as I choked and whimpered, my own cock responding in turn as I humped his foot one last time, and came all over the inside of my pants.

Sticky.

We were both so sticky.

Before I'd had a chance to recover, Prudence was pulling me to my feet with the grip he had on my hair. My scalp zinged. I stood on wobbly legs, surprised I still was capable of walking as he yanked me to him, and fucked his tongue right into my mouth. He chased every last taste of himself, claiming me so thoroughly my cock was nearly summoned back to life again by the time he'd decided we were done.

When he finally pulled back I wobbled again, reaching out for his biceps to steady myself. To my surprise, he let me. He patted me down, wiped my mouth off on the hem of his t-shirt, and then made out with me till I forgot my own name again. He nipped, and sucked, biting at my lips till I was so drunk on his kisses all I could do was chase his tongue and sway on unsteady feet.

When he finished, Prudence's arm hung possessively around my waist as he led me out of the room without a word. Someone cheered at us as we passed through the blur of bodies, but I couldn't bring myself to care.

Cover officially blown.

Among other things.

We got in the car in a daze. Belatedly, I glanced down to make sure the wallets I'd stolen were still hidden from view. They were. *Ah*. So that's why he'd been jerking on the hem of my hoodie.

Prudence booted my phone up for the second time that night, flipped through a few pages, the blue light flickering over his features, before he put the car in drive, and leaned over my seat to check behind us as he backed out of the parking spot.

I stared at his hand as it pressed to my headrest, my eyes nearly crossing as I traced the shape of the familiar tattoos with ease. L.I.A.R taunted me across his knuckles. I held back the urge to kiss each individual letter. My lips were still tingling. Salt danced on my tongue.

"Hotel," he grunted, answering the question I hadn't even asked.

"Hotel," I agreed, my voice so quiet I wasn't even sure I'd spoken. Before he retracted his arm he gave the curls at the base of my neck a gentle pinch. And when we pulled out onto the street, GPS blaring from my phone screen, his hand lay cool and protective on the top of my thigh.

I spared one last thought to the men at the club. The one's I'd robbed. The last one in particular.

I should've felt guilty.

Part of me did.

But part of me? Yeah. Part of me was tired of caring. Part of me was tired of hiding this side of my personality.

I just hoped none of them came looking for us before we got to our destination.

Chapter Twenty-One

Prudence

I SHOULD'VE PICKED a shittier spot to stay the night. Hindsight and all, I realized a fancy high rise hotel in a big city wasn't the best place to lay low, considering the fact we were spending someone else's money. It was late enough now though, that I decided to throw caution to the wind. If something bad happened, I had plenty of options.

For example, I could tell Luca about the power he held over me.

But, I wanted to avoid that if at all possible.

Weirdly enough, after seeing how easily he had fallen into his role at the club, I was less apprehensive than I'd been before about telling him. Hilarious how I'd sworn just a few short weeks ago that I would never in my un-life give someone that power over me again. I thought I was safe, latching on to a person who didn't know.

But just a few short weeks together, one wild crime-filled night, and here I was, wavering.

And here *he* was, confusing me once again.

I should've picked a shittier hotel.

But the way Luca's eyes lit up when he spotted the fluffy king-sized bed made the risk worth it. His grin was positively sunny as he flopped down on his back like an overgrown kid, far more lively now that he'd had a chance to settle. That foggy, dazed look on his face as we'd left the club would live in my thoughts for all eternity.

He wiggled.

Cute.

I shook my head, disgusted with myself—and him—for the inappropriate thought. I glared as he flailed around happily, making pleased little noises that went straight to my dick.

Then his stomach growled.

Again.

He stopped wriggling, peeking at me through his bangs sheepishly, like being hungry was somehow a crime. He was lucky to get hungry at all. I jerked my head toward the phone that sat on top of the pale golden wood of the nightstand beside the bed.

"Twenty-four-seven room service."

"Shiiiit," Luca grinned, bouncing onto his knees. The bed rocked. "Seriously? I thought room service died in like the '90s." He blinked at me, then his expression shifted, apprehension creeping back in. "Hey— What happens if someone finds us here?"

"They won't."

He rolled his eyes. "Okay, yeah. But what if they do?"

"I'll deal with it." Just like I'd already decided. If I had to, I'd tell my secret. When he knew the power he held, there wasn't a problem in the world we couldn't solve. Possessing someone and driving off in their own car—while inconvenient—was a viable option. As was murder. Not that I could do either of those things without his permission.

I doubted Luca would mind if I had to take things into my own hands. After all, he hadn't minded when I'd taken the form of one of the men from the club and used his ID to check us in to the hotel. He'd just blinked at me, squinted, then said "cool." Like the fact my body was an easily changeable illusion was as interesting as a color changing coffee cup.

I shuddered.

Even just thinking of the word permission made my skin crawl.

There was so much Luca still didn't know about me, and the secrets were beginning to feel like far too heavy a burden for one person to carry. Even me.

Like every hotel I'd stayed at in my youth, the room was covered in opulent, horribly patterned wallpaper, and gaudy white trim. The bathroom was close to the entrance, and with the door swung wide open, I could easily see the marble countertops and complimentary bottles of soap sitting beside the sink.

"Order what you want." I repeated, waiting for the apprehension on his face to melt away. It did. Quicker than I expected. Clearly, he trusted me. I didn't know what to do with that realization.

"What's your favorite food?" Luca asked a few minutes later, laying on his stomach as he rifled through the menu he'd found in the top drawer of the nightstand. He flipped a page, and hummed.

"I don't have one." I glared.

"Everyone has a favorite food, Prudence. Even Prudence the Grouch. Since they don't have Oreos, I suppose I'll just have to guess." I forced back my amusement. He'd had enough punishment for one day. He didn't know it yet, but I was going to be really, really nice to him later. He'd won our competition, after all.

After he ate.

After *we* ate, apparently.

Which I only realized when half an hour later the clock blared a bleary five o'clock at us and room service arrived with enough food to feed an army.

Luca tipped the guy generously from one of his stolen wallets, shut the door, and turned to me with a sheepish smile. "You wouldn't tell me what you liked, so I just grabbed a bit of everything? I figured we could make it a game, you know. But without the whole robbing people thing."

"You and your games," my heart fluttered. "Show me what you got."

Luca spread the food across the bed, stacking pillows behind his body before he pulled the round silver lids off of the plates with a flourish, as dramatic as if he'd cooked the food himself.

"We've gooooot—" he gave plate number one a far too enthusiastic introduction, jazz hands and all, "baked Mac and cheese."

I grimaced.

"Oookay. Got it." Luca snorted. "How abouuuut—" He jerked another lid off and waited, his eyes bright.

"More burgers?" I arched a brow.

"Of course." Another lid was tossed to the side. "And fries. I couldn't forget the fries. You know, seeing as you are a fuckin' fry thief. Clearly you like those."

"Better," I admitted, biting back a smile. The mattress looked comfortable, but I refused to sit. Being next to him right now felt like too…much. So I just floated to the side, like before in the car, letting my guard down enough I stopped pretending like gravity affected me.

"You can fly," Luca said curiously, then yanked another lid off, casually, like it wasn't a big deal at all. "Of course he can fly, he's a fuckin' ghost, Luca," he admonished himself under his breath, then spoke louder. "What about ice cream?" He blinked expectantly. Skeptically, I eyed the giant bowl of Neapolitan ice cream he'd uncovered in shock. Bananas were stacked along the edges, the top slathered in chocolate sauce, strawberry preserves, and a healthy pile of whipped cream.

"You ordered ice cream?" My brow knit. It did…look appetizing. "It's going to melt by the time you finish your dinner."

"Who says I'm not eating it first?" Luca grabbed one of the two spoons on the plate and waggled his eyebrows playfully at me. He shoved it into the chocolate section, making sure to scoop up whipped cream and berry sauce before he popped the spoon into his mouth with a happy moan. "Thee?" He slurred, chocolate smeared across his lips. "Ith delithouth."

I floated back to the ground.

He swallowed, then beamed at me. And it was the sunniest, happiest grin I'd ever seen in my life. "You know you want some, boo. Just admit it."

I cringed in disgust.

"Boo? You know. Since you're a ghost."

"Do. *Not*. Call. Me. That."

"Okay, okay." Luca cackled and shook his head. "Pru it is." I don't know where I'd gone wrong, because for some reason he no longer seemed scared of me. Not that he ever really had been. I cleared off the bed.

Plate by plate, stacked carefully out of the way on the floor in a neat row. Luca had an adorably confused wrinkle between his brow as he observed. "Aren't you hungry?"

I didn't have the heart to tell him I didn't get hungry.

Besides. His smile had made me change my plans.

I placed the final plate on the ground, then climbed onto the bed and reached for the remaining spoon. The massive bowl of ice cream teetered and Luca reached out to steady it. "Open," I commanded as I scooped up strawberry ice cream and held it out.

He opened his mouth, eyes twinkling. At the last second, I bypassed his lips, smearing the ice cream down his long, kissable throat. Luca hissed a breath through his teeth, then giggled a high, hysteric sort of noise.

"You asshole—" His words were cut off as I leaned forward and sucked the dollop of icy treat from his feverishly warm skin. His breath stuttered, and he whined, fingers immediately tangling in my hair as he clutched my head to his neck. I could practically sense his dick rise. "Shit, do that again."

With every scoop of ice cream, with every lick, every bite, every kiss, Luca became more and more pliant.

His dirty clothes were soon tossed onto the floor, a messy pile, far away from the abandoned food. He was hungry, but *I* was hungrier. When I flipped Luca onto his belly, he spread his legs unashamed. His ass was three shades paler than his sun-kissed back, and covered in as many freckles as the rest of him. There was a distinct line around his waist and upper thigh that marked where his shorts typically fell. The swathes of speckled skin called to me, and I couldn't help but admire him. The fragile skin at the back of his knees. His long, gorgeous neck. His lean, limber waist, and the way it tapered impossibly wide leading up to the sculpted shoulders.

Scooping directly from the bowl, I spread vanilla ice cream over his crease. He hissed through his teeth, and I bit back a groan when his cheeks clenched. I wanted to make him do that again, except, with my tongue inside him this time. I wanted to feel the way he squirmed away, like he wasn't sure he could have this. Like he wasn't sure he could have me.

"Oh shit, oh fuck." Luca's hips jumped, pushing away from me, before snapping back. Like he didn't know whether he wanted to run or chase. "What are you doing?" I leaned down, my heart pounding in my chest as I sucked at the drip of cream that tickled down to his balls. He spread his legs wider, and I bit back an appreciative growl as I got my first real look at his delicious little hole.

I would never forget the flush of shame that blossomed across his skin when he'd admitted he liked to be played with there. He'd been shy. Too shy to even say the words. Even now that we had weeks of touching behind us, his body shook in anxious anticipation.

How much experience did he have with being touched there? Had someone else looked at him like this? Seen the way his asshole fluttered? Admired the freckles that dotted his supple cheeks, and dipped all the way into the secret place between them. Darker skin. Dusky. Pink. The idea that someone could have worshiped him like this before me made me see red, so I forced the thought away.

Instead, I bit my lip, and admired his hole. He squirmed away from my touch. His entrance was pink. Wrinkled and sweet. Flushed with blood. My balls ached but I ignored my own growing need as I closed the distance between us and sucked up the last of the ice cream. When he was trembling, but clean, I fanned a kiss against his hole again, just to feel it twitch.

He relaxed.

I couldn't have that.

He was getting too comfortable.

"I'm going to train you," I murmured, biting at his fleshy ass cheeks hard enough he twisted away from me, a desperate sob muffled against the bed covers. "Whenever you think of sex, you're going to think of me." Half threat, half promise.

Luca's breath burst out raggedly, as he shoved his hips against my face chasing more touch. Once again, immediately after they grew shy and pulled away. Contradictory. Like he was.

"C-cold." He complained unhappily as I smeared another dollop of ice cream across his freckled ass cheeks. They flexed, *hard*. And goose flesh trembled across them. I sucked at the pebbled skin, letting the chilly ice cream melt before I licked it away. God, he smelled good. I would never get enough. Coconut, salt-water, sweat. His smell was even more concentrated down here, and I couldn't help the way I inhaled greedily.

For a while I played with his skin, licking away cream as it pebbled, kissing and sucking everywhere but the place I knew he wanted me most. When he became truly desperate, his hips stopped trembling away from me. Instead, he shoved his ass toward my face, needy, and no longer frightened of the touch.

Maybe he'd been embarrassed before. To be sucked and licked open. But he wasn't now. My patience had killed the last of his reservations.

By the time I returned to his entrance Luca was sobbing, these hiccuped, panicked puffs of air that had my cock hard enough to pound nails. But, *no*. This wasn't about me. This was about him. About the stunt he'd played at the club. About his many, many mysteries. About the smile, that made my skin too tight, and my head staticky.

I laved a hot stripe across his fluttering entrance and he howled again, trembling all over, completely at my mercy. His broad shoulders trembled as he bunched the sheets in his hands and I reached beneath his body to wrangle his cock back toward me. With it pulled downward I could see all of it clearly. Long, freckled, pink. Just like him. He was leaking all over the place, his crown an angry red. I spit on it to wet it—not that he needed me to—then gave it a rough jerk as I dove back between his cheeks.

"Pru—" Luca reached back, fingers tangling in my hair, his hips arching. He was reluctant to give in. He kept leaping away from me, like he didn't know what to do with the sensitive press of my tongue.

"Give in." I demanded, biting one of his cheeks hard enough to bruise. I was getting tired of his resistance.

"I can't—" he complained. I bit again, and he hissed out a breath. "It's so sensitive—I've never."

"Give. *In.*" Another bite, another whine.

"Pru—" My name was sin on his lips. I reached for his cheeks again, spreading them open and holding him tight, his cock abandoned as I shoved my tongue inside where he was tightest—hottest—just to feel his struggle. Surprisingly—holding his body immobile was what finally got him to settle. He sagged, a wretched moan leaving his lips as his tension bled away and his hole relaxed beneath the dominating press of my tongue.

Good.

So fucking good.

"That's it, Pinkie." I murmured, withdrawing long enough to kiss apologies over the angry red bite marks I'd left all over his ass. "So good for me." I kept him spread, enraptured by the way his hole fluttered around nothing, before I dove back in with enthusiasm. Unbidden, the memory of his earlier admittance came back to me. He'd told me he wanted to lay back, to do nothing.

I wanted to make that fantasy reality.

"Please—" Luca gasped, clinging to my tongue as I fucked up inside him, rubbing, rubbing, rubbing his slick inner walls. "No one's ever—*shit*." Every time I pushed deeper, the hold he had on my hair tightened, my scalp tingling as my dick ached to bury itself within the tight wet space. "It shouldn't feel so—*oh, Pru*." He relaxed again for me, his body pliant, welcoming. When he finally did, I spat on his trembling hole, then released one ass cheek to push the pad of my thumb in alongside my tongue. In, in, *in*, he squeezed and shuddered. His tight body clenched around me as I shifted till I found that sweet spot inside him, I knew would make my big bird sing.

When I rubbed it, he *howled*. His legs jerked and his hole gave beneath my questing touch. His hand left my hair as he scratched at the mattress, bunching the comforter in his grip, tight.

"Good boy." With my thumb still clutched tight inside his body, I leaned back to admire my handiwork. Luca lay sprawled, his legs wide, his thick ass spread obscenely. His cock and balls hung beneath him, streaks of precum smearing the mattress. Freckles. So many freckles. Along his ass cheeks, up his narrow waist, trailing his spine, scattered like splatters on a Jackson Pollock painting. His hands were bunched in the comforter on either side of his body, his knuckles white, veins in his forearms ropey as they flexed.

Prettiest of all, was the way his tear-streaked face was tipped toward me. His lashes were spiky and wet, his mouth gaping, lips still raw from earlier.

Fuck yeah.

Every time I pressed against his prostate Luca's eyes fluttered beneath his lids and he gasped, drool slipping down his chin and onto the mattress. His hole clenched around my thumb when his eyes opened, and that stormy gray gaze met my own. We stared at each other for a few devastating moments, and when his lips turned up into a sweet little smile I was lost.

I dove back into his ass, fucking deep with my tongue, eating him out till he came all over the bed and his whole body convulsed against me. For a while, as he came down from his high, I admired my work. The sheen of sweat that glistened on his sun kissed skin. The way spit trickled from his now loosened asshole. I had to shove my hand against my cock to soothe the urge to stuff it inside his still twitching entrance while it was soft and he was unsuspecting. I wanted to hear him squeal, but—this hadn't been for me. The bite marks I'd left on his ass cheeks faded as he slowly, but surely came back to himself.

Big gray eyes.

The very slight gap between his two front teeth.

His smile haunted me as I shoved him into the shower.

It haunted me as I roughly toweled him off.

As I hauled him into bed.

As I stacked all his abandoned plates of food around him like the gangly pink prince he was, and we shared the meals he'd bought for us, cold, but just as good.

Chapter Twenty - Two

Luca

"YOU'RE FUCKING KIDDING." My laugh was almost hysterical as I stared at the smoke billowing from the hood of my car before I pulled to the side of the road, a sinking feeling in my gut. Of course, I'd expected this. I'd just hoped it would happen you know…a few years from now. Not hours away from the daydream of a hotel we'd left behind, so close to my hometown I could practically taste the scent of my mother's geraniums in the air.

"How close are we?" Prudence asked from the passenger seat. He didn't sound surprised. He didn't sound much of anything, actually. Here I was—full-blown panicking, and he was still cool as a cucumber.

What was the point of robbing people for gas money if we no longer had a car?

Karma was such a bitch.

"A few hours? If we were driving." I offered, not sure how to explain. My phone battery was at fifty percent, and like the previous day, I'd been conserving it. I could've charged it in the car. You know, if my car had contained a working phone charging…hole…thingy.

But it didn't, and it wasn't.

Prudence was out of the vehicle mere moments later. The backpack full of our things was slung over his shoulder as he bent over the hood and I did my very best not to drool as I ogled him. There was nothing hotter than a man who knew about cars. Then, a more pressing concern hit me.

Peeing.

Yes.

I needed to do that.

A quick Google search showed there was a gas station just up the road. Small mercies and all that. I had never liked peeing outside. Ever. Even when I'd spent a lot of time outdoors I'd done my best to avoid it. Unlike Adam, or even Paul, who had always made fun of me as they went off to do their business like little pee-headed dude-bros. The fact they could bond over peeing in the wild made me simultaneously want to laugh, and also bash my head against the nearest surface.

I knew my aversion to it was weird, so I purposely played it cool so as to not arouse suspicion from Prudence as I asked, "You okay, if I head to the gas station to pee?"

Prudence arched a brow in annoyance. "Do you really need my permission to go to the bathroom?"

"Okay, fuck." I laughed. On my way past him I slapped the hood playfully right next to his hand, just to enjoy the memory of his glare as

I headed down the beat-up asphalt away from him. There was a prickle between my shoulder blades, a tingle at the base of my neck that had me checking both abandoned sides of the road for threats.

I'd been feeling that same awareness for hours now. Ever since we'd left the hotel, actually. But I'd shoved it aside. Like Prudence had said, no one was going to follow us. And even if they did? He'd promised to deal with it.

There was nothing to worry about.

Which is what I told myself, every time I jumped as a twig cracked behind the tree line. Or when a bird fluttered its wings, and my soul promptly left my body.

"You're being paranoid," I reminded myself as I pulled around the corner and breathed a sigh of relief as soon as I spotted the gas station I'd sniped on Google. Before I headed inside, I gathered a handful of cash and shoved the stolen wallet into my back pocket. At the hotel we'd consolidated our bounty into the biggest of the seven, and seven different IDs and credit cards had made their home against my ass the entire drive there.

Prudence had explained that he wanted to keep the IDs in case he needed to assume a new identity, like the one he'd taken back at the hotel. I figured he knew more than I did about shape-shifting, so I wasn't about to argue.

Soooo because I didn't want to risk the gas station attendant seeing anything suspicious, I needed to be extra careful should I need to buy something.

Sunshine McIdiot was now Sunshine McParanoid.

Go figure.

As I pushed the door to the convenience store section of the gas station, the bell chimed. The guy manning the cash register glared at me, and I tried not to judge him for the ratty tatters of his baseball cap. Or the fact I could smell him all the way from the door—B.O. and too much Axe body spray to cover it.

Everything else about the gas station was unremarkable, aside from it being maybe a bit dirtier and older than what I was used to in San Diego. I couldn't remember if everything had been run down this close to my hometown when I was a kid, or if this was a recent thing, but I refused to dwell on it too long as I made my way toward the back where the bathrooms should've been. Only…there were no bathrooms.

"Bathrooms are for paying customers," the dude grunted. I swiveled around, my heart thudding unsteadily as I caught him leaning over the counter to watch me suspiciously.

"Right." I'd thought something like this might happen. I ignored the need to do a little I-need-to-pee-jig and made my way toward him, snagging the first thing I saw—a lighter, and placing it on the counter. Something beeped under the table, and cashier dude's eyes flickered in surprise, before shuttering once again.

"ID?" He asked and I scowled, gesturing at the sad stubble beginning to form on my face.

"Do I look like a high schooler to you?" The look in his eyes most definitely said *yes*.

"Five bucks." I offered, waggling the extra cash I had in my hand. "I don't have my ID with me."

He debated with himself, his beady little eyes swiveling from side to side. His attention caught on Prudence's necklace, dangling from my throat out in the open. Fuck. I hadn't even noticed. Something in his gaze changed then, and the darkness in his eyes grew even darker.

"Fine." He snatched the five right out of my hand and didn't give me any more trouble as I paid for the pink lighter, and shoved it into my front pocket. When we were finished, he handed me my receipt and I waited.

And waited.

"Bathroom?" I reminded him, my leg beginning to bounce a little.

"Out back." He tossed me the key, and I was so grateful that I ignored the way his gaze followed me all the way out the door. I tucked the necklace protectively under my shirt, weirdly uncomfortable when I remembered the way he'd ogled it.

It wasn't something I was supposed to share.

It felt private.

Even though it was just a necklace.

The bathroom was indeed out back. A single stall inside a tiny little building covered in chipped blue paint, probably older than I was. It took a couple tries to get the damn key into the lock. And I forced out a relieved breath the second it clicked open, and a flickering fluorescent lightbulb burst on.

When I had finished doing my business, I washed my hands liberally, ignoring the fact the bathroom was even dirtier than the gas station had been. My phone buzzed in my pocket. I pulled it out, ignoring my reflection as I checked my notifications. I'd meant to turn the damn thing off, but I'd forgotten in light of my bathroom adventure.

It was one of those emails from a random beauty company wishing me an early birthday with a coupon so small it wasn't worth using at all. With a sigh it finally hit me. My birthday. Three days away. Jesus. I bit my lip, nervously reaching up to fiddle with Prudence's cross through the fabric of my hoodie.

I'd have to see my family soon.

I'd been forcing back those thoughts, but now? In this dirty as hell bathroom, with the Pee-Gods sated, was as good of a time as any to deal with my demons. My mom's words still bounced around in my skull like a fucked up game of ping-pong as I pulled up Adam's contact page and reread the text he'd sent me nearly two weeks ago.

Adam: I finally finished that anime you told me to watch.

Adam: ???

Adam: Are you ignoring me?

Damn. I really should've replied. I sighed, releasing my lip as the bite of copper burst along my tongue. Now that I knew the mess I'd made would be fixed, talking to my family no longer felt quite so impossible. I had Prudence to thank for that. The pain grounded me, and I built up my courage as I leaned against the dirty sink and finally replied.

Me: Hope u liked it!

Me: Heard ur out of school.

Adam replied immediately. Because of course he did. He'd probably been waiting gleefully for this moment to tear me a new one.

Adam: You're alive! Wow. Amazing.

Me: Shit head.

I couldn't help but laugh, scratching absentmindedly at a paint streak on my jeans as I waited. It was a good thing Prudence had packed me another pair. Otherwise I might've been stuck in my cum-soaked set and that was…definitely not an appealing idea. It still boggled my mind that he'd been able to get me to come in my pants at all. That had never happened to me before.

His paranormal penis was truly life changing.

In the time I'd been musing about Prudence and his pierced dick, Adam had texted back.

Adam: *tongue out emoji* :P Mom says you're coming home for your birthday.

Adam: Are you actually coming? Or did you just say that to get her to stop freaking out?

I'd never lied to my siblings before. Well. Before the last six months. Mom? Hell yeah. All the fucking time. She didn't know half the shit we'd had to do growing up just to survive. All three of us had opted to keep her in the dark permanently. So Adam had no reason to think I'd lie to him now. In fact, knowing him, if I told him right now I wasn't coming he was sure to make up an excuse for me. Betty would back him up.

It was nice that I had good news for once.

Me: Rude. I'm not a liar.

Adam: Ha!

I snorted, unable to hide my smile against my shoulder any longer.

Me: *devil smiling emoji*

Me: I'll be there.

Adam: Seriously?

Me: Seriously.

Adam: Good, cuz Betty has been practicing baking all week. Her first three birthday cakes were pretty horrible, but she's getting better. She'll need all the comforting she can get when her boyfriend doesn't show up like he said he would.

Me: How does my birthday cake have anything to do with her boyfriend?

Adam: She's trying to impress him with her non-existent skills *eye roll emoji*

Adam: Probably.

I wasn't surprised how invested my sister was in impressing her boyfriend. Adam was just a dick. As pessimistic as I was optimistic.

Adam: the cakes for you 2.

He added, belatedly.

Adam: But mostly her boyfriend.

I couldn't help but snort.

Adam: She claims he'll be here Saturday.

Me: Maybe she'll stress bake enough cakes to summon him early.

Adam: Shit. That's funny. I'm gonna go tell her you said that.

I knew there was no point arguing with him. My cheeks hurt from smiling so hard, and the ache in my chest had subsided. I'd missed them. Damn. Someone knocked on the bathroom door and I huffed in annoyance. Prudence had probably finished up at the car, and was here to harass me about my very human needs. He could wait. Two seconds later, I got another text.

Betty: Fuck you.

Me: *kissy face emoji*

Betty: What's your favorite cake flavor?

Me: Chocolate

Betty: Great. I'll make vanilla. *middle finger emoji*

Betty: Glad you're alive btw

The knocking got louder and I rolled my eyes heavenward as I shoved the door open, still staring down at Betty's last message. "You don't even need to use the bathroom, you—"

My back met the wall. My phone flew out of my hand, skittering across the gravel as a fist smashed hard into the side of my head, and I plummeted to the ground with a dazed thud. There was a ringing sound in my ears that drowned out the rest of the world as I stared blearily up at the stout man looming over me.

He definitely was not Prudence. Too tall. Too thick. His dark eyes were hidden in shadow, as the sun blared from above. My head was pounding, my heart racing as I scrambled backward toward my no doubt shattered phone.

At first I didn't recognize him.

But then I did.

The guy.

The one Prudence had imitated at the hotel. The guy from the club. The one I'd slipped my hand into the back pocket of and—

He grabbed me by the hair, and it hurt. It hurt so fucking bad a baffled little wail left my lips as he jerked me around and I felt his big hand pawing at my ass. Oh, shit. Fuck. *No.*

This wasn't like when Prudence manhandled me. There was no pleasure to accompany the pain, only fear, so visceral I could hardly think.

I peeked over my shoulder, terrified. He pulled the wallet I'd stolen out, and I sagged in relief, now that I knew what he'd actually been after. Belatedly I realized how fucking stupid we'd been to think we could get away with this at all.

My attacker's eyes gleamed as he sat down on top of my back, squashing me into the rocks. He was heavy enough the breath left me in a distressed *woosh* and I gasped, scratching at the ground, my protests futile.

Card after card smacked against the back of my head as he towered over me, the sun blocked out by his massive shape. He stopped when he finally found what he wanted. Blearily, I stared at him till recognition hit and adrenaline began coursing through my veins the moment I realized he was holding up his own driver's license. He glared down at me, teeth bared.

And then he spoke—

Chapter Twenty-Three

Luca

"I KNEW IT was you, you thieving pink-haired fucker." The man's words were twisted with fury, so different from the way he'd crooned into my ear as he'd caressed the hickeys Prudence had left around my neck the night before.

I was so fucking fucked it wasn't even funny.

Where was Prudence?

Goddamn it. I needed my murder ghost—like—yesterday.

I didn't respond, and douchebag obviously didn't like that. Because another blow met the back of my head, and I was spinning, spinning, *spinning*, spitting gravel out of my mouth as a muffled gasp left my lips. He hauled me to my feet, and I was too dazed to do much more than scratch at him as he latched his hands around my wrists and hauled me toward a red car parked a few yards away.

That definitely hadn't been there when I'd gone into the bathroom.

Had he been following me?

I swallowed back bile.

I'd seen enough *True Crime* to know if I got in that car I might as well be dead. I kicked at his legs, struggling with newfound strength, my sweaty hair poking my eyes as I swore.

"You and your nasty little boyfriend think you can steal from me?" He chuckled, talking to himself like I wasn't even there. "Let's see how he feels, when I steal you." He laughed again, a short barking sort of sound. Manic.

Shit.

Of course I'd had to rob the one fucker who would hunt me down because of it. Wasn't Prudence supposed to be lucky? Speaking of Prudence—Where. Was. *He?* "Think you're smarter than me, don't you?" He continued to mutter as the distance between us and his death-trap (a real death-trap, hilarious, I know) closed step by step. "But you're not." His chuckle was a bit deranged. "You're the dumb ones. All it took was one call to my credit card company to find which hotel you were staying in."

Mother. Fucker.

Apparently things could always get worse.

Villain monologues were really very enlightening.

TV got that bit right.

It was an entirely different feeling though, to be the one led to their death. This was not fun. Not at all. I kicked out again, struggling as hard as I could as I opened my mouth to yell—

He slammed me up against the hot metal on the side of the car, twisting my wrists in front of me in one of his big hands as he squeezed my cheeks in the other and his wild eyes met mine. "You crazy little psychopath," he hissed as I bit his palm, but he held tight. Blood burst on my tongue, and I wiggled, hard, trying to break his hold.

"I dare you to scream," he cackled, a smear of hot spit hitting my cheek as I blinked through the haze in my mind, my vision wobbling. His nails bit into my already stinging cheeks. I could feel a piece of gravel stuck to my forehead, and my head was still spinning—spinning—*spinn*— "I dare you to. Let's see what the cashier says when I show him all the IDs you had on you, huh?" He grinned. More spit hit my cheek. "Who do you think he's gonna wanna help, then?"

He was wrong.

I *knew* he was.

There was no way to prove that the wallet had been mine in the first place. Buuuut the smallest tiniest, stubbornest, *guiltiest* part of me believed him. Believed all it would take was a single look at me for the cashier to know that all of this was my fault. Unfortunately, my silent terror distracted me long enough he was able to get the car door open.

As I stared into the dirty interior, at crumpled-up wrappers, and abandoned soda cups, my life flashed before my eyes.

I saw Betty and Adam, still chubby, still young. Their round faces peering up at me like I was God, as I evenly distributed the candy bars I'd slipped into my jacket when the cashier hadn't been looking. I saw my first baseball game. The way Paul had torn his baseball cap off, sweaty and summer sticky, and slapped it onto my head. I saw mom. Every Betty Crocker birthday cake she'd burned for my birthday. Betty's smile when she'd packed up her shit in her car and headed off to her first year of college. I saw her green graduation cap. The way it had flown into the air. The degree I'd paid for as she held it high and beamed at us, her dirty-blonde hair matted from wearing the hat so long.

I saw Adam's disappointment when I didn't show up Saturday like I promised.

I saw Prudence.

I saw the shape of his downward smile. I saw the insecurity that lay hidden in his eyes every time he talked about his past. I saw his walls, the ones that had crumpled, one by one to the ground the longer we spent together.

What would happen to him?

If I died.

What would happen to him if I was gone?

Who would he talk to?

Who would give him fries…or blow jobs…

Or, or—any number of other, equally important, equally special things.

No.

No, no, *no.*

I couldn't do that to him.

I couldn't do that to any of them.

With a surprisingly dope bout of strength, I managed to sink my teeth into murder dude's palm again at the same time I launched my knee at his balls. He screeched bloody murder, crumpling forward as I felt the squish of his testicles popping beneath my knee.

Good.

And then I ran.

I used every ounce of strength I had left and I ran.

Into the woods. Into the spotty shadows. Ducking between tree trunks, and beneath branches. Crazy dude didn't wait long. I could hear him behind me, the thud, thud of his steps. His breathing was ragged as an animal's, his legs eating up the distance between us as I huffed and puffed, dazed and disoriented, searching, searching, searching for somewhere I could—*there*.

I ducked behind a tree trunk, strangling my mouth with both hands to quiet my breathing, as I strained to listen for footsteps behind me.

Closer and closer.

There was no time—

No—

"Boo."

Dirt filled my mouth and nose as I hit the ground, a desperate scream torn from my lips.

Hurt.

Hurt, hurt, hurt.

Everything hurt.

There was a weight on my back, hands around my neck. A bird fled the branches above, cawing its anger as it took to the skies and the ringing in my ears only grew worse and worse and worse. Maybe it was pain, maybe it was panic. Both. Probably.

"No—" I gasped raggedly, my words hoarse. I scratched at the dirt, trying to get the guy off of me, but there was no use.

There was no fucking use.

He was too heavy.

Too strong.

And I was just…

"I'm gonna kill you, you little—"

There was one last thing I could do. I could…yes.

Yes.

He might not hear me—but if he could? I had to take that chance. I had to.

"Prudence!" I yelled. Or tried to. The words were barely a whisper, all choked and broken. "Prudence—"

"Shut up you dumb bit—"

"Prudence, help me!" I hiccuped, tears streaming down my stinging cheeks. "Save me—I—"

Before the words left my lips, the weight on my back was gone. I sucked in ragged, desperate breaths, my throat aching as I curled my fingers into the dirt and sobbed against the fallen leaves.

Distantly, I recognized the sound of fists meeting flesh but it took me a few seconds to find the strength to lift my head to watch.

Prudence was glorious.

The sun bled through his body, refracting like sun beams as he hauled my attacker by his hair across the forest floor away from me, eyes blazing. He looked other worldly. He spoke, but I couldn't make out his words as I stared at him in awe. My beautiful, avenging god. The electric blue of his gaze burned as he kicked the guy where he lay on the ground for good measure, and immediately returned to my side.

Thick thighs flexed as he squatted down, half see-through, lip curling in disgust.

"Why didn't you call sooner?" His voice was gruff. Angry.

Shit.

He was hot.

"Sorry." The word felt like cotton in my mouth as Prudence huffed out an aggrieved sigh. Like I'd done this to spite him. I couldn't contain my laugh. But the sound abruptly died as I spotted murdery dude behind him, a rock in his hands, his eyes wild, and blood smeared across his face. "Prudence watch ou—"

The rock came slamming down on Prudence's head. Buuuut—instead of making contact, it went right through him. The guy was so surprised he fell forward, toppling on top of my head with a startled squawk.

Sweat. Ew. Ew, ew, ew.

Gross, murdery man, sweat.

I couldn't brea—

"I told you—" Prudence hauled the guy off of me, grabbing him by the throat, and lifting him into the air, as he rose from his squat in one fluid motion. The guy dangled and Pru gave him an angry shake. "If you touched him again, I'd kill you."

Dude scratched at his hands, but his fingers only met his own flesh.

Prudence clucked his tongue disapprovingly.

"Close your eyes, Pinkie. Unless you want nightmares."

There was no way in hell I was missing this.

I expected Prudence to…to *something*. To break the guy's neck maybe? A sick sort of fascinated horror filled me as I waited in anticipation. But he didn't. *He didn't have to.* Slowly, seconds ticked by, and the dude's skin grew paler and paler. Prudence began to glow. At first it was a soft, pulsing thing. But it grew stronger, and stronger. Almost like he was sucking the life right out of him. The brighter Prudence glowed, the more color drained from the other man's face.

The guy kicked his legs, feebly trying to get out of his grip, but there was no use. The longer Prudence held on, the weaker the guy became, until his kicks were nothing more than twitches, and I watched, slack-jawed, as his body finally grew still.

Prudence tossed him aside like he weighed nothing at all. Like he *was*, nothing at all.

Nope.

Not a dead body.

Not a whole ass human, now murdered.

No siree.

Just a big ole six-foot-something sack of potatoes.

Prudence squatted down by my head again, this time more solid than before. The earlier glowing was gone as quickly as it'd come. He made an annoyed sound, then gently fingered my curls, probably checking for lumps. I held still. So very still, as he explored my body, testing for bruises and bumps, his movements jerky and uncoordinated.

He was acting just about as overwhelmed as I felt.

His pale eyes were angry, scared.

My heart hurt.

"Guess your 'almost murder' record is now officially, an 'actually murder' record," I joked. Prudence laughed, and the sound was so sudden and sweet it startled me.

"Are you okay?" It was the first time he'd asked me that, and the realization made my head spin. I should be scared of him. I should be terrified. *Murder, duh?* But his killer hands just felt good, and his laugh made my heart race. "Are you okay?" Prudence repeated a second time when I didn't respond, uncharacteristically patient.

For the first time in my life I wasn't even tempted to lie. I'd been asked 'are you okay' thousands of times probably, but never like this. Never with open honesty and care laced into every syllable. Coming from a man like Prudence, this meant something.

I swallowed, my head spinning as I nodded, then immediately regretted it because it made my head hurt even more.

And then something horrible occurred to me.

Panic.

"Prudence—"

"What?" His voice was surprisingly gentle.

"Shit. Fuck. *Shit.* The cards—" I grasped for his hand, tipping my head to look at him even though it hurt like hell. His grip on mine was just as tight, as he stared down at me with a look on his face I'd never seen before. "My phone. They're still at the gas station. Shit-shit-shit." The gas station clerk had seen me. He'd seen my face. He'd probably seen the guy who followed me too and— "He saw me—the guy. The cashier." I squeezed his hand tight enough I was certain I'd pop the bones. "He saw the guy—oh god. He's gonna know that we—we're. Shit. We're fucked. We're so fucked."

"Where?" Prudence was calm as usual, though the wild look in his eyes remained. His broad shoulders leaked sunlight as he waited for my response.

"What?"

"Where at the gas station?"

"By the bathroom." I responded, more than a little dazed.

"Tell me what to do." Prudence's words were soft. Softer than I'd ever heard him speak before. The tone of his voice made a fluffy sort of feeling buzz under my skin as I licked my lips, and tried to wrestle the ringing in my ears back so I could think.

"What?"

"Tell me to cover this up."

I blinked at him, confused. Why would he need me to—?

"Tell me to do what I need to do, baby. No limits."

Baby? Damn. I'd have to unpack that later.

I blinked again, still confused. Buuuut, I trusted him. And as much as I didn't understand this weird ass ritual he had me doing, I wasn't going to argue again. My head hurt too much for that. Prudence would take care of us. He'd promised. "Okay, um." I swallowed. "Prudence. Do what you need to do. No limits."

"Even if it hurts someone?" Prudence clarified, and I stared at him blearily through my lashes, brow furrowed.

"Yes."

He nodded, and the tension in his shoulders grew. "You have to tell me."

This was getting weirder by the second.

"Shit, okay." I blinked rapidly, squeezing my eyes shut when the world began to spin. "Do whatever it takes to cover this up, including hurting people, or whatever."

Prudence's cold lips against my forehead shocked some of the pain from my body. He stroked over my cheekbones, and carded his fingers through my hair one last time before he pulled back and caught my gaze again.

He checked my body over a second time, and I let him, too dazed by the kiss to do anything but lay obediently still.

When he'd decided I was well enough, he rose and headed toward the man's crumpled corpse where it lay abandoned and lifeless on the forest floor.

"Close your eyes, Pinkie." Prudence's voice was a suggestion more than anything. "You don't want to see this."

To hell I didn't.

For the second time that day I ignored his command, gaping in morbid fascination as he sat down directly on the body—no *inside*, the body—then laid down. When the corpse rose up, I nearly threw up the remainder of our feast from the hotel. I forced myself not to though, trembling as the empty body stared back at me with Prudence's blazing blue eyes.

Prudence dusted himself off, picking pine needles from his shirt, and clearing away as much dirt as possible. He scrubbed the blood from his cheek. I watched, slack-jawed, my aching body forgotten for the moment, as I stared at this wondrous, terrifying thing happening before me.

"Car?" he asked, and it took me a second to respond. The voice didn't sound like Prudence. But his eyes—yeah. *Those* were his eyes. Haunted. Pale. Predatory. *Mine.*

"By the bathroom too."

Prudence—corpse dude? Nodded.

To say I was weirded out would be the understatement of the century.

"No. *What kind?*" He clarified.

"I don't know. Red?" I blinked up at him, my heart still racing.

Prudence's head bobbed once to accompany the dry look he gave me, before his eyes narrowed in the direction of the gas station. "You will not leave this spot," he commanded. I simply nodded, not sure what else to say. "I will be back for you soon. Stay still, and stay safe." He glared at me. "Call me if you need me. I'll come."

I'll come.

"Okay."

And then…he walked away.

Maybe he'd been right. Maybe this really *would* give me nightmares. But…as I watched him let a tree branch swing right into his meat puppet's face, because he was a petty bitch that didn't want to spare my attacker damage, even in death, I thought…maybe…maybe not.

I was pretty fucked up.

How the hell were we going to get out of this?

Chapter Twenty-Four

Prudence

BY THE TIME I returned, Luca had made himself at home with his back against a tree trunk, lean thighs slung wide. I chucked the backpack at him without warning, watching him critically to check his reflexes as he caught it with a grunt, and immediately pulled it open.

A fast response time meant the likelihood of a concussion was low.

Still.

I'd keep an eye on him.

"Please tell me you packed me a hat," he muttered under his breath, acting surprisingly normal considering how bruised and swollen his face was, and the fact that he was well aware I'd just returned from disposing of the corpse I'd murdered.

"I packed you a hat." I didn't understand why he needed one, but I'd figured considering the size of his collection, if I hadn't, eventually I'd have to deal with a bitch fest. I was nothing if not a planner.

"Aha!" Luca pulled out the half white, half purple monstrosity, then carded his fingers through his sweaty, dirty hair with a grimace, shoving it out of the way before pulling the cap on. His hands were shaking. I hadn't noticed at first, but I certainly noticed now. "Thank god." He huffed out a laugh, then smiled at me and flashed a double thumbs up. "My hair kept poking my eyes. It was driving me crazy."

I stared at him, at a loss for what to say.

Why was he acting so normal?

Maybe he really did have a concussion after all.

Then again, I was coming to realize Luca was all layers. Maybe on the surface he was calm. Maybe he was smiling. But beneath that—if I peeked into the depths of his stormy gray gaze, I could see the turbulence whirling like a hurricane.

"I was thinking…" Luca continued, ignoring the way I was staring at him. "You know, while you covered up the fact we killed a guy—"

"*I* killed him—"

"Yeah, well. I definitely helped." He laughed, and the sound was just a hair higher than normal. I cocked my head to the side and stared at him. "*Jee*-sus, stop looking at me like that." Luca rose shakily to his feet. He was pretty banged up. I'd cataloged his injuries earlier. Nothing would leave any lasting damage. Scrapes, bruises. Healing would take a few weeks at most. "Anyway, as I was saying before you interrupted me…" Luca glared at me, his long legs wobbling. I took a half step forward, ready to catch him, but he steadied himself, then offered me a friendlier, more genuine smile like he could tell what I'd been about to do before I'd done it. "I was thinking we could hitchhike."

"No."

No.

That was not an option. I clenched my fists, ignoring his protests, as he cocked his head to the side, mirroring me. "What aren't you telling me?"

"He knows."

"Who knows?" Luca blinked in confusion. "Knows what?" He scrunched up his face, as if realizing too late, that his questions made no sense. "Explain."

"The cashier you were worried about."

"*Okaaaaay?*" He waved a hand. "You're making no sense."

"He knows what I am. What *you* are," my jaw clenched. "He's probably already out on the road, waiting for us to show up." We'd be sitting ducks. I kindly did not point out the fact that Luca was surprisingly memorable with his long, muscular legs, pretty grin, and floppy pink hair. His hair would be like a beacon in the dark woods, even with the baseball cap to cover it.

"Okay cool, so maybe he'll help us."

"No."

"You are being confusing and cagey as hell."

"We need to get away from the road." I jerked my head West and Luca huffed out a long, annoyed sigh.

"Not before you tell me what's happening."

There was no point arguing with him when he was like this.

Especially after he'd proven to me over and over again that he might be trustworthy.

So I told him.

I told him how I'd made my way to the gas station. How I'd gathered the stolen cards, and his phone. How I'd stepped inside the convenience store with the intent to frame the corpse for our theft. I explained how I'd waved the full wallet, how I'd made sure the security cameras caught every movement. How I'd paused—beers in hand—only to realize the cashier was not looking at the damn wallet.

No.

He'd been looking at me.

"I was wondering when you'd show up," his lips twisted into a feral little smile. Immediately I stopped thinking about the pink-haired forest creature I'd left battered in the woods. There was a gun behind the desk. I could see it tucked half-hidden beneath a pile of scattered magazines. The man's eyes were wicked, his teeth yellowed.

He smelled of stale smoke and too many days without showering.

None of those things, however, were what caused me alarm.

No.

It was one of the magazines. It lay toppled over, laying open on the dirty tile, its pages brightly illuminated by the flickering lights above. *The Occult News.* The only national newspaper run by the Supernatural Alliance Committee that acted as a second government for all monster sanctuaries. The same exact government that had killed me. The same one that held Lydia prisoner.

Everything hit me all at once.

In a manner of seconds I knew that he knew what I was.

But I played it cool, despite the way I trembled inside my host, ready to abandon the body so I could make sure this new development did not mean that Luca was in danger for a second time that day.

"I'm not sure what you mean," I'd flashed a smile as I picked up the beer bottles, waiting a painfully long time for the guy to ring up my stolen card.

"Your host came by earlier," the cashier continued, the glint in his eyes wicked as he deliberately held the card hostage. Technically, I didn't need it. But…I flicked my gaze toward the security camera to my left. It would be strange—should the footage be reviewed—if someone saw me leave behind one of the cards I'd stolen.

It wouldn't fit the alibi I was creating for Luca.

So, I grit my teeth, and forced my smile to remain even though my heart was pounding and I itched to chase my twink down and stand guard over him. I'd piss a circle around him to mark my territory if it meant keeping him safe from all the assholes that he attracted. If this man knew *what* I was, there was no doubt in my mind that he was a hunter. This close to the supernatural prison, that could not be a good thing.

Calling him a poacher would probably be more accurate.

There were a lot of hunters like that. People that had perverted the law, that chased rare creatures down and sold them at auction like they weren't sentient beings, but cattle for the slaughter. Ghosts were rare enough there was no doubt in my mind he wanted to collect me.

He slid my card back to me with two fingers, deliberately slow.

If he really was a hunter, that meant he'd know there was no use attempting to detain me. Without my host there was nothing he could do. Which was why…I needed to get back to Luca, as quickly and efficiently as possible.

With his shattered phone burning a hole in my back pocket, I took the credit card back, and headed to the door, beers in hand.

We weren't safe here.

There was no doubt in my mind about that.

Luca had been lucky to walk out safely the first time.

The keys were sitting on the front seat of the corpse's car, and I huffed out a laugh as I climbed inside, and headed south, back the way we'd come. It took a while, but eventually I saw a cop parked on the side of the road. With a grin, I chugged the last of the beer, and stepped on the gas.

Siren's blared behind me, red and blue lights flashing weakly in the bright sunlight.

Faster, I went.

Faster and faster.

The road burned beneath the tires as the scent of hot rubber filled my nose.

I gave the cop a good chase before I decided we'd gone far enough, and veered sharply to the left into a ditch. I slipped into the passenger seat just in time for the car to crash with a sickening crunch, a high-pitched whistle filling the air as the corpse's body launched halfway through the windshield.

If he hadn't been dead before, he certainly was now.

The sirens drew closer and I artfully arranged the beer bottles, wallet, and cards on the passenger seat, so they were out in the open.

As I stepped through the warped metal of the crumpled vehicle I admired my handiwork.

Yes.

It was the perfect cover up.

With the evidence I'd laid behind, there would be no question that this man had been the thief that night in the club. That he'd become obsessed with Luca. That he'd followed him here, and when he couldn't find him, took his sins and himself—out of the picture.

Maybe it was far-fetched.

But then again, the most far-fetched part of the story had been true.

I had no sympathy for the discarded body. I made my way back to Luca's abandoned piece of shit car where I'd dropped off his shattered phone. Our backpack lay exactly where it had fallen on the ground beside the vehicle when I'd gone to help him.

I glanced up at the sun, annoyed when I realized how much time had passed. Especially because I'd need to take the long way back to him so that the hunter from the gas station could not follow.

I could get there unseen without my physical form, but that was not an option. Not when I held the only warm clothing we had strapped to my back. Especially, considering how injured Luca had been when I'd left him. It would only get colder, the later it got.

This would be a long day.

"You can say 'I told you so, now.' Your 'death trap' is dead." I offered charitably. They were the first words spoken between us since we'd started walking nearly an hour ago and Luca had gone radio silent. He was slower than normal, there was an awkward stumble to his gait that I wasn't sure was caused by the serpents of his thoughts, or if his ankle had been twisted.

"Time out," Luca declared, before stopping abruptly, his shoulders drawn high and tight.

I stared at him, slack-jawed as he leaned hard against the tree trunk he stood beside, and shoved the heels of his palms into his eyes, an ugly-wretched noise leaving him. He kept his back to me, and I watched his shoulders wobble as panic bubbled up inside me.

Shit.

Crying.

Shit.

I didn't know what to do.

In the past, when he'd cried, it made my dick hard. Sometimes how emotional he was even made me want to laugh, but now…I wasn't amused. Or even turned on, much to my confusion.

"I'll buy you a new car when this is over, you don't need to—"

Luca interrupted me immediately. "I'm not upset about the fucking car, Jesus." His shoulders kept shaking. There was a big rip in the back of his hoodie, and I could see a splash of gorgeous tanned skin between its folds. Freckles. So many freckles. They danced as he trembled.

I didn't understand what was happening.

How could I fix it?

If not the car, then why was he—

I startled when arms wrapped around me, Luca's face smashing into the side of my neck as he squeezed me tight, and his wobbling breath met the sensitive skin at my throat. He was so much taller than me, it should've pissed me off, but…I was running out of things about him to be annoyed by.

Wasn't that a horrifying thought?

"Hug me back, you shithead." Luca's arms trembled around me, and belatedly, I tentatively patted his back. He was warm. So fucking warm.

He was summer days, new discoveries, and second chances.

His shoulder blades trembled as I smoothed my hands down them, salty sweet tears tickling my skin. I swallowed, *hard*. Luca's hair was soft where it brushed against my cheek. So fucking soft. Like him. I'd thought that before, but now…with him clutching me close…my desire to covet him was something I could no longer ignore.

This tall, gangly, muscular madman was mine to look after—until he wasn't.

Wasn't it okay to…to…

Like him?

Even if he was confusing.

Even if he was loud, and happy—and constantly surprising me.

I was scared, I could admit that now. Scared, confused—overwhelmed. Because, even when I'd been alive I'd never had feelings this strong. I'd never met anyone like Luca, and I wasn't sure if that was a good or bad thing. If I'd never met him at all, maybe now I wouldn't be having second thoughts.

Maybe I wouldn't feel…regret when all was said and done.

Maybe I wouldn't be worrying about how he was feeling, or what he was going to do when I was no longer in the picture. Every day was a day closer to freedom. Only freedom didn't feel so free anymore.

Was I truly becoming a slave to this fluffy pink disaster?

Yes.

Luca cried harder, and distressed words stumbled their way from my lips without permission. "I'm doing it wrong."

"No," he laughed, though the sound morphed into a soft little sob. He laced a few butterfly kisses against my cheek, and my belly flipped. I was light. Light enough I worried I'd float away. It was only his arms, and how solid he was in my grip that reminded me that I was corporeal. I'd never felt so full of wings. So tingly. "You're perfect." *You're perfect, you're perfect, you're perfect.* "This is perfect."

No one had ever said that to me before.

Apparently, my stilted attempt at comfort was…enough. I stroked a hand into Luca's hair, my fingers bumping against the rim of his hat as his sobs quieted and he held me there, for a long, long time.

"I don't understand why you're crying," I admitted, hating how wrong-footed I felt. I knew Luca though. I liked to think I understood him well enough, to know my confusion would only be met with patience, rather than frustration. "If it's not the car—"

"I'm just glad."

Well that made no sense. Luca snorted, probably in reaction to the disbelieving noise I'd made. What did he have to be glad about? He was beat to hell and back. We had no car. The money we'd stolen was gone. His stomach was already growling, and when I'd asked him how far we were from his hometown he'd told me it would take at least two days to walk there.

There was nothing to be glad about.

"Glad?"

"I'm glad you're okay."

Oh.

Oh.

Apparently there *was* something to be glad about. My hands clenched into fists, and my cheeks grew hot as I struggled to figure out how to respond. *Was I okay?* I wasn't sure. It'd been sixteen long years since I'd felt okay. But then again…even before Lydia had taken me, had there ever been a moment that I was just…

That I was…

"Your phone is broken." I ignored his words, blurting out the first thing that came to mind.

"Yeah, I figured." Luca chuckled, like it was no big deal. I swallowed the lump in my throat, confused as he squeezed me tight.

It hit me then that I could've lost him today.

This confusing, strange, creature—who waited till we were miles away from the road, safe from danger, to break down because he knew how important it was we find safety first. This man who laughed and cried freely—sometimes at the same time. Who danced in his bedroom, who sang at the top of his lungs, who force-fed unsuspecting civilians fries, watched way too many romantic comedies, and always listened when you needed someone to talk to.

This man who was brave.

And silly.

And stupid.

And surprising.

Innovative, flirtatious, cunning—

And maybe…maybe…

Maybe…*mine*.

Yes.

"The screen is done-zo." I found myself using one of his favorite phrases, just to hear his laugh. And I thought…*I thought*…maybe—for him. Maybe if I stuck beside him, being alive wasn't so awful, after all.

"Definitely," Luca chortled, his tears forgotten already. He shook me hard enough my teeth clacked, happy, despite our dire circumstances. His stomach growled.

I hugged him tighter.

I hugged him tighter.

I hugged him tighter.

Chapter Twenty-Five

Luca

EVERYTHING HURT, BUT my heart was full as I forced Prudence to hold my hand and we continued on our way. Leaves rustled, wild life chittering from hidden shadows, as slashes of sunlight danced through the overhead branches and lit the way. The air was crisp and cool. A little chilly despite it being summer.

After my embarrassing cry-fest we'd made good ground.

I'd camped inside these woods dozens of times in my teens. After I'd gotten my license, any time Mom was working a full weekend, or was out with boyfriend numbers eleven through seventeen, we'd drive through the switchbacks and spend the night under the stars. It always felt like escape. Like the world was bigger out here, with the stars dancing and the thick tree trunks stretching sky high, timeless as a cathedral.

Privately, I'd always wondered how it was possible that the world could be so fucking large…and yet my world…felt so small.

Adam and Betty had always done their best to help me with preparation, though the first time we'd gone camping on our own it'd been a bit painful as we figured out how to make a fire, or set up a tent. We'd been forced to get over our growing pains quickly. By the time Paul had come around, we'd pretty much perfected our survival skills.

And he'd joined us.

For those few, glorious years, back before—back when I hadn't known what it felt like to have the weight of a fortune on my shoulders—we'd spent months memorizing the paths that led through these mountains.

It should've felt relieving to climb the familiar peaks once again.

Instead I just felt…confused.

"Why did the hunter want you?" I asked, stumbling a little, and swearing under my breath as I shook the pins and needles out of my feet, then pushed onward.

Prudence was silent.

I paused, tipping my face toward a wayward patch of sunlight as I waited for him to reply. Sometimes it took him a while. It was patience that won my battles against him.

With an aggrieved sigh, he dropped my hand.

But I reached for it again, latching on, refusing to let him go. His palm scratched against mine, cold and familiar.

"You owe me an explanation, Pru," I said the words, gently, letting the blow fall soft as a pillow fight rather than the challenge it was. I had things I suspected about him. Things that fell into line with what Violet had told me, and my experiences with him thus far, but I was waiting for the right opportunity to voice them.

Baby steps, and all that.

"We're hiking through the woods, in the middle of nowhere because you're being hunted," I reminded him, still gentle. "I deserve to know why."

"Ghosts are rare."

"So you've said." I gave his hand a squeeze, but didn't speak again. Instead I listened to the birds flitting from branch to branch overhead, and tried to ignore the thundering of my heartbeat against my ribs.

I had my own secrets.

But at least we weren't in danger because of mine.

Wasn't like Hunter was going to pop out between the trees with jazz hands, and try to steal my non-existent wallet.

Prudence still wasn't talking, so I threw him a bone. Maybe he wasn't ready yet. We continued walking, and I inhaled the scent of sap and fresh rain with a happy sigh. Yeah. This wasn't so bad, actually.

"I used to come hiking up here all the time with my kid siblings."

Prudence's gaze snapped to mine. He thought he was slick, but there was no hiding the genuine interest sparking in his eyes. I supposed that was fair, I hadn't really talked to him about my family much. I'd been giving him scraps, really.

Whiiiiich I realized was probably the problem.

Shit.

No wonder he wasn't opening up, when I wasn't either.

A catch-22.

My palms were a bit sweaty, and I tried to separate from Prudence's grip, but this time—it was his turn to hold me tight, as he arched a brow, and waited. We were more similar than either of us was ready to admit.

The pit in my stomach was slowly but surely becoming a cavern. I ignored it as I huffed out a little laugh and I lost the battle with my grin.

Later there would be time for secrets.

I needed to build up the courage first.

"I've never hiked all the way home before, but…I know the way." *In theory, anyway.* It'd be really fucking embarrassing if I got us lost. I doubted I would though. I had these woods memorized like the back of my hand.

Walking through them felt like riding a bike.

Something you don't forget, even if sometimes…you maybe want to.

I had good memories here, sure. Laughter. S'mores. Stars. Sunshine. But being here also reminded me what it was like to go hungry, or cold. To lack what others had. To have your needs unmet, despite the sacrifices your mother made every fucking day.

I blew out a ragged breath.

"Where are we heading?" Prudence asked, and I shrugged, squinting as we crested a little hill and the trees parted enough I could see the solitary mountain in front of us. There was only one more peak to cross, then it was all downhill to the valley.

"Eastgrove is in that valley over there." I gestured at it. The two or so days it would take to get there felt like a lifetime away. Normally I'd be quicker, but I felt like I'd been joy-riding a cheese grater. So…

"How old?" Prudence asked, and I was so surprised by his question I didn't think before answering.

"Almost twenty-five, you?"

He stared at me like I was stupid. Probably because that was one of the first things I'd ever told him about me. Oops. "I know. I was asking about your siblings," he deadpanned.

"Right." I snorted out a laugh. "Betty's three years younger than me, so twenty-two. And Adam's three years younger than her." I blinked. "He just graduated."

Prudence nodded, his jaw ticking as he mulled over the new information.

"I don't know how old my sisters are."

Ah. *Wow*. So we were talking about *his* family too. Maybe there was something to be said about this whole, sharing is caring thing.

"You don't know how old they are?"

"I don't pay attention to stuff like that." His nostrils flared, and I snorted as we made our painstaking way back down the hill, the mountains no longer in sight.

I bit back a smile, because obviously he did, in fact, pay attention to 'stuff like that' when it pertained to me.

"Younger or older than you?" I asked, curious.

"Younger."

"Hey! Older brothers for the win!" I held up my free hand for a high-five and Prudence gave me the most unholy stank face I had ever seen in my life. I couldn't help but snort out a laugh as I shook my head and lowered my hand. "So you don't know how old they are…do you at least know their names?" I joked and he glared at me.

"Chastity and Vanity."

"Jee-sus," I whistled. "And I thought Prudence was an unfortunate name." Prudence's lips twisted down, into my favorite—now familiar— smile as he shook his head. "What, is your mom a religious nut or something?"

"Or something. She's a hunter, or was. Lots of religious history in old hunting families. We have a colorful past."

"Yee-sh." I gave his hand a little shake. "No wonder you're a lil' rebel. Religious trauma, and old money? Damn." I gave it another shake, just to watch his poker face rattle as his lips wobbled. "Mr. Tattooed-and-gorgeous." I remembered what he'd said at the diner. That he hated his mother. That she'd been the cause of his rebellion. Maybe I shouldn't have poked fun, but he didn't seem to mind. In fact…it was almost like he was…thawing. "So, what about you? How old are you?"

"I appear in my mid-twenties."

"Okay…" I waited.

"If I was alive, I'd be somewhere in my mid-thirties."

"Hot." I nodded, winking at him, though it took me a second to process the new information. Thirties. Huh. An older man. I could *totally* fuck with that. Not that thirty was old, per say, but it was definitely older than I was.

"Tell me about them."

"My sisters?"

"Sure." I waggled my eyebrows. "Are they as cute as you?" I gave him a once over, just to watch amusement flicker behind his glare.

"They look nothing like me."

"Really?" I arched a brow.

"We're all adopted."

Oh. Interesting.

"C'mon, I need details," I urged playfully. This time I was patient, waiting—as I did my best to ignore how much my feet were aching from hopping over tree roots (Prudence just floated, the bastard.)

"Vanity feels too much, but pretends like she feels nothing. Chastity pretends she feels a lot, when she doesn't. One is tall. One is short. One is blonde. One is rainbow. Both are annoying."

"Interesting."

"They're close in age."

"Huh."

"Closer than I am, to either of them."

"Do you at least know your approximate age gap?" I flashed him another grin. "I have no idea if we're talking about full grown adults, or babies right now." I could guess, based on the fact they were searching for him. Buuuuut, I wanted to hear Prudence talk. And if I kept pushing maybe…maybe we'd get to a place where this actually felt like a full blown conversation, and not me poking a bear with a stick.

"Ten years." Prudence was quiet for a few minutes, and even though it was reallllly fucking difficult I managed to stay patient. So, they were close to my age. "I don't know them well." He frowned, a real one this time, not the smile I'd grown to lo—*like*. "They think they know me, but they don't."

"I see."

"I died when they were too young to remember much about me." Prudence's expression was stoic as he glared out at the trees surrounding us like they were the ones that had offended him, and not his sisters. "When I came back, they put me on a pedestal." *Shit. That sucked.* I knew better than anyone how being put on a pedestal could hurt someone. "I wasn't my own person…" He struggled to find the words he wanted and I waited with baited breath to hear what he'd say next. "I was the big brother they'd lost, and their memories had already twisted their expectations of who I would be. They had a role picked out for me to play. A martyr. A prisoner. A saint. They bent over backward to please me, terrified they were bad people because they hadn't known I was still around, and somehow my torture was their fault—even though it wasn't. They felt so guilty, knowing I'd been trapped, that they were willing to do anything to fix it. "

"Oh." So much was making sense. People who didn't know Prudence, would probably suspect he'd feel relieved by his sisters breaking their backs to cater to him. Buuuut I knew him. "Must've felt like another cage."

Startled by my words, his gaze snapped to mine, eyes wide. An expression almost like wonder crossed his face as he stared at me, lips parted, his breath escaping in a panicked little burst.

"I didn't want them to be nice to me," he said, quietly. "I don't want to make up for 'lost time'." He swallowed. "I don't want to be the brother they missed."

"You just…" His eyes were still on mine, and I was lost in their writhing, tumultuous depths. "You just want to be Prudence." He nodded, the tension between us snapping like a rubber band pulled too taut. "You just want to be a person. To move forward. Instead of shackled by a past you can never escape."

When our lips met his kiss tasted like summer air and heartbreak.

His hand squeezed mine so tight the knuckles nearly popped.

When he pulled back, my lips were swollen, and my head was spinning. Any more of those drugging, delicious kisses and I'd be lost.

"You don't have to be anything when you're with me," I promised him quietly. "You can just be…whatever it is you are." The words were stupid, honestly. They didn't mean much of anything, if you really broke them down.

But Prudence got their meaning because he kissed me again.

He kissed me, and kissed me, and kissed me.

My back met a tree trunk as he shoved me against it, teeth sharp, his hands greedy. He clutched at my body, fingers digging into bruises, his tongue demanding as he cataloged every inch of me with newfound wonder.

His mouth was cold and wet when he took my cock inside it. Every suck had me gasping and whining, my back scraping against the bark as I clutched his dark hair in my hands and fucked his throat, searching for God along his palate.

His fingers dug into my ass, toying with my cleft, tapping against my hole as the backpack he shouldered fell to the forest floor with a quiet *thump*.

By the time I came, I was a babbling, sobbing mess. And when he pulled back, his eyes bright, lips swollen, a grin splitting across his face—I knew.

I knew.

He didn't mind.

Messiness and all.

Prudence liked it.

Chapter Twenty-Six

Prudence

AS WE WALKED, I talked. A lot. I had never, in all my life—and un-life—talked as much as I did for those first few hours in the woods. Maybe it was the warmth of his hand in mine that gave me the courage to open the doors to my past. Or maybe it was the way he looked at me, compassion etched in every facet of his expression. I told Luca about my childhood. I told him about what it was like growing up trapped inside a snow globe of my mother's making. I told him about the galleries, the charities, the galas, the travel that was never for me—but always for her.

I told him about the day my mother had brought my sisters home.

How I knew I should've been furious because she'd told me she needed more children because I wasn't doing enough. Instead all I'd felt was relief.

Relief that someone else could please her for a change.

Relief that I wasn't alone with her anymore.

Relief that every time one of them messed up, stones broke from the chapel erected of her expectations.

I told Luca about Amanda.

I told him about the first time I'd seen her. How she'd welcomed me with a hug, despite having never met me before. How her long dark hair had tickled my nose. How she smelled like cinnamon-sugar. How she fed me cookies, and made me hold her son—like she trusted me. Like she'd taken one look at me and known I was good.

No one had ever done that before.

I told him things I had never told anyone before, and instead of judging me—instead of growing bored or annoyed, he latched on to every word with enthusiasm, his eyes bright, his smile patient.

And when I was done talking, he let me be done.

He squeezed my hand, his palm sweaty, his exhaustion obvious as he huffed out a tired little breath and his stomach growled again.

We kept walking. The daylight was growing weak when Luca spotted a berry bush with a triumphant skip to his step. He bit his tongue in concentration as he picked a dozen or so pieces of fruit, sweat glistening at his temple, his eyes shaded by his ridiculous half-purple baseball cap. "Look!" He held out his handful to me, the red berries gleaming. "Thimbleberries." He popped one into his mouth with a happy moan.

"Aren't those poisonous?" I asked, just to mess with him.

His eyes bulged as he spat the berry out with an indignant squawk. "Shit!" He glared at me in suspicion. "Wait." His eyes were practically slits as he cocked his head to the side, assessing. "How do you know? You're from Maine. These are West Coast berries."

I blinked. A wolfish grin spread across my cheeks and Luca gasped in mock outrage. "I don't."

"Hi-lar-i-ous." He deadpanned as he shoved more berries into his mouth with a head shake. "Thimbleberries are not poisonous, dickhead." Luca glared at me through his ridiculously curly lashes, grabbed another handful, and shook his head in exasperation as we continued on our way.

Five minutes later, when his stomach gurgled again, I caught him muttering under his breath, "I would kill for some betrayal lasagna right about now."

I'd had enough of his growling stomach by the time we accidentally stumbled upon the road again. He needed food.

Luckily, there were no cars in sight. But that didn't stop my nerves from acting up as we ducked inside the tree line again and Luca huffed from the shadows.

His stomach growled, for the millionth time, and I turned to him, only to catch the very real embarrassment on his face.

"Sorry," he said, voice wobbling. "Sex makes me hungry."

That wasn't the only thing making him hungry—the guy could eat enough to feed an entire congregation on a normal day. But…that wasn't his fault. He looked genuinely miserable, and that in turn, made me want to fix whatever was making him upset.

"We'll follow the road until we reach a gas station," I decided, blindly ignoring the fact there probably wasn't one. I wanted to give him something, even if all it was, was hope.

"What about the hunter dude following us?"

I glanced up and down the road, noting the lack of cars.

Maybe he'd given up?

Or we had outrun him. Though, that didn't seem likely, seeing as he probably had a vehicle, and we'd been traveling on foot. I checked the road again. Nothing. For now we were safe but I'd have to stay aware, and should a dire situation arise…

Shit.

I needed to tell Luca about the spell. I couldn't keep forcing him to tell me what to do—I needed to move freely. And for the first time, I trusted someone else to give me that freedom. He didn't want to trap me. I knew that now. Maybe it was disadvantageous of him to celebrate my agency as much as I did, but—he was a kind-hearted fool.

"I'll deal with it if we see him."

Wind whistled and a chill was settling in the air. It wasn't even night yet and Luca needed food. Fire. Something warmer to wear. I was suddenly grateful I'd thought to pack him a second hoodie. *Grlggrlgl.* Luca's whole face burst red as he stared down at his beat-up sneakers, tears in his jeans, blood slowly dripping from the dozens of micro cuts that had whipped his lovely shins. He slapped a hand over his belly in punishment.

I would fix this.

I would.

In a surprising bout of luck it only took twenty minutes to find another gas station. Luca was so relieved, I could practically smell it in the air. He had made a big fuss about peeing in the trees earlier, and despite his reassurances that he liked camping and he'd spent a lot of time in these woods, I couldn't help but think he wasn't cut out for this.

He needed to be pampered, not beaten.

"You remember what to do?" He blinked at me, long lashes fluttering. That same boyish grin was back that had haunted me since our time at the club, and I couldn't help the way I returned the smile.

During the time we'd skirted the edges of the road we'd come up with an elaborate plan. It would work, I was sure of it. Once again—I was surprised by how quickly Luca had dove into the idea, though…how cagey he got when I asked him questions made it clear there was something else behind his easy acceptance of breaking the law.

Funny how just a few weeks ago he'd been biting my head off about robbing an ATM for him.

The two sides of his personality were so opposite they should not have co-existed. And yet…somehow they did. Complementing each other perfectly.

The man who was responsible, and followed all the rules.

Versus

The man who would do anything to survive.

Luca tore his hoodie over his head as I hid our backpack behind a tree for later retrieval. He handed it to me and I tugged the hoodie on with a grunt, annoyed when his shit-eating grin met my gaze the second my head popped out of the neck hole.

"You look tiny," Luca cooed. I pinched his ass, *hard*. He yelped, but didn't comment about my size again.

Tiny, my ass.

My shoulders were practically bursting out of the seams on this thing— even if it did fall nearly to my knees. Wasn't my fault he wore them baggy, and his body was freakishly long.

"Make sure to cover your hands," Luca plucked at the sleeves till they fell over my knuckles. "People are small-minded up here." He grimaced, obviously embarrassed by the fact since he'd grown up in this area. "The amount of tattoos you have doesn't necessarily scream, lost, scared, college student."

"That's judgmental." I poked at him, only to catch him rolling his eyes. I could've gotten rid of the tattoos entirely, but the idea made my skin crawl. My body was an illusion, but it was still mine. These tattoos were the only thing I actually had control over. I could've assumed a new identity too—but...I didn't want to share this with Luca looking like someone else.

I wanted it to be us.

Just us.

"Believe me, I know." He looked ridiculously good in his simple t-shirt. It hugged the swell of his pecs, his nipples hard from the cold where they pushed against the fabric. Damn. I resisted the urge to lean over and suck one into my mouth. "Stop looking at me like that."

"Like what?"

"Like you're going to push me against the nearest tree and fuck me."

God...the images that aroused—I fought the urge to do just that—only stopping when his goddamn stomach growled again.

Food.

Food, then sex.

Luca shivered.

Fine.

Sex could wait until he was warm, and comfortable—I amended quickly. The casual reference he'd made to fucking wasn't lost on me. I'd thought about it—especially lately. Before I'd met Luca I had never hesitated to sate the need to fuck. It was carnal. Natural. It made me feel real.

With him though…nothing we did could be construed as casual. If I slipped inside the tight clutch of his body, I'd never want to leave again. I wasn't sure I was ready to deal with the implication of that. It wasn't his body that made me feel alive, it was him. His laughter. His smile. The twinkle in his mischievous big gray eyes. I'd let him know me—*really*, know me.

If I fucked him there would be no going back.

Funny how something that had never meant anything to me before, meant everything now.

We fell into line, dashing across the road as sunlight glinted off the gas pumps out front. I didn't recognize the name of the gas station, only that it had food, and we needed food. Good.

"You ready to Bonnie and Clyde this shit?" Luca asked out of the corner of his mouth as we approached the front door. I stared at his ass as he shifted nervously from foot to foot, then caught himself doing it and stopped, shoving his hands into his pockets.

"Bonnie and—"

"Fiiiine, Bobbie and Clyde. *There*, happy?"

Luca waited—and I snorted. I couldn't help myself. The laughter escaped before I could catch it.

We were ridiculous.

This was ridiculous.

Absolutely fucking ridiculous.

I'd never had so much fun in my entire fucking life.

"Oh my god, he knows jokes, *and* he knows how to laugh!" Luca cheered, as he reached over to give my shoulder a friendly shake.

"Alright, Bobbie. Let's go." I shoved him toward the entrance, rejoicing when he tripped a little and shot me a glare over his shoulder. His back flexed when he pushed the front door open, the chime above it dinging to alert the store to our presence.

He thought he was real slick.

But I caught the smile he tried to hide when he turned away from me. There was laughter etched in every inch of his gorgeous body, and I couldn't help but rejoice in the fact that I had caused it.

I'd never rejoiced in anything before.

It was weird.

But I liked it.

Everything went according to plan. While Luca flirted to distract the cashier, I stuffed my hoodie with snacks on the way to the bathroom, pretended to use it, then waved my thanks on the way out the front door. I paused though, the door handle caught in my fist as my attention snagged on a cork board covered in pictures to the left of the entrance.

What… *Who* was that?

Luca was still using the bathroom—I was meant to head outside without him to wait, but instead I paused, turning toward the friendly cashier who was still bright pink from my man's attention.

"What is this?" I asked, curious.

"Oh." She flushed even redder, as if she'd only just noticed me. I shouldn't have talked to her to protect our anonymity, but I couldn't help myself, my curiosity burning. "Whenever someone steals, if we get a good pic of them on camera it goes on that board."

There had to be two hundred people up there.

"All of these people stole from you?" I asked, feigning shock.

"Well, not just from this location." She laughed, biting her lip, her lashes fluttering as she checked me out. She was young. Which was good. Less likely to notice the bulge of stolen food beneath my sweatshirt. "We print them out from all over the valley and they sit at the exit, just like that, in every location."

I nodded and shrugged, "Cool."

She flashed me one last little smile, though her attention was immediately stolen by Luca as he pushed his way out of the bathroom and the door hit the wall with a quiet *thump*. His full pecs bounced as he strutted his long legs toward her, tiny waist even tinier without his hoodie on. Fuck. He was delicious. I didn't blame her for staring.

With her head turned, I snatched one of the pictures from the wall quickly, ducking out the front door as I listened to Luca flirt his way toward the exit. The door shut with a quiet *jingle* behind me as the whisper of a breeze danced between the towering tree trunks on either side of the building. It tickled my fringe away from my face, carrying the scent of pine trees, summer, and pollen. I leaned against the wall, double-checking that Luca wasn't behind me yet, before I pulled the little picture out of my pocket and stared.

It was…him.

It was Luca.

I was sure of it.

He had to have been in his early teens. He still had some baby fat on his cheeks despite being a tiny, scrawny thing. His eyes were huge, his signature freckles somehow even more crowded and haphazard splattered across his cheeks. Dark blond hair sat in unruly spikes on his head, and he was wearing a hoodie, hands stuffed into his pockets, his eyes challenging as he stared right up at the camera as if daring it to tell him what he was doing was wrong.

Beside him were two tiny blurry figures. One with pigtails, the other barely more than a snot-nosed toddler.

The chime above the door dinged a third time as I heard Luca's voice again.

"Next time I'm in town you owe me that burger!" He called cheerfully. His flirting didn't make me angry, not when he was only doing it for our benefit. Though, it did make me curious. How young had he been when he'd learned he could get what he wanted by fluttering his lashes and showing off his sexy ass? I didn't like it. I didn't like thinking about the kid in that picture doing what my very adult, very capable companion had just done.

I shoved the stolen photograph into my jean pocket, hidden away from the rest of our goods as Luca spotted me and jumped a half foot in the air.

"*Jee*-sus." He huffed with a laugh. "You spooked me." A rakish grin split across his cheeks when he realized the joke he'd just made.

"C'mon." Luca jerked his head toward the street and I followed him, feeling a little dazed, his picture burning a hole through my pocket.

Who…*was* he?

I was dying to find out more, but I bit my tongue. Now wasn't the time. I'd let him eat first.

And then…well. Then I'd get what I wanted.

Chapter Twenty-Seven

Luca

AFTER GATHERING OUR abandoned backpack and stuffing it full of our bounty, we headed into the woods again. My hoodie still smelled like Prudence, and I surreptitiously tucked my nose into the collar as we walked, soaking him up. Leather. Smoke. Musk.

This time as we traveled we trailed parallel to the road, following the loops and curves of the switchbacks out of sight. Diving between tree trunks, and dodging wayward branches, we chased the last rays of afternoon sunlight.

The sun would set soon.

When we'd gotten far enough away we were sure we couldn't be followed should the cashier discover our deceit, we paused for a few minutes to feed the demon my stomach had become. I was so hungry I could hardly see straight as I pulled out the giant pack of Oreos Prudence had grabbed, and raised an eyebrow at him.

"Typical," I deadpanned, in that exact same way he had when I'd told him my safeword what felt like a million years ago.

Prudence glared at me. "They're high calorie and were easy to grab."

"Uh huh. *That's* why you grabbed them," I nodded slowly. "Not because they're your favorite thing ever or anything." I waved a cookie at him enticingly, but he batted my hand away with an angry huff.

"I don't want any."

"You are a giant fucking liar, Pru-Pru." I waggled the cookie under his nose, ignoring the ache in my legs as I crouched over the backpack. His nostrils flared dangerously. Bear meet stick.

Instead of batting my hand away a second time, Prudence latched on to my wrist. His grip was soft as he pushed my hand back toward me, his blue eyes flickering. "Eat, Luca." He said, in a tone that—if you squinted—might've been considered gentle. "I got the food for you."

"But—"

He shook his head at me, his jaw flickering with tension.

"I don't know the next time I'll be able to get you food." Admitting this only seemed to piss him off, and it struck me suddenly, that it really *really* bothered him. The fact that he couldn't provide for me, or fix the mess we were in. It wasn't his job to take care of me. I'd never asked him to do that—which meant the only logical reason he wanted to was that…

Shit.

Did Prudence…care about me?

"I'll eat them," I hurried to reassure, shell-shocked when I saw the infinitesimal droop of his shoulders, like he'd been prepared to fight me for this. "Okay?" I promised, and he nodded.

"I'm going to check the road."

"Okay, sure." I watched him go, still amazed as he just—fucking yeeted himself through the trees, phasing through them rather than wasting time dodging between. Perks of being a ghost, right?

I sniffed at my collar happily again as I tucked into the packaged goods with reckless abandon. It barely took me five minutes to get through almost the entire pack of Oreos. I stared at the last, lone cookie, my stomach flipping as I licked chocolate crumbs from my lips.

Prudence would've been angry if I left him half the package like I wanted to.

But surely…one was okay?

I tucked the cookie into my pocket for safe keeping and promptly forgot about it as I scarfed down two protein bars in quick succession. The sugar sat like lead in my stomach, so I slowed down, grateful as hell that Prudence had had the forethought to pack us a water bottle.

If there was one thing these hills didn't lack—it was running water. Thank god. Wiggling streams danced nearly every hundred feet between the tree trunks, their water twinkling in the sunlight.

I'd already filled the damn thing up three times.

Which meant tree peeing.

Which I hated.

But I didn't have much of a choice at this point, especially now that we'd robbed the only gas station for no doubt, miles.

When Prudence returned, I'd already packed up the backpack again, and I gave him a little grin as I shouldered it and cocked my head toward the next hill we'd need to climb. Without preamble Prudence snatched the backpack right off my back and slung it over his own.

It was nice to see that he was feeling stronger lately.

His pendant burned where it was tucked safely between my pecs.

"I saw him," Prudence told me, scowling. "We need to get away from the road for the night."

Immediately, fear blossomed beneath my skin as I licked my lips, and the sting of sugar clung to my tongue. I shuddered, glancing back the way he'd come from.

"No fire then?" The lighter in my pocket no longer felt quite so useful.

"You won't survive the night without one."

I wasn't sure that was true, but…already the air was getting more chilly. So I supposed there was some merit to the thought.

"We need to cover as much ground as we can before the sun sets."

The weak afternoon light was growing fainter with every minute that passed. With adrenaline and sugar to fuel me, I ignored the aches and pains in my body as we headed east as far as we could, moving in a straight line so we could find our way back to the road the next day.

For a while we climbed uphill, dodging rocks, and searching for footholds on the unruly mountain. I was sweaty, and exhausted by the time we reached the peak. A long line of boulders marked the top of the hill, and I gasped as I stared out at the open valley below us.

Thousands of trees dotted the landscape, all different, yet cohesive. Splashes of a variety of greens and blues, tall trees, small trees, skinny, wide. Sunbeams shattered the peach-colored clouds that streaked the pastel skyline as I stumbled to a stop and Prudence paused beside me.

"We're far enough," he decided, just as I realized I was about to collapse if I didn't sit down.

"Oh thank god." My muscles ached as I flopped onto one of the boulders, sprawling my legs wide with a quiet laugh. I stared out at the lonely mountain peak ahead with a wry smile. That was it. My mountain. Another day of this—maybe two—and we'd cross over it, down to the valley I'd grown up in. Where my family waited.

For so long I'd avoided them, too overwhelmed with guilt to stomach seeing their smiling faces when I didn't deserve them. But…after my deal with Prudence I no longer dreaded the inevitable meeting. I was excited. With a plan in place to fix my mistakes, there was room for me to miss them.

I rubbed the ache in my chest with a little smile as Prudence sat down next to me, and crossed his arms. There was a bird chirping overhead as it flitted from branch to branch but despite its incessant warbling my attention never wavered from where Prudence sat solid and quiet beside me.

Usually silence bothered me.

It always felt like there was a lack of something, a lack of understanding, a lack of communication, a lack of basic interest.

But when I was with Prudence, silence was just…silence.

He didn't talk a lot, so when he did I found myself cherishing the words. Each one was special, no matter how mean, rude, or utterly pessimistic it was. I'd covet the stories he'd told me earlier, because I knew how precious they truly were.

The boulder we shared scraped against my ass as I adjusted myself. Prudence ignored me. I wiggled again, this time intentionally, in the hopes of annoying him enough he'd pay attention.

"What?" He finally asked, turning to arch one pierced, dark brow my way, his eyes narrowed. Normally, he wouldn't have acknowledged me at all, so it was a testament to how close we were becoming that he did now. He'd told me so much about himself today, I was honestly humbled by it.

I swallowed the lump in my throat.

The bird chirped again.

Prudence scoffed, turning away from me when I didn't answer quickly enough.

"Why do you want to die, Prudence?" I asked softly, surprised by the words as they escaped. I'd been thinking about it a lot lately, but I hadn't intended to actually ask him. Bigmouth strikes again. Now that the question was out though, I couldn't make myself regret bringing it up. My heart was in my throat, my palms sweaty as I waited.

He'd probably ignore the question.

It was invasive after all.

But he surprised me when after only a few minutes of silence he answered, his shoulders tense, his legs spread in the effortlessly dominant way he always presented himself. Like the world was a stage and he had a point to prove to the masses.

Big things sometimes come in small packages.

"It doesn't matter." Prudence's voice was a quiet growl. Clearly he'd thought I'd give up after the dismissal. Buuuut he should've known me better than that by now.

"It matters," I said, nudging his shoulder gently with my own. "To me."

The mountain in the distance was topped with snow, though we'd been lucky enough we hadn't been cursed by it. That was one thing I loved about living in San Diego. I'd left the blizzards and black ice behind. Now though…staring at the snowcapped peaks with Prudence beside me, even bad weather didn't seem quite so daunting.

He didn't speak for a long time.

And then he did.

"Life is a disappointment."

Oh.

My eyes began to burn as his words hit me. They were so honest, so depressingly, *horribly* honest. They sawed my heart in two.

"Pru—"

"*People* are disappointing." Prudence interrupted me. His words were brutal but he didn't move, body still beside mine, our thighs almost brushing. Somehow despite all the sex we'd had, all the laughter, all the secrets, this admission was the most intimate thing he'd ever shared with me. My heart hurt. And for the first time, I really let myself think about him.

Not in the shallow way I'm sure everyone who knew what he'd gone through must have when they found out—even his sisters that we knew were already looking for him.

No.

I thought about who he'd been when his life had gone to shit. The scared boy who had been punished for the murder of the woman he'd sought a mother in. I knew he blamed himself. I knew he'd always regret the day she'd died. The fact he'd seen Lydia pulling gasoline cans out of the back of her car—and hadn't said a word. When he'd found out what had happened, something inside him had no doubt broken. Parts of his heart scattered so far he'd never been able to piece it together again. Never *wanted* to piece it together again.

He'd lived a life worse than hell.

The puppet to a twisted woman, a soldier for her warped agenda.

Of course he thought people were disappointing. They had been. They'd lived up to that expectation over and over and over again. Constantly underperforming. Betrayal hidden behind smiles. Lies spun prettily with the cobwebs of their empty promises.

Prudence's world was a dark place. Full of people that always lived up to his lowest expectations. Full of nothing but validation at every turn, that the darkness he believed hid behind every friendly face was real, always lurking, always waiting for the opportunity to show itself.

"You're quiet," Prudence accused. I was so surprised by his voice I jolted out of my reverie. I could feel his gaze boring a hole into the side of my cheek. "You're breathing too fast." He pointed out, not subtly at all. "Why?"

"Because—" It took me a second to get my thoughts in order and by the time I did, my earlier turmoil had been replaced with a sudden rush of affection for him so strong it made my fingertips tingle. Dappled sunlight peeked through the now lavender clouds, casting shadows on and through Prudence's body, his pale eyes dark with curiosity and trepidation.

I saw that now.

The way he looked at me, always surprised when I didn't disappoint. Always terrified I was about to.

Teetering.

I didn't want to be another reason he lost faith in humanity.

I wanted to be his sunshine.

I wanted to rise for him, a constant reminder that sometimes things could exceed expectations.

I wanted to prove to him that even though there were millions of shitty people out there, some of us were still good. Some of us were kind. Some of us could see past the prickly exteriors of sadistic ghosts, to the haunted men hiding behind barbs and fury. Some of us loved others *for* their faults, and not despite them. Some of us deserved a little faith.

"Still quiet," Prudence reminded me.

I laughed. Maybe it was a bit manic. Maybe not. But I latched on to his shoulder and turned him, forcing him to look at me. Touching him without permission still felt wrong. Like I was breaking an unspoken rule between us. His eyes were glacier pale, the dark fringe of his lashes blending in with the smudges of exhausted bruising beneath his eyes. For someone who claimed he didn't need to sleep, he sure looked tired.

"Prudence…" I took a steadying breath. "Some people are going to disappoint you—" His lips thinned and he started to turn away, clearly fed up with my bullshit, but I caught him, brushing my palm gingerly along the swell of his jaw to keep him steady, our gazes meeting.

His attention felt heavy.

I was sure he could feel my heartbeat in my fingertips where they pressed against his cool skin.

"But some people won't." My pulse quivered as I recalled all the times in my life I'd disappointed myself. Every time I'd ignored a phone call just because I was ashamed of the mistakes I'd made. Ashamed enough I kept making more. I swallowed the lump in my throat, searching his gaze for the steadiness he always exuded.

"They can't disappoint me if my expectations are low enough," Prudence said, and I stroked over the hinge of his jaw before releasing him, my hands trembling from that simple touch alone. Touching him was like touching a rabid animal. Always scared you'd get bit. Though I realized… it had been a long time since he'd done anything to make me wary.

"If your expectations are low, they can always surprise you." I flashed him an optimistic grin and watched the way the ice in his eyes melted. His expression was almost fond, if not a little miffed—like usual—as he looked at me.

Ah.

I'd almost forgot.

I reached into my hoodie pocket, rooting around, biting the tip of my tongue in concentration as I searched for my prize.

"What are you doing?" he asked, clearly annoyed. Confused? Both? It was hard to tell since his face only had one default setting. Chronically pissed off. I ignored him and continued to fight with my pocket till I had what I wanted, my heartbeat wobbling, my eyes warm as I latched on to his hand and pressed my prize into his waiting palm, my own blocking it from his sight.

Where our skin touched fire blazed.

To prove my point, I waited, making sure Prudence was paying attention before I pulled my hand away to reveal the object I'd placed in his grip.

An Oreo.

The last Oreo.

"Tah-dah!" I waggled my fingers in a jazzy little dance, watching the way Prudence stared down at the cookie, flummoxed. I'd never seen him look so adorably confused before. Like he didn't know what to say—or think. Like he didn't know how to react to the simple act of kindness. "I know you said not to, but I saved this for you," I chuckled a little awkwardly, brushing the cookie dust off my hands and grimacing when I noticed how beat up the Oreo had become from riding around in my pocket. It probably had dirt on it too. Which was…not as appetizing as I'd hoped. "It's a bit smooshed though."

Embarrassment tinged my cheeks red and I shuffled awkwardly, biting my lip while I waited anxiously to see what he'd say. Maybe he'd think the gift was as stupid as I was now realizing it was.

He kept staring at the cookie.

For.

A.

Million.

Years.

And then he just…popped it into his mouth. His cheeks puffed up as he chewed and he glared out at the sunset, the exhaustion written across his features slowly bleeding pink and persimmon as sunbeams fell behind the shadowed mountain and lavender clouds turned indigo. And when finally he had finished chewing, I watched enraptured as the corner of one side of his mouth turned up, and the glacier blue of his eyes turned sweet.

"The world is a big place," I promised him, the warmth in his eyes making me lightheaded.

It was then that I realized as Prudence spread his legs just wide enough his thigh brushed mine, his gaze remaining on the tree line—that I was completely totally fucked.

Because I loved him.

I loved him so goddamn much.

And I was the one driving him to his death.

Chapter Twenty-Eight

Luca

THAT NIGHT WAS cold. Almost unbearably so. Even the flickering of the fire we'd built did little to fight off the chill that settled inside my bones. What was the point of summer if it was going to be a cruel, vicious bitch?

I couldn't sleep. Not with rocks digging into my back, cookies sitting heavy in my belly, and my two stacked hoodies too thin to ward off the ever-present chill.

"What are you doing?" Prudence asked, staring at me as I dumped the backpack out onto the ground and began organizing its contents. Everything inside was stained with dirt. My broken phone. The last handful of protein bars Prudence had stolen, our half-full water bottle, my still cum-soaked jeans, fresh boxers—a set of rainbow-colored markers, my sketchbook.

Everything was there.

Wait.

I picked up the pack of markers in confusion. When I glared at Prudence in accusation he just huffed out an annoyed breath, like *I* was the confusing one.

"Why the hell did you pack markers in our very tiny survival backpack?"

Because he was a cagey bitch he just shrugged and crossed his arms, obviously trying to intimidate me into submission—or distract me with his biceps. But no. No. This…*No.* This was not a fight I was going to abandon. I was too hungry for this shit. And this was honestly the most ridiculous thing he'd ever done. There had to be a reason behind it.

"I packed the bag before you told me you weren't making art anymore," Prudence glared at me, waiting for me to retaliate. "I thought you might want it."

What could I say?

Fuck you, for being weirdly thoughtful and packing art supplies since you knew I was an artist?

The fight left me as quickly as it had come and I sighed, fiddling with the plastic packaging thoughtfully. I hadn't created anything new in months. My last attempts had made me want to gouge my eyes out—so I'd given up rather quickly.

Prudence's hope was yellow, yellow, yellow as I bit my lip and squinted at him thoughtfully. His arms flexed where he had them crossed, all those gorgeous tattoos on display. Tentacles trailed up his forearms, other gothic depictions of crows and grim reapers, tombstones and spiderwebs dancing atop his very pale skin. Between each design, however, was an ample amount of blank space. Too much blank space, maybe.

Huh.

"You owe me," I decided, holding a hand out expectantly. I didn't know what exactly he owed me for—but—I figured I could decide that after I got my revenge.

"I don't have any money."

"Jesus, this isn't a robbery." I laughed, shaking my open hand at him. The dirt was cool beneath my ass, but the conversation was distracting enough I nearly forgot how uncomfortable and tired I was. "Give me your hand."

Reluctantly, Prudence placed his hand in mine.

He eyed me warily, like he expected me to attack. Which was hilarious, since between the two of us, he was the violent one. I was the sneaky one, obviously. Very sneaky. Which was why he didn't suspect a thing as I tugged him closer, and his eyes narrowed while I dumped out the package of markers and snagged a red one. I bit the cap between my teeth to pull it off, spat it out, then pressed the marker to his skin.

He sucked in a breath, and I did my best not to grow hard immediately at the sound.

"You're...*something else*," I said honestly, softly. The words were simple on the outside, but the true meaning behind them hung like stars in the air between us as I traced the first fledgling petals of a delicate rose beside one of the tentacles on his ropey forearm.

You're something else meant...

You're perfect.

You're wonderful.

It meant...

You're surprising.

You're better than anyone I've ever met before.

You're confusing in the best way.

Three innocent words, with a love poem hidden between the cracks.

"What are you doing?" Prudence asked, and for the first time, he almost sounded eager.

"Your tattoos looked lonely," I traced another delicate petal, shading in the edges gently, biting the tip of my tongue as I focused. "You brought the markers—so I figured…"

"I don't mind," Prudence was quick to reassure.

Shit, he was cute.

I bit back my smile as I grabbed a green marker and began etching leaves. His skin dragged beneath the pressure of the marker, and there was something weirdly sensual about the sliver of ink that was left behind when I lifted the tip.

We were both a little breathless as I moved on to the next rose.

"So," I said, because our earlier conversations were still weighing on me. I had secrets, sure. But his were more relevant to the current situation, and now that we were settled for the night I could no longer hold on to the knowledge I'd discovered. "You can't say no to me."

"What?" Prudence froze. I felt the way he stiffened up immediately, and I huffed out a soft breath as I gave his hand a gentle squeeze, before I dragged a long winding vine up the inside of his elbow. Gooseflesh tickled in its wake, and I blew on the ink to dry it, my cock twitching as I heard his quiet exhale.

"I figured it out earlier." I gave the sensitive skin on the inside of his elbow another gentle blow, just to watch him shudder. Or maybe that was my words causing the reaction? Either way. It didn't really matter. "When you made me tell you it was okay to…you know. *Hurt people?* To cover up shit with the dude we killed."

"You didn't kill anyone."

This argument was getting old.

Of course, he latched on to the wrong detail. Probably out of a misplaced sense of chivalry. If he thought I was going to freak out now that the day had settled, he was wrong. I'd already told him earlier that I was just as involved in the death as he was—maybe he needed to hear it a third time for my words to really sink in. "If you think I'm going to cry about it, I'm not." I said matter of factly, moving on to the blank spot on his wrist that was just crying for a sunflower to be added. "It was him, or us. We chose us."

When I glanced up to see Prudence's response I was shocked to find him staring at me, pupils blown black with lust, his nostrils flaring. He licked his lips and I shuddered in response, accidentally leaving a squiggle on his arm. "Shit." I tried to scrub it off, but the markers were permanent, so there wasn't much I could do.

Prudence was silent for a few minutes as I traveled up the skin of his arm, trailing leaves and flowers in my wake as I filled in the gaps between his tattoos. I was busy adding a flower crown to the grim reaper on his bicep when he finally spoke.

Clearly, he'd been fighting his own demons in silence.

But he was done.

"Why are you bringing this up, now?" He asked softly, voice a quiet rumble next to my ear. I hadn't realized how close we'd gotten as I climbed up his body, so the tickle of his breath through my hair made me shudder.

"Because we've been through a lot together," I said softly, pulling the marker back so I wouldn't leave a streak like I had before. "I owe you the truth." I'd been thinking about this all day, though they had been background thoughts, swallowed by very real danger and the threat of impending doom. Now—with the stars for company, with the gentle hoot of a friendly owl overhead, and the crackle of the fire beside us— there was nothing stopping me from laying my cards on the table.

The realization that I loved Prudence made my heart flutter and my pulse skip as I licked my lips, finding words to put to the writhing serpents of my thoughts. When I glanced up, I met Prudence's gaze again. The lust was still there, but behind it, deeper—past the turmoil, the desire, and the anger that always stubbornly guarded the surface of his emotions—I saw...hope.

Hope was a dangerous thing to give a man who had never had it before. But...if there was anything I prayed he'd learned about me after all our time together, it was that when it came to emotions, I was a good bet.

"I hope you know," I started, making sure he was paying attention to me as I gave his hand a squeeze and the marker in my grip wobbled. "I would never, ever make you do something you didn't want to." I put every ounce of conviction I had inside those words, my honesty bled like an open wound between us, naked and vulnerable.

His lips thinned, like he didn't know what to say—so I spoke again.

"And if I accidentally put my foot in my mouth and ask that of you? I expect you to tell me." I bit my lip, suddenly insecure. *What if he didn't care about this? What if...what if I was wrong?* My very real fears were valid, but I shoved them away. Because this moment wasn't about me. It was about him. *For* him. He needed to hear this. And even if he could never love me back, even if these last few days we had together were all he had, I wanted him to know, till his dying breath, that he hadn't made a mistake trusting me.

That he was safe with me.

"You don't have to say anything," I murmured, turning back to the masterpiece I was erecting on his bicep. He hadn't moved since I'd begun speaking. Frozen like a statue. He hadn't even breathed. "I just needed you to know that I'm on your side. Just because—for whatever reason—I can control you, doesn't mean I'm going to."

Prudence inhaled raggedly, and when he spoke, I couldn't help but laugh—the marker skidding across his arm again. "You're an idiot."

"Maybe." I agreed, turning the unfortunate squiggle into a new branch. Happy accidents, and all that. Thanks, Bob Ross. "Maybe, I am an idiot. But I'm okay with that." Another flower, another vine. I connected his bicep to the tattoos hidden by his t-shirt. "I'd rather be a kind idiot, than a clever asshole."

Prudence pushed me off of him, discarded his t-shirt, then offered me his arm again. The t-shirt disappeared from view the second he was no longer touching it. Gone. Like it had never been there at all. I would've paid more attention to it, if I hadn't been momentarily blinded by how absolutely gorgeous—and shockingly pale—he was. Skin like moonlight. But I forced myself back into action, continuing my bouquet of flowers up his shoulder to connect to his neck tattoos. His breath stuttered, and I tried not to stare at his tight pink nipples. His pecs danced as I dragged a fat petal across his deltoid, and he released a startled little breath.

Sensitive.

Huh.

Was all of him that sensitive?

I definitely wanted to find that out ASAP. For science. Of course.

Buuuut there were more pressing concerns at hand. Like the whole *ghosts are rare enough a guy is hunting us* thing. Or the *a murderous psychopath is the one who made me* thing. Despite being an idiot, I was pretty sure there was more to that story. "So…" I added another petal to the sunflower I was sketching. "You gonna tell me how…you know…all of 'this' happened?"

I thought I'd have to fight him for answers.

But he surprised me.

"So, I'm a ghost," Prudence started, his voice playfully teasing, a clear reference to the statement I'd made when we'd first started our game of questions. I snorted. "I was framed as an accomplice for murder when I was twenty."

I blinked, paused, then continued drawing. Hopefully my patience would coax more answers out of him.

"I didn't do it, in case you were wondering." Prudence's voice sounded distant. Detached. Like he was relaying information about someone else and not himself. "The woman who did was psychotic. She'd planned it all out, every last bit."

"Lydia?" He'd told me briefly about her earlier. Sadistic bitch. I wasn't sure how I was going to handle seeing her in a few days without wanting to strangle her for what she'd put him through. This though—the origin of all of this—was new to me. As much as I'd wanted to ask earlier, I'd held my tongue patiently for this exact moment. "The woman that made you."

"Yes."

"Who killed you?" I asked, keeping my tone light as I moved on to his knuckles, scrubbing out the letters and tracing over them with a flourish. Prudence shifted uncomfortably for a second, and I almost retracted my question—but like earlier, I figured he probably needed to talk to someone about this more than I needed to hear it.

When I finished with his hand, he immediately gave me the other one. The wind ruffled my hair as I latched on and started the process all over again, trailing letters across his knuckles as I waited patiently for him to speak. "The council—the supernatural government that runs sanctuaries like my hometown—killed me to reset the balance."

"Because they thought you'd done it?"

"Because they thought I'd helped."

It was both baffling and terrifying that there was an entire fucking hidden government for the supernatural that I didn't know about. *What else was out there?* Secret prisons, spooky creatures, supernatural sanctuaries parading as regular towns and governments—I shook away the thoughts with a shudder, waiting for him to speak again.

When he didn't, I asked another question. "How?"

Maybe it was insensitive to ask—but I had no way of knowing that, so I asked anyway. Curiosity was a bitch, but I was bitchier.

"Lethal injection."

"No beheading?"

Prudence snorted in amusement, and immediately my belly filled with butterflies. I liked making him laugh. My marker skittered across his skin a third time, and he jerked a little in my grip, then settled. His breath puffed along the sensitive shell of my ear as I forced my lungs to work again and began adding flowers to his bicep. "No, beheading," he repeated. "My death was humane. As humane as murder can be, anyway."

"I bet they felt real stupid when they realized you were innocent." That was the understatement of the century, but still.

I jumped when the friendly owl hooted again, startling a little laugh from my lips. This was spooky shit. All of it. I couldn't believe how casually we were talking about murder—like it was an everyday occurrence as common as coffee drinking, or riding a bus.

But then again, we'd literally killed someone today, so—

Maybe this conversation wasn't that far-fetched.

I knew I should feel bad, but I didn't.

What I'd said to Prudence earlier was true. It had been him, or us. And there had truly been no choice. It would've always been us. Always.

"I don't care whether or not they felt bad," Prudence grunted. "Dying never really mattered to me." I listened carefully because I got the feeling he was about to admit something incredibly personal, and his voice was so quiet I worried that if I so much as breathed, I'd spook him into silence. "After Amanda was killed, I didn't have much to live for anyway."

I knew he hadn't been close to his family. He'd explained earlier the disassociation he felt when they were near. The way they'd attached themselves to him out of loyalty, even though he felt as though sometimes they were strangers. He loved them, true. In the only way he was capable of loving. But he didn't…*live* for them. He couldn't. I knew that now.

Amanda had meant a lot to him.

She'd taught him to look forward to the future.

The sheer amount of times he'd mentioned her was a testament to that fact. Made me wonder if he'd ever spoken about her to his sisters. If this was the first time he was truly telling someone how much she had impacted his life.

We were both finding something in these woods, and I could only hope the end of our adventure wouldn't eviscerate us.

My heart fluttered.

"She made me feel like people weren't…" Prudence trailed off, but—I waited quietly. The owl hooted again, and a spark from the fire popped next to us. The bright orange flames licked greedily at the dry wood we'd gathered, seeping between the rocks stacked to block in the fire. "Like people weren't—" he tried again, "all horrible." I watched his Adam's apple bob, my hands frozen still. "I was proven wrong." His entire expression shuttered as he glared down at the flames beside us and the muscle in his jaw jumped again.

I forced myself to move to distract him. Halfway done with his second arm, with my body still aching from trauma, and my head spinning, I clutched the pieces of my heart together. I wanted to kill whatever had made him sound like that…so…so *defeated*.

Prudence wasn't allowed to be defeated.

He was supposed to be pissy, angry, and unforgiving.

Not…this.

Whatever this was.

"When Lydia woke me up I thought that I had dreamed the whole thing. Amanda's murder, Lydia's betrayal, my own death. That illusion didn't last long. The first time I fell into the Nothing, I realized it was real. All of it. Trapped in limbo, I was forced to come to terms with everything that had happened. Everything I'd ever known became confused. Lydia molded me into what she wanted. She used me as a tool for devastation." Prudence swallowed again, and when I caught his gaze, his eyes were lost.

"It didn't take long to find out the truth." My heart beat thundered.

"That she'd fabricated all of it to kill her twin sister," he shrugged.

"Wait, what the fuck?" Shit, I hadn't meant to say that out loud. "Sorry, I don't think you mentioned they were twins before. That's even more like...wow. Sorry." I waved a hand at him. "Continue please."

Prudence blinked, his expression carefully blank, like none of this mattered at all—even though we both knew it did. "*She* was the murderer. And like idiots, we'd all fallen right into her trap." The fire cast flickering shapes along his cheeks as my breath left in a startled burst. "Lydia came from a long line of hunters, longer even than my family line. With her hunting background she'd realized early on that she could get revenge against me for attempting to save her sister—and benefit from my death."

The marker skittered inside my grip, but I forced myself to steady, starting another rose on his shoulder, even though my hands were shaking.

"No one goes looking for a dead boy."

Jesus Christ.

No one goes looking for a dead boy.

Those words shook me to my core. I couldn't even imagine what Prudence had lived through—everything he said was honest to god terrifying. How could such cruelty be real?

Suddenly my shady past no longer looked quite so dark.

The stars glimmered above, their beauty a direct contrast to the indigo night surrounding them, and I couldn't help but think that Prudence was like that. Bright. Despite the blackness that had threatened to stifle his light.

The fire crackled and I drew another rose on his skin.

"You said that becoming a ghost was rare, right?" I reminded him gently. Now that he was talking, it was important he didn't stop. I didn't want to make him relive this more than once. I almost didn't want to have the conversation at all—but I needed to know. For both our sakes. "That's why that guy is after you. Because you're…"

"A weapon?" Prudence huffed out a sigh. My grip on the marker was slick with sweat as I finished up another petal. "Yes." He took a fortifying breath. "Originally, the 'creation' spell was made to help the hunters. The war against the supernatural—before sanctuaries like Elmwood were established—was a bloody one. Even humans that were aware of the supernatural didn't stand a chance against their monster counterparts." The fire popped again, and I jumped a little, my breath skittering out in a rush. I inhaled. "They needed to even out the playing field."

My chest was tight. "And?"

"The Companion Spell was created." Prudence's skin somehow felt even colder than before. A ghostly glow began to softly emanate from his skin, as he grew more and more transparent. For a moment, my marker pushed through him—before he reined himself back in, and grew solid enough I could keep drawing.

Upset.

He was upset.

I didn't want to push anymore…he didn't need to—

"Using a complicated ritual, hunters would resurrect their deceased comrades, bringing them back primed and ready, stronger than even the monsters they were fighting."

"How is that possible?" I blinked. "It seems too good to be true."

"In a way, it was—is. In others, it isn't. Creating a ghost is a difficult process. One that is protected with magic. The steps cannot be written down. It's passed through generations of old hunting families, and even those that are aware of it aren't willing to give the sacrifice required, or put in the years of preparation a single summoning takes."

I eyed him warily. "I'm guessing that's not all that goes into it."

"No." Prudence nodded. "You're right." He flashed me a grin that was anything but happy. "Most people aren't willing to hack into the dead body of their loved ones to carve out a talisman."

I jerked away from him, the picture he was painting so gruesome it made my stomach rebel. The cross necklace burned against my skin, as what he'd just admitted hit me hard enough I lost my breath.

I pulled the chain out of my shirt, the white bone cross catching the light of the flickering flames as I cupped it in my palm reverently, then raised my gaze to meet Pru's. His expression was grim.

"You're holding part of my thigh." He pointed out, and instead of dropping the necklace, I just clutched it tighter, suddenly terrified of losing the only real part of his body left.

I had never been more horrified.

Not even when I'd realized I was dirt poor—

When I'd found out I was a has-been.

Or that Hunter had betrayed me.

I couldn't believe that someone could take Prudence's body and—no. No, no, no, *no*. I refused to think about it. I gripped the necklace tight enough my knuckles turned white. *I had to keep it safe.*

"I'm going to throw up," I told him as my stomach lurched. I probably looked stupid, scattered markers around my knees as I sat in the dirt, his necklace clutched protectively to my chest. "So…*Why?*" The only way through this was forward. "I get the weapon thing—I do. But why make ghosts slaves? If the spell was created so people could resurrect their loved ones, why did they make it so you had to follow orders?"

It didn't make sense.

"That's how magic works." Prudence stared at me, his eyes flickering with something…something I couldn't name. "Everything has a price. You cannot bring something back from the dead and expect it to return as the same being it was before. It isn't possible."

"So the price…of your soul, was your freedom?"

"Yes."

"And the hunters…"

"Were clever enough to build a failsafe into the spell. Their companions came back as servants, but through the generosity of their loved ones, they could use commands to give them back their humanity."

Shit.

I thought back on every encounter we'd had since we'd met. Everything I'd done to make Prudence more comfortable—however unknowing at the time. Apparently I had been inadvertently using the spell exactly as it had been intended.

Accidental rule following for the win!

"So with the wrong host…" It hit me all at once. "Without those bits of freedom given back, what happens to you?"

"I get sucked into the void inside the talisman where my soul is trapped."

"Jesus Christ." How many times had he disappeared before I'd told him to stay? How many days had he spent suffering because he was terrified if I knew how to free him, I'd only tighten his shackles.

I scrubbed my hands over my face, catching my breath as I processed what he was saying. "That's why I had to tell you to stay—" I whispered, my voice choked. "Because if you hadn't…you'd…" God. The thought of him trapped in darkness was enough to make me—to make me—No. *No.* Now was not the time to freak out.

This was for Prudence.

Not for me.

I could sit through this, if he had been forced to live it. It was the least I could do. I swallowed the bile down and dropped my hands, shakily picking up my markers again as I reached for his arm. His skin was just as cold, just as solid, as it had been before we'd had this conversation.

"I'm guessing, Lydia didn't want you to feel human again."

"No."

"Shit, Pru. That's fucking horrible." I didn't even know what to say. He'd been stuck with her for over a decade—forced to help her on her twisted quests, like a fucked up soldier. When I glanced at his face, he looked bone-tired, like this conversation was sucking the life out of him.

Prudence shrugged.

"And the 'password' we're getting?" I didn't want him to have to see Lydia at all, but I needed to know the significance of what we were doing, now that he was opening up. "Why was that built into the spell?"

"On the day of the human's death his companion ghost would lie beside him, and he'd say the 'key'. Together, they'd pass on. The way they were meant to in the first place."

Without the key…what would happen to Prudence? Would he just exist forever? Forever hunted by greedy people not willing to perform the illegal ritual themselves? Forced to watch everyone he loved die. Forced to live in a world that was not his own. Alone. In the dark.

No.

No.

Fuck it.

Fuck everything.

"The spell became outlawed when hunters began to abuse it," Prudence continued, unaware of my spinning thoughts. "They wanted slaves, and with the treaties that were being put into place there was no room for error anymore."

I was glad now, more than ever, that I'd decided to help him.

"Tell me how the commands work. Do I have to say them in a particular way?"

"No." Prudence sounded wary, but I kept my voice perfectly light as I finished up the petals on yet another sunflower. "You just need to mean it."

"So if I tell you, right now." I inhaled raggedly. "If I tell you—that I want you to make your own choices. That I want you to interact with anyone, and everything you want to. That I want you to be free from my control—does that…*did that,* fix it?"

My heart was pounding unsteadily as I lifted my gaze to meet his. His pale eyes were flooded with warmth, a tender smile stretched across his lips, so full of wonder I hardly recognized him. Awe was etched in every inch of his expression as he cocked his head to the side and regarded me.

"I don't know," Prudence admitted. "There are rules, even I am not aware of. My knowledge comes from documentation I read from my mother's library in my teens—and Lydia's fucking villain monologues— which were not exactly reliable."

I deflated a little, frowning. "Okay." I bit my lip. "Dammit."

Prudence snorted, using his free hand to ruffle my hair. My cap knocked off and I glared at him, before he leaned over and gave me the sweetest, gentlest, most amazing kiss I had ever been blessed to receive.

"We'll figure this out," I whispered against his lips, just to enjoy the way they twitched.

His breath was cool against my skin as he shook his head and leaned in for another kiss. This one meaner, sharper, harder. His body was a blur of rainbow marker, pastel, and black—an amalgamation of our complementary personalities, as he grabbed my face, and flicked his tongue piercing against the top of my palate. "Whatever you say, Pinkie."

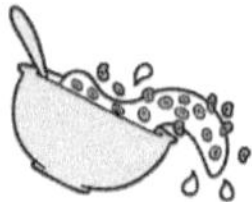

The next day felt like it was a decade long. We walked, and walked, and walked, and walked. All day—till the sun set again, and we were forced to camp a second night. My feet felt like they were more blister than skin at this point, but I didn't complain about them.

We were almost there.

Just a few more hours and we'd hit the town limits—

But we'd had to stop because if I'd taken another step, I was sure I'd collapse.

All day, my unspoken secrets had squeezed like a noose around my neck. After everything Prudence had shared with me it felt cheap to keep him in the dark. But…then again—the struggles I had paled in comparison so starkly they felt silly to bring up now.

I couldn't imagine what he'd gone through.

But somehow—instead of pity, all I felt was amazement.

Because here he was.

Grouchy, strangely earnest, and deliciously violent. He'd been through so much—but his trauma hadn't made him unrecognizable. It gave me courage—that maybe—the sunshine I'd thought had been stolen from me wasn't so far away after all.

Prudence set up camp while I lay weakly in the dirt, my body fatigued, and my stomach gurgling. I'd already eaten the rest of the food we'd stolen, and as much as I wished for more, I wasn't strong enough to rob another gas station, even if we'd found one.

I'd even stopped complaining about peeing in the woods. That's how horrible I was feeling.

"I'm sorry." My voice was so hoarse I hardly recognized it as my own. "We're so close but I—"

Everything hurt.

My face, where it had been smashed. My shins. My feet. My lips were cracked and dry, despite the copious amounts of water I was consuming. I'd kill for some chapstick right about now.

Prudence ignored my apology as he used our pink lighter to get the kindling to catch. I'd had to teach him how to make a fire that first night, (fucking rich kid) but he'd caught on quickly. As the flames burst to life, I sucked in a ragged breath, my eyes fluttering shut. I inhaled the scent of smoke and pine trees.

The ache in my stomach was a familiar pain. It wasn't one I'd experienced since my youth, but the call back to those days, hungry and desperate, made me feel shaky all over. I'd never wanted to feel this way again. But I didn't complain. We were doing the best we could in the situation we'd found ourselves in.

"You know…" I found myself saying, a little out of it as I blinked sleepily at Prudence's solid figure. "It's been a long time since I've been hungry like this." He paused, the flexing of his muscles completely still as he tipped his head toward me. He'd shared a lot with me, and maybe my secrets were smaller than his, but in that moment I just…I wanted him to *know* me. The way I knew him.

"We were so hungry all the time," I admitted quietly. "I could handle it. But Betty and Adam…they were just…so small." Prudence waited patiently, completely silent as I spoke. "I've never told anyone about what we did—" I swallowed, "—what we used to do." My cheeks were hot. "You probably noticed already that stealing shit wasn't exactly unfamiliar. Mom did her best, she really did. She probably would have tried harder too if I hadn't decided to take things into my own hands. I…I was trying to help. I was tired of having less than everyone else. It wasn't fair."

"You did what you had to do to survive," Prudence said, and for some reason his quiet acceptance made my eyes burn.

"The worst part…" My gut churned. "I…" Fuck. I needed to get this out. For years this had weighed on me, tucked so deep I'd never even admitted it to myself. Prudence had shared so much with me, and though that helped motivate me to share this single vulnerable truth, that wasn't the real reason I was doing it.

I trusted him.

"*I liked it*," I admitted in a hushed whisper, the words hanging heavy in the air between us. "I hate that I did—but I can tell that you…"

"I?" Prudence waited, still as a statue.

"You don't mind," I admitted quietly, another truth laid bare. "You don't mind my darkness, in fact…I think you even enjoy it." His eyes were molten hot as he gave me a single almost imperceptible nod. The weight on my shoulders lifted, my breath leaving me in a ragged exhale as I relaxed back into the dirt. "You've seen all my faults," the stars were so bright. So very bright. "But you still like me."

I was ashamed of what I'd done. I knew it was wrong, but that had never stopped me from doing it. My crimes had shaped who I had become as a person, even though I'd tried to ignore this part of me for so long I hoped it would go away entirely.

It never had though.

I'd never thought I'd meet someone who could embrace me. All of me. Light and dark. Equally accepted, like the two sides of my personality made a single, lovable person. I'd never thought I'd let my walls crumple, that I'd welcome someone inside them, that I'd be able to admit who I really was behind the carefully cultivated persona I showed the world.

Maybe it would take me a while to accept myself, the way Prudence did. But the flicker of warmth and admiration I saw hiding in his gaze every time he looked at me—whether I was Good Luca or Bad Luca— was going a long way toward showing me the light. In his eyes, I was simply Luca.

Just Luca.

In the same way he was just Prudence to me.

Memories of my childhood flickered behind my eyelids as my empty stomach whined. Empty cupboards. My Mom's love, and the burden it sometimes was. The hero worship that had glowed in both my sibling's eyes. The way they'd looked up to me. Relied on me. The birth of Bad Luca to begin with.

"I just didn't want to see them cry anymore," I said softly. Now that he knew my darkest secret, the next words came easier. I hadn't known opening up could be this painless. Funny how the prickliest, most closed off person I'd ever met had been the one to teach me how to tell the truth. "I did a lot of things I shouldn't have. I taught them to help me." I swallowed the lump in my throat. "I wasn't a good big brother. That's why I…"

"You…?" Prudence waited.

"That's why it's so important I don't hurt them again." Sleep crept at the corners of my vision as my eyes drooped, and my exhaustion finally caught up to me. I hadn't realized I'd fallen asleep until I startled awake, Prudence's cold hand cupping my cheek. I forced my eyes open even though my lids felt like they weighed a thousand tons. The fire was now raging and warm. "Wha—"

"You're still covered in bruises," Prudence observed, stroking a thumb over the injured skin at my temple. *Thank you, Captain Obvious.*

"I thought you liked me covered in bruises." I was tired, not dead, thank you. I could still sass my ghost not-boyfriend. I flashed him a little smile, even though sleep was pulling at my consciousness already.

"Not like this." His words warmed me from the inside out as I laced a gentle kiss against his palm and let sleep drag me under once again.

Tomorrow.

Tomorrow we'd have food, a bed—and a shower.

Tomorrow.

Tomorrow.

Chapter Twenty-Nine

Luca

"IS IT TRESPASSING if I know the code?" I asked as I leaned heavily against the side of my mom's house, the garage keypad panel open as I blinked blearily at it like it was a viper waiting to strike. Prudence huffed beside me, and I was once again grateful he'd listened to me when I'd insisted I wanted him physically next to me for this.

After we'd passed inside Eastgrove town limits we'd ended up getting picked up by my old English teacher from high school. Which was equal parts hilarious and mortifying. I looked like total shit, and the side-eye she gave me made that clear. She kept squinting at Prudence too, almost suspiciously, like she thought maybe he'd been the cause of my misfortune. He glared right back at her, arms crossed in defiance. The car ride could not end soon enough. She'd asked about a million and a half art-related questions—which only made it obvious my mom was still bragging about me to everyone around town. Too bad my career was dead and I'd never create anything again—

But.

Wait.

I'd stared at Prudence where he sat to my left, attention snapping to the flowers still etched painstakingly across his skin. I *had* created something. I'd done it. I'd broken my art drought, and I hadn't even fucking noticed. He blinked at me, brow furrowed, his lip curling up in annoyance.

"What?" He mouthed, and I shrugged helplessly, and stared at his rainbow arms in awe.

I'd done it.

Motherfucker, I'd fucking done it!

I could art again!

My burst of excitement had died the second I'd stepped out of the car and my legs attempted to buckle from under me. Prudence caught my elbow, huffing in annoyance as we waved goodbye to Mrs. O'Leary and I turned to face my childhood home.

I'd been dreading this. But after everything we'd been through the last few days, that dread had died a slow and painful death. Instead, as I looked up at the familiar yellow siding, and the jolly white trim of my childhood home, I felt relief.

My mom's pink geraniums hung merrily inside baskets hooked haphazardly across the porch, and I couldn't help but smile when I saw them. She was a monster when it came to her plant babies. She'd even bring them indoors during the winter in the hopes that she could coax the blossoms to return the following spring with nothing but whispered promises. She was endlessly hopeful, despite the fact she knew they were technically annual flowers.

I wondered what Prudence thought of it. Of *all* of it. It was no mansion, that was for sure. The paint was chipped. The porch furniture was secondhand. The home had…personality. A lot of it. A pride flag wagged at us from where it hung beside the front door, and I cringed down at the weeds that stubbornly sprouted from the cracks in the sidewalk.

Prudence didn't say anything though.

Nothing.

In fact, he hadn't made a single noise since we'd gotten out of the car. Not even when we'd banged on the front door, only to discover that no one was fucking home. He hadn't complained when he was forced to support me all the way to the garage, where I now stood, stomach gurgling. I was tired of being hungry. I was tired of being tired—so rather than wait, I decided to "fuck it" and jabbed the date of my birthday into the key pad.

The door rose painfully slow, inch by inch, screeching loud enough to wake the dead.

When it was finally open, I huffed out a sigh. Unsurprisingly all the cars were missing.

Food was close.

I could sense it.

I hobbled through the empty garage to the door that led into the kitchen, my stomach complaining with enthusiasm as I grabbed the knob and shoved it open. *Wooooosh.* Crisp, blissfully cold air-conditioning blasted my face as I stepped into the crowded hallway that led to the kitchen. There were piles of dirty shoes scattered along the walls and I couldn't help but sigh in delight as it finally hit me that I was home.

"Oh, AC," I crooned happily, as I attempted to kick off my dirty tennis shoes. "How, I love you." I stumbled into the wall instead, shoes still stubbornly stuck.

Prudence followed behind me, a quiet judging presence at my back.

Maybe all our talking in the woods had eaten up his capacity for speech? And that was why he was so quiet. No matter the reason, I didn't mind. I liked him silent just as much as I liked him talking. *Not as much as I liked him mean though*—I privately contested.

I attempted to kick my shoes off a second time—and failed spectacularly. My legs were too wobbly, my balance shot. Everything hurt, and not in the fun way.

Prudence growled his annoyance and my eyes widened in shock as he dropped deliberately to his knees, and held out a hand expectantly. With my jaw practically on the floor, I answered his unspoken demand, leaning hard against the wall for support as I placed my foot in his waiting palm.

It was weird to see him on his knees for me.

Sure he'd blown me in the woods—God bless tongue piercings—but this was different.

This was almost…caring.

What the hell.

I was touched.

Prudence's fingers were icy cold but soft as they brushed the bare, battered skin peeking beneath the hem of my pants. He gingerly pulled both my shoes off, movements uncharacteristically gentle. Standing there, I was a little dazed by his kindness as I stared down at the cowlick on the top of his head and my heart skipped a beat. When he rose to his feet, all kindness was forgotten as his eyes narrowed challengingly and his nostrils flared. Because apparently—for him—there was a strict niceness limit, he ruined his gentility by promising, "I'll make you pay for that later." I shuddered, a tingle racing through my body like his words had pretty much electrocuted me.

Shit.

And now I was hungry—with a boner.

"Promises, promises." I rolled my eyes.

"That's two."

"I don't know what we're counting, but cool." I stumbled into the kitchen, my socked feet skidding, the cold tile bleeding through the holes in them. My mother's pantry practically sang "Hallelujah" as I pulled it open with a delighted hum, and began hunting.

"That's three."

I tossed a grin over my shoulder at Prudence, only to discover he was right fucking next to me. My heart skipped a beat, and a nervous laugh escaped as he watched every movement I made, a predatory gleam in his eye.

We'd moved into the house after Mom had gotten married, and while it was familiar, it still always floored me how different things were now.

When I'd been a kid we'd never had anything like this. Our cupboards had been mostly bare, and when they had been full, it'd been with expired cans Mom got with a discount at the grocery store she worked part-time at. I'd grown up shoveling cold SpaghettiOs in my mouth, and coveting boxes of off-brand mac and cheese.

This pantry was a testament to how different her life was now. Floor to ceiling options. Name brand.

I dug through the shelves again, wiggling happily when I discovered a bag of my favorite bagels hidden on the top shelf.

Fuck you, Adam. He thought because he was the tallest now, no one would find his hiding spots.

Ha!

Some things never changed.

I shoved a bagel in my mouth because I'd run out of hands—chips, peanut butter, and a gallon of chocolate milk mix tucked into my arms as I turned around only to—to—

Come face to face with my mother.

The bagel dropped, and Prudence's hand zapped out liquid quick to rescue it before it hit the floor.

"Mom! Hey!"

She stared at me.

Her gray eyes were wide, her jaw slack as she flicked her gaze between us. We probably looked…hilarious, thieving her pantry like a couple of bagel burglars. And I…well, I surreptitiously sniffed myself and cringed when I realized how sweaty and dirty I smelled—and looked.

Hopefully the soil would conceal the worst of my bruises.

She shook her head to clear it, her short, shoulder-length blonde hair sticking up haphazardly as Paul stepped through the open door behind her, and immediately froze when he saw us. Their expressions were mirrored, and ridiculous, as he shut the door behind them and waited patiently to see what my mom would do.

"Luca!" Mom said, sounding equal parts delighted and confused. "*Aaand?*" She waited, cocking her head toward Prudence where he stood beside me. I couldn't see his face. He had frozen stiff as a board, and I blinked down at the top of his head with a grimace.

"Prudence—" I hurried to introduce him. Mom blinked expectantly at me, clearly waiting for more information. "My fri—"

"Boyfriend," Prudence interrupted, in his usual quiet growl. Surprisingly, his tone was more polite than he ever spoke to me, the shithead.

And then his words hit.

Boyfriend.

Boyfriend?

What the hell?

I almost wanted to laugh, the ridiculousness of the situation hitting me like a slap to the face. I would have, too, if I hadn't realized—too late—what was about to happen. Oh no. Oh no, no, no. I should've warned him—

Horror was probably written all over my face as Mom's lips split into a wide, wicked grin, her eyes gleaming evilly. "Ah." She nodded, knowingly. "I see."

Standing behind her like a gangly blond beanpole, Paul's eyes were just as wide, his grin just as bright. The shimmer to his gaze meant tears might spill should he smile any bigger. He towered over my mom's figure despite the fact that she was rather tall herself.

Their twin expressions made me simultaneously want to laugh and cry.

His eyes said, *I knew you could do it.*

Mom's said, *It's about time.*

And I was suddenly, viscerally aware of what she was about to say, before she even said it. I should've planned this better—

I should've—

"So thiiiiis is what's been keeping you busy." Mom's smile only grew bigger, her eyes twinkling with mischief. Both my parents were decked out in matching teal tracksuits, their arms laden with grocery bags bursting at the seams. I couldn't help but cringe as it occurred to me, for the first time, that both of them were about to embarrass the hell out of me in front of Prudence. "Why didn't you say so?! Keeping us all in suspense."

Paul nodded along earnestly, sniffling, a single happy tear slipping down his cheek. Oh no. Now Paul was crying. I shouldn't be surprised—the man cried about everything.

The Bears won a game? *Instant tears.*

I got a C on my math test? *Instant tears.*

One of the tomatoes from the grocery store was freakishly tiny and needed a home? *Tears.*

He took a step forward and I was too shocked by my mother's words to stop him as he placed the groceries on the counter, then crossed the distance between us to gently pluck all the food I was carrying out of my arms. He gave my shoulder a single familiar squeeze before he turned toward the counter to begin cooking.

"Wh—" I didn't even know what to say. Before I could protest this new development, I felt a sharp slap hit my ass cheek and a startled squawk left my lips. Prudence glared at me, and my cheek stung as I huffed out a disbelieving breath.

"Don't ignore your mother." Prudence's fingers dug in briefly before he retreated.

I hadn't thought it was possible to be more mortified, but apparently it was.

"Oooooo, he's a keeper," Mom chirped happily, an impish grin on her cheeks. "You see that Paul?"

"Sure did."

"Oh my good god." I could not believe this was happening.

"Sit down," Prudence commanded.

I sat down. My ass burned.

If Mom grinned any wider her smile would fall off her fucking face.

The dining room table had clearly multiplied its cells since I'd been here last, because it was twice as large as it had been at Christmas. Prudence stood guard behind my chair, staring at my mom, his eyes narrowed, like he wasn't sure if she was for real or not.

She was for real, for sure.

My cheeks tingled.

"Take a seat, baby," Mom commanded Prudence, pointing to the chair beside mine. "We don't bite."

Oh my god.

No.

No, no, no, no.

I stared at Prudence in horror, expecting—I don't know what. Something not good. I wasn't sure what his response to being called baby would be. Because he was a contrary creature, he did exactly what I didn't expect. He dropped down into the seat obediently, and politely nodded at my mom, before turning his flickering blue gaze to mine.

My ass still stung from his palm.

My eyes were probably bugging out of my head but I couldn't help it.

Helloooo?

Who the hell was this polite, obedient gentleman?

"You're here early," Mom said, immediately snatching my attention back from Prudence's stoic figure. "I didn't expect you till tomorrow—" She paused, then her eyes widened and narrowed in quick succession as she looked me over.

"Surprise?" I waggled jazz hands at her, my dirty fingers dancing.

Her tennis shoes were brand new.

Lucky.

"What the hell happened to you?" Very real concern flooded her expression as the pleased grin on her face died. The dirt had only distracted her for so long. "Oh, my sweet baby. You look like you took a cheese grater for a ride."

Funny how I'd thought that exact same thing earlier.

I snorted out a laugh, even though my amusement died pretty quickly in light of her concern. Elizabeth Baker, my mother, was a nice lady. Forty-four years young. Tall. Blonde. With a long nose and freckles all over her face. She had so many, when I'd been a kid I'd taken to counting them, in the hopes of competing against her over who had more.

I had 998.

It was not a battle that I had won.

Luckily, we'd rehearsed our last day in the woods for this exact moment. So rather than panic, I just lied. "Car accident." I made sure to inject the right amount of fear and sadness into my tone. "Prudence got lucky. He made sure to get me out of there—" I added that last part, because I wanted my mom to see Prudence as the hero he was. Maybe he hadn't rescued me from a burning car—buuuut he *had* murdered a guy in cold blood to save me.

Everyone needed to know how great he was.

"A car accident?" Mom screeched, her voice so high-pitched I had to force myself not to cover my ears. "Fuckin' hell, kid. Why didn't you call me?"

"My phone was an unfortunate casualty." We'd rehearsed this too. I pulled the battered thing from my pocket and waved it at her as proof.

"Pru is against pretty much all technology—so he doesn't have one. We walked most of the way here." This technically wasn't a lie, either. Prudence had died before cell phones had become a common commodity. Technology—he'd mentioned—was silly, and unnecessary. Privately, I thought he just didn't want to admit he didn't know how to use more than half of it.

I…waited.

Hoping she'd buy it.

My injuries didn't perfectly align with the story—but it was the best and most believable thing we'd been able to come up with on short notice.

The ticking of the clock above the stove marked the passage of time as Paul hauled a pan out of the cupboard and slapped buttered bread onto it. The scent of grilled cheese filled the air and my stomach gurgled, reminding me, despite the excitement, how absolutely starved I was. Glasses clinked as Paul mixed up a twin set of chocolate milk cups, then deposited them in front of Prudence and I on the table.

"Honey—" Mom started, clearly alarmed. Paul made a quiet shushing noise, halting her next round of hysterics.

"Stop harassing, Luca, baby. He needs a first-aid kit, not a shake down." God bless Paul.

"You're right." Mom laughed, though she still looked concerned, and shellshocked. Her expression shifted however as she turned her attention back to Prudence. "Prudence?" She hummed, voice quiet.

He stiffened, and I waited with baited breath to see what would happen next. Had she not believed me after all? Were we fucked? Was she about to ask a shit ton of questions I didn't have answers for?

Prudence was staring at Mom like a deer in headlights. His expression would've been hilarious in any other situation. I so rarely saw him uncertain.

I suddenly felt about a thousand years old.

"Thanks for getting my Luca home safe," Mom said simply, her words earnest and kind.

My jaw dropped as I watched a furious flush burn across Prudence's face in response.

"It was my pleasure."

What the fuck.

What the actual fuck!

He nodded, and smiled.

Smiled!

I reached over and gave his hand a squeeze, and to my surprise, he squeezed back.

Chapter Thirty

Prudence

LUCA'S FAMILY WAS…strange. They smiled at each other often. And every time they did, they meant it. Their laughter was never mean. Never condescending. It was genuine. Affectionate. Conversation flowed easily. His mother was constantly asking him questions, then complimenting him—no matter what he said. No matter how inane, stupid, or obviously a lie. The praise was unending. I had never seen anything like it.

Mom: What's your favorite food nowadays, baby?

Luca: Fruit Loops?

Mom: Well that's just a fine choice. Isn't it, Paul?

Paul: Sure is!

Luca's relationship with his siblings was at least more recognizable, though their easy camaraderie was still unfamiliar as hell. At dinner they picked on each other, but it was all good-natured. Adam—the youngest—was a giant of a kid, all gnarly pointy elbows, and bird-like nose. He was also grumpy as hell, which made me immediately like him. Luca had been so concerned that he'd let his siblings down, but looking at the way they interacted, there was no indication at all that they resented him for his part in their fucked up childhood.

Betty—the sister—was silent for the most part during dinner, though every so often she'd quietly inject vitriol into the conversation, only for everyone to laugh—and move on, like she'd been joking. Even though she clearly hadn't been. She was smaller than both her brothers, petite in both width and height, and she wore ridiculously massive black band t-shirts that drowned her frame, and a studded black choker around her neck. Somehow, despite their differences, she still seemed to fit seamlessly within the family dynamic.

Both siblings had the same dirty-blond hair their mother had. The same exact shade I'd seen hinted in the picture of teenage Luca I coveted.

Throughout all of this I stayed silent as much as I could, only speaking when spoken to, overwhelmed and shocked by how…happy and well-adjusted everyone seemed.

Luca was the black sheep by choice.

In a way, he had a shield up here—with his family. There was a guardedness to him that I had hardly seen before. He became gas station Luca. Club Luca. Thief Luca. Falling easily into the charismatic persona he had created to survive even the most dire of circumstances.

How was it possible that he could have a family as obviously loving and accepting as this, and yet still worry what they would think if he showed his true face?

He looked healthier now that he'd showered and all his cuts and bruises had been properly treated. His exhaustion was still apparent however as he sat at the dining room table and hid behind his grin. At least *that* wasn't fake. Despite his obvious personal issues, he was still happy to be here. Still happy to be surrounded by family, by laughter.

His stolen picture burned a hole in my back pocket, and I wondered, distantly, if his parents would ever know what he'd done. If any of them would ever really know him, at all. His easy acceptance of crime. His double-sided personality. Kindness, and cruelty hand in hand.

Looking around the table, I finally began to understand him. The way he was willing to give up everything to protect this, even himself. I could see why the thought of disappointing them, of hurting these people—was devastating to him. But if they were so important, then…why had he moved so far away?

I couldn't imagine wanting to leave a family like this.

It was like Amanda all over again, even though thinking that felt disloyal.

Over the course of dinner Luca's eyes met mine what felt like a thousand times. I learned something new with every glance. When his attention was on me, my belly filled with butterflies and my breath would stutter to a stop in my chest. Confusing. He was confusing. Overwhelming. Perfect. His fingers brushed my arm when he turned to include me in the conversation, an invitation into his family's inner circle, a secret hidden within his smile each time he caught me looking back.

Without meaning to, I'd begun collecting his smiles.

When he'd told me about his art block and the radio had blared and startled me.

When he'd teased me with his plan to pick-pocket unsuspecting club-goers.

When he'd collapsed onto the hotel mattress, with his eyes full of stars.

Every time he answered my trauma with understanding, his smile gentle.

The ones now, shared with me like we had a secret—which I supposed we did.

I wasn't sure what had come over me earlier when I'd called myself his boyfriend. Maybe it had been the memory of the men at the club. The way they'd eyed him hungrily, and I'd had no claim to him.

No matter the cause, I was glad I'd done it. Because now he didn't have to hold back. He touched me. Constantly. Every brush of his fingers, every tease of his thigh against mine painted a picture of domesticity in my mind that had me so light-headed I nearly floated away. If I'd thought those days spent drifting around his apartment had been sitcom-worthy, this was a fucking Disney movie in comparison.

By the time we headed upstairs for the night I hardly felt like myself.

All the illusions of life that the Companion Spell had given me—the sweat, the heartbeat, the butterflies—felt real.

I'd fallen into an alternate dimension.

A world where people truly were as promising as Luca had sworn they could be.

I couldn't take my eyes off of him. Not when he changed the sheets on his childhood bed. Not when he hopped into the shower for the second time that day. Not when he brushed his teeth, foam spilling down his chin as his eyes crinkled with amusement when he met mine in the mirror's reflection. Not when he led me into the bedroom, locked the door, and began rifling through the overfull closet.

He was wearing Adam's clothes. White t-shirt. Gray shorts.

Which I never would've known, considering the fact they had the exact same sense of style. Which was to say was absolutely none. Water droplets trickled down the back of that long, elegant throat, the bruises from my touch pale yellow and nearly gone.

I hated that the ones I'd left behind were disappearing, and yet the ones from his attack remained. I clenched my hands into fists as I forced back my anger he'd been hurt in the first place. Before, when we'd been surviving in the wild, there hadn't been time to process all of this. In fact, I hadn't known there was anything to process at all.

Apparently now that we were safe, feelings…were appearing left and right.

I'd never felt so much.

It was…

It was…

It was *scary*.

"What are you doing?" I asked, to distract myself. The rest of the house was silent, and the blue-ish silver of moonlight streamed through the open window as a breeze rustled the posters that hung on the wall. Stupid nerdy shit I didn't recognize. Sports. Ugh. The whole room was illuminated by a single sad night-light half hidden by a desk pushed up against the wall.

"Grabbing—Some—" Luca waved me off distractedly, his ass wagging in the air as he hunted through the cluttered closet floor. He crowed in triumph when he found what he'd wanted, popping back up with a happy grin as he tossed the item at me expectantly.

I caught it, then inspected it in confusion.

A paintbrush set.

When I glanced back up he was wiggling through the closet again. Several more minutes of this, and he had a nice pile of art supplies formed in the middle of the spaceship rug on the floor. It was paint-splattered— as paint-splattered as the unfortunate carpet it had done a poor job of protecting.

Luca sat down cross-legged with a happy hum, picking through his bounty with enthusiasm.

He peeled the plastic off of a canvas, then grabbed a jar of gesso and liberally coated the whole damn thing. The scent of acrid paint in the air shocked me to life as I slipped to the floor across from him, the paintbrushes he'd thrown at me still clutched in my grip.

"We're painting," he told me. Didn't ask. No. *Told*.

"I thought you…" I was still feeling wrong-footed from earlier. That was the only reason my words seemed incapable of carrying their usual bite. Luca smiled at me. A *new* smile. One I coveted away with the rest as he chewed on his full pink lip, and his eyes crinkled with affection.

No one had ever looked at me like that before.

"I know I said I couldn't paint," he said softly, reaching over the still drying canvas to grab my hand. "But I was wrong."

Butterflies danced in my belly as his warm fingers wrapped around my own and he gave my hand a gentle squeeze. I was getting addicted to his hand squeezing.

"I'm not ready to paint on my own," Luca admitted, voice still painfully gentle. "But with you?" I couldn't stop staring at his eyes. The genuine fondness within them shattered every bit of my resolve as I nodded. "I want to try."

Luca's thighs flexed, the shorts he'd borrowed riding up to reveal swathes of gorgeous tanned skin dotted with wiry blond hair. The cuts on his shins had been painstakingly re-bandaged before we'd entered his bedroom, and the white bandages practically glowed in the bleeding moonlight.

He shifted and the shorts rode up higher. High enough I caught a glimpse of the strip of pale flesh that marked where the hem of his shorts usually fell. Desire, unlike anything I'd ever felt before, made me lightheaded.

In Elmwood, I'd chased sex, searching for humanity in the bodies I discarded. With Luca, I'd never been able to bring myself to do that. To dehumanize him with my cock. To discard him beside all the no-named faces, and blurry bodies in my past.

Part of me—I was finally ready to admit—had been terrified of him. Terrified of what he made me feel. I'd erected walls between us, rules for myself put into place so I could protect the last bits of my unguarded soul I had left.

I couldn't fuck him without admitting I loved him.

Even though I wasn't even sure I was capable of love. If it was something someone like me could feel. All the complicated emotions I'd avoided for years—all the experiences I'd endured because of my lack of human understanding, had made me feel like half a person. Half a man.

When I was with Luca I wasn't whole.

But for the first time in my life—I was enough.

My half was enough.

I stared at the blur of paint on canvas, enthralled as Luca's gaze traveled a million miles away. The turbulence that swirled in the depths of his eyes burst to the surface, trembling through his body, slashed like killing blows with each stroke of his talented fingers.

It was perfect.

The mix of color, black—blue—pink. Twisting, writhing, curling.

Immaculate.

As one corner dried I slid a finger through it, dragging paint across the canvas, the wet-cold feeling of it clinging to my skin causing me to shudder.

"There you go," Luca purred, clearly pleased. "C'mon Pru." His grin was back, though his eyes remained beautifully distant. Like he saw worlds in his head—galaxies—invisible to the rest of us. God, he was glorious, paint spotted across his high cheekbone, his eyes wild.

Breathless.

I was breathless.

He'd never looked more beautiful than he did in that moment. Free. Totally himself. No walls to hide behind anymore.

"What are you so afraid of?" His words shattered me, spoken so gently— sweetly, like it didn't matter. Like it mattered too much. A contradiction, just like him.

I smeared my entire hand across the canvas, black paint slicking my palm as the angry imperfection made my blood sing.

"Fuck yes," Luca cheered, squirting more paint on the canvas for me to smudge. Which I did. Enthusiastically. There was something therapeutic about ruining something that was so…perfect. About contributing. Like by adding my poison to paper, I was pulling it out of the parts of my soul where it had festered for far too long.

Luca continued to paint, swirling colors through the black I left behind, his laughter breathless, and maybe a little desperate. He grabbed white, and beneath his paintbrush a face began to form. Haunted, shadowed eyes. Wild black hair. His hand moved to another spot on the canvas and beneath it appeared clenched fists, knuckles covered in tattoos and colorful marker.

He was painting me.

All of me.

I pulled black paint with my fingers through the painted fists, tracing over the letters of my tattoos, twisting the words till they formed the only thing that I could think in that moment.

Luca.

Luca, Luca, *Luca*.

"Shit." Luca laughed as I grabbed a bottle of acrylic and a brush for myself—adding black everywhere I touched as I began smudging a messy portrait into an empty corner on the canvas. Freckles. A naughty grin. Chewed up hoodie strings.

With every part of his body I depicted, one of my own appeared on the page.

We painted, splashed, laughed, and splattered colors all over the canvas and the rug—the brutality of our creation leaving a gruesome crime scene in its wake.

I understood now what he'd meant.

That he painted emotions.

Messy and all.

Hope, fear, anticipation, relief—

Smeared in pastel beneath my fingertips as our frantic jerking movements slowed and I glanced up at Luca once again. He was breathing hard, his chest heaving, sweat glistening on his temple. We were both covered in little flecks and smudges of paint, and as he cocked his head, brow furrowed in concentration, a drop of sweat glistening on his upper lip I finally realized I couldn't do this anymore.

I couldn't live one more minute without knowing what it felt like to be inside him.

Without knowing his heat.

Without joining with him, the closest way I knew how.

I wanted to crawl inside him, make a home for myself beside his soul. Intertwine us together till none of me was left—till we were just…us. Conjoined. Messy. Fucked up, and beautiful. Two half-men, made whole when we were together.

"You make me feel alive," the words left my lips shakily. They were the first I'd spoken since we'd started our painting, and Luca's smile…was worth any risk to my sanity as he beamed at me, reaching over with a paint covered finger to stroke over my cheekbone.

"You *are* alive, Prudence," he said gently, as if it was that simple.

And I realized he was right.

I *was* alive.

I was.

For the first time in my un-life I was officially glad I hadn't died. That I'd lived to see this moment. That I'd lived so I could meet him. My past, however dark, the injustices I'd suffered, the lives I'd ruined—all of it had been worth it, because it led to this moment.

I grabbed him by the cheeks, my fingers leaving prints along his skin, marking him more permanently than even my kisses could. When our lips met all the shattered pieces of myself I'd lost snapped back together. My knee skidded across the painting as I pulled him closer, smearing art across the masterpiece of his body.

My Mona Lisa.

My Starry Night.

My Luca.

He pushed me down, groaning happily as we lay side by side, facing each other, on top of the mess we'd made, our kisses frantic—desperate—wet.

His mouth was molten hot, and deliciously pliant as I licked inside it, memorizing every inch of him with my hands as paint stuck to our skin and leaked into our hair. I sucked on his upper lip, then his lower lip, then chased his slick tongue back inside his mouth so I could taste his breathy moan. His chest heaved as I dragged my palm over his round pec, uncaring of the mess it left behind as I toyed with his pebbled nipples and he hiccuped an overwhelmed little sigh.

His skin was hot to the touch when I slipped my hand under the hem of his shirt, tracing the contours of his belly with reverence as he cradled my face in his hands, gently. Somehow, without words, he knew this was different. This was different. It was different. It was—

Scary.

Uncharted territory.

I poured every new, startling feeling into my touch as I shucked our clothes off, till we lay naked and his dick left a hot stripe of precum against my hipbone. His cock was long and lean, freckled, like he was. The sweet pink head peeked at me, precum leaking down his shaft as I took him into my palm. I marveled at the velvety soft feel of his skin, stroking tight, rough, the way I knew he liked it. He sagged against me, separating our lips for long enough to gasp a quiet plea as his hips bucked into my fist and his lips dragged against my cheekbone.

I kissed him again, a promise pressed to his parted mouth.

I want to love you, I poured into that simple touch.

I want to love you, but I don't know how.

I wiped my other hand off on his body till they were free of paint as I reached for the dirty backpack we'd leaned haphazardly against the bed frame to our left. My hands trembled as I hunted for the lube, breath leaving me in surprisingly panicked bursts till I found it. I had never wanted something more than I wanted him.

Luca's pupils were blown wide and dark, his lips parting in a happy smile, swollen and sweet.

He spread his legs, our painting crushed beneath him, somehow still intact, even though the paint was smudged.

I crawled between his thighs, unable to describe how beautiful he was to me in that moment as I lubed up my fingers and stroked them over what was left of his bare skin in a glistening trail, before I reached my target. His muscular ass flexed as I teased the secret skin of his crease.

"Fuuuuck," he groaned, low and throaty, covering his mouth with his forearm to stifle the noise as his hips jumped toward my touch and I slipped the tip of a finger inside him. The moment I felt him sucking around me, I was gone. All my patience left me and I shoved deeper, fingers slick and probing as he welcomed me into his body, my wrist straining to finger him properly. His dusky pink entrance gave beneath my fingers, spreading wide as it clenched and fluttered, tight with promise.

I had to taste him.

I had to.

I moved quickly, rearranging us to my liking. My mouth met my fingers as I pushed deeper, sucking, licking—caressing every inch of his supple hole as I readied him to take me. He spread his legs wider, hooking a paint-stained hand behind his knee to hold himself open for me as he hiccuped his pleasure, his abs jumping.

His long cock glistened with precum, where it jerked above my head, his sexy balls drawn high and tight. I laved a line from his hole to them, giving each a liberal suck that had him sobbing.

I spared a single thought for the family that occupied the rooms down the hall, but quickly forgot all about them as his body clenched hard around my knuckles, tight as a vise, and all my attention was once again commanded by the glorious man I was fucking.

When he was ready, I rose onto my knees to admire my work, my whole body trembling as my cock twitched. I'd managed to ignore it until now, too enthralled with the idea of pleasuring Luca.

There was no denying how badly I wanted this. The idea of sinking inside that tiny little opening was almost enough to end me on its own. He was delicious, spread out for me like a feast, his hole twitching, lips swollen and red from our kisses, thick thighs spread invitingly, his wild pink hair hanging off the canvas. I hoped we would leave the imprint of his ass behind on it. Every time I looked at this painting I wanted to remember this moment.

What it felt like to breed him till I marked him from the inside out.

My cock flexed and I groaned.

He had no idea how fucking perfect he was, my Pinkie.

Desire tugged deep in my belly as I licked my lips, his dazed expression meeting mine. I hoped he saw then, how much I wanted him. How deeply I craved to own him. How he was mine, and only mine. And he would be, till the day he was lowered into his grave, and I rose from hell to greet him.

Unable to wait any longer, I pressed the fat head of my cock against his fluttering entrance, a fresh drop of precum joining the copious amounts of lube as I pushed against him in question. His hole twitched against me and my lip curled as I bit back another groan.

"Please—" Luca gasped, peering at me through his lashes, tear streaks glistening in the moonlight where they slipped down his freckled cheeks. He was so beautiful—so goddamn, fucking perfect.

I wanted to own him, to claim him, to maim him.

I wanted to lose myself inside him and never find the way out again.

His eyes glistened silver as I pushed into his body, sucked in by the heat, overwhelmed by pleasure, as I found heaven within his tight hole. The fat crown of my cock split him wide, the dusky pink of his entrance spreading obscenely to accommodate my girth. Lube glistened, and the sound of my cock, slick as it slipped deeper, made my head spin, and my teeth ache to bite. The contrast between our skin was gorgeous. Moon and sun. Night and day. Complementary colors.

There was no stopping once I'd begun. He clutched at me, pulling my hair, scratching my shoulders as I started up a punishing rhythm, blinded by the hot clutch of his body.

Fuck he was tight.

So fucking tight.

I'd never felt more human than I did in that moment, as I bred his pretty ass with abandon. He whined and sobbed, arching his back to grind against me like he wanted me deeper, deeper, deeper still. His forearm flexed, shapely hand squeezing the back of his thigh tight as he held himself open for me.

My stomach tightened with every ragged breath he took, his pleasure making me foggy with lust. Hot-wet. Snug and slick. The slap, slap of my pelvis meeting his ass made my blood sing. Memories of my time with him spun through my mind and I snatched at them, punctuating each thought with my hips.

Maybe I didn't know how to love him the way he deserved—I hissed through my teeth when he squeezed me tighter—but I was selfish, and I was going to take him anyway.

I remembered every word he'd ever spoken to me like they were branded inside my brain, and I'd use that to my advantage, where emotion often failed. I wanted this to mean something to him. I wanted him to understand what I was saying, even though I wasn't capable of actually speaking the words.

With sudden clarity, I knew exactly what he needed to hear.

My pulse raced.

"I want you to lie back," I commanded, sweat trickling down my nose, and dripping onto him as I framed his shoulders with my arms and pounded his ass as hard as I could. "I want you to take it." He squeezed around me, clenching and unclenching, the vise-like grip of his body making my eyes roll back with pleasure as I panted and growled. "I want to worship you." He whined, a lost, broken sound. When I was with him, I became nothing more than a feral creature, completely whipped. His eyes were glassy as they searched mine. "Just because I like you that much."

Unable to help myself I recalled the game we'd begun to play.

As he squeezed tight around my cock I brought a hand down low, my body trembling as I smacked his ass, hard. His flesh jiggled, and my dick flexed inside him as his cheek squished beneath my fingers.

"That's one," I grunted, punctuating the slap with a roll of my hips.

"Oh fuck," Luca mewled, trembling. My hand tingled where it had met his skin, and I couldn't help but chase the sensation a second time.

"That's two." This time when I pulled my hand back he howled, all shuddery and sweet, his brow knit together. I smacked three against his other cheek, and though the pain had been brief, it wasn't until his ass stung red with my hand prints that he finally seemed to really let go.

Relaxed.

Open.

Eager.

Happy.

Luca stared up at me enraptured, his gaze traveling over my shoulders as they flexed and burned, his brow scrunched up as he dropped his grip behind his knee, and used both hands to trace reverently over the muscles in my torso. Slowly, slowly, inch by inch he worshiped my tattoos. His skin left burning trails in its wake. The flowers he'd drawn on my body blurred in my peripheral vision as I circled my hips and he hissed his pleasure, fingers skittering and pausing—before they started moving again.

Down, down, down they went.

Till they traced the rim of his hole. His groan sounded amazed as my dick bumped against them, the slick sound of it squelching in and out, only made more filthy by the sight of his tan fingers toying with where we were connected.

I reached for his cock, shifting my weight onto one hand, suddenly desperate to lose myself within him, to feel him take every last drop of my pleasure like he was meant to do so. All it took was two twists of my wrist before he came between us, his face scrunching up, his eyes rolling back as his tongue curled inside his lovely open mouth.

I followed after him, snapping my hips, once—twice—as I filled his body with a quiet growl.

I kissed him.

And kissed him.

And kissed him.

He tasted like heaven as I rubbed my tongue against his and made myself at home on top of his body. Luca trembled and twitched within my grasp, overwhelmed and gorgeous, his muscles quaking. He looked glorious. Well-fucked. Well-loved. He was a vision with paint smeared across his skin. Littered with bruises that were a symbol of his strength, not weakness.

He checked the hallway twice before we stumbled into the bathroom to clean ourselves off. Luca's laughter fed my soul as we huddled under the warm water and I sucked bruises into the side of his neck overtop the ones already there.

He was soapy and sweet—giggly, and sex-stupid, as I got on my knees, twisted him toward the wall, and sucked my cum from his puffy pink hole. The musky sweetness of his taste was quickly becoming my favorite flavor. His fingers dug into my hair, pulling tight as I ate him out till he was nothing but a panting, breathy mess.

When we stumbled to bed, we skipped over the mess we'd left on the floor.

Our masterpiece lay abandoned.

And it was the most beautiful thing I'd ever seen, aside from its co-creator.

I stared at it as Luca snuggled into the bed beside me, slinging his long limbs over mine, his nose pressed against my neck. I let him hold me because he wanted to, my head spinning as I realized the implication of what we'd just done.

Things couldn't go on as they had been.

They'd changed.

I didn't care that he had secrets.

The picture I'd stolen of him lay hidden where I'd tucked it safe inside our shared backpack while he showered. The weight of the truths he had given me, proving if nothing else, that he was far more precious than anything I'd ever known.

Maybe our future was uncertain, but one thing wasn't.

I couldn't let him risk his life for me, deal or not. I pressed my lips to his hair, inhaling the sweet scent of him—sex and strawberries—and closed my eyes as I committed to memory every last second of the time we'd spent together.

"Happy birthday," I murmured, just to try it out. Just to see how it would feel—for a second—to be normal.

Luca snuffled, slapping my chest sleepily, his face scrunching up. I cradled the back of his head, shoving him into the crook of my neck as my heart thumped unsteadily.

Two days.

Two days and I'd be dead.

It was what I wanted.

So why was I…?

Why did I feel…?

Sad.

Chapter Thirty-One

Prudence

LUCA CACKLED AS he blew out the candles on his vanilla birthday cake, amused by something I did not know about.

"You bitch!" He laughed, giving his sister a squeeze as she rolled her eyes, a delighted smile on her face despite the fact that her boyfriend hadn't shown up like he'd said he would. The whole family had been walking on eggshells around her all day. Luca shook her happily as his shithead little brother began cutting a slice from the cake, ignoring them both.

"Wait your turn!" Eliza—Not Elizabeth, lord what is that boy teaching you—Baker smacked the spatula out of Adam's hands as she turned to me with a warm smile. "Guests first."

"I thought the birthday boy goes first," Luca complained, just to be contrary.

"One," I said, offhandedly, and he immediately straightened, his cheeks and ears growing splotchy red. His reactions…were more gratifying than any punishment could be.

Luca eyed me warily, brows furrowed in anticipation.

"One what, dear?" Eliza asked, glancing between the two of us.

"It's obviously a weird sex thing, Mom." Betty rolled her eyes, tucking her chin-length hair behind her ear as Luca squawked in embarrassment like the big bird he was. He had no way of disproving his sister's words, so I got to enjoy the way his face turned bright red as he looked at me for help, even though I was the one who had caused the problem in the first place.

"Not at the table," Eliza *tsked* at us both, though her eyes gleamed as she handed the piece of cake she'd rescued from Adam to me.

I stared down at it, not sure what to do.

My family had never done…*this*.

The birthday thing, with a party and—I shuddered—*sprinkles*. Luca wore the most ridiculous party hat I had ever seen in my life, a brand new pair of off-brand tennis shoes decorating his feet. They'd been a gift from his mother. One I fully approved of. The fuchsia tracksuit that had accompanied them on the other hand needed burned.

His dirty, beaten sneakers had disappeared from the hallway sometime before we'd gotten up that morning, and when she'd returned with the brand new box and a package of socks from Costco I'd had to bite back a smile.

That amusement had been short-lived, especially with Luca's birthday cake practically glaring back at me.

Obviously, I knew I was supposed to eat it. But this still felt like a trap. I wasn't sure if there was a specific protocol required for eating your boyfriend's birthday cake. I'd never had a boyfriend before, or gone to a birthday party. Was I supposed to sing? Because, fuck that. I'd rather hump a cactus.

This was the fries all over again—only more treacherous should I mess up. Oddly enough…I cared what his family thought of me. I didn't want to look like the socially incompetent asshole I was. I didn't want to be the guy who had become a social pariah back home. I didn't want them to know how broken I was.

I just wanted to be…

Prudence.

I handed the cake to Luca so he could deal with the mess.

Almost like he could read my mind, his eyes lit up with mirth.

"Prudence is more of an Oreo guy," he explained graciously, as he shoveled a piece of cake into his mouth then moaned his approval, pink head bobbing. "Hey! Thish ish pwebby gewd!" He declared proudly, slapping his younger sister's back so enthusiastically that she pitched forward. When she caught her balance she batted him away from her for the second time that day, eyes narrowed.

Her pointy nose sniffed arrogantly as she shrugged, "Why are you surprised?" She looked at her nails, her oversized punk-emo band t-shirt shifting as she dodged another of Luca's well-meaning, back slaps. Adam snorted judgmentally, and I glanced at him out of the corner of my eye, unable to ignore the amusement that threatened to return.

He looked like Luca. Tall. Gangly but muscular. Though he was a lot thinner than his older brother was. His eyes were a dark gray, nearly black, and he had a suspicious lack of freckles that I decided I didn't like. At all.

No.

Freckles were superior.

This was unbiased fact.

Luca swallowed, the aforementioned freckles on his nose scrunching up as his grin turned wicked, and his eyes sparkled with mischief. "By the way—I lied." His cheeks were pink, his broad shoulders relaxed, a leftover paint smear sticking out of the collar of his shirt. His mother hadn't seen the mess we'd made in his bedroom the night before, and I wasn't sure I wanted to know what she'd say when she did.

"What?" Betty narrowed her eyes at him.

"While I'm a big fan of chocolate—" he began importantly, "when it comes to birthday cake, I actually prefer vanilla." His grin was shit-eating as she gasped in mock outrage and Adam chuckled wickedly beside me.

I didn't understand what they were laughing at.

Eliza smacked both her kids as she passed by them, shaking her head despairingly though no one believed the unspoken reprimand. How could they? When she was as shit at hiding her grin as her children were. Paul chuckled from his spot behind everyone, gathering the half-eaten gallon of rainbow sherbet ice cream from the fridge.

Apparently everyone was in on the joke other than me.

Adam nudged my shoulder, cocking his head toward Luca with a private smile. As Luca continued to mess with his little sister and his parents unsuccessfully tried to hide their amusement Adam ducked down to speak.

"He looks happy," he said quietly, his voice deeper than Luca's by half an octave. I didn't like it. "You're better for him than Hunter was." Adam scowled, his ire mirroring my own as Luca's asshole ex was mentioned for what felt like the millionth time. I wanted to set him on fire. To erase him from memory, like he'd never happened at all. "Luca never smiled this much when he was around."

"Good," I said, honestly.

Adam laughed, and straightened.

Luca's eyes met mine, glancing between the two of us with unguarded fondness.

And I decided, despite the fact he'd mentioned Hunter, Adam was alright.

They were all…alright.

High praise, coming from me.

Luca's eyes twinkled as he raised another forkful of cake to toast me.

When evening rolled around we found ourselves outside, lounging on the front porch, ice cream cones dripping. Luca was still too sore to play so instead we watched his family perform the most painfully horrible game of basketball I'd ever been cursed to witness in their driveway. Luca was surprisingly relaxed, considering the weight he was holding on his shoulders. The secret he still hadn't told me. The promise—of what he'd agreed to do for me tomorrow.

I didn't want him to meet Lydia.

She didn't deserve to look at him.

But most of all…I was struggling with the idea of a world without him in it. There was no evidence to suggest that releasing me from the curse would kill him. But it had never been done before—a host, releasing their ghost while still in the prime of life. It wasn't the way the spell had been intended to be used.

I couldn't imagine a world without his stupid grin.

Sunset painted his floppy hair orange as he spread his ridiculously long legs wide, thigh bleeding heat into mine. Every so often Luca pushed the porch swing forward—a slow swoop, drop—our bodies swinging back and forth as he lapped melted ice cream from his fingers, content. Like clockwork after every deliberate lick, he'd raise his voice to heckle Adam, his eyes twinkling every time he got his little brother to stumble.

"Stop!" Adam yelled angrily, once—just for Paul to swipe the ball right out of his hands.

"Foul!" Adam screeched, but no one listened as Paul dribbled toward the basket, and scored.

Eliza gave him a high-five, their matching tracksuits (fuchsia today) somehow even more horrible in the setting sun than they had been indoors.

Luca's gaze met mine as he chortled. The bruising on his cheek had faded some, but his features were still tainted by another man's touch, and I hated the fact that my marks wouldn't be the last left on him. He leaned over with a playful smile, tongue hot and wet as he sucked melted ice cream from my fingers.

My cock twitched.

I hadn't even noticed my cone had been running.

When he pulled back, he licked his lips, and I tracked the movement, entranced.

"Don't look at me like that," Luca murmured, voice low and sweeter than the ice cream he had stolen. My tongue piercing clicked against my teeth as I grit my jaw. "Unless you're gonna do something about it." He arched a brow. "You look hungry, Prudence." The sun made his lashes glow as he held his ice cream cone up and deliberately pressed the pointed tip of his overly pink tongue into the melted multi-colored treat.

It squished, a quiet parody of the way it had sounded when my dick had pushed inside him. My cock throbbed. "Are you *hungry?*"

I grabbed his cone, deliberately slow, and when he released it, I smashed it right between his big, delicious pecs. His nipples immediately hardened as he snickered out a shocked little laugh.

"You should be banned from ice cream," he snorted, swiping a hand through the mess and moving lightning-quick to smash it against the side of my face in retaliation. "It's almost like you don't know how to eat it." I glared at him, unbothered. Though the glare was maybe, probably, more a smile than a glare.

"That's my shirt, assholes!" Adam called, clearly annoyed. He still didn't know about the other clothes we'd ruined, and I was honestly disappointed I wouldn't get to see his reaction when he discovered it.

Luca's whole family had paused the game to watch us, and weirdly enough, the attention didn't make my skin crawl. Luca's whole face scrunched up as he began adorably laughing his ass off. Eliza's eyes were warm as she regarded her giggling, pink-haired son. Betty's gaze was approving, and Paul and Adam…looked maybe a bit too fond.

When was the last time they'd seen him like this?

Care free.

Just…him. Without his walls up. Without his perfect-son persona to hide behind. Luca snorted on another giggle, and licked the ice cream from his fingers, finally noticing his family was watching us.

"Foul!" He yelled, startling them all into action again. "Carrying the ball."

"You the ref now?" I asked, reaching up to swipe away the smear of ice cream from my skin. Luca shrugged, his gray eyes glittering. "You into that sort of thing?"

I'm into you, I thought, but didn't say. He pulled his shirt up, flashing those tight, tan abs my way as he sucked the ice cream from the fabric.

We sat there till the sun set entirely, and the streetlights turned on to illuminate the ungodly awkward continued game. As the sun disappeared, Luca grew more guarded. Like he sensed, as strongly as I did, that our last day together was coming to a close. Sometimes, I'd catch him stiffening, then relaxing, like he was forcing the anxiety back for as long as he could.

When he looked at me with stars in his eyes, I couldn't help but remember what we'd done the night before. The paint. The feelings. The fact that for the first time in my life I had felt like…enough for someone.

I couldn't ignore the blatant affection in his eyes, or the desire there—the blind loyalty. This was a man who would follow me to the ends of the earth. Who would forgive murder for me. Steal for me. Kill for me. And that thought would inevitably smash the last of the butterflies flitting inside my belly. My heart would shrivel up, cold, and desperate the second I remembered what I'd made him promise to do.

With every star in the sky the weight on his shoulders increased.

I could sense his warring thoughts.

Desperately clinging to our last time together, while dreading what we were about to do.

Since the moment I'd found out I was a ghost, all I'd ever wanted was to actually die. There was nothing to live for when the future felt like a trap. But the time I'd spent with Luca had helped me change my narrative. The words he'd spoken that day on the mountain, his hair lit up like a halo, his eyes full of forever, had haunted me for days because I knew now he was right.

Some people are going to disappoint you. But some people won't.

Life had been a disappointment. People had been even *more* disappointing. But him? No. He'd exceeded every expectation I'd ever had. He was complicated, confusing, frustrating, and…lovely. Every day with him was a surprise. Living didn't feel like a trap when he was by my side. And the mountains I'd once labored climbing just to survive my own existence, now felt like molehills.

Luca said the world was a big place.

Maybe there was room for me in it.

Maybe.

Something had changed inside me.

Something fundamental and frightening.

Emotions weren't any easier, but the prospect of learning them no longer felt quite so overwhelming.

I couldn't fathom a universe without Luca in it.

I wouldn't allow it.

When we retired to his bedroom, late into the night, after hours of playing Monopoly with his playfully argumentative family, I fucked Luca to sleep, slow and easy. His sweet whines lay buried inside the pillows, as I took him from behind, and decorated the back of his neck with hickey shaped promises.

His hole was hot, and wet. His hips arching to take me, eager, slutty—the way he was born to be. The muscles in his back bunched as he sobbed, those pretty tears I loved so goddamn much making my head spin as I watched my cock disappear inside him, enraptured.

The slower I moved, the harder he cried.

And when I was done, when he was a limp, sated, sweaty mess, I curled up around him protectively, and waited.

I waited.

And waited.

And waited.

His quiet snores signified the end to my limbo. With a heavy heart, my emotions jittery, I drifted out of his grip. Immediately, Luca clutched the sheets, hands passing through my body, searching for me as I floated away from the bed, a sick, terrified feeling making my skin grow tight.

I'd been feeling *a lot* these past few days.

Too much, really.

I'd had a lot on my mind.

Decisions to make.

Things I could no longer walk away from.

The Baker's had a home phone in the hallway between the kitchen and the garage. I'd noticed it the first time we'd come inside, when I'd helped Luca pull his abused feet from his even more abused shoes. The rest of the house was silent and peaceful as I made my way downstairs. I stared at the phone receiver for a long…long time, building up the courage to do what I needed to do. Luca's new sneakers lay haphazardly beside me, and I tapped one with the toe of my boot, leeching strength from it as I steeled my resolve.

I would do this.

I would save him from himself.

I would save him from me.

One phone call.

I'd memorized the number long ago.

One phone call and I could save him from the fate he'd agreed to.

I sucked in a breath, reached for the phone, and did the one thing I thought I'd never do.

I asked for help.

Chapter Thirty - Two

Luca

FOR ONE GLORIOUS day, everything was perfect. My family loved me. Prudence was by my side. The world was full of possibility—and then…then, it wasn't. I woke up the morning after my birthday, my heart in my throat. My palms slick with sweat.

Today was *it*.

The last day.

Prudence's last day.

Maybe mine too.

My hands shook as I patted the bed, searching for him, but he was nowhere to be found. My heart pounded an unsteady staccato as I rose sleepily and gathered my clothes for the day. I figured he was probably downstairs antagonizing Adam, or sweet-talking Mom like he had the previous day. So I took my time getting ready, prolonging the inevitable as I brushed my teeth, and scrubbed every inch of my sore body clean.

My ass twinged as I walked down the hallway toward the stairs, and I bit my lip, memories from the previous night making my head spin. The way Prudence had plowed into me. The way he'd gripped my hips, fingers biting into my flesh as he humped my ass, his balls slapping against the sensitive skin of my perineum as he drilled inside me.

I'd drooled into the pillow, holding the headboard tight as he circled his hips, his thick cock splitting me wide, the piercings that lined his dick lighting fireworks inside me every time they brushed along my inner walls.

When he'd finished, he'd pressed apologetic kisses against my hole, held me open, and pushed his cum back inside me with his tongue.

Apparently he liked doing that.

A lot.

Sunrise follows even the darkest night.

I clung to that phrase, desperately.

Everything had been perfect.

I dragged my hands over my face, a wobbly breath escaping as I forced myself not to cry. I didn't want to let him go. I didn't want to say goodbye. But I'd meant what I'd said to him in the woods. I would never take his choices away from him—*never*.

That was why…

That was why I wouldn't cry.

I would suck it up.

I would be a perfect little soldier.

I would take my mom's minivan north to the goddamn spooky prison and give away the other half of my soul. I mentally prepared myself for what I'd need to do, for seeing Lydia, after everything I knew she'd done to Pru.

I'd need to keep my cool.

Getting angry wouldn't get Prudence what he wanted—no, *needed*. After he'd explained to me how important having the key to the spell was, there was no way in hell I was going to fuck this up. I refused to let him become stuck in limbo when Lydia eventually kicked the bucket.

And at the end of the day…when I said it.

When I freed him.

Maybe I'd die—

No one had ever attempted to free a ghost without being on their deathbed themselves. At least—as far as any of us knew.

I should've been afraid, but I wasn't. What I'd told Violet, like a million years ago was still true. I had never been happier than I was with Prudence. All of this—murder, drama, pain—was worth it.

I couldn't believe it was almost over.

There was so much I hadn't told him.

So much I hadn't told my family—

And those secrets weighed me down as I scrubbed the water from my body with a decade old towel, and stumbled my way into another pair of Adam's clothes. The steadily growing pile of outfits I'd ruined lay messily on the carpet in my bedroom, and while I felt guilty, I couldn't bring myself to care too much.

I had a limited capacity for feelings, and all of it was taken up by Prudence today.

I heard voices murmuring down the stairs by the front door as I took a fortifying breath and made my way down to face the music. I expected to see Mom chatting with the mailman, or Paul chittering away to the geraniums out front.

What I didn't expect was to see two perfect strangers standing inside the entryway, flanked by Violet. A tall blonde girl. A short green haired one.

"What…" I stared at them all, frozen halfway down the stairs, as my mom turned her head toward me.

"Luca! You're up!" She beamed. "Chastity and Vanity were just telling me that they're here for their broth—"

No.

No. No. No.

They'd found us.

I leapt down the last of the steps, my heart racing, adrenaline burning like fire in my veins as I sprinted down the hallway and burst into the kitchen.

"Prudence!" My voice was hollow and low enough I hardly recognized it. I searched the room frantically—cupboards, counter, cookie jar—*there he was.* Sitting at the table, forking cake into his mouth, like our entire plan—our entire mission—wasn't about to explode in our faces. "We gotta go." I was breathless and desperate as I latched on to his arm, dragging him bodily toward the garage and the van parked inside. "C'mon—"

He dragged his feet, suddenly weighing a thousand pounds as he pulled away from me, brow furrowed.

"Luca."

"No!" I grabbed him again, ignoring the alarmed looks my siblings and step-dad were exchanging. "No." I pulled, *hard.* "We have to go." I couldn't think. I couldn't see. Everything was ruined—all of it. I couldn't let him down like this. I couldn't do it. Not after what we'd been through.

A deal was a deal.

It wasn't about the money.

It had never been about the fucking money.

Jesus, I'd barely even thought about it since we'd started this.

It had always been him, him, him.

I couldn't leave him trapped here.

I couldn't.

"Luca—" He tried again, but I wouldn't hear it. The ringing in my ears was too loud. I managed to yank the kitchen door open, and pull him down the cold cement steps into the garage. He was letting me drag him, I recognized that. We stopped a few feet from my mom's car, the chill bleeding into my bare feet.

Alarmed voices rang behind us—more than there should be. Which only meant...

"The keys—" I needed the keys.

I needed—

"Baby." Prudence grabbed my face in his frigid, dominant hands, squeezing till I was forced to look at him. Electric blue. Dark lashes. Smudged shadows. Familiar. I gasped, my whole body burning with anxiety as his familiar, steady gaze met mine. "Stop it."

"You don't—" He didn't understand. He didn't know—*why wouldn't the words come out? Why couldn't I—*

"Is he okay?" Violet's voice called from the open doorway.

"Pru—" I couldn't stop shaking, trying to get him to release me so we could get in the car—so we could—right. *Keys.*

Keys, keys, keys—

"Sweetheart." Prudence's cold fingers swept over my cheekbones and distantly I recognized startled voices from the open doorway behind him.

"Did Prudence just call the tall pink dude, sweetheart?"

"Yeah, I think he did." The voices sounded awed, but I didn't even have half a brain cell to spare for our unlucky audience as I tried to get Prudence to understand what was happening. If I slowed down—maybe I could get my words to work. I took a fortifying breath.

"Your sisters are here—"

"I know."

"Your sisters are—" Wait. Wait-wait-wait. "*What?*"

"I know." Prudence's fingers continued to gently stroke my cheeks as his hypnotic gaze kept me captured. I was a moth, trapped willingly in his web. "I know, Pinkie."

"Pinkie!" came a muffled cackle.

I tried to shake my head, to clear it of the panic that was still making my blood sing.

"You…*know?*"

"I called them." He said dryly, though the words—no. The words didn't make sense. Was he sick? What was happening right now?

"*No.*"

"Yes."

"You—" I didn't understand. "I don't understand," I repeated aloud.

"They're here to help," he said simply.

"What?" I blinked. "But I thought—"

"I know," he said gently, thumbs stroking soothingly over my skin as I stared down at him, shocked and confused. "I thought so too."

"But—"

"You don't have to take me anymore," Prudence said carefully, that familiar muscle in his jaw ticking just the way I liked it. "They're here now."

"And…Violet?"

"For you."

"I don't…"

"For when I'm…" Oh. *Oh*. For…for when he was gone. He'd called in his sisters to…to what? Replace me? And Violet was here to pick up the broken pieces left behind when he was gone.

No.

No. No. No.

No-no-no-no.

"I'm taking you," I grabbed his wrists, holding his hands in place as they continued to cup my cheeks. "We had a deal."

"I'm letting you out of the deal," Prudence said carefully. He still was covered in the flowers I'd drawn all over him. His eyes were expressive, honest, stubborn. So full of life. So different from the first time I'd seen him what felt like a lifetime ago.

"No." I shook my head. "*No*, Pru."

"I'll still uphold my end of the deal—"

"I don't give a flying fuck." My grip on his wrists grew tighter. I hated that we had an audience right now. I hated that this was happening at all. *Why couldn't he just stay?* Why couldn't I just—not care about him as much as I did? It would be so much easier to let him go if I didn't love him. If every beat of my heart wasn't tied to his.

His talisman felt like it weighed a thousand pounds where it lay against my now sluggish heartbeat.

"I don't give a flying fuck about the money—"

"What money?" Betty's voice echoed behind us and I ignored it, in favor of glaring Prudence into submission.

"I don't care anymore. About any of it." Maybe he didn't believe me. Maybe he thought I was too weak to do this—too weak to support him. Maybe because I'd lied to my family since we'd arrived, putting on a big fucking fake production as I fixed the mess I'd made behind the scenes— maybe he thought he couldn't trust me.

Maybe he didn't trust me because I'd never told him what actually happened.

Fine.

I'd tell him.

I'd tell them all.

"Are you listening?" I said, watching as his eyes widened in alarm.

"What—" I'd never seen him as freaked out as he looked, when I turned my head toward the collection of people ogling us from the hallway. Chastity, Vanity, Violet, Mom, Paul, Betty, Adam. All smashed together like nosy sardines.

"I lost everything!" I yelled at them. "I lost it all. All my money. Every last cent of it. I'm stupid—naive. I'm an idiotic son-of-a-bitch. Hunter took it. And I'm sorry—I'm so fucking sorry. I'm a horrible son. A horrible brother. I broke all my promises. I lied to you. I avoided the truth. I did anything and everything I could so you would never find out." Collective gasps erupted, and my gaze caught on Violet's—because of course it did. As the only person who'd known the full truth, I needed—I needed something. Reassurance, maybe? Yes.

She smiled.

She nodded.

Her strength pushed me forward.

"Prudence isn't my boyfriend." I was shaking all over. "We made a deal, and he's helping me. He's going to pay for Adam's college courses."

"Dude—" Adam's face was turning green. "I don't—shit. I never asked you to—"

"I don't care anymore. *I can't*—" Not when it meant Prudence thought I was too soft to help him. I glared Adam down, I glared them all down. "You probably won't love me anymore—" My mom gasped. "And now that you know, you probably think that I'm this big stupid, fuck-up—none of it matters. I'll fix it. I'll fix all of it. Maybe I fucked up—maybe I'm a waste of space—" All words I'd told myself while I'd wallowed, but never voiced aloud.

Prudence made a wounded noise.

"But I made a deal." I shook his wrists, then turned back to meet his gaze again. "I'm not weak. I'm not a coward. We're a *pack,* Pru. Bonnie and Clyde. A package-motherfucking-deal. And I'm going to help you, I don't fucking care what it takes. *I. Don't. Care.* I will throw myself in front of a train before I let you do this on your own."

I thought he'd fight me.

The aftermath of my confession left a minefield behind me.

I should've paid attention to the fury on my family's faces—because I was sure that's probably what they were feeling. I should've paid attention to the tears. I should've done a lot of things that I didn't do, because my ghost was here. And he was hurting. And he was giving up on me.

"I won't let you give up on me."

"That isn't what this is," he said softly. It was the softest he'd ever spoken. Reverent. "I was giving you a choice, Luca." His lips thinned and

I released a desperate, brutal sob as I realized what he meant.

I was giving you a choice, like you've always given me.

"I don't want a choice, Prudence." I dropped my head to lace a kiss against his lips. He didn't kiss back. He was too tense. "I don't need one. I already chose you." I kissed him again, and the stiff line of his mouth relaxed fractionally. "And I'll keep choosing you, even if you don't want me to. Even if it hurts. Even if choosing you means losing you."

Prudence dropped his grip on my cheeks, finally.

His arms wrapped around my waist as I laced tear-flavored kisses along his mouth till he relaxed and met me in the middle. The dominating press of his tongue inside my mouth felt like coming home. I choked back a sob as I clutched the back of his shirt and he kissed me till I forgot all about what I'd just done. The truths I'd brutally discarded.

All I knew, when we pulled apart, our breath mingling, was that I'd made the right choice. The spark in his eyes was back.

"Okay," he agreed, turning toward the door—which was now apparently…empty. Our audience had left us, the gift of privacy more meaningful now than it had ever been before. Without their eyes I could truly let myself relax, sagging against Prudence, letting him take my weight—and the weight of my confession into his capable, sturdy arms. He could handle it. "But my sisters are coming with."

"Okay." I agreed easily, refusing to let him go. Relationships were all about compromise, after all.

My stomach gurgled.

He laughed.

Chapter Thirty-Three

Luca

CHASTITY AND VANITY had a staring problem, but other than that they were pretty cool. It was clear they were fascinated by the way Prudence and I squashed together during breakfast. After piling plates high for all three of us, my family had left us alone to get acquainted. I was honestly grateful. I needed a bit more time before I would be ready to confront what I'd admitted in the garage.

I hadn't seen Violet since my confession. Maybe she'd left?—or maybe, like everyone else, she'd taken mercy on me by giving me the distance I needed. Now though, I regretted being left alone. Without a buffer, Chastity and Vanity had nothing better to do than ogle where I clung to Prudence stubbornly. The staring made my skin crawl. I wanted to call the sisters out for it, but forced myself not to. Instead, I focused on

Prudence as he gave the back of my neck a soothing, apologetic squeeze.

"They're annoying," he explained quietly. "Ignore them."

I melted.

This exchange somehow only made the sisters stare at me harder. Like I was a wild unicorn, and they'd never seen anything like me before. It was weird. I didn't like it.

"Knock it off," Prudence growled at the both of them—and like me—they just laughed, apparently not afraid of their older brother despite the fact he could probably bench press both of them at the same time. Oh and also—you know—suck the life out of them with a single touch. No biggie.

Vanity was the quieter of the two. She had an effortless sort of grace to her, like an old-school movie star. Her eyebrows were perfectly manicured, her acrylic nails painted red to match the dipped ends of her bleached blonde ponytail.

Chastity was her shorter, curvier, softer counterpart. She was clearly the most socially adept sibling as she carried the conversation effortlessly, her lime-green hair tucked into little space buns, reptilian looking scales painted with highlighter along her cheeks. Very dragon-esque, and on brand, probably, considering the fact Prudence had once referred to her as a rainbow.

Meeting them should've been more awkward, especially with everything else that was going on. After what I'd confessed to in the garage—how I'd projectile vomited my secrets all over the floor for everyone to judge—it should've been downright uncomfortable.

Aside from the staring, though?

I sensed no judgment from either sister.

Shouldn't they be angry their brother wanted to give me a shit ton of money? Or that he wanted to die? Shouldn't they be mad at me, for being the one who had decided to help him?

After Mom had backed the van out onto the driveway, Chastity headed outside to collect the keys. Vanity followed obediently behind her, her long black fabric-encased legs, eating up the distance quickly as they made their way to the car, and Prudence paused, just outside the open doorway. Mom politely ducked around him, and joined Paul as I caught Pru's gaze, my heart thumping.

We'd opted to use my mom's car as opposed to their rental due to the fact the only thing the sisters had managed to book on such short notice was a compact—and fitting four people inside it for hours? Yeah, no. Leg room was a thing, even if one of us was dead and therefore didn't actually care.

Besides, he wasn't the one with the long-leggy problem, anyway.

Short-stack.

Part of me—the squirrelly anxious bit, privately admitted my vote for Mom's car had less to do with the extra space, and more to do with the fact I wanted something familiar. Comforting. Especially if this was my last goddamn joyride—or…worse—if I rode home with a Prudence-sized hole beside me.

"Coming?" Pru asked, his eyes flickering with challenge as he jolted me from my depressing thoughts. He stood in the open front door, and I longed to go after him. But I didn't.

"One sec."

He nodded, nostrils flaring as he peeked over my shoulder at where my family was waiting patiently. I could've put this off till we came back—*or didn't*. In fact, maybe that was the smart move.

But I was a sunshine McIdiot, so I let him go—and turned around to face the madness.

The glares, anger, and disappointment I had anticipated encountering upon reuniting with my family were noticeably absent.

My little brother was the first to step forward and close the gap between us. I wasn't sure what I expected him to do—to yell at me, maybe? Cry? Instead, Adam hugged me. *Tight*. And when he pulled back, the skin at my neck was damp where his face had pressed. His eyes glistened. "It's okay, Luca." He said simply, blocking the rest of my family from view. I hadn't realized how much I needed to hear those words till he said them.

It's okay, Luca.

It's okay.

I pulled him back into my arms, buried my face in his shirt, and I cried.

For so long I'd agonized over this. Disappointing him—hurting him, was my worst nightmare. The guilt of our broken childhood had choked me for years. His simple acceptance, his love—shattered me.

"I'm fixing it," I promised.

"You don't have to," he returned.

When he pulled away, Mom took his place. She grabbed my shoulder and gave it a little shake, her eyes bright, lips wobbling. "You're not a fuck-up, you know." Her words were gentle. "Lord knows, I've made more than enough bad bets of my own."

I laughed, my heart wobbling.

"You still love me, don't you?" she asked gently, and I nodded—because *duh*. "See?" She ruffled my hair, the same way she had when I was a snot-nosed kid, too prideful to admit I'd gotten soap in my eyes, despite the obvious physical evidence. "We all make mistakes. But we never stop loving each other. That's what family is for. Everyone messes up."

"*I* don't," I said—quickly. I could've left it at that. Let this go. Like it really was as simple as one stupid decision and not that I was a bad bet, myself. But I didn't. Because for the first time in my life I was ready to let her see me. *Really*, see me. My walls came down. "I don't." I bit my lip. "Not when it comes to helping our family. I *can't*. I can't make mistakes. I—I can't. I have to be here. To fill in the gaps. To fix things. I don't get to fuck things up. I protect us. I provide. That's my job."

"Oh, sweetie." Mom cupped my face in her palms. They were dry and warm, just like they always had been. There was no soap in my eyes now, but they still burned. "No one asked you to do that."

"You didn't have to."

"I know." She swallowed, her eyes shining. I hadn't meant to make her cry, but hell. I was tired of lying, of hiding. "I wasn't a good mom to you."

"Yes you were—" I interrupted quickly.

"*No*, I wasn't." She laughed and the sound was wet. "I did my best. You know I did. But you deserved better. Maybe if I'd been a better mom, you would've learned that when things go to shit, other people are there to help. You wouldn't be so hard on yourself. Maybe if I hadn't failed so much myself, it would've left room for you to." She stroked her thumbs over my cheeks and looked at me—really looked at me. I looked back. She was so familiar, and yet so different. The years had been kind to her, but there was still a decade between the face I saw now, and the woman I had done my best to protect and support. "I can't be a totally horrible mom though. Not when somehow, despite everything I put you through, you still ended up perfect."

Against my will, tears slipped down my cheeks and I shook my head. "How can you say that, after what I just told you I did?"

I'd lost so much—

Adam's future.

Everything I'd worked toward.

My legacy, *gone.*

And she still…

She still loved me, faults and all—

I was still perfect in her eyes, even though I wasn't.

Maybe all along, I hadn't had to try so hard. Maybe the only person who'd been expecting perfection had been myself. Maybe my imperfections were what made me perfect. Happy accidents that built the person I had become. It might take me a long time to really believe that, but…I'd have to try.

The smile that broke across my face was so wide it hurt.

"There's my chipper-skipper," she murmured, and for the first time in my life I didn't hate the nickname.

"Did I ever tell you about the time I crashed my dad's car?" Paul piped in, head popping over Mom's. I hadn't even realized he'd gotten that close to us, I'd been so caught up in our conversation. I shook my head, and Mom groaned. "Right into my neighbor's house."

"No." A startled laugh burst out of me.

"Uh-huh." He nodded. Straight-laced, always quiet, always perfect Paul and he'd— "High on shrooms."

"Paul!" Mom's eyes bugged out as she laughed. Maybe she hadn't known— "Don't tell him about that—you'll give him ideas."

She'd definitely known.

"How old were you?" I asked, picturing teenage Paul as Betty's laughter chimed behind him.

"Thirty-five?"

"Oh my god." I had not been expecting that. Paul reached over Mom to give my shoulder a playful slap. He was wearing the same exact baseball cap he'd gifted me for my birthday last year, tickled pink at the thought of us matching.

"I survived *that*," he said deliberately, his smile wide. "And I still talk to my dad every Sunday, and when I visit? The neighbors just laugh." His big palm was warm. I soaked up his attention like a sponge, before I turned to the front door with a grimace.

I couldn't keep putting this off.

It was time to go.

Feeling stronger than I had in months, I headed outside, hopping down the porch steps, pausing at the bottom. The humid summer air tickled my skin. My family followed behind me, trailing along the banister, their eyes kind. They had no idea what was going on, but they could tell it wasn't anything good. I was grateful that no one had asked. That, at least, had been a mercy. I'd had a lot of those today. Violet's familiar black bob peeked out between Adam and Betty's shoulders and my heart began to flutter unsteadily, as I glanced toward the driveway.

Chastity and Vanity waited patiently in the front seat of my mom's minivan, watching us with curiosity. I couldn't see Prudence in the back, but I knew he was there. I could sense him, like his very soul was connected to mine. Which I supposed, in a way, it was. Two sides of the same coin. I swallowed the lump in my throat as Paul's kind eyes caught my attention and he made his way down the steps to close the distance between us. He raised his hand in farewell.

"When you get back from whatever weird ritual you kids are up to—"

he laughed, oblivious to how spot on his statement was. Violet released an ungodly snort somewhere behind him, but he ignored her. "I'll get some burgers on the grill."

"Thanks, Paul."

He nodded, pulled the baseball cap off his head, and slapped it on mine. "Go get him, tiger."

I spared one last glance at my family before I pulled the cap on more firmly, and turned toward the waiting siblings. By the time I traveled those last few steps across the driveway and pulled the sliding door on the van open, I felt like I'd aged a thousand years. I climbed into the back row beside Prudence, staring at the distant figures of my family members still standing sentinel on the porch. They all waved at us. Badly out of sync. And hilarious. Betty flipped me off, and I smiled.

Violet's eyes were knowing, sad.

She raised a shaky hand.

"I'm sorry," she mouthed, her painted black lips tipping up into a mournful little smile. "Love you."

"Love you," I repeated silently, raising my hand to return her wave, even though she couldn't see me.

Despite all the hurt between us, I knew when I came back, she'd be waiting. She'd pick up my broken pieces just like she had before. She'd crawl into my bed beside me, and fill up the cupboard with my favorite cereal. She'd put on an episode of *Supernatural* with a lot of ass shots, and she'd let me cry my heart out.

Because that's what best friends were for.

Chastity was so short her head was blocked by the back of her seat as she put the car in reverse, and peeled out of the driveway. Vanity hissed out a breath, clutching her seatbelt tight. "Jesus. Drive much?" She laughed and Chastity very pointedly, very slowly, flipped her off.

The second we were on the road, Prudence's cold hand squeezed the back of my neck for the second time that day, and I turned to look at him. His eyes were a fathomless electric blue, a kaleidoscope of feeling twisting inside them as we stared at each other for a long, long time.

It was hard.

All of this was.

But hardest of all was resisting the urge to climb on top of him and taste him the way I would've if his sisters had not been three feet away.

There were crumbs all over the backseat. Probably half a decade old, if I was being honest. This car had been the first thing I'd bought after I'd sold my first painting. Funny how, after all these years, it still looked the same. The gray seats were stained brown in some spots. The air smelled like stale summer and my mom's favorite Mexican restaurant. Empty McDonald's drink cups lay beaten and discarded beneath our feet as my lips began to wobble.

"Don't cry," Prudence said.

My laugh was shaky. "Pru—"

His thumb scraped over my cheek, tracing the trail of a rebellious tear as it escaped.

"Are you sure you want to be here for this? I'll make them take you back."

"I'm not going anywhere." I cupped the back of his hand, forcing him to keep it pressed against my cheek as I lost myself in his eyes again. The turbulence that had always hidden deep inside them had fought its way to the surface.

He kissed me, and for a moment, I forgot what we were about to do.

What *he* was about to do.

He kissed me, and I was whole.

The drive to the prison upstate was mostly uneventful. To pass the time, I made small talk with Prudence's sisters, though even that felt like it took far too much energy. Everything inside me screamed at me to beg Prudence to stay. To tell him I loved him. To bargain—to plead.

But I refused to hurt him like that.

To manipulate him.

Lord knew, he'd been manipulated enough.

If all I could give him was a choice, that was what I'd do. Even if it killed me. I knew...I *knew* if I admitted how I felt, he would stay.

But it wouldn't be what he wanted.

I couldn't do that to him.

So I stayed silent.

Prudence allowed more physical affection than I thought he would. Ignoring the sisters' watchful gaze I climbed half onto his lap, wrapping my arms around him like an overgrown octopus, soaking up his scent, memorizing the way his knees jabbed into my leg—or his thighs squished beneath my bulk.

Smoke, musk, and magic.

Home.

That's what he smelled like.

He didn't complain the way he would've before. Instead he just held me back, just as tight, his eyes stormy—lost.

Hours later we pulled into a surprisingly normal looking parking lot and Chastity flipped the ignition off with a quiet sigh. Her phone buzzed, and she pried it from her pocket, checking it with a snort.

"What?" Vanity asked.

"Blair just sent me a pic of Boots biting his own foot." Vanity leaned over to look at the picture, a weirdly mournful expression flitting across her face, before her red lips thinned and she sighed while she straightened.

"Who is Blair?" I asked Prudence, curiously.

"The kid."

"The…kid?" *What kid?* I stared at him for a second before the realization struck me. "Oh. *That* kid." Amanda's kid.

Huh.

Prudence's sister was friends with the kid he'd tortured?

What a small world.

"C'mon, Vanity." Chastity urged, glancing at us in the rearview mirror, her dark eyes sympathetic as she pocketed her phone and cocked her head toward the door. "Let's give them a minute."

I didn't want a minute.

I wanted a lifetime.

But clearly I wasn't going to get that.

When the car was finally empty, I turned to Prudence, a surprising calm washing over me as I waited patiently for him to speak. There were questions dancing in his eyes, confessions he hadn't made.

"Vanity will take me inside," he said. Not the words I wanted to hear, but hey, at least it was something. "She'll be the one to free me."

To free him.

Like freeing him wasn't just a euphemism for killing him.

I swallowed the lump in my throat.

"But…"

"You will stay safely inside the car, where Chastity will keep an eye on you."

"I don't need a babysitter." The thought was absurd. I glared at him. He knew better than anyone how capable I was. I'd shared more of myself with him than I'd ever shared with anyone else. "I'm supposed to go in with you—I'm supposed to flirt out your password from the murder bitch—I'm supposed to—"

"You're supposed to stay in the car. Protected. Where I want you to be."

"I know I might die," I said, ripping apart the last lie between us. Prudence's eyes grew wide, his jaw dropping open in an expression of shock I hadn't realized he was even capable of. "I've always known."

His lips thinned, brow furrowing. "How?"

"Violet."

"Oh." It was almost hilarious that I'd shocked him into silence.

I remembered how I'd felt when Violet had told me that freeing a ghost might kill me. Back then she hadn't known what I was about to do, so her warnings had only been surface deep. It had taken me hours to come to terms with what she'd meant, but I had. And I had no intention of going back on my word, especially now that Prudence had become the most important person in my life.

"I'm going in with you," I told him, sure now that he knew I was aware of the risks, he wouldn't fight me, "like we agreed."

"No."

"What?" Now it was my turn to be shocked.

"You will stay safely inside the car where Chastity will keep an eye on you," Prudence repeated, word for word. There was something hidden beneath what he wasn't saying…hollow—desperate. An emotion I'd never heard from him before. So instead of arguing, instead of getting angry, I just took a fortifying breath and reached for his hand.

I gave it a squeeze, gathering my thoughts before answering.

"Why?" Softly, sweetly, I asked.

That was the crux of it, wasn't it? There was something happening behind that haunted gaze of his. Something twisting like poison. Thoughts— fears he never would've shared with me had I raised my voice.

His jaw clenched tight, the muscle jumping. Hope. Hope was a live thing in my chest, my heart fluttering as I stared at the stubborn twist of his lips.

"Why, Prudence?" I repeated, hope leaking into my tone without permission.

"Because," he said, like an asshole.

"Because, *why?*" Apparently we were five now.

"Because—" He took a shaky breath, refusing to look at me, his cheeks—oh god—his cheeks flushing dark with embarrassment as his nostrils flared. "I need you here."

"You need me…*here?*" I glanced around the familiar interior of my mom's car. "In the car. With Chastity."

"Yes." His jaw muscle jumped again. "I need you *safe.*"

"*Why* do you need me safe?"

"Because."

"Because *why?!*" I asked, exasperated. Oops. "C'mon Prudence." I knew what I hoped he might say—but I wasn't sure if I was way off base—or if he…if he…

Oh god.

If he really did care about me.

If that was why he wanted me to stay behind.

Because he cared. Because he didn't want me to see the woman who had hurt him—because he couldn't stomach even the possibility of her hurting me too.

Prudence's chest heaved with a ragged, aggravated breath. His shoulders were drawn tight, hands squeezed into fists.

And that was when I saw it.

His fingers.

Oh god.

"Prudence—"

He raised his hands, holding them out, fists still clenched, till his tattooed knuckles were on display. The letters that had painted them were still there, though a different word was depicted. Instead of L.I.A.R, there was a name. *My name.* My pulse was wild, my eyes wide as I took in each individual letter.

Luca.

L.U.C.A.

Written across each of his hands, like a promise.

"My body is an illusion," he said softly, lowering his hands. I knew that already—I'd always known that. Especially after that night in the hotel when he'd taken on the form of another man to get us a room. So much about him was otherworldly, it was hard to keep track of it all.

It hadn't occurred to me that this—that his tattoos—may not have been there when he was alive.

That he could change them.

"I didn't want to be changed," Prudence said softly, and I knew he wasn't talking about the damn tattoos. "I didn't think I could." I swallowed the lump in my throat, reaching for his cheek, his stiff jaw fitting perfectly in my palm. "But you changed me anyway."

A wet laugh bubbled up my throat as I pressed our foreheads together and squeezed my eyes shut tight.

His skin was as cold as ever, a testament to the fact that he wasn't human, and yet—he'd never felt more alive than he did in that moment.

"You don't have to go, you know?" I murmured softly, my lashes damp and shockingly cold as I squeezed my eyes tightly shut. My heart thumped erratically. "You could stay with me. Here. Or home—wherever you wanted to go." His skin was so soft, so solid, so real. "This doesn't have to be the end."

The end of us.

"Is that what you want?" His voice was ragged.

"What?"

"To trap me here?"

It was an honest question. As far as we knew, I still could. The curse was supposed to give me power over him, after all. For a moment I considered it. He was right. I could trap him here. I could command him to remain by my side. I could even command him to forget that I'd forced him to stay in the first place. I could hurt him. I could keep him. He'd be mine.

But he didn't need to be mine.

Prudence needed…

He needed to be Prudence.

And I loved him too much to take that away from him.

"You could tell me to stay," Prudence reminded me, like I hadn't just been thinking that exact same thing. "I would have no choice."

"That's the thing though," I interrupted him, unable to help myself, because the thought of taking this decision away from him was enough to make me sick—even though what I wanted most in the world was to keep him right by my side. Cherished. Happy. Safe.

Damn it.

The exact same thing he was trying to do, by forcing me to stay in the car with Chastity.

"I refuse to be another person who takes that choice away from you," I murmured, my lips brushing his as my heart thundered in my chest. "Love..." I swallowed, opening my eyes to look at him. "Isn't selfish, Prudence." Blue. Blue, blue, blue. I fell inside the depths of his gaze as the truth trembled in the open space between us.

"Even if it makes you miserable?" He didn't acknowledge the weight of my words, though I could feel the way he was trembling.

My tough, no-nonsense, dommy, pint-sized sadist. *Trembling*. Because of me.

"I'd rather be miserable without you, than hurt you." My voice wobbled.

"Why?" He asked, mirroring my earlier question. It was almost funny how similar we were. A cruel joke, from a God I didn't even know I believed in.

"You make me feel alive, Prudence," I said softly. "You make me happy. You make me brave. You make me accept the parts of myself I've always buried." My heart was heavy. I wanted to tell him I loved him. To confess what this growing, beautiful thing between us was. To give it a name. "You make me better. I make you better too."

But that would trap him here as surely as a command would.

So I gave him one last gift.

And I stayed silent.

"I support you," I said instead. "Whatever you need to do."

He nodded. His eyes were clouded with indecision.

"Tell me."

My hands were slick with sweat.

"Do what you need to do, Prudence." The words wobbled out, but I steeled my resolve, my heartbeat thundering. "Hurt who you need to hurt. Possess what you need to possess. I give you permission—no, I *command* you to."

His lips were soft and yielding as I slipped my tongue inside his mouth and climbed onto his lap. He tasted like forever. A forever we'd never have. Holding him tighter would only make it hurt more to let him go. But I did it anyway.

"One more time," I pleaded softly, straddling his lap, my cock straining against my pants despite how conflicted my emotions were. He was just as hard, just as eager as I was. I could feel the thick, insistent line of his dick against my ass when he nodded in agreement, burying his face in my chest, his hands on my hips, grip bruising.

"One more time," he agreed.

We fell together like we always did. Gasoline to flame. An explosion of everything that made us real. His cock was hot and hard as it slapped against our bellies when I freed it, our shirts rucked up as I forced my pants down and wrapped us together in my fist.

God he felt good.

Liquid pleasure flickered down my spine as I squeezed, our heads tipping back in tandem as we both groaned.

"*Fuck*," Prudence hissed through his teeth, his hand wrapping around mine, squeezing us tight enough the rigid pressure of his piercings dug into my dick. Oh sweet baby Jesus. I whined, flexing my hips into our shared grip, chasing the sensation at the same time he rutted forward.

Friction, tight, hot—delicious.

Our balls rubbing together.

His cold skin against my own, as precum slicked the way. It was still on the wrong side of dry—but it was perfect regardless as Prudence bit punishingly into my shoulder, yanking my hand out of the way so he could take us into both of his own and set a brutal pace.

It wasn't the soothing, loving sex from the previous two days. His teeth burned, stung. I chased the pain desperately.

This was goodbye.

It was an apology.

It was ours.

When we came, we sagged together, smooshed and sticky, our breath mingling, limbs intertwined. I didn't want to pull away. I knew the second I did we'd have nothing left to look forward to. So I clung to him. I forced my tears back. I forced my confession back. I let him tuck us gingerly inside our clothes, and then—he let me cling again.

For a long time we stayed like that. Together. Long enough I knew, without a doubt, that he needed this as much as I did. And when we finally separated, and Prudence phased right through the side of the car, my heart left with him.

A dry sob escaped my throat as I chased the sight of him through the glass. He walked away. Vanity joined him, and I watched in despair as they made their way toward a trail out of the parking lot that led to the front entrance of what looked like a perfectly ordinary office building—if office buildings were often built in the middle of the woods, an hour from the nearest city.

The car door slid open and Chastity climbed in.

"He loves you," she said gently, awed, as I stared at Prudence's retreating figure. One second he was there.

I knew she was right.

Even though he'd never said the words.

And then he was gone.

"I love him," I replied, still unable to look away from the spot he'd used to be. No doubt he had possessed Vanity now, taking a ride into the prison since they only accepted human guests.

"It's not over," she promised, but I knew she was wrong. I offered her a smile, though I was pretty sure it was more scary than reassuring.

She was wrong.

Prudence had made his choice.

And I…I would just have to live with it.

Even if it felt like I was dying with him.

Chapter Thirty-Four

Prudence

SINCE THE MOMENT I'd found out I was a ghost, all I'd ever wanted was to actually die. To let the nothingness free me from the monotony of existence. To finally escape the tedium of everyday struggles. To break away from the people, the emotions, that had always felt like a cage. There was nothing to live for when the future felt like a trap. There were countless experiences I didn't want to have, people I didn't want to meet, things I didn't want to feel.

But for the first time in my life I had something to look forward to. Something to leave behind. Regret. Heartbreak. Possibility. There were paint-smeared kisses, I hadn't tasted. Masterpieces that we hadn't created. Smiles I hadn't collected. Giggles I hadn't heard. Bruises I hadn't left. Memories I hadn't made. A future that was both promising and terrifying all at once.

Luca had said that the world was big enough.

Whether or not that was true, I no longer cared. I would make space for myself inside it if I had to. I was tired of feeling like I was not enough. I deserved life, and I would take my happiness, whether or not I'd earned it.

Something had changed inside me.

Something fundamental and frightening.

That change had never been more apparent than it was as Vanity sat down across from Lydia, and everything I'd been experiencing—everything I'd endured, survived, and struggled through came rushing back full force.

I thought of green eyes. I thought of sobbing. A tiny boy who resembled the person I had used to care most about in the entire world, held down and beaten in front of me. I thought of darkness, of the Nothing. Of choices I never would have made.

I thought of the freedom I'd felt the moment the chain around Lydia's neck had snapped, and her hold over me had shattered.

I thought of months under my sister's watchful care. Of the bodies I'd plowed. The life I'd chased through fleeting pleasure. The boredom. The gnawing desire for the monotony to end, devouring me from the inside out.

I thought of gray eyes.

Kind, gray eyes.

A smile brighter than the sun.

Freckles, all 998 of them.

Freckles I'd counted as Luca lay sleeping, sprawled naked, and gorgeous—always trusting, even when attached to a monster like me.

I thought of the words I hadn't spoken, not just to him, but to anyone. Words that had never meant anything to me until he'd shown me what they looked like.

You don't have to go, you know? You could stay with me. Here. Or home—wherever you wanted to go. This doesn't have to be the end of this.

And suddenly…suddenly…none of it mattered anymore.

Not the green eyes.

Not the loss.

Not Amanda, and everything that had happened. Her tragedy—I realized now—hadn't been my fault.

Maybe it would matter, today, or tomorrow—the next day after that. But that meant there had to be a tomorrow, didn't it?

"I'll bring him to visit you," Vanity bargained, putting on the charm like she so rarely did back home. She was just as manipulative as Luca was, should she need to be. Growing up with our mother had taught her that. Hiding inside her consciousness like this I could feel her fear, the way it trembled.

I had no sympathy.

She'd been the one to insist on taking me.

To right her wrongs, despite her own very real fear.

Promise, I urged her. Anything to get what we needed.

"You'll see Jeffrey again," Vanity crossed her arms, head cocked to the side as she regarded Lydia. The woman was a husk of what she had once been. Shriveled up, her cheeks hollowed, her green eyes muddy and dark. She would do anything to see her adopted son. The man she'd stolen. The one she'd killed for so she could keep him, against his will.

Dark roots had bled into the bleached blonde she'd sported the entire time I'd known her. The color crept in like sickness. Without makeup, without her pure-white designer armor she looked ridiculously small.

Not a figure from nightmares.

But a cautionary tale.

Funny how technically speaking she had been Amanda's identical twin. They looked nothing alike now, even with her dark natural hair creeping back in. It was like the ugliness that had festered beneath the surface of her skin was finally becoming visible. Prison had done her no favors, and for a woman as vain as Lydia—that was the highest punishment of all.

"I swear on my life," Vanity waited.

"How do I know you're not lying?" Lydia's eyes narrowed, and I knew Vanity could sense my amusement, because her surprise flickered through me. The tiny Luca in the back of my head painted my thoughts pink, pink, pink. Maybe she'd thought I'd be as scared as she was.

Tell her she doesn't. Tell her that she doesn't have a choice. It's us, or nothing. Those are her options.

Vanity relayed my words and I watched with apathy as Lydia waffled back and forth, deciding what to do. Pitiful. Without people to take advantage of, she was just a nasty little hag. Unable to help myself, I remembered Blair's words months ago right before he'd shot her and ended her reign of terror.

No amount of money or designer clothing could ever cover up the fact that you're just a sad miserable hag who is nothing but the dollar-store version of my mother.

Stop it, Vanity chided me. *Don't make me laugh.*

"Fine," Lydia agreed, after what felt like an eon waiting for her to get over herself.

"Don't even think about giving me the wrong word. I'll know. And I'll leave—and never fucking come back," Vanity threatened.

Lydia hissed her displeasure, and I held back my amusement. Her eyes flickered with uncertainty before she sighed, and deflated, the pure yellow of her prison uniform making her skin nearly green.

"Love," she said, lip curling.

"What?" Vanity blinked, surprised. "The key to freeing him is love?"

"The word, dear," Lydia said, rolling her eyes. "The password."

"You're such a bitch," Vanity blurted out, then slapped a hand over her mouth in surprise. She probably hadn't meant to say that out loud. Apparently she wasn't quite as scared of Lydia as she'd thought. She lowered her hand and leaned forward, clearly having found her backbone. "Did you pick that so that whoever held his talisman couldn't say they loved him without killing him?"

Lydia shrugged. "I also figured no one could ever love him, so it was the word least likely to be used by accident." Those words were meant for me. She could probably still sense my presence, my eye glimmering from Vanity's face. When I'd been Lydia's property she'd religiously worn colored contacts, not that she'd ever let me front the way my siblings or Luca did.

I was grateful, once again, that I hadn't brought Luca with me. Grateful, because, as I'd just made my decision—the idea of never hearing him say I love you would have killed me. Funny how those words had never meant anything to me before. The fact he was unaware of the password meant there would be no rift between us, and one day maybe, years from now— one of my sisters could let him know, and we could pass on together, like we were supposed to.

"Oh my god." Vanity stared at her, genuinely flabbergasted. Then, without a word, she rose from her seat and headed toward the metal door.

I could see the guard outside of it, just waiting for a knock to let her out. The chains attaching Lydia to the metal table rattled.

"You promised!" she called—shrieked, more accurately.

"I know." Vanity turned around and offered her a saccharinely sweet smile that immediately quieted her down. "I never break my promises." Lydia nodded, appeased, and Vanity rapped on the door.

The guard let us out.

We were silent for the entire walk through the facility. Silent as we rode the elevator that had brought us into the depths of the underground prison. Silent as Vanity gave back her visitor badge. Silent as we moved down the gravel walkway, and started on the long winding path that led back to the parking lot.

"I'm never fucking bringing Jeffrey here, I hope you know that." Vanity swore with a wry laugh.

I thought you didn't break your promises.

"I'll make an exception, just this once."

I laughed.

Chapter Thirty-Five

Luca

REALISTICALLY IT DIDN'T take that long for Prudence to come back, but a century still passed while we waited. I wasn't sure if I wanted him to stay gone—to prolong the inevitable—or if I desperately wished him beside me, to steal any last time with him I could.

While we waited, Chastity tried to make conversation, but for the first time in my life I did not have the patience. I grunted politely where I could, because I wasn't an asshole, but my heart—and my mind—were firmly attached to Prudence.

I hated that he was inside the prison without me.

I hated that I was out here.

I hated that he was seeing Lydia again, and that I had to sit idly by. That I hadn't been able to protect him. That we'd had no choice.

"Why didn't they kill her?" I blurted, several minutes into the wait.

"What?" Chastity blinked up from her phone where she was scrolling through Instagram. Cat pic after cat pic. A painfully pale bicep. A tall blond man with a tiny black-haired twink laying with their heads together and an itty bitty kitten curled up between them. A sad looking plant. She'd given up talking to me only a few minutes ago.

She put her phone down and swiveled to look at me.

"Lydia," I elaborated. It was the first time I'd spoken since our brief conversation as Prudence had been walking away. "They killed Prudence because they thought he helped murder people. She *actually* murdered people. So why is she alive?"

"Oh." Chastity frowned, tapping her lip thoughtfully. "Well…" Her brow furrowed. "Unfortunately the fact she's from an old hunting family protected her."

"But so are you. So is Prudence."

Chastity shrugged helplessly. "The Rains haven't actively practiced hunting in over a century. Sure, we have some musty ass books, and some like…distant cousins or whatever that maybe still know the old ways, but us? Yeah. We're hunters in name only. Lydia's family is still actively practicing."

"So?" It didn't make sense.

"They have secrets," Chastity sighed. "Knowledge that is useful to The Council. If she dies, that knowledge dies with her." She shrugged helplessly. "Take Prudence for example. How many ghosts have you seen walking around?"

"Oh."

"Exactly." Her cheerful expression shuddered, her brown eyes growing dark as hate dashed to the surface. Quickly, she blinked it away, offering me another more reassuring smile. "Believe me, I think it's bullshit."

Surprisingly, that last statement was what quieted my anger.

With a sigh, I turned back to the window, watching for Vanity's tall silhouette through the glass.

And then something she'd said hit me.

Like a ton of fucking bricks.

"Did you say Rain?" I asked, head snapping toward her again.

"Sorry, what?"

"Your last name." My breath came out in a flickering burst. "Did you say it was Rain?"

"Oh?" She blinked, obviously surprised. She set her phone down again. "Yeah. Pru didn't tell you?"

"Nah." I shook my head, feeling dazed. "You don't happen to be related to a really uptight—horribly dressed—brunette heiress, do you?"

Chastity cocked her head to the side, eyes blazing with curiosity. "Was her name Temperance?"

Mother. *Fucker.*

The names.

Chastity, Vanity, Prudence, Temperance.

The stupid fucking names. I should've figured this out way sooner. A startled laugh tore its way from my throat as I recalled my first visit to Elmwood. The insults Temperance had thrown my way as I'd tried to sell her my last hope, literally. Because of her rejection. Because of her unkindness, I'd found myself at the club that night, willing to toss the painting away in favor of a lucky necklace.

"Holy shit," I stared at Chastity, jaw dropped.

"What?"

"Your mom is a bitch." Shit. I should not have said that out loud.

"Believe me, I know." Chastity grinned, shrugging one shoulder. "Why do you think we all turned out so odd?" She gestured at her lime-green outfit and the little dragon wings sewed to the back.

I hadn't known either sister long enough to be able to judge their oddness. But I figured, flying across the entire country in search of your suicidal ghost brother, who you didn't even know liked you, made them both fairly strange.

Knowing Prudence, he just needed more time to warm up to them.

And also maybe for them to stop coddling him so much.

Maybe I could help with that.

"Prudence isn't who you think he is." Shit. Again, the words just burst out. This was awkward as hell. I cringed, waiting for Chastity to berate me, or—or—whatever small pastel goths did when they were annoyed by tall traumatized men.

But she didn't.

She just turned fully in the seat, and climbed into the back with me. I scooted over to make room, not sure if she wanted to hit me or—

"Explain," she said simply, fanning her hands out. She was tiny. Smaller even than Prudence. I stared down at her, a little shocked.

"He's not…" Damn. Maybe I should've thought this through. But…I figured if we only had a few more minutes left with Prudence, he at least deserved to be treated like the individual he was. "He's not your big brother." Shit. "Wait, that came out weird." I chewed on my lip and Chastity waited patiently. "He is—your big brother, I mean—but he's also…just…him." I bit my lip. "A guy who never got to figure out who or what he is." His mother had never left him room to do anything but rebel and then— "I mean…shit. He *died*. And when he came back, he ended up living inside his own shadow." My lip stung. "That's why…don't be mad at him, okay?"

Chastity regarded me, her eyes still shimmering with kindness, though there was a pensive furrow to her brow. "He told you all that?"

I swallowed the lump in my throat. "I mean, yeah? Kinda." I squirmed. Hopefully I hadn't just betrayed Prudence's confidence. Wasn't like we'd pinky sworn not to tell anyone, or anything though, so I figured I was fine. "He thinks he can't move forward." Chastity nodded. "It's not your fault or anything, obviously it's like…a mental block." Damn, that sounded wrong. "I just—I mean. We all have those, right? And for him…well. He's been through a lot. The last thing he needs is to be put on a pedestal. When you're that high up, there's just…" My hands shook. "There's so far to fall."

I knew that better than anyone.

I'd put myself on a goddamn pedestal my entire fucking life.

I'd given up so much, my morals, my time. I'd lied and lied and lied. And for what? To be the perfect big brother. To protect a family that didn't need protecting anymore. We weren't starving. Mom was happy. Betty was happy—*ish*. Adam was going places. He was going to make something of himself, whether or not I was involved.

In a way, I understood Prudence.

Leaving would be easier than staying. Than dealing with the aftermath of everything that had happened. Easier for him, anyway. But for us?

I couldn't imagine my life without him in it.

Maybe I hadn't known him long, but my stomach churned just

thinking about it.

"You're pretty perceptive," Chastity said, interrupting my thoughts. "Thanks for sharing that." She flashed me a little smile and leaned over to give me a half hug. "Thanks for…you know, everything else too." Her smile wobbled. "Honestly, I've never seen Prudence act the way he does with you."

I was a thirsty bitch, so I needed more details—overwhelming emotions or not. "What do you mean?"

"There's this light in his eyes. He's soft." She shrugged. "And he tries. Even though it's hard. He tries, for you. To talk, to respond. To touch you. To support you. There's life to him that was never there before."

"This is new?"

"Yeah." Chastity shrugged. "It's difficult for him. Being around other people. Emotions have never come easy. I think it used to make him angry. Maybe it still does." She bit her lip. "But I think…maybe…" Her eyes searched mine as I sucked in a startled breath. "He's decided you're worth trying for."

"He's perfect," I said softly, because it was true. He was perfect. He was prickly, mean, occasionally condescending, and the best fucking person I'd ever met. The fact that it was hard for him, made his effort even sweeter. It meant more.

"I never thought I'd hear someone say that," Chastity laughed, expression gentle. "Not to be mean. Because obviously I love him. But man…" She shook her head. "You two are a perfect fit. You've got the same kind of crazy."

Movement outside the car caught my attention, and I immediately forgot what we'd been talking about.

Vanity approached, way too fucking slow. Well. Maybe she was walking normal—but it felt slow. Glacially so. Rather than go around Chastity to get out the door, I launched myself over the middle seat and pushed out the sliding door.

The second my feet hit the ground Prudence separated from Vanity's body.

His talisman thrummed against my chest as the ten yards between us was easily eaten up by my stride. He met me halfway, an unnatural spark in his eyes that was unlike any expression I'd ever seen him wear.

He was here.

He was here.

"Did you get it?" I asked, my words all raw and wobbly. He nodded, and the relief that flooded my body nearly made my knees give out. Prudence must've noticed because his cold fingers bit into my hips, steadying me as all my fears—worries—and anxiety trembled out through a ragged breath.

I pulled him close, wrapping my arms around his shoulders, my face smashing in his hair.

I couldn't tell him I loved him, or he'd stay.

I knew that.

It would be selfish.

So fucking selfish.

I wasn't a selfish person, at least not usually. I'd always done my best to give and give and give. I'd given my childhood away. I'd risked. God, I had. All those days with my siblings, biting back my own hunger so I could make sure they were fed. The relief I'd felt when I finally had money in the bank, and I'd immediately poured it into their futures.

And here I was.

Future-less.

I didn't regret it, any of it. I didn't regret Mom's smile when she'd come home and we'd have groceries in the fridge, courtesy of the iPod I'd stolen then pawned. Betty's private happiness when she'd made me help her hang her diploma in the hallway at Mom's house. Adam's grin at fourteen when he'd told me he wanted to grow up to be just like me.

I didn't regret any of that.

But.

But if I let Prudence go—if he died, never knowing how I really felt—I would regret that for the rest of my fucking life.

And it struck me—all at once—how stupid I had been.

Maybe…maybe it was okay to be selfish sometimes. Maybe being selfish could be its own form of love. Because I wanted him. I wanted him so goddamn much. I'd given—lord. I'd given. Maybe it was time I…took.

Maybe it was time I stood up for myself.

And if I did—if I did, maybe he'd stay.

Maybe he wouldn't.

The choice was up to him.

Like it was supposed to be.

Not telling him would make me just as bad as all the people in his life who had taken away his agency. It was a disservice to him to deny the chance at a future. Maybe the coward in me had been frightened of rejection, after all, I'd been burned.

Hunter and I had been engaged before his betrayal. He'd made pretty, empty promises. I'd *trusted* him. And look where that had gotten me. Violet's words, *trust no one*, uttered as a careful warning to my cracking heart had sat like a noose around my neck for far too long. I'd held them close. But I realized now—*that*—wasn't who I was.

I wasn't distrustful.

I wasn't cautious.

I was naive.

I was stupidly optimistic.

I was the kinda guy who'd attach himself to a phone pole if he thought it looked at him twice.

I was bound to make mistakes, lots of them.

But that was okay.

Because Prudence liked me anyway.

I liked me anyway.

He'd taught me that.

I didn't want to be a coward anymore.

He deserved better.

And I refused to let this be another mistake I made.

"What's going on in your head?" Prudence asked, shocking me out of my thoughts. He released my hip with one hand to thread in the back of my hair. His fingers tickled under the hem of my cap. He smelled like home. He *felt* like home. I buried my nose in the soft skin at the side of his neck, my eyes burning.

This was maybe, possibly the stupidest—bravest thing I would ever do.

My laugh wobbled. Prudence's grip in my hair tightened.

"Pinkie?" He hummed questioningly. I squeezed my eyes shut tight, fingers catching in his shirt.

"I don't want you to go," I said, so quietly I wasn't sure he'd be able to hear. "Pru—"

I forced my head back to look at him. *Really*, look at him.

His pale blue eyes flickered with the flames of emotion. His lips were drawn thin, his brow lowered as he stared right back, unafraid to make eye contact with me. The sunlight glinted on his eyebrow piercing and I took a fortifying breath. The grip he had on my hip, and in my hair grew tighter.

"I know I said I wouldn't tell you to stay." My lips wobbled, and tears spilled free. God, I was a sweaty, sobby mess. Prudence's hand slid from my hair till he cupped the side of my jaw, his thumb tracing gentle circles through the wetness. I sniffled. "And I'm not—"

"Then what are you doing?"

That was a good question.

What was I doing?

I'd never felt this way for anyone. Like if he stopped breathing, so would I. I'd kill for him. Die for him. Die *with* him.

"I said I wouldn't tell you to stay. But, I never said I wouldn't ask." Maybe it was selfish. Maybe it was brave. Maybe it was stupid. Maybe it was wildly optimistic. But Prudence liked all those things about me, so it was worth a chance. "So let me—"

"Luca—"

"Stay with me." I blurted, and my face scrunched up as I made an attempt at a reassuring smile. "I'm not commanding you—" I sucked in a ragged breath. "I'm asking—So please—" *Jee*-sus I was a mess. Why the hell would he want someone like me. "Please stay with me."

"Why?" His brow lowered, his eyes molten hot as he waited.

It didn't escape me that our positions had reversed from the conversation in the car earlier.

"Because I—" Another wobbly breath. My hands were sweaty, shaky. My knees threatened to give out. Vanity was still standing to Prudence's left, and when I caught her eye she had a satisfied, relieved smile on her lips. Chastity's gaze tickled the back of my head as I laughed, wetly. "Because I—"

"You what?" There was something behind Prudence's words. Anticipation. Fear. Excitement.

"I love you, Prudence." Shit. As soon as the words were out, the weight that had been wearing me down to nothing, finally lifted. I could stand taller. My hands no longer needed to shake. "I love you," I repeated, stronger this time, steadier. Fresh tears made him blurry, so I quickly tried to blink them away. "Stay with me." It wasn't a command, we both knew that. "Stay with me and I swear—*I swear,* I'll love you. I'll love you every day. Even when you're cranky. Even when we fight. Even when you steal my fries. Even when the sky is gray, and the sun seems a million miles away." Wind whispered between us, dancing from the tree line surrounding the parking lot. "And when we're old—" Prudence snorted. "When *I'm* old—" I corrected myself, "—and gray, and wrinkly all over…" I took in a shuddering breath. "We'll go together."

We could have this.

We could have a future.

If he wanted it.

"I'm…I'm offering you a choice." My breath stuttered out. "Grow old with me, Prudence. Live with me. Die with me." The hold he had on my hip was painfully tight. "Choose me. But know—know even if you don't, I'll keep on loving you. No matter what you pick, that won't change."

With all my cards on the table there was nothing I could do but wait.

And I did.

My vision was blurry, so it was hard to catch his expression as I sniffled, my heart in my throat.

"I'm not a good person." Prudence's voice echoed quietly in the space between us. I could feel his vulnerability quaking within every syllable.

"Maybe not," I agreed, my heart fluttering with something akin to hope. "But you're *my* person. And for me, that's good enough."

And then he sighed. It was a low, put upon sound. I swallowed back a sob, so sure in that moment that it was done. That it was over. That it hadn't been enough. I took a half step back, ready to let him go—but his grip only grew tighter as he dragged me back.

"If you keep crying like that, I'll have no choice but to take you right here."

A startled laugh bubbled up my throat.

"Wh—"

"I'd rather wait until we have some privacy." Prudence's eyes were all mine, but his words were clearly directed at his nosy as fuck siblings. "And I have time to really take you apart."

I didn't blame them for eavesdropping, this wasn't a casual conversation. We were talking about Prudence's future after all, or lack thereof.

"One last time?" That was better than nothing.

"No." Prudence shook his head, and he released my hip to cradle my face in both his palms. His thumbs swiped away my tears, and I blinked till my vision cleared enough I caught the earnest unwavering strength in his gaze. "No, Luca."

I didn't get it.

I blinked stupidly at him.

"Do I have to spell it out for you?" He rolled his eyes, and another almost hysterical laugh left my lips.

"Yeah, probably."

Prudence growled, curling his lip in annoyance. The gentle, almost reverent way he cradled my face however, betrayed his true feelings. Hope. Yellow, yellow, yellow. Hope began to flutter in the collapsed cavern of my chest. "I told you I was going to fuck you as many times as I can before I die."

I nodded stupidly.

"I don't…" I didn't understand. Prudence huffed again, leaning up to lace a greedy, needy kiss against my lips. Rather than stay on solid ground he floated upward, crowding against me, his tongue pushing into my mouth. His piercing rubbed along the top of my palate and I whimpered, distracted, as he devoured me kiss by possessive kiss.

With the higher angle he was able to get deeper, push harder. The kiss tasted like salt and possibility. He nipped my lip. The pain centered me. His tongue fucked deep enough for a moment I forgot my own name.

By the time he pulled back I was dazed and flushed, and my lips were all tingly.

"I'm staying."

Oh.

Oh.

Oh.

Prudence kissed me again, probably to stop me from asking the zillions of questions that threatened to burst free.

"I'm staying," he repeated quietly, privately. Just for me. His cold nose brushed mine. "So save your tears." He nipped my bottom lip and a surprised little whimper escaped. "You'll need them for what I want to do to you later."

Prudence's "I love you" was laced in every needy kiss we shared as we made our way to the van. It hid inside his arms as he bundled me onto his lap despite the way I dwarfed him in size. It crept into my heart, secret and safe, as he sucked kisses against the freckles on my neck, and he stroked the last of the tension from my shoulders.

When we pulled onto the freeway to head back to Eastgrove I couldn't help but glance at Vanity and Chastity where they'd stayed mercifully quiet up front. Chastity caught my eye and winked. The drive back was spent in exhausted silence as I soaked Prudence up, relief making my body floaty, and my heart settle.

"Bank," Prudence said so abruptly I jumped.

"What?" I blinked in confusion, untucking my face from the crook of his neck to look for clues on his face. "What do you—"

He ignored me, glaring his sisters down, the empty seat between us doing nothing to protect them from his ire. "Take me to the bank."

"The…" Oh.

Shit.

I'd forgotten about our deal.

"Prudence, we don't need to—" Prudence covered my mouth with one delicious tattooed hand, quieting me.

Fine.

If he wanted to play it like that, we'd play it like that. I licked his palm, and he was so startled he dropped his hand. His gaze snapped to mine, an almost hilarious look of surprise on his face. I ignored the fact the only other time I'd done this was in less than ideal circumstances. Instead I focused on him, unable to hide my giggle. He covered my mouth again.

"Bank," he repeated, his surprise quickly squashed. His eyes glowed as an evil grin flitted across his face, fingers tightening their grip on my cheeks. With a wicked look in his eyes, he leaned in close, his lips against my ear as he promised, "*Two.*"

Motherfucker.

He was such a fucking shithead.

But he was my shithead, so I loved him anyway.

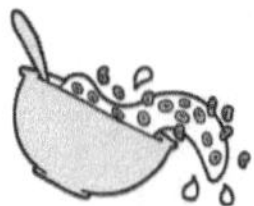

Apparently Prudence Rain was dramatic and extra as fuck. I wasn't sure what to expect when we pulled into the parking lot of a massive, frankly terrifying bank inside the nearest big city an hour away from the prison. It was high rise—covered in black glass, and ninety percent of the cars parked were sports cars.

I didn't argue, because it hadn't worked well earlier. But I did give him my best side-eye as we entered the lobby and immediately a rotund man with a honestly amazing mustache approached us.

Chastity had called ahead, so clearly they'd been waiting for us. I glanced down at my borrowed pants and t-shirt and felt about an inch tall. I should've taken off my baseball cap. Shit. Prudence's grip on my hand grew tight, almost like he could sense my self-consciousness and wanted to distract me.

"Mr. Rain," the man greeted, looking more than a little starstruck. "Follow me back to my office and I'll get you and your..." he waited, blinking patiently.

"Fiancé," Prudence deadpanned. I squawked, unable to help myself. Prudence looked incredibly proud of himself, his lips twitching into my favorite downward smile as he caught my distress. Always a sadist.

"And your fiancé all taken care of." He led us through a giant lobby with a chandelier big enough to squash at least three people, down a long winding hallway, and into an office with an entire wall made of that same black glass I'd seen outside.

The armchairs looked like they were made for giants. Made from leather, my chair squeaked as I sat down. I grimaced. Prudence's grip on my hand only grew tighter.

Bank guy—I peeked at the plaque on his desk—Martin. Martin gave us both a friendly nod. "Give me two moments, gentleman, I'll get someone to bring in refreshments." He headed toward the door, presumably to call out to a butler or something—whatever a fancy ass bank like this would have—to bring us food.

Taking the opportunity I leaned over, glaring at Prudence.

"Fiancé?" I asked, confused and a little miffed. "Really?"

"You said we weren't boyfriends." Jesus fuck.

"You are one petty bitch," I decided, though I couldn't hide my smile. "What are we doing?" I lowered my voice. "Why are we lying to this nice bank dude?"

"Who said we're lying?" He stared at me blankly, and I floundered for something to say.

"Um. Me? I don't remember getting proposed to."

"Of course you don't." Prudence's grin grew wicked. "*You* were the one that proposed to *me*."

All the words and promises I'd made at the prison came rushing back all at once. I suppose, in a way I *had* proposed.

"Oh." I flushed bright red. I could feel how tingly my cheeks had become as I heard Martin's muffled voice behind us. I didn't regret what I'd said, but I also…felt weirdly disappointed.

It must've showed on my face because the twinkle in Prudence's eyes softened. "Did you want a proposal?" He cocked his head to the side, and I squirmed.

"Even Hunter proposed."

Prudence's eyes grew hot and angry, his lips thinning as his casual posture grew rigid.

"You didn't tell me that."

I sniffed, pretending like that choice had been totally intentional. "You don't know everything."

"Apparently." He eyed me contemplatively, then relaxed. "Fine."

I narrowed my eyes at him.

I wasn't sure I liked where this conversation was going. "What does *that* mean?" It wasn't like him to give up so easily.

"I'll just have to propose better." His eyes flashed, like he was daring me to argue. "And then—I'll kill him."

"No killing Hunter!" I commanded, breathlessly. Before I could argue further, Martin returned. He handed over ice-cold water bottles—which I guzzled enthusiastically—and a wooden board covered in…meats? Cheese? I wasn't sure what to describe it as. Everything looked very fancy—and very expensive.

When I asked, Martin called it a Char-coochie board, or something like that, but I was too hungry to care what body part the thing was named after.

I didn't want to look weird while eating, so I waited to see what Prudence would do. He was the one with the fancy-ass upbringing after all. Obviously, I shouldn't have worried about how I looked, because he began devouring the tray, shoving everything into his mouth with no rhyme or reason to it, like he always did.

Martin looked a bit horrified, but he hid the expression quickly.

The rest of the meeting was boring. I lost half of the conversation, focusing on sneaking crackers from the tray before Prudence ate fucking everything. It was only at the end, long after I was forced to sign a bunch of shit, that I realized what was happening.

"Congratulations," Martin said, straightening the stack of papers with a happy smile. "Let me know if you have any questions."

He ushered us out of the office, and I stared at Prudence confused, and suspicious. Before we could exit the building he paused inside the massive lobby. I was momentarily distracted by the chandelier again before he tugged me toward one of the bank tellers that lined the wall.

"Check the balance," he commanded when it was our turn.

"What?"

"Check the balance in the account," he repeated, brow twitching. "Did you not pay attention to anything we just did?"

"No," I answered honestly, my heart fluttering as I stepped up to the teller with a nervous smile. "Uh, hi."

Prudence saved me from myself, thank god, and when the woman passed me a little sheet of paper that detailed the amount of money in the account I nearly threw up the crackers I'd just eaten. My brow scrunched in confusion.

"This is—" I shook my head. "This is too much." It didn't make sense. This wasn't part of the deal. And then I relaxed, because I saw the name at the top of the paper. Ah. "Ohhhh this is your account."

"No."

"No?" *What did he mean, no?* "What do you mean, no?" I repeated, confused. Prudence pointed to the top of the paper and my eyes bugged out of my head as I noticed my name right below his.

"It's *our* account."

"It's our what now?"

And that was how, just an hour after accidentally proposing to my ghost boyfriend—Fiancé—I somehow became a multi-millionaire. Apparently joint accounts were a thing and Prudence was nothing if not extra as fuck. And as we drove south, chasing pine boughs with the fear from earlier in the day behind us, I realized, tucked safe in his arms, that I'd never in my life been happier.

The future had never looked so bright.

My heart had never felt this light.

Optimism tingled at my fingertips, a promise of more laughter, of a life worth living. With my mistakes in the rearview mirror and Prudence's hand on my thigh, I realized maybe I'd been wrong all along.

I hadn't lost my sunrise, after all. He was sitting right beside me, his eyes flickering, sunlight shimmering through his half-transparent body. My sunrise sounded like sex, smelled like leather, and knew exactly how to torture me into getting off. And when I met his pale, gorgeous gaze, the warmth that flooded my chest was filled with possibilities for the future we'd share together.

It was new.

It was sweet.

Fluttering and tentative.

It was ours.

Epilogue

Prudence

LET IT BE said that life with Luca was the opposite of boring. As much as I liked him—loved him—(I was still getting used to using those words) he was nosy as hell. Surprising him was the most difficult thing I had ever done. For months I'd bided my time, waiting for him to drop his guard, and for the summer months to bleed into autumn.

It was then that I struck.

"Holy shit, really?" Luca beamed at me from across the table, his spoon full of Fruit Loops halfway to his lips. Milk dripped as his eyes crinkled happily. "Halloween with Violet in Elmwood? Fuck yes."

After he'd gotten over the initial shock of the supernatural being real, Luca had been more than a little—annoyingly—enthusiastic about the whole thing. Because the secret had been revealed outside Elmwood there was nothing the Council could do but accept that he was aware. Funny how the rest of the world didn't comply with their rules, and they weren't punished for it. I was glad for that small mercy. The idea of Luca being injured or even killed just because he knew the truth made my stomach churn.

Two days later, we landed in the quaint little airport near Elmwood, Maine.

I hadn't been back since everything had gone down in the early summer. I thought it might be strange to return. Uncomfortable. Elmwood had never been my home. But with Luca squeezing my hand eagerly, his eyes bright as he shared his box of fries with me, I found it wasn't nearly as daunting as I'd worried it would be.

As a sanctuary, it was safer there for us, even though the town carried memories I desperately wanted to rewrite. At least with Luca by my side, my demons were quickly forgotten.

Things with him were effortless.

He made them that way.

When he was around I breathed a little easier.

Which was why I had every intention of shocking the hell out of him, blowing Hunter out of the water, and simultaneously nailing the best proposal of all time. Luca had no idea that an hour outside of town my surprise sat waiting.

"Do we have to visit your mom?" Luca asked as we climbed inside the rental car. His disgust was palpable, his face scrunched up, eyes narrowed. He dropped the empty fry box on the floor and I reached for it, opened the window, and tossed it out. "Um, litter much?"

Before I could start the car, Luca climbed out, rounded the hood, glared at me, and pointedly picked up the trash. I rolled the window down, arching a brow at him.

"Wait here."

He returned a minute or so later after tossing the trash with his head shaking disparagingly. When he climbed back in, his ire was quickly forgotten as he tipped his head back against the seat and released a stressed out little sigh.

"No," I replied.

"Huh?"

"No, we will not be visiting my mother," I answered his earlier question, and Luca relaxed, spreading his long legs with a little smile.

"She still trying to get ahold of you?"

"Don't remind me." Since I'd arrived in Elmwood with Lydia, my mother had done her best to get back in my good graces. Hilarious, considering the fact that I had never liked her. I didn't want to piss her off too much, however, since I had little time to deal with her ire.

Besides, I grudgingly owed her for never reporting my death. Realistically, I knew she had been commanded not to by the Supernatural Alliance Committee for fear of the government getting involved in their business, but it still had made my integration back into society much easier, and for that…yes, I was grateful.

I didn't mind a challenge, but now that I had a leggy pink fiancé to worry about, the lack of struggle was greatly appreciated. It left more time to focus on him. To spoil him. To punish him.

"I can't wait to see Violet," Luca sighed happily, staring out the window as I pulled onto the freeway and we sped south. Trees whipped by on either side, taller, and somehow greener than the ones we'd seen in Oregon the last time we'd visited his parents.

The Bakers were obsessed with us now that we were engaged, and while I grumbled—secretly, I didn't mind the positive attention.

It was the first time anyone had fawned over me, not because of my money—or my family's status—but because they liked me as a person. Because they thought I was a good match for their son.

"How long is she staying in town?" I asked, feigning ignorance. I didn't care about Violet, even though her involvement in my proposal plan had admittedly made the surprise much easier. I did, however, care about Luca, so I made a point to pretend I was interested so he wouldn't feel neglected, despite the fact I already knew the answer.

"She's helping her brother with his shop," Luca hummed thoughtfully, reaching down to pull the lever at the side of his seat so he could scoot it back for more leg room. He sighed, his smile sleepy and pleased. "So she'll probably stick around till Christmas…maybe later? Maybe forever. She already brought all her filming stuff over and it isn't like the internet is only available back home. She's even got a sweet little apartment in town she's set up inside." He shrugged. "I think…" He bit his lip. "I think we're going to stop rooming together."

The pieces of my plan were falling together nicely.

"Does her staying have anything to do with the fact she's been fucking my sister since May?"

"Yeah, probably." Luca narrowed his eyes at me. "Wait. How did you know about that? I thought it was on the down low."

"I have eyes."

Luca snorted, dubiously. "You don't pay attention to people other than me. Forgive me if I find that hard to believe." He would've sounded conceited if he wasn't one hundred percent correct, and—like the little shit he was—reciting my own words back to me.

I refused to admit to him that Violet had told me. She'd had to, when I'd come to her for…help…I shuddered just thinking about the way she'd squealed when I'd told her my plan. Disgusting. As much as I disliked her, like I disliked everyone on principle, I was grateful the awkward months directly after Luca and I had gotten together were over.

There had been a lot of hurt between the two of them, but they'd found their rhythm. Luca was much happier now that they had fallen back into their easy friendship.

I liked him happy.

The apartment building my family owned in the middle of Elmwood towered high into the sky as I pulled into a parking spot and looked at my slumbering sweetheart. He was drooling, his head tucked against the window, cheek squished against the glass.

I flipped the ignition off, and leaned across the console to brush his hair out of his eyes.

"We're here, Pinkie."

Luca grumbled, face scrunching up adorably as he blinked his eyes open. "Take me upstairs?" He asked, voice scratchy and soft.

We'd be occupying the empty apartment above my sisters for the time being, and I didn't blame him for his exhaustion. I'd kept him up late the previous night, and he'd been working through a new art piece that had been stealing his midnight hours for days before that.

There were dark smudges of exhaustion beneath his eyes and bite marks littering his neck as he tipped his head to look at me, sleepy gray eyes beseeching.

"Please?"

"Fine." The moment I agreed, Luca relaxed happily, letting his eyes shut as he waited. When I climbed inside him it was like slipping into a vat of warm butter. His sleepy consciousness wrapped around me like a blanket as I pushed open the door using his body, and headed to the trunk to grab our things.

We'd done this a handful of times before, and every time, the trust he so easily gave me warmed me from head to toe.

I loved being inside him, in every sense of the word. Whether or not it was slipping my cock inside his snug little hole—or possessing him. It didn't matter. If I could've permanently welded myself to him, I would.

The doorman smiled at me as I passed, and I flipped him off before heading toward the elevator, suitcases in tow.

The apartment was dark as I pushed the door open. Light twinkled through the floor to ceiling windows on one side, courtesy of familiar starlight as I tossed our bags onto the floor, locked the door, and searched the apartment for threats. When I'd deemed it safe, I headed into the bedroom. Above the headboard hung the painting we'd created on his bedroom floor what felt like a lifetime ago. I'd had it shipped over, though its position was temporary. Soon, it would have a very different place of honor. I lay down on the comforter, letting Luca's body rest as I started to pull away from him.

No.

No?

Stay.

Warmth flooded my chest as I settled back inside him, letting him soak up my presence.

Sleep with me, Luca murmured softly inside our shared space, and I huffed my amusement as I settled down to do as he asked. I gave back the reins of his body so he could shuffle around the way he liked, flopping like a starfish. He tugged off all his clothes sleepily, sprawled naked and gorgeous as moonlight bled from the window onto the sheets he bunched as he threw a leg up.

I wanted to leave him, just so I could admire the globes of his ass, but I didn't. This was more important.

Goodnight, Luca murmured.

Goodnight.

The intimacy of sharing his body like this made me feel both humbled and awed. He liked me inside him. He always had. It seemed my desire to get closer to him than what was physically possible was a shared one.

Violet distracted Luca while I finished the last of my preparations. I needed more time than I thought I would, however, and as the days blurred by with Luca occupied at Violet's side, I toiled away with my surprise, frustrated, and…excited.

Finally.

Finally, it was finished.

Two weeks into our return to Elmwood, I decided everything was as good as it was going to get. All week long Luca had been begging to spend time with me today. I wasn't sure why, but I figured maybe he'd wanted to go see that movie up in Ridgefield he'd been ranting about, so I didn't question it.

His legs were sprawled wide, encased in tight black dress pants. It was the first time I'd seen him in anything other than casual athletic wear and I couldn't help but groan at the sight of him as he stretched the confines of his pale pink button-up. His chest tested the button's patience every time he breathed, his plush lips tipping up into a secretive little smile.

We drove for almost an hour down the main road, trees creeping toward the sky, rain clouds for once, absent, as the swirling leaves began to turn shades of red and orange in time for autumn. When I took a left onto a long winding gravel road, Luca cocked his head curiously at me.

"We're not going to Ridgefield?" He asked, a spark of alarm in his eyes. I cataloged the reaction for later appreciation, too focused on what I was about to do to be able to properly respond. Normally I'd hunt down the reason behind his worry, but anticipation was buzzing too loudly in my head.

"Later," I scowled at him. My hands felt tingly. My chest was tight. The sun peeped between branches as the asphalt turned into dirt and the wheels crunched upon the gravel road.

Luca looked vaguely panicked, but he bit his tongue, eyeing me suspiciously.

"You could've told me our plans were changing," he huffed in annoyance.

"Three."

"Jesus Christ." Luca laughed, though his suspicion immediately melted away in favor of anticipation. A different kind than the one I was feeling. "What's it going to be this time?" He licked his lips. "Flogging?"

He'd been pretending he didn't want to get flogged for weeks. Ever since he'd stumbled upon a video about it online. We'd bought one, and it had sat at the bottom of my suitcase specifically to taunt him.

He still hadn't admitted he wanted it.

I wouldn't give it to him till he did.

I didn't respond as I rolled down the windows and cool wind crept into the cabin with us. Luca's hair whipped, wavy and fluffy—longer now than it had been when I met him. It was weird that he'd dressed up today. If Violet had warned him something was happening today I was going to be incredibly pissed off.

The closer we got to his surprise the more nervous I became. I was not the kind of person who got nervous. Ever. It wasn't a feeling I entertained. Now, though? There was no other word to describe this antsy, bubbly buzzing beneath my skin.

Except maybe…maybe excitement.

Nervous and excited.

How the hell had my life become this?

There was a break in the trees up ahead, and I knew the moment we passed through it there would be no hiding our destination. I only hoped Luca would be distracted enough by the ocean he wouldn't notice what we were really there for.

"Holy shit!" Luca called in excitement the moment we crested the hill. The ocean fanned out in front of us. The rocky beach was covered in peach sunset-tinged sand as sunbeams flickered off the waves, and puffy pale lavender clouds sat fat and gorgeous along the horizon.

He stuck his head out the window like a dog, his broad shoulders blocking most of the view as he tasted the salt in the air with a delighted laugh.

"I didn't realize the ocean was this close to Elmwood!" He called back to me, tongue out, like he was tasting the salt. I'd always loved the ocean. It was one of the only things near Elmwood that had ever felt like it was mine. That was one thing we shared.

I continued onward, pulling onto the long winding driveway I had paved a month ago.

"Don't you get enough of the beach in San Diego?" I teased, though Luca just laughed.

"Hey!" He slid back into the car, his attention all mine as he flashed me a happy grin. "There's no such thing as too much ocean."

Said like a true summer baby.

I pulled the car to a stop, and Luca frowned in confusion before turning to face his surprise for the first time.

"Pru…" He sounded confused.

Confused had not been what I was going for.

Nervous.

Nervous.

Nervous.

"What?"

"Why are we parked in someone's driveway?" Luca frowned, turning back toward me as he picked a piece of lint from his dress pants.

"We're not."

"Ummm. I'm pretty sure we are." He glared at me like *I* was the stupid one as he huffed out an annoyed breath. "We're gonna block their cars in—"

"We're not parked in someone's driveway." This wasn't going like I'd planned. Why wasn't he getting it? Luca stared at me like I was the biggest idiot in the entire world, and I had to hold back my laughter. "C'mon." Fine. If he wasn't going to get it, I'd just show him. I stepped out of the car, waiting for him to follow my lead.

"Fine, *fine*." Luca shook his head at me in disbelief as he opened his door and climbed out. He stood in the driveway, his hands on his hips as he stared up at the house. The front side of it was made entirely of one way glass, the ocean and our faces, reflecting back at us as sunset painted the windows pastel. There was a second building attached to the main one by a glass walkway, and the warm beige of the wood that comprised the rest of the structure fit right in with the sandy beach it sat beside.

Luca released a wistful sigh, and my gaze snapped to him as I waited to see if he'd finally understood why I'd brought him here.

"Now that is one badass house." He crossed his arms thoughtfully.

"You like it?" I couldn't keep the hope from creeping into my tone. Which was entirely unlike me.

"Shit, yeah." He smiled at me, his cheeks pink. "Is this what you were showing me?"

"Yes." Finally he was getting it. I rounded the car so we were standing side by side as he stared at my gift.

"Because you think we should buy something like this?" Luca nodded thoughtfully.

Jesus fuck.

"No."

"You don't like it?"

"I didn't say that." God, he was infuriating. I shuffled even closer to him, soaking up his beachy coconut-esque scent. He laced a kiss against my cheek, and my skin tingled.

"You not a fan of the color?"

It was becoming clear to me that unless I spelled it out for him explicitly we were going to stand here all fucking day.

"This isn't someone else's house," I tried, going for direct. Luca's eyes narrowed, then widened, his mouth dropping open. *Finally*. He got it. "It's—"

"Our house?" he squeaked, his voice breathy and shocked. "Holy shit, you did not."

Was that a good or bad reaction?

"Prudence." Luca latched on to my shoulders and gave me a shake. "You bought us a fucking mansion on the beach!" His words tumbled together in his excitement. "Holy shit."

My cheeks were hot as I shrugged, suddenly not sure what to do with his excitement even though this was exactly what I'd been going for. So I just didn't respond. I headed toward the front, and Luca dropped my shoulders to follow, a shocked look firmly plastered on his face.

I skipped over the main areas of the house, because ultimately they didn't matter.

No.

His real surprise was waiting.

Luca kept wanting to stop to look around at all the furniture but I latched on to his wrist and dragged him away, enjoying his angry half-squawks. We crossed the glass walkway that connected the main house to the second building and I took a fortifying breath before I pushed the first adjoining door open.

"What is…" Luca stopped, tugging on my hand to slow me down as I gestured around the open room. One wall was made entirely of glass, just like the main house had been. Another wall had a line of short easels and floor-to-ceiling cabinets full of art supplies. There were desks stacked in a corner, and four sinks lining the back of the room. A second doorway was placed smack dab in the center of the glass wall, with a neat little pathway leading away from it to what looked like a small parking lot on the edge of the tree line. The walls were painted white, and they glowed in the setting sun as I waited to see what he thought.

"This is where we'll host classes." I wasn't sure how he'd respond. It was something we'd talked about a few times—picking up where Amanda had left off in my childhood. The idea of a non-profit art school for children had seemed a little ridiculous, but Luca had always assured me it was genius. But now…*now* with the very real evidence of what could be our future, I was suddenly left unsure.

What if he didn't like it?

What if he—

"Prudence." Luca cupped my cheeks, smoothing away my panic as he dipped his head down to press a gentle kiss against my lips. "It's fucking perfect." He kissed me again, and I melted. I tangled my fingers in his hair, pulling him closer, tasting his happiness with reckless enthusiasm.

Our tongues tapped, and I groaned, forcing myself to pull back.

"I'm not done," I said, my voice deep and full of gravel. "There's one more room."

"Alrighty." Luca laughed, though his voice was soft and reverent. "Lead the way Mr. Extra AF."

So I did.

Luca

"No fucking way." I could not believe my eyes. "No fucking way, Pru!" I repeated out loud as I stared at the last room with my jaw dropped, and my eyes bulging. "You made me a fucking art studio."

I had never, in all my life, seen something more beautiful.

Well.

At least, until I looked over at Prudence, and saw the flickering, proud smile that tugged at his lips. His smile said *I did good*. And I couldn't help but cross the distance between us to smash my mouth against his again. I'd floundered around the room enthusiastically for probably too long, considering the fact it was *his* fucking birthday—and yet I was the one being spoiled.

Knowing Prudence, he probably didn't even remember what today was.

Which only made it more devastating that we were currently missing the surprise party I'd planned for him at the mall up in Ridgefield. Violet had been working with me all week to put it together. This though…there was no way I could ignore what he'd done. I had a feeling this moment was far more important than anything I had planned.

"I love it."

Prudence's smile flickered against my lips as he held me to him, one hand in my hair, and one on my hip. I groaned, sucking on his tongue as he crowded me up against one of the white walls and shoved a thigh between my legs.

I was hard already, it was difficult not to be when he was around.

"Shit," I gasped, pulling away to catch my breath. As Pru's kisses traveled eager and greedy down the side of my neck I admired the studio again. The white walls were pristine, cupboards just like the previous room lining the south wall, no doubt already full of paint supplies.

Everything had been cleared away and pushed to the side of the room, however, and in the center of the floor lay seven buckets of paint. I didn't understand why they were there, but knowing Prudence, there had to be a reason.

His teeth scraped the tendon in my neck and I hiccuped a little groan, my head thunking against the wall as I circled my hips against his firm thigh. "Pru—" I gasped out a laugh. "What's with the paint?"

He growled, clearly annoyed that I'd interrupted him. When he pulled away, I immediately regretted opening my big mouth. He turned toward the buckets, glaring them down like they'd personally offended him.

"Strip," he commanded.

"Huh?" Maybe I was sex-stupid already, because I had no idea how the paint buckets at all correlated to me getting naked. Were we still doing sex? What was happening?

"Now." Prudence's eyes were flooded with heat as he turned back to me, the plain hunger I saw reflected in his gaze enough to make my head spin. Always a predator. Always ravenous. I licked my lips, and immediately began fumbling with the buttons on my shirt. When it took too long he grew impatient with my progress and dove for the buttons himself. Instead of sparing my best—and only dress shirt—he tore it open.

Buttons flew across the room and I gasped out a laugh.

Goddammit.

"Hey—wait." Prudence pulled the shirt down my back, trapping my arms for a moment before he peeled them meticulously free and moved toward the button on my pants. "Wait—"

"What?"

"The windows—"

"It's one way glass," he huffed with an eye roll as if *I* was the one being unreasonable. I snorted out a laugh, though the sound died quickly as he shoved my pants and boxers down my legs and my hard cock slapped against my belly leaving a hot streak of precum behind.

Shit.

Prudence got on his knees to help me out of my pants. He tossed my shoes and clothing toward a corner of the room, his eyes dark with desire as he stared up at me from his spot on the floor, thighs spread. It would never get old seeing him on his knees for me. My balls, which had until now been mercifully patient, officially began to ache. His gaze was searching, the swath of his bangs like ink where they spilled across his forehead.

"The paint?" I asked, because I was stupid.

"Shut up."

"Jeez." I rolled my eyes at him, but did as I was told, amused. Prudence's brow quirked in frustration as he fumbled with his back pocket. I watched him dumbly, still completely confused. Still naked. *What the hell was happening right now?*

He fought with his own pants, growling in frustration, before he finally seemed to get what he wanted.

"That better be a condom or I'm going to have to stage a riot," I joked, only for my joke to fall completely flat as I realized what he was holding. "Oh."

It was definitely not a condom.

"Luca."

"Hi." The word blurted out before I could stop it. I floundered for a moment, floored by the glitter of the ring tucked tight between his thick, tattooed fingers. His familiar chipped nail polish caught the light as my eyes bulged and I tried to find my words again. No. *Nope.* I had none. I couldn't form a single coherent thought right now if my life depended on it.

"Luca," Prudence started again, brow lowering seriously as he pinched the ring tighter and my heart beat unsteadily in my chest. "Marry me." It was more a demand than a question, in typical Prudence style.

"Really?" Oh man. Oh man, *oh man.*

"*Really.*" I dropped to my knees, my laugh wet as I cupped his hand between both of mine and I caught his gaze.

"Shit, you are one competitive motherfucker."

"My proposal was better than Hunters."

"I mean—he didn't give me a house, so I think that's fair." I laughed again, leaning forward to lace a kiss against his cheek. His cool skin left my lips tingling as I pulled away, blinking through my tears. "I haven't said yes yet."

He stared at me, expression scarily blank, so I didn't torture him any longer.

"Yes," I snorted, kissing him again. And again. And again. *And again.* Somehow, at some point, between the kisses he positioned the ring onto my finger. It fit perfectly, and I huffed out another awed little laugh as he pushed me to the cool wooden floor and my breath left me in an overwhelmed rush. "Yes. A million times yes," I repeated, just because I could.

Prudence's clothes disappeared sometime between the twentieth and sixtieth kiss. Distracted, and buzzy all over, it took me an embarrassing amount of time to realize what he was doing with his free hand while he'd been fucking me with his tongue.

One of the paint cans was open beside him, the lid plopped on the ground, a splatter of pale green paint marring the pristine white floor.

"Oh my god," I whispered, forcing his lips away as I stared at the cans of paint with new understanding. "Is this part of the proposal?"

"Yes."

"Are we painting the room?" My excitement must have been apparent, because Prudence snorted. He reached down to give his dick a tight squeeze. I groaned, licking my lips as my attention immediately snapped to the thick root of his cock. His crown was glistening, the piercings that lined the length of it winking in the sunset as I bit my lip and resisted the urge to lean down and taste.

A fresh drop of precum slipped from the tip and I groaned, lashes fluttering.

"Please tell me you're going to fuck me," I pleaded, voice low and breathy. "Or I might take back my yes."

"Four."

"Shit, you are perfect."

"Open the others," Prudence commanded. I quickly scrambled to obey, distracted because every time I bent over to pop the lid from a new can he would crowd in the space behind me and suck kisses on my shoulders. He wasn't really helping me—but I didn't complain, too enthralled by the hot drag of his cock against my ass as I fumbled to get paint can after paint can open.

A rainbow of pastel sat before me, lids tossed haphazardly to the side as Prudence pressed to my back, his teeth biting almost threateningly at the nape of my neck. Every touch had me spinning, spinning, spinning. My dick was so hard it hurt, and when I glanced down at it I couldn't help but groan at the sight.

The tip was flushed with blood, precum glistening as it slipped down my length, well on its way to my balls. I bit my lip, so incredibly excited by the sight of my dick next to the paint I could barely breathe.

"It's skin safe," Prudence promised, his words whispering along my shoulder as he fumbled for something behind himself, then returned to his rightful place against me. "But I'm going to get you nice and open first before we play."

"Oh fuck yes," I mewled, already too far gone to argue.

Clearly he had a plan, and I wasn't about to mess that up.

"Face down," Prudence demanded quietly against the shell of my ear. "Ass up." His breath tickled, little tingles shooting up my body as I immediately dropped onto my elbows, and arched my back. He grabbed my hips, forcibly extending the arch for me as my lips bumped against the cool floor and I held my breath.

"That's it, Pinkie. Show me how much of a whore you are for me." He groaned, low and sweet, fanning his hands over my cheeks for a moment, before spreading them open to admire the flutter of my hole. "Like a bitch in heat." He liked the way I squirmed when he did this. The way my hole twitched, and my body flushed with shame.

The first push of his finger against my ass had me hiccuping against the wood. As always, his touch was cold. I quickly got used to it, however, as he rubbed lube against my twitching, eager entrance, waiting for me to welcome the intrusion. I ached for him, the way I always did. It hadn't taken long for him to train me. Now every time he was near my ass twitched in memory, begging to be filled to the brim.

I'd become Pavlov's dog and Prudence was my reward.

"You know how I know you want me?" he murmured, his voice rumbling in the space between us.

"Because I bend over like a slut for you?" I offered, breathless.

"No." He pressed against my hole again, circling, circling. I spread my legs, breath leaving me in an overwhelmed puff. I wanted him *in*. "Your hole gets all twitchy when it wants to be filled." He pressed harder, and his point was only proven when my entrance trembled and sucked at his fingertips. "You can't get enough of it."

I'd never been this insatiable with anyone else, so I was still getting used to the way my body chased his touch. Like he was a craving I would never satisfy, and I was fine with that.

He pressed the pad of his finger in, and just like he'd said I would, I twitched around him eagerly, a desperate little puff of breath escaping as my lashes fluttered and I forced myself to relax, to welcome the intrusion.

Getting fucked felt weird sometimes, for the first few seconds. Wrong. In the best of ways.

"So pink," Prudence praised. "So tight." My cock jerked and a drop of precum slipped down my shaft. "So needy." The fact he was staring at the most intimate part of my body made me lightheaded. It felt so good—forbidden almost. Taboo. "I want to crawl inside you," his lips were suddenly beside my ear, tickling away as his finger pushed in deeper at the same time his tongue flickered out to trace the shell. "If I could become you, I would." I whined. "I would share a heart with you, if I could. Share every breath. Close is not close enough."

When he'd pushed the rest of the way inside, I cried out. A second finger quickly joined the first and I clenched around the width of them. They squelched as they fucked in and out, the filthy sound making my skin flush with shame as it filled the room and Prudence crooned praise against my ear.

"Open up for me," he purred. "That's it. Push back against me—" he growled. "That's my good boy," his voice was a quiet hiss. "You're going to take what I give you, and you're going to like it."

His possessiveness should've frightened me.

But it didn't.

The truth was, he could possess me all he desired because I wanted him to.

By the time I was ready, I was loose and breathless. I couldn't help the punched out whines that left my lips every time he pushed against my prostate and pleasure zinged through my body. "P-please—" I begged, toes curling.

"No."

"Please fuck me—" I tried again as his fingers pulled out a fraction, then squished back up inside me. God I was so full. I clenched around his knuckles, trying to hold them inside as my hole gave beneath their touch. His fingers were big. *Shit.* But not big enough.

"No," Prudence repeated, curling upward to give my prostate a pointed, circular rub that had my cock jerking. My hands were curled into fists, the cool brush of the floor welcome against my overheated skin.

"Plea—"

"Did you forget what I said?" Prudence's words were detached, low. But he couldn't play me. Not anymore. I knew him well enough now to recognize the heat behind his words, the desperate, dark desire to claim, to maim me. To own me. To fuck me till I forgot everything but him. Till we became one, and he finally got his wish.

Prudence's knuckles slipped free and a desperate, ragged cry left my lips. My hole clutched at nothing, fluttering in the cool air, open and gaping. It attempted to close, but he'd played with me so long and good it would take a while to tighten up again.

"Grab the paint."

"What?" I was too horny to be able to put his words together.

"The paint, baby." I shivered, fucked out, and confused as I fumbled for the nearest bucket. It screeched a bit as I dragged it across the floor toward him, paint slopping over the lip in splatters of yellow. Prudence's cold hands clutched at my hips as he gently sat me up. I turned, tucking along the side of his body with a breathless whimper, my hole still unbearably empty.

"Please," I tried again, murmuring the words against the crook of his neck.

Prudence chuckled.

Somewhere behind us my phone buzzed where it still sat in my pants pocket. I ignored it, however, distracted as Prudence grabbed the full can, then my hand. I stared at the tight pale loop of his grip around my wrist as he dipped my hand into the paint and the cool wet substance made me shiver.

"We're going to mark this place," Prudence commanded, releasing my wrist and dipping his hand in beside mine. "We're going to make it ours." He brushed a kiss against my cheek. "Every time you look at these walls I want you to remember this." Our fingers laced together inside the wet paint, the chilly slippery feeling of it slicking the way as I stared out at the blank canvas of the all-white room, and excitement flickered inside my belly.

I pulled our hands from the bucket, finally—*finally* understanding what he meant.

Why he was doing this.

In this space there was no room for anything but us.

With a laugh I smeared the paint from our joined hands onto the floor. I knocked over the full can, pale yellow bleeding across the floor as I released my grip on him and tugged him to his feet.

"Perfectly imperfect." I hummed, my ass aching and empty as I grabbed another paint color, and hauled the bucket a few feet away to dump it out. It was hard to ignore how much I wanted him, but in the name of art I managed. Prudence followed my lead. His grin was wicked as we dumped all the cans, one by one, the paint slipping between the cracks.

When the room was prepped I held out my hand for him, skin flushed, sweat glistening on my chest and thighs. The sun had fallen low enough the indigo of twilight was creeping in, but I wasn't deterred.

"You ready to fuck this shit up?" I asked, heart wobbling with excitement.

"Yes."

I laced our sticky fingers together for the second time that night and with delight I pulled him across the floor, our feet skittering through the paint, spreading it everywhere. Laughter bubbled up my throat as I slid a little, and Prudence steadied me.

Minutes passed. Maybe hours. With the remnants of paint in the buckets we splattered the walls. Our hand prints smeared every surface in a riot of rainbow, our footsteps dancing together, mingling, intertwining, combining colors till the marks of our bodies were indistinguishable from each other.

And when we were done, when there was no paint left, when the desire that had burned like fire through my soul burned brighter than ever before—Prudence pushed me against the wall and sucked my tongue into his mouth.

His grip was slippery and wet as his fingernails bit into my hips, leaving paint streaks behind. My dick flexed, and my balls throbbed as my empty hole twitched with need. He jerked me around till my sweaty chest was pressed against the still drying wall, and his cock pushed insistently up against my ass.

The hot stripe of cum it left on my skin had me nearly panting.

Maybe I really was a bitch in heat.

I couldn't think of anything I wanted more in that moment, than Prudence's dick pushing inside me, claiming me as his property once again.

"C'mon." I urged breathlessly, grinning when his palm slammed onto the wall beside my head, leaving a smeared handprint in red beneath it. "Fuck me."

He didn't need to be told twice.

My engagement ring glittered as the fat head of Prudence's cock pushed insistently up against my entrance. Luckily it hadn't been long enough for the lube to dry, so the slide would be easy. Smooth. Intoxicating. I reached backward to clutch at his hip, leaving crescent marks with my nails as he forced himself past my rim. Inch by inch, his dick marked my insides as thoroughly as we'd just marked my new studio. A choked whine escaped as my body struggled to accommodate his girth.

"Shit." He was big. *So fucking big.* It was a wonder something so thick could fit. It shouldn't have felt as good as it did. Those delicious piercings rubbed up against my inner walls and I spread my legs wider, feet slipping along the floor as I dropped my hips low enough he could pound my ass without stretching onto his tip toes.

"Nnng." When he pulled out a fraction, I whimpered—the noise punched out of me as he fucked forward. Each push was more brutal than the last, his pelvis slapping against mine as the slick sounds of our sex made my head spin. The sweet scent of sweat wafted through the air, dancing through the acrid chemically smell of wet paint.

"That's it," Prudence growled against the nape of my neck, biting hard. Tingles shot down my spine as I hissed, arching my back and pushing against him, my dick leaking a steady stream of precum onto the wall. Uncaring of the paint still on my hands, I released his thigh and reached down between my legs, wrapping my fingers around the root of my cock and squeezing to stave off my orgasm.

I wanted this to last, but I was too far gone already.

Electricity danced beneath my skin, my tongue curling as my lips rubbed up against the wall and Prudence fucked me hard. He made these gorgeous little growly noises every time he pushed in all the way and his balls slapped up against my taint, like the animal in him was pleased to force me into submission.

I didn't mind submitting to him.

Not if it meant I was his, and he was mine.

"Take it, Pinkie," Prudence commanded, snapping into me deep enough I saw stars. His breath puffed along the nape of my neck, my hair standing on end. Every time the fat head of his cock pushed against my prostate, I couldn't help but sob. I squeezed around him, just to feel it better. "Fuuuuck." He bit my shoulder again and the pain zinged all the way to my fingertips. "That's it, c'mon." He smacked one of my ass cheeks, wet paint cooling on the feverish skin. "Clench down."

I *squeezed*, head dropping back toward him as my lashes fluttered.

"Yeaaaah," Prudence sucked on my shoulder, somehow managing to pick up the pace even more, his cock striking against my sweet spot on every thrust. I was so hard, it hurt. My balls sung as he snapped his hips. "You like it hard. Rough." I couldn't help myself as I began to stroke my cock, up and down, pulling my foreskin over the tip as the slick of my own pleasure made the glide easy. "You'd bend over for me anywhere, wouldn't you, Pinkie? You need it. You need to be fucked, don't you?"

I sobbed, my head bobbing, "*Yes*, yes."

Once again, I was grateful I'd always leaked a lot during sex, as the steady stream of precum made fucking my fist effortless. Shit. Shit, that felt so good. Prudence changed his angle and I sobbed, tears slipping down my cheeks as my orgasm rushed toward me. His dominant hand reached up, palm scratching along the column of my throat as he closed his fingers around it and squeezed till fireworks burst and my eyes rolled back in my head.

"Fuck." It hit me, and the broken cry that escaped as I came all over the paint streaked wall, sounded more like an injured animal than a man.

Prudence growled, panting and overwhelmed as he fucked me through the aftershocks, his pecs rubbing up against my shoulder blades, thick hands moving around my torso to toy with my nipples and squeeze my pecs as he finally came inside me with a low groan of his own.

Our chests were still heaving when he laid me down on the paint-smeared ground, then flopped beside me as we stared up at the ceiling. It was made of glass, like the wall, and I was momentarily floored by how gorgeous the night had become. Stars glittered in the skylight above, dancing, like they could sense our contentment as I tangled my fingers with Prudence's and basked in the afterglow.

My hole twitched uselessly, and my toes curled as I glanced down at Prudence's now flaccid dick and wondered how long he'd need before he could get it up again to fuck me. Even soft, it was gorgeous, plump and flushed at the tip, his piercings glinting. His thick thighs were spread, his body relaxed, the rise and fall of his chest tantalizing in its humanity. I couldn't stop staring at his profile as he tipped it toward the ceiling, the slope of his adorable button nose, his lips—usually flattened by vitriol—soft and kiss-swollen. Those dark lashes fluttering with every single blink.

He was perfect.

He *really* was.

His big chest heaved as he caught his breath, the scrawled squiggles of the rainbow flowers I'd drawn all over him still present. Because his body was an illusion, he'd told me he could choose how he appeared. And—ever since that night in the woods—the pictures I'd left on his skin had remained despite the time that had passed.

He'd claimed I'd changed him.

But the truth was he'd changed me.

We'd changed each other.

I used to live my life, looking for the sun, with this underlying guilt that because of what I'd done, because of who I was—someday the darkness would catch up to me. There was a side to my personality I kept hidden, tucked away, like a secret. I was ashamed of my faults. Terrified of failing. Ready to give away everything I had to others till there was nothing left. The world would take and take and take—and I always figured, that was what I deserved.

That there was something secretly wrong with me. Something to hide.

For fear of what would happen should I accept it.

Prudence didn't care though.

He didn't care about my past. About my mistakes. About my darkness. He embraced every side of me with open arms and no judgment. He liked my tears, my laughter. Funny how he knew every single part of me, and yet had never been deterred.

Prudence squeezed my hand and I glanced over at him again, noting the questioning quirk to his brow as he waited. My ring was practically glued to my skin with paint, but I didn't mind. That's what showers and baby oil were for after all. Knowing Prudence, he'd have some sort of overly pricey paint remover in the bathrooms just waiting to be used.

"I love you," I said, because I needed to say it as much as he needed to hear it. His lips tipped up into a little smile. "Thank you." I was humbled by the gift he'd given me. He may not be good with words, but the man showed he loved me with his actions every single day.

He squeezed my hand tight, his eyes glittering.

"We're going to be happy," he responded, voice soft, sure. "Together."

"Hell yeah, we will." I leaned over, grimacing as my hole twinged, and kissed the little cross tattoo right beneath his eye. "Blissfully, disgustingly, wonderfully happy."

Prudence looked pleased.

He looked decidedly less pleased and more flummoxed, after we spent nearly an hour scrubbing paint from my body—Prudence just poofed his into thin air, the bastard—and I told him about the birthday party he'd missed. He'd stared at me in confusion as he roughly toweled me dry, then bodily pushed me into our first ever real bedroom. "It's my birthday?"

"We'll celebrate tomorrow. I'm sorry it didn't happen today." I patted the empty spot on the bed—our bed—next to me, waggling my eyebrows. "I made you a cake."

He looked almost alarmed. "A cake?"

"Oreo." I nodded. "It's pretty much just Oreos and cream cheese. You'll love it."

He blinked in confusion and climbed onto the bed beside me. "I—"

"Shit." I turned over to look at him. "What time is it?"

He glanced at the clock then turned back to me, "Eleven fifty—"

"Happy birthday!" I blurted out quickly, interrupting him. I smashed a kiss against his lips, squeezing him tight enough he was forced to give in to the snuggle. He huffed out an angry little grunt that I knew meant he was secretly pleased. "Old man," I added, just to be cheeky.

"Five," he responded, wrapping me tight with a quiet hum.

"Promises, *promises*," I teased immediately.

We held each other for a long time and I began to drift, my fingers cradling his chest, his hand stroking through my hair. The next morning when I woke up Prudence was gone. I fumbled around until I found my paint-streaked phone and checked my missed messages.

There were about a thousand from Chastity and Vanity.

And one from the tattoo artist I'd booked an appointment with next week.

I texted them all back, blinking blearily as I made my way down the unfamiliar hallway of our new home, still naked.

"Pru?" I called, stumbling a little down the stairs. I spotted him before I'd made it halfway down, and I immediately paused—quickly tripping up the stairs in retreat and covering my junk out of modesty. Prudence had the front door open and when I peeked through the banister there was a tall, muscular redhead peering down at him.

He had a frantic look on his face, his big dark brown eyes wide with fear, as his freckled hands shook at his sides.

"You sure you haven't seen him?" he asked, panic laced into his voice.

"No." Uncaring of the redhead's trauma, Prudence immediately shut the door in his face. When he spotted me, his hard expression softened. He was wearing a black tank top and jeans, and he had never looked more delicious than he did in that moment. His eyes narrowed when he noticed I was naked.

"Who was that?" I asked, heading down the stairs for the second time that day. Sunlight streamed through the glass, making the house glow as I crossed the distance between us and pressed a kiss against Pru's lips. He softened beneath my touch, though when I pulled far enough away I could see him properly, his eyes were flickering with mischief.

"If he saw you naked I'll have to punish you."

I snorted.

"Or gouge his eyes out." He shrugged. "I'll be happy either way."

"Don't distract me," I laughed, my stomach an aching, empty pit. We hadn't eaten dinner the night before, and I was officially feeling the effects of the marathon sex now that the hunger had caught up to me. "Who was that?"

Prudence rolled his eyes. "I don't know. I don't care."

"Pru," I admonished. He looked uncomfortable.

"Some kid," he shrugged. "One of the ones I…" He waggled a hand in a gesture I was coming to realize meant he knew from before.

"Okay…and what did he want?" It was pretty weird he was all the way out here in the middle of nowhere at our house. *Our house!* I didn't think

I'd ever get over that. We'd have to FaceTime my mom after breakfast. She'd want to know everything—and she'd been bothering me all day yesterday trying to wish Prudence a happy birthday. My phone buzzed, and before I could check to see who it was, Prudence growled in annoyance and yanked it from my hand. He shoved it into his own pocket, pouting.

"He lost his dog."

"His…dog?" I blinked. "What kind of dog?"

"I don't know." Prudence scowled. "Does it matter?"

"Prudence," I rolled my eyes. "This is Elmwood." I nudged him pointedly. "If the dude lost his dog, who's to say it's not like…a *cursed* one. Or magical? Or even—" I grimaced, "a werewolf."

Prudence's eyes narrowed thoughtfully. "You think he lost a werewolf?"

"I dunno," I bit my lip thoughtfully. "It's possible."

"Whatever you say."

My stomach growled. Prudence rolled his eyes, though he didn't complain as he showed me to our brand new, freakishly massive kitchen. He looked almost shy as he pushed open one of the floor-to-ceiling cabinets, and I swear to god sparks flew as I fell in love with the shelves, on shelves, on shelves of cereal inside.

"Eat," Prudence grunted, a put upon expression on his face, like he wasn't fucking chasing away my childhood demons. Like he hadn't planned this. Like he hadn't filled our new house with food he abhorred, just because I liked it. Just because he didn't want me to ever go hungry again.

Funny how I'd found my perfect match in a dead man, but hey. I wasn't complaining.

He was a secret softie, my sadistic ghosty. All bark…and some bite. And just like he'd proudly proclaimed the night before, when he'd promised me a future I had no intention of letting go, I knew, staring at the rows and rows of colorful boxes, Prudence and I?

Yeah.

We were going to be very, very happy.

fae.fae

Acknowledgments

THANK YOU SO much to everyone who finished *Possess Me*! I hope you enjoyed your adventure with Prudence and Luca, and I can't wait to see you for my next spooky release. Special thanks to all those who made the creation of this book possible, especially Molly with her creative artsy genius, Jess, the world's best cheerleader, and Kat, who dedicated hours to reading and rereading the book for me, despite having a release in June of her own (Go check out *Werewolves Hate Clogs* by K.L. Hiers for more paranormal MM fun!).

I am grateful to my husband for loving me even when the excessive caffeine I consumed while writing made me crash. His love and support kept me going, and his endless patience has allowed me to grow and change because he catches me every time I fall. Thank you to everyone who contributed their time, energy, and love to this project; you are all my dear friends. And most of all, thank you to the reader, because without you, the creation of this story would have been meaningless. I write the words, but you are the ones who bring the story to life. Each and every one of you is priceless. Thank you for falling in love with these characters alongside me. I love all of you so much. See you next time!

Love,

Fae

About Fae

FAE IS OBSESSED with anything romance. From a young age she realized she had a passion for falling in love over and over again. She loves to tell stories through both her art and writing. With a passion for classical monsters, meet-cutes, and contemporary romance you can often find her with her nose stuck in a book and her pet corgi Champa on her lap.

She currently resides in Utah with her amazing husband and her collection of squishmallows. When you read one of her books you can expect to find love stories between humans, monsters, and loveable assholes that will make you laugh (and cry) as you get lost in their worlds for just a little. Every story comes with a happy ever after guarantee.

Find her online at:

WWW.FAELOVESART.COM